The Good Luck Girl

Kerry Reichs

W F HOWES LTD

This large print edition published in 2009 by
W F Howes Ltd
Unit 4, Rearsby Business Park, Gaddesby Lane,
Rearsby, Leicester LE7 4YH

1 3 5 7 9 10 8 6 4 2

First published in the United Kingdom in 2009
by Orion Books

ISBN 978 1 407 44237 2

Typeset by Palimpsest Book Production Limited,
Grangemouth, Stirlingshire
Printed and bound in Great Britain
by MPG Books Ltd, Bodmin, Cornwall

FSC
Mixed Sources
Product group from well-managed
forests, controlled sources and
recycled wood or fiber
SA-COC-1565
www.fsc.org
© 1996 Forest Stewardship Council

The Good Luck Girl

ALSO BY KERRY REICHS
FROM CLIPPER LARGE PRINT

The Best Day of Someone Else's Life

CHAPTER 1

FACEBOOK

I can honestly say I didn't *intend* to be bad. It's just that I have rotten luck. I was nine and on a camping trip. It was very After School Special: four suburban families with expensive tents that didn't get out of the garage much, and Coleman stoves that the fathers couldn't really figure out but which required hours of happy tinkering while the women gossiped and made burger patties. A dozen kids charged about in Osh Kosh B'Gosh brand overalls.

We were marshaling forces for the day's excursion. My father had slathered my bug bites with calamine lotion and I was instructed to stay put while the adults debated Grandfather Mountain versus Blowing Rock. A nearby trailhead tantalized. I begged to explore. My father considered the likelihood of speedy consensus among the adults, and the eleven hurtling short people in need of calamine, and gave me permission to go for ten minutes, not a minute more.

But the lure of each new bend of the trail was too much for me. I *had* to see what was around the corner. And the next. And the next. By the

1

time my father caught up to me an hour later, I got a bare-bottom spanking right there on the trail. My punishment was to sit in the tent and 'think about things' while the other kids were having fun at Tweetsie Railroad. To be honest, I think my dad was secretly glad to prop his feet on a log and listen to the Bears game on the radio while he did a crossword puzzle. What I thought about was how great that trail had been and how I wished I'd gotten to the end. Back then, I was different. Back then, I was fearless. It was much later that the death of my best friend made me dread things I couldn't see coming.

I've always been restless. I can't seem to settle on anything. That's probably why it took me seven and a half years to finish college. I finally graduated at the ripe old age of twenty-five with a major in Anthropology and a minor in Film Studies. I had no idea what I wanted to do and a lot of time on my hands. That was the situation four weeks ago. That was when the trouble began. That was when I discovered Facebook.com.

'What're you doing?' I asked my brother Brick over the phone as I lounged on the sofa. I was snacking on pretzel rods, which have zero trans-fats, and looking for a diversion. But not the kind that would take actual effort, like the scattered photos next to empty albums, the unfolded laundry on my bed, or the blank thank-you notes that would theoretically write themselves before winging to relatives who'd given me graduation gifts.

'Setting myself up for life in a cardboard box under the freeway by screwing around on Facebook instead of studying.' Brick was in college, following a normal four-year plan. My intense need to graduate before him had fueled an academic fervor last semester. I beat him by six months. I'd been in college since he was fifteen.

'What's Facebook?' I picked at my nail polish.

'It's a social networking website, and death to productivity,' he groaned.

I perked up. Oliver, my cockatiel, ruffled his feathers in annoyance. I'd disturbed his perch on my head. I ignored him. I hadn't been doing much since graduation, and the possibility of a time-sucking website was far more appealing than figuring out what I was going to do for the rest of my life. Normally a reader, lately I was into short-attention-span diversions like the Internet and TV.

'Let me get a pen . . .' I said.

An hour later, I'd posted a photo, established a Super Wall and was diving into the Cities I've Visited application. It involved sticking virtual pins into a world map of all the exotic locations you'd been to. Unless Frying Pan Landing, North Carolina, counted as exotic, it was going to be a short diversion for all of us. I hadn't ventured far from my hometown of Charlotte. Now, if there were a map for colleges I'd attended, that would take more time. I could proudly claim at least four. And don't get me started on majors. There wouldn't be enough virtual pins.

Not that I had many people to impress. So far I had one friend in my network, and it was my brother. My interest was waning when a message popped up: a friend request!

'It's a movie producer,' I predicted to Oliver. 'Who wants to make me a movie star after seeing my photo.' It *was* a fetching shot, and I was wearing my favorite polka-dot knee socks. You can't see them in the picture, but the right socks are essential to total appearance.

'Are you thinner?' squawked my bird, as he did at least once a day. One of my more successful projects. I grinned as I clicked open the request, and stared at the face of a stranger named Laura who wanted to be my friend. Was this how it worked? Random people became your friends online? I hesitated, unsure if I was comfortable with that. Something about the name nagged at me. Laura Mills. I frowned in concentration, then immediately stopped and rubbed my forehead. A wrinkle between your eyes is so unattractive, and our family was prone to the Connelly divot.

Suddenly I remembered. Laura Mills had lived across the street and been my best friend when I was eight. We'd been inseparable, with matching skinned knees and sunburned noses, but then her family had moved to Texas when I was eleven and I never saw her again.

I examined the photo. There was no doubt about it. Eleven-year-old Laura was looking out from behind the glamorous makeup of my new future friend. I had no idea how she'd found me after sixteen years, but Facebook was officially the coolest website ever. I clicked 'accept', bracing for a flood of long-lost acquaintances and new adventures.

Two hours later, I slid behind the bar at Gin Mill as unobtrusively as possible.

'Maeve? Are you here?' shouted my boss Joe from his office. His voice was followed by his stocky frame, sporting folded arms and a forehead divot big enough to hide a body.

'Hey, Joe,' I tried. 'I was taking out the trash.'

Annoyed evolved to thunderous. 'Maeve, you're an hour and sixteen minutes late!' Rats. My typical luck he'd noticed. Some days he never left the office.

'I'm sorry, Joe. It was traffic.' I really was sorry. I didn't want to lose another job. The pins in a virtual map of all the bars I'd worked would be blinding.

'Look, Maeve, I like you. I really do. But from four to eight, I count on you to handle the bar.'

Regular customers Billy and Brooks – or was it Brooks and Billy? – the only two people in the bar, nodded at me seriously. I blew out my bangs in irritation. They usually helped themselves anyway.

Joe continued. 'Between you and that unreliable

car, I spend half your shifts at the bar.' My car Elsie was an ancient 1970 Plymouth Road Runner prone to breakdowns.

'I'm sorry, Joe. It won't happen again.' I hung my head, long blonde braids drooping penitently.

He considered me. 'Not again, Maeve,' he relented, before lumbering back to the office.

Billy snorted, but Brooks asked, 'What was it this time, Maeve? *America's Next Top Model* marathon?' I sniffed dismissively, but in truth, that *was* why I'd been late last time.

'Have you guys heard of Facebook?' I asked the two grizzled men, who probably thought an 'internet' was something you used to catch fish.

I was thinking about the last message of an afternoon emailing with Laura. She lived in Los Angeles and worked as something called a First AD, which meant she worked on the Fox Studio lot, met all kinds of famous people, and got to see movies before they were released.

'You should *totally* come visit. Los Angeles is awesome, it's just like on *The Hills*. I see celebrities <u>every day.</u> Last week I sat next to George Clooney at a screening. You could crash with me as long as you needed, and get a job at the studio. We'd have so much fun going to clubs and movie premieres and shopping and having lunch – like Paris and Nicole!'

It sounded a lot better than wiping down a dirty bar counter in Charlotte. I popped the tops off two Coronas for Billy and Brooks, then leaned on my elbows, daydreaming about sunshine, palm trees and George Clooney.

CHAPTER 2

GETTING FIRED FROM MY JOB

T he day had started well – I'd savored the arrival of spring during my three-mile run, and returned to read the details of Laura's morning with Katherine Heigl! I wished I had the money to take her up on her invitation. The fantasy was delicious: me in adorable Capri pants and ballet flats, laughing with Katherine Heigl as I drove our golf cart, casually waving to pals Matt Damon and Will Smith. It was whimsy, of course, but if I did something as radical as go to California, no telling what I could accomplish. Look at Laura.

Reality was the picture I'd spotted on Facebook of an old boyfriend, arm slung around the shoulders of a petite redhead, matching happy smiles. We'd broken up after I'd dropped out of University of North Carolina, Charlotte freshman year. Bad luck that he'd wanted a college girl. I hadn't wasted a lot of time exploring how that made me feel. You can't make big decisions based on a boy. But, I'd been thrilled to reconnect on Facebook. He'd accepted my friend request, but ignored my email about getting together. I couldn't help probing the wound by monitoring his profile. It'd been a blow when he changed his status to 'in a relationship' and posted new pictures saturated with the same smiling girl.

I glanced at my watch, knowing the cure for a foul mood. I had plenty of time.

'Road trip. Don't forget the bird,' chirped Oliver as I put him in his cage.

'Next time, pal,' I promised. Elsie grudgingly started after gentle coaxing. My car was sunshine yellow with a black stripe across her hood. Unlike 'collector-quality' Plymouth Road Runners, Elsie had done over 150,000 miles and was limping through her golden years. I loved her.

'I know, baby,' I said, as I double-checked the rope knot that secured the passenger door. 'I'll give you a bath soon.' Her rustspotted frame was distinctly dingy.

Twenty minutes later, I was happily browsing Nordstrom's. I should've gone to Target, but Nordstrom's shoe section was the best. If it was a good day, I wouldn't find anything I liked.

Today was not a good day. From forty feet away I felt the jolt you get when you first lay eyes on the boots you know shortly will be yours. I sprang towards them like a lioness on an antelope, canvassing the room for a salesperson as I moved.

'These.' I waved the red suede boot at a clerk who looked like a fish. 'Size eight.'

As he glided off, I glanced at the $225 price tag. Ouch. I thought of the ignored bills stacked on the kitchen counter next to my ignored thank-you notes. I'd already charged dinner at the club to my parents' account six times this month. Or had it been seven?

When the shoe salesman returned, I wrestled with myself. Maybe I shouldn't try them on. I could get attached. But they *were* gorgeous. Would I regret their absence for years, haunted by the lost opportunity of a truly perfect pair of boots?

'This is your lucky day,' he said. He really did look like a halibut. 'They're twenty percent off.'

'Fantastic.' I grinned as I reached for the box. God did love me.

Fifteen minutes later I doubted God's love as I fumed at the register. It bore my glares stoically. No human was there to receive them. I looked at my watch: 3.50 p.m. I was half an hour away from work. Maybe I should forget the boots. My hands clenched the box reflexively. No, they were too good. Just when you think your perpetual bad luck is turning by giving you twenty percent off the perfect pair of boots, it runs away laughing, leaving you sweating at an untended register.

At last the shoe salesman reappeared, wiping crumbs from his mouth. I'd have thrown my credit card at him with a pert 'make it snappy', but I had to split the cost of the boots over three cards, so I held my tongue.

Back in Elsie, I gripped the steering wheel, as if my uber-control of the car would make the traffic move faster. My uber-control lacked authority.

The taillights in front of me didn't waver. The car clock refused to stop advancing. Four twenty-three. Shit. I crept along Fairview Road. What the hell was going on? It shouldn't be this slow on a six-lane road.

I spotted red and blue lights flashing at the intersection of Fairview and Park Road, and groaned. An accident was narrowing traffic to one lane. It would take fifteen minutes to get past. I should've worn my favorite Speed Racer knee socks. The right socks can improve your luck.

'I had plenty of time when I got to the mall,' I defended to the clock, which replied by jumping the minute hand three minutes in a single movement to 4.27. Chastened by the inanimate object, I banged the steering wheel. Elsie responded with an ominous rattle.

'I'm sorry, Elsie,' I repented, patting the console. 'Please don't die.' I glanced at the gas gauge, which remarkably was a third full. Though with Elsie that didn't necessarily mean much. She liked to play fun games where needles plummet from half full to below empty in the course of one mile. The 'empty' light had long since burned out, so it was no help. The last thing I needed was to run out of gas.

I ran out of gas. The needle dropped like a stone just after I turned on to Park Road, and all resistance left the gas pedal. I leaned forward in my seat, as if shifting my five-foot-nine, 140-pound frame would give the 4,000-pound car momentum, and

11

willed Elsie to coast. Still pissed about the steering-wheel thing, she rolled to a stop a mile from the Texaco.

'How much bad luck can one person have?' I moaned, reaching for my cell phone to call Joe. He was going to be furious. At least I had a bona fide excuse, I thought virtuously.

I flipped open my phone. I had No Service. How come I had no service in the middle of town? I had a text message, so I opened it curiously as I stepped out of Elsie. Maybe I'd get a signal when I walked towards the gas station. I froze as I read my text message.

> Your Sprint mobile phone service has been suspended for non-payment. To reactivate your service, contact a Sprint representative at *2 or 1-888-211-4727. Payment of your outstanding balance in full is required to reactivate phone service.

I couldn't believe it. Was Ashton Kutcher going to pop out and tell me I'd been Punk'd, sharing a good chuckle as he handed me the keys to my shiny new Mercedes convertible? Nothing greeted me but a couple of empty super-size cans of malt liquor and a condom wrapper in the ditch.

'Big night out,' I muttered, shaking my cell phone, as if that might reactivate service. I was *sure* I'd paid the bill. I recalled the stack of bills on my counter. Hadn't I? I frowned, then smoothed the groove between my eyes. No way was I going to end up looking like Great-Aunt Ida. I blew out my bangs. Nothing for it but to trudge to the gas station.

It was close to six when I pulled into the Gin Mill parking lot. The place was packed. I mean, *really* packed. People in suits were six deep at the bar, trying to get served. I could see Jules' long, dark ponytail flying as she whirled to grab bottles of beer. Next to her, Joe was sloshing something pink into shot glasses. People clamored to get their attention, waving bills in the air. My heart plummeted. Today was our inaugural Young Professionals happy hour.

I dashed to the bar, dropping my purse on the floor by the cooler to stow away later, and jumped to work. The look Joe gave me would have made a frailer woman faint, but now wasn't the time to explain. I started taking orders and slinging beer.

By eight, most of the crowd had moved on and we could draw a breath. Joe was back in the office. The bar was a chaos of bottle caps and spilled booze. I sagged against it, rewarded by a line of beer soaking my T-shirt.

'That was crazy, daisy!' I said. 'Who knew so many baby suits would turn up!'

'You should have seen it earlier.' Jules leaned her tall frame against the back counter, staying dry. I rubbed a rag at the beer on my T-shirt, managing only to transfer a stain, and sighed. 'It was even worse. Wall to wall Wall Streets.'

I cringed, giving up on the shirt. 'Jules, I'm so sorry. I ran out of gas.' When she laughed, I protested. 'No, really, I did! On Park Road. There was a condom wrapper in the ditch.' I said this as though details would make me more credible.

Jules shook her head. 'You don't have to convince me, girl. I'm fine with it.' We'd been friends since junior high. She was used to forgiving me. She winked. 'I was the only gal at the bar, and I got phone numbers. Complainers can suck it.' She became serious. 'Joe was pissed, though.'

I hesitated. 'How pissed?'

'Well, remember that time Billy spilled beer on the new speakers?'

I remembered. Joe had kicked a hole in the office door and used words I didn't know existed. I felt a little better. After all, I hadn't ruined anything expensive.

Jules shattered my illusion. 'This was worse. I thought he was going to have a heart attack when this guy told him he was unfit to own a bar if he couldn't serve his patrons.'

'What should I do?' I asked.

'Well . . .'

'Maeve!' Joe's holler cut her off. 'Get in here.'

'Good luck, little camper.' Jules patted my shoulder as I passed.

Joe's look was black. 'Shut the door,' he instructed. I did, and sat in the uncomfortable chair that wobbled because one leg was missing a caster.

'Today was unacceptable—' Joe began.

'Joe, I ran out of gas.' In the office, my defense seemed less legitimate.

'Maeve, that's a worse excuse than a dead grandmother.'

'But there was an accident, and then I ran out of gas and had to walk to the Texaco . . .'

Joe sighed. 'I'm sorry, Maeve. But I gotta let you go.'

'But . . .'

Joe held up his hand to cut off my protest, and I stared at the way the flesh bulged around his metal watch band. 'It don't matter whether it was your car or traffic or running out of gas. The bottom line is that you're regularly late and other people aren't. So, you're off the schedule. You can come by next week to pick up your last check, or I can mail it to you. Your choice.'

I blinked rapidly at the welling tears. I would *not* cry, I vowed. This was humiliating enough. Didn't he know he was talking to UNCC's former president of the Young Entrepreneurs? I'd been a *star*. I used to turn *down* jobs.

Joe's gaze softened. 'Maeve, I know you're sorting things out . . .'

I sprang from my seat. I didn't want his pity. 'Mail me the check,' I directed.

'Maeve . . .'

I ignored him and strode out with a wave and a chipper 'Thanks, Joe. No worries.'

Behind the bar, I hugged Jules and retrieved my purse from a puddle of beer.

15

'I'm off.' I radiated cheer. 'Sorry again about tonight, Jules.'

'Did he fire you?' She looked worried.

'It wasn't working out.' I was vague. 'This is for the best.' I fluttered my fingers at Brooks and Billy one last time, blowing a kiss to Joe standing in the office doorway, and practically skipped to my car to show how carefree I was.

It was only when the door was shut and locked behind me that the tears came.

'Elsie, what am I going to do?' I whispered, the thought of my unpaid bills making me queasy with fear. I hit my new boot box with self-loathing. I couldn't bear to look at it. What was wrong with me? I used to have a plan.

I needed spaghetti. If my mother was cooking spaghetti, my luck would change, I told myself. It was a constant game I played, betting against my luck. I could already taste the meatballs as I started the car. Good news was just around the corner.

CHAPTER 3

GETTING FIRED BY MY FAMILY

'Maeve!' My father's face lit with surprise when I walked into the kitchen. He was leafing through the mail, still in his suit, collar rumpled. 'Joining us for dinner?'

'Yep.' I received one of his excellent hugs. I was feeling better already.

'Hello, dear.' My mother popped up from behind the counter, casserole pan extracted from the precarious dish cupboard like a trophy. 'You're in luck. I'm trying something new tonight. A curry chicken.'

I wobbled, but rallied. No big deal. I'd already had my daily dose of bad luck.

'Hey.' My attention returned to my father. 'You're looking at your mail.' My father only looked at mail on Sunday, when it was guaranteed that no more would arrive while he was sorting. He tossed half into the garbage and gave me a rueful look. 'Your mother has insisted on some *reforms* since she finished the Spirit Square project.' He winked.

'Ah.' My mother, a sculptor, alternated between periods of complete oblivion when she was immersed

17

in a project, and ruthless organization when she emerged and tried to make up for lost time. That explained the new recipe.

'Hurry up and change for dinner; we're ready,' urged my temporarily Type A mother, as she set a bowl of grapes and a Mason jar of M&Ms on the table, returning to the kitchen counter to get a plate of pepper jack cheese slices and the curry chicken. My mother believed that 'your palate is a blank canvas', so dinners Chez Connelly were unconventional. My father grinned at me, and headed upstairs.

'Do you think wheatgrass or no?' She surveyed the table. Yech. I was all about eating healthy, but there were limits.

'This will be fine,' I assured her. 'I'm eating light.'

She shot me an exasperated look. 'Maeve, there's no need to restrict your diet so severely—'

I cut her off. 'I know, I know.'

She looked undecided for a minute, then said, 'Speaking of mail, there's a letter for you. It's from Cameron's parents.'

I got the fluttery, panicky feeling I got whenever I thought about Cameron.

My mother continued, voice gentle. 'I believe they plan to do something to commemorate the anniversary of her passing.'

I met her eyes. 'I don't think I can,' I said.

She opened her mouth to say something more, then thought better of it. 'No need to decide right now. Let's sit and wait for your father.' She kicked off her Birkenstocks and sat cross-legged on the bench. I sat on the 'grown-up' side of the table, in a normal chair. 'Tell me about your day.'

Definitely not.

'I taught Oliver a new phrase. He can say "Great hair!"'

My mother looked sort of sad but forced a smile. 'Well, that's something. He's turning into free therapy and an entourage all at once.' Mom had clearly been watching her HBO shows. 'Why did I think you were working tonight?'

'Schedule change,' I said, not entirely untruthfully.

'Have you given any thought to what you'd like to do now that you've graduated?' Her tone was careful.

'I don't know.' I hesitated. 'I don't know what I'm good at.' There. I'd said it.

My mom squeezed my hand and smiled at me. 'Maeve, you're good at so many things.'

'You have to say that. You're my mother.'

'It's the truth. Look at what a good bartender you are!' Not encouraging words. I grimaced. 'You're good with people.' She looked thoughtful. 'What about something in the health-care field? You—'

I blanched at the thought of hospitals. I hated hospitals. 'No way.'

She sighed. 'What about photography? You did a remarkable job taking pictures of my sculptures and helping me update my portfolio.'

19

'I don't think you can make a living—'

'Maeve!' My father's bellow echoed down the hallway. What now? He strode into the room, deep crease between his eyebrows, waving a sheaf of papers, looking like an angry orange in sock feet and an Illini sweatsuit, hair sticking up. 'What the hell is this?' He thrust the sheets under my eyes and I winced. The country-club bill had arrived. I couldn't believe it. The *one* day this month I needed to be far away from home happened to be the day I got fired, dropped in unexpectedly, and Dad uncharacteristically opened his mail before Sunday. Talk about bad timing. 'Care to explain this?' he demanded.

'Um.' I looked at the bill. Had I really eaten at the club *nine* times?

'We don't begrudge you the occasional meal, Maeve,' my father chastened. 'But four massages? A new tennis racket?' I'd forgotten about the tennis racket.

'I . . .'

Dad's outrage deflated at the sight of my hunched frame. He sat down heavily. 'Your mother and I understand that you've had a hard time. Harder than most. We've been patient, allowing you time to figure things out. But now you must take responsibility for your life. You're a bright girl, you've got your degree. You need to start thinking about your future.'

I stared at them aghast. My future loomed impossibly large and intimidating. I had no idea

20

how I'd fill the chasm. I'd *just* graduated. It seemed unfair to expect too much too soon.

'You have to curb your tendency to spend beyond your means,' my father lectured in a gentle voice. 'You can't buy something every time you're upset. It doesn't fix anything, and you'll be in financial trouble your whole life. It may seem tough to you, but honestly, this is for your own good.' He paused, as if afraid of his own words, then plunged. 'I'm going to require you to repay us for the massages and the tennis racket.'

'What!' I couldn't believe they were doing this to me. My sister Vi had gotten a car for graduation, and I was getting this? I ignored the fact that they'd bought me Elsie during my junior year, against my father's better judgment, after I'd begged and begged for the decrepit car.

My father steeled himself to maintain his resolve. 'You can take as long as you like to pay us back, and of course we won't charge interest. But you need to learn responsibility. The way you live now is,' he waved his hands in the air, 'flibbertigib-bety,' he pronounced. 'It requires us to step in and help out more often than we should.'

'Flibbertigibbety?' My voice rose an octave. It was an unfair categorization. It wasn't like my parents were perpetually rescuing me. I had a *job*. Well, I did yesterday.

'Flighty,' my mother affirmed. 'But we know it's temporary, Maeve. You'll find your way back to center—'

21

'I am *not* flighty.' I adopted a haughty tone. 'I graduated with a 3.5. I take excellent care of Oliver.' I wanted to say more, but the fact that I never missed an episode of *Bones* or Clinique's Free Bonus Time at Hecht's didn't seem quite right. I was uncomfortable with the brevity of my rebuttal. I wasn't flaky.

'I'll help you work out a payment plan.' My father seemed happy to sidestep the debate. 'We'll look at your shifts at Gin Mill and your current expenses and create a budget for you.'

'Then you can decide how long you want to keep bartending, and if you want to try something else.' My mother sounded hopeful.

My stomach turned. 'Um . . .' I hesitated. I looked at my parents' concerned faces and felt about an inch tall. Which ranked me two inches shorter than my stack of unpaid bills. 'Isortoflostmyjob . . .' I mumbled.

'What was that?' Mom's confusion-divot mirrored Dad's anger-dent. My forehead was doomed.

'I'm not working at Gin Mill anymore,' I said more loudly. I didn't know which was worse – the expression on my dad's face, or my mother's disappointed 'Oh, Maeve.'

'It wasn't my fault.' I protested my refrain. 'Elsie's gas gauge wasn't working and I ran out of gas so I was really late to work.'

'Joe fired you for being late?' My father looked confused.

'It wasn't just the once,' I confessed to my plate.

My mother rubbed her face tiredly. We sat there for a moment, mutely staring at cooling curry chicken. Then my parents' eyes met, and my father voiced a decision I suspected they'd prearranged in anticipation of the next come-to-Jesus.

'Maeve, it's time for you to learn about personal responsibility. I won't require you to repay the club bill – though be warned that I'm going to restrict your charging privileges to one meal a month. But from now on, you're on your own. Your mother and I will start you out with next month's rent and utilities. That gives you a month and a half to find a job and become self-supporting. After that, consider yourself cut off.'

They both looked stricken as he spoke. I could only imagine what my face looked like.

'We want what's best for you, and being extreme seems to be the sole way to get through.' His regret seemed genuine.

'How is it whenever someone tells me they are doing what's best for me, it ends up hurting me?' I demanded, fighting tears for the second time that day.

'Maeve, you cannot be dependent on your father and me for ever. For one thing, we won't be here. It's time to stand on your own.' My mother's eyes were serious. 'The only thing holding you back is you. It's all there for the taking, if only you would reach for it.'

'What, life's a freaking cornucopia of low-hanging

fruit?' I snorted. 'Not in my world. It's not that simple.'

'It can be.' My mother was resolute. 'I agree with your father. You got knocked off track. We haven't helped matters by enabling your inertia. I recognize that. But it's time to take the next step in your life.'

A wave of anger doused my panic, and drove me to my feet. I was *not* some basket case. I had a wicked bad-luck curse. My day was textbook proof – actions that are perfectly normal for other people are catastrophic for me. How many people get fired and cut off by their families because they bought a pair of shoes? *On sale?* Something was out of kilter in the universe, but it wasn't me. I had a vision of palm trees.

'I am *not* a flake,' I squeezed out of a tight throat. I fought tears as I grabbed my purse. 'And I'll prove it.' I ran-walked to the door, imagining their envious faces as they watched successful me on television giving red-carpet interviews on my way into the Oscars. I wasn't sure what I was going to win, but it was something good.

'Honey . . .' My mother tried to follow, but her crossed legs got tangled in her long skirt.

I made it to Elsie and leapt in, praying that for once she would start right up. My father rapped at the window.

'Maeve, come back in for dinner,' he said, when I rolled it down.

'I don't have an appetite.' I was telling the truth. 'My stomach hurts.'

He looked at me thoughtfully. 'Take a week to think about our conversation. Then come to dinner and bring your bills and we can talk about what you want to do next.' He pressed twenty dollars into my hand and then patted my head the way you pet a dog, stroking from the crown forward, making my bangs a static mess. It was his signature form of affection. 'It'll all work out, bug.'

I nodded. 'Tell Mom . . .' I tried, but my throat wasn't working properly.

'I will.'

He withdrew his hand and I drove away with the window still down, hoping the cold March air would blow my head clear. I inhaled deeply, a strong believer in the curative powers of fresh air. I dug in my purse for a bottle of charcoal tablets and popped two. The evasion I'd offered my parents was true – my stomach was roiling. I hoped I wasn't getting a virus. I cursed myself for forgetting to take Emergen-C that morning. I fumbled for my car supply of echinacea and popped one of those too.

I'd already gone for a run today, but I needed more, like a hit. I steered Elsie towards the university track. I parked and shocked some old people walking for their health by wiggling out of my jeans in the car to slip on sweatpants. I wasn't generally committed to the underwear movement, so Grandpa might have glimpsed something he hadn't seen in years. I stretched for only a nanosecond before I was sprinting. My feet pounded rhythmically along the track in a steady alternation, wind rushing by my ears, blocking all other sound. I had my iPod, but I preferred the womb-like combination of my thudding heart, pounding feet and the blowing wind. I lost myself in the physical exertion of repetitive motion. Of my body obeying me. Of the rare moment when I was in total control.

I wanted to crush my parents' pity and the look on Joe's face beneath my pounding feet. I was *not* someone to be pitied. My heart beat true and strong. My pace ate the track. Look at me, see how I *run*. I can push myself. I have discipline. My resolve solidified. I *would* prove them wrong, but it wouldn't be out of spite. It would be because I could. I would elude my rotten luck if I had to run all the way across the country to do it. In fact, that sounded like just the trick. I was ready for Hollywood. After all, I'd flashed my privates at strangers today. I jogged lap after lap, seeing myself walking in sunshine, confident, competent, happy and successful. Most of all, I imagined a different look in my parents' eyes. It was pride.

CHAPTER 4

FIRED UP

To: LALola@neticom.net
From: Maeveyourday@gmail.com
Sent: March 3
Subject: LA Here I come!

Laura,

Guess what? I'm doing it! You've talked me into it. I've decided to come to California. I'm still working out the details but I'm thinking sooner rather than later. Why wait for paradise, right? I'm so excited. Watch out Paris and Nicole – the new 'It' team of Laura and Maeve is about to hit the town!

Give me a call at 704-555-1881 to talk about details.

Can't wait to see you in person!

Later gater,
M

'Are you sure about this?' my older sister Vi asked me for the hundredth time. I loved her, but sometimes she was too perfect a model for my unrehearsed follow-up act.

'Never more.' I used my shoulder to hold the phone in place while I reached for a carrot. Something about talking into the phone always made me hungry. Maybe it was having something hover so tantalizingly close to my mouth. With my other hand I refreshed my computer. Still no reply from Laura. I squelched a twinge of anxiety as I bit into the carrot. When she was running around the lot, she didn't have email access. Anyway, how hard could it be to find her? I'd drive until the ocean stopped me.

'It's an awfully big move without a *plan*,' she pressed. My sister was not a risk-taker.

'I have a *plan*, Stan.' I mimicked her tone. I was in high spirits.

Vi snorted. 'What, drive west until the ocean stops you?' She had an uncanny ability to read my brain. But nothing could dampen my conviction that moving to California was the solution to my problems.

'Laura invited me. Remember Laura Mills?'

'Laura Mills from when you were ten?'

'We reconnected.' Vi let it go. I was grateful. Laura was the unknown variable in the plan. I didn't actually expect to be frolicking with Johnny Depp upon arrival, but I was counting on being able to crash with my old friend while I got sorted.

Me, the car, the map, I had that under control. Still, there was no reason to think Laura's invitation wasn't sincere.

'A marathon, huh?'

'Yep. The Los Angeles Marathon.' The first step towards a new me was a personal goal. I would train over the summer and the fall marathon would literally be the starting gun for my new life.

'A marathon is 26.2 miles because that's when the first man to run it dropped dead.'

'Are you saying I can't?' I bristled.

'Of course not. You can do anything you put your mind to.'

I wouldn't go that far, but I agreed. 'Yes, I can.'

'It just seems so . . . far. From all of us. If anything happened . . .' Her voice was hesitant.

'Nothing's going to happen,' I said firmly. Did she sound wistful? It occurred to me she might not want me to go for selfish reasons. But it was hard to imagine my sister missing a screwball like me. Her life was pretty perfect. Perfect job, perfect boyfriend, perfect house.

'I'll miss you.' She peeled open my mind yet again.

'I'll miss you too, babaloo.' I meant it. 'But I need to make a change. I need people to take me seriously. Hell, I need to *be* serious. Here, I don't know, I feel trapped in, well, in *before*. I want to prove that I am a completely responsible and capable person.'

She laughed. 'You might be the first. An archeological entry from 3090 will celebrate the discovery of the first completely responsible and capable human being, *Homeo Fictitious Mavis*, adorned in the ritual costume of flip-flops and knock-off Dior sunglasses, and clutching a Map of the Stars' Homes.'

'I'm being serious,' I protested. I knew she'd still worry. She always did. 'It'll be good for me,' I assured her. 'I've got to go, Vi.'

She sighed. 'I know. But let me help. I'm sending you a check.'

I wanted to say no, but I was stone-cold broke. 'Not much,' I capitulated after embarrassingly little inner struggle.

'Trust me.' She laughed. 'I'm buying peace of mind that you won't end up stranded in the middle of the desert with no gas or cell service in a town named Skeleton Junction with a population of four people and one tooth. Promise you'll call before you leave?' It made my departure sound so definite I caught my breath, reality frighteningly present. I almost recanted it all as a big joke. Instead, I assured Vi I'd call her and hung up.

I explored my instinct to retract from the trip. True, I was wafting towards departure with only a vague idea that I'd load up the car with lots of water and hit the road. That didn't really accord with the new responsible me I was shopping to everyone. An inner whisper asked whether I was doing this because I wanted to or because I wanted to prove people wrong.

No, I decided. I *did* want to make a real change. It wasn't just the inspirational Post-it notes I'd taped all over the apartment in a fervor. I focused on my favorite from Master Yoda.

Do. Or do not. There is no try.

I'd been living down to everyone's (low) expectations of me. In their eyes I was Maeve the Clown. Vi was the go-getter. My brother Brick was the smarty. And me? I told good jokes. I made people laugh. I wasn't expected to accomplish a lot, but folks sure liked me. It's a truism that we respond to people's perceptions. I'd lazily adopted the Maeve-is-a-slacker notion as my own. But not anymore. If I went far enough away, I could be anyone. I had a vision of myself in a lab coat and intelligent glasses, holding up a test tube and saying, 'Yes, when the black ants came back to life, I knew I'd found the cure for cancer.'

'Okay . . . maybe that's over the top,' I conceded to Oliver. 'But I *am* capable of doing something amazing, even if it's not the cure for cancer. I use words like "truism" in a sentence when I'm only talking to myself.'

'Let's get drunk!' Oliver said.

'You're going back in your cage,' I threatened. 'This is serious time.'

'Are you thinner?' Oliver nipped my ear.

'You're forgiven.' I laughed. He resumed tugging strands of blonde hair from my braids.

I assembled my morning vitamin regimen as I pondered, absently lining up vitamins A through D, a woman's multi, ginkgo biloba, manganese, flax oil, selenium, dong quai (not that my libido was being called into action these days) and the other dailies. I made a note to pick up ginseng and coenzyme Q10 to counteract the increased stress of travel. If I was going to do this, I resolved to do it right. I needed a battle plan, supplies. I had to prepare for dinner with my father and figure out my financial mess. I frowned into the empty bottle when nothing shook out of my zinc container. How had I let that happen? Zinc is an essential part of a daily supplement regimen. I decided to start with a shopping list.

My eye fell on a Post-it that read:

Before you can arrive where you want to be,
    you have to know where you are going.

The first thing I needed was a Super Map . . .

I spend hours studying maps. For a person who's traveled only within a two state radius, they fascinate me. Riding back from the beach one weekend with Jules, studying a map, I'd noticed a nearby town called Half Hell, North Carolina. I'd insisted she detour. Half Hell hadn't been more than a trailer park off Middle Swamp Road, but the friendliest chatterbox alive had sold me an icy-cold Coke in an old-fashioned bottle, and my passion had been born. I'd organized day trips all over the state to visit Climax, Toast, Erect, Welcome and Whynot, occasionally crossing the border to visit Ninety-Six or Sugar Tit, South Carolina. I loved capturing the curves of the road and the quirks of the towns on film. I'd drag along whatever unlucky friend I could find on these shutterbug Saturday back-road adventures. I'd lost most of my co-conspirators after a trip to Smackass Gap where I'd accidentally forgotten to mention it was practically in Tennessee. My friends were less than impressed with the four miles of houses along Route 64 after eight hours of mountain roads. Even Elsie radiated attitude in the pictures. For me, it was like that trail when I was nine. I couldn't rest until I'd reached my destination. Even if I had to swear affidavits in blood that a town was within three hours and had at least one charming feature, with supporting maps and internet research to prove it, before anyone would go with me.

I liked to snap an Elsie centerfold from each destination, and developed quite a collection of my car in front of one-of-a-kind town signs. Friends contributed postcards from Satan's Kingdom, Vermont; Boring, Oregon; and Gas, Kansas. I meticulously categorized my scrapbook. First you have just plain peculiar names, like Peculiar, Missouri; or Goofy Ridge, Illinois. Second you have 'I was here' places, such as Hell, Michigan; or It, Mississippi. Third are the great imitators: Milan, Ohio; or Moscow, Idaho. Fourth you have superlatives, such as Best, Texas; or Top of the World, Arizona. Best, Texas, is not to be confused with Veribest, Texas. The number of Wild West murders, knifings, shootings and brawls in Best fostered the slogan 'The town with the Best name in the world and the Worst reputation.' Last census: Population, 2. Veribest, by contrast, reported a community of forty inhabitants, two working churches and seven businesses. I fully intended to stop by both on my drive across, and crossed my fingers that the two dedicated souls in Best had hung in there. I wanted to photograph America from the inside out.

Elsie couldn't handle the high speeds of the Interstate, so I happily planned a back-roads course wending between these alluring designations. Back roads would extend my trip, but I was in no hurry. The marathon wasn't for months. Only the longer the journey, the more money I'd need. That *was* a problem, since I didn't have any.

Affordable camping would figure heavily in my trip, and I'd chosen the southwestern route because southern states not only had some crazy town names, but the warm, dry weather would be best for camping. Food would be a bigger problem. I pondered. I'd lived for a week on a carton of eggs once. Eggs were cheap. Hard-boiled eggs kept well and traveled easily. I could get pretty far on a couple of dozen boiled eggs. Eggs are high in iodine, choline and vitamin B2, I reasoned, and a good source of protein. This was a good plan. I'd throw in trail mix and cheese sticks for variety. And oranges. I lived in constant fear of scurvy, so oranges were essential. I'd reserve my cash for necessities, like Diet Coke and water. You want to take lots of water when you drive through the desert. I hadn't driven cross-country before, but it seemed to me that as long as I had a map, water, boiled eggs and sunscreen, I'd be fine.

'People have survived weeks in the Australian Outback with less,' I informed Oliver. 'Naturally I wouldn't want to drink my own . . . you know . . . but that's why I'd have the water.'

That left the last hurdle. Cold, hard cash. I sat back, rubbing my neck. Oliver didn't object, as he'd abandoned my shoulder and was practically beak to nose with Simon Cowell on TV, entranced by an *American Idol* rerun. 'You'll go blind if you sit that close to the TV,' I warned. He ignored me, just as I'd ignored my parents. Kids never listen.

The phone rang. I grabbed another carrot stick and answered. It was Jules.

'Can I borrow your ladder?' she asked without preamble.

A year ago in a fit of DIY that petered out almost before I got home from Lowe's, I'd blown $300 on a ladder. It now served as the world's most expensive drying rack for my delicates. Well, second most expensive. Maybe third. My road bike and treadmill were also costly clotheslines.

The only time the poor emasculated ladder was used for its intended purpose was when I loaned it to friends. Jules regularly borrowed it to change the seasonal fairy lights in her apartment. As it was April, I suspected illuminated mini-bunnies were going up.

'Sure. Easter lights?'

'Yep.'

'For a hundred dollars you can keep it,' I joked. 'I have enough spokes on my bike to dry all my naughty bits.'

'For real?' she demanded. 'Cause if you mean it, you're on.'

'Really?' I was surprised. A hundred bucks was a lot for something as boring as a ladder. But then Jules took her seasonal decorations very seriously.

'Hell, yeah. Save myself the hassle of driving to your place and back every month. And that's over half off.' Some things Jules and I had in common.

My eye fell on my new, trouble-making tennis racket, tag still on, sitting next to a bowling ball that I'd never gotten holes drilled into. 'Do you play tennis?' I asked Jules.

'No. Why?'

'Never mind.' An idea was forming. 'You know my turquoise BCBG pumps you love?' Jules and I wore the same size shoe.

'Of course.'

'I'll sell them to you for another hundred dollars.' I held my breath. It seemed like an outrageous sum to ask of a friend. But the shoes had

36

cost me $160 and I'd worn them in only two battles before the pain in my toes won the war. Jules wore them much more often – she has a commendable tolerance for pain when it comes to shoes. She'd survive the siege of Stalingrad in spikes so long as she looked good. I folded like a Lady Jane Grey monarchy at the first sign of a blister. Had I been Robert E. Lee in uncomfortable heels, the Civil War would have ended in thirty minutes if the North had offered me a pair of flip-flops to concede.

'Seriously? Hell, yes! I love those shoes.' Jules jumped at my offer. I couldn't believe it. I'd made $200 just like that. My brain raced.

'Jules, if you help me organize a yard sale, I'll give you an employee discount on all my shoes.' I barely listened for her response as my eyes flicked from item to item around the room: treadmill, bowling ball, tennis racket, chess set, television, sofa, yoga ball, juicer, waffle maker. I was going to California for a fresh start. I'd sell it all.

'Sure. I'd help anyway.' She was quiet a moment. 'So I guess you're really leaving.'

'Mm-hmm.' I was cataloging the room, eager to get off the phone and start organizing.

'I'll miss you.' Jules recaptured my attention.

I thought of her bright eyes and easy laugh. Her willingness to try anything, even Smackass Gap. I wanted to say something in return, but it was hard for me. I opened my mouth to tell her I'd miss her too. Jules was more than a former co-worker.

She was a friend. Instead I said, 'When I leave, I'm giving you my yellow suede Fiorinas as a memento, pimento.'

'Girl, I can't get you out of town fast enough.' Jules laughed.

When I hung up, I hoped she knew I'd really been trying to say thanks for being a friend.

I was fidgeting anxiously as I stared at my possessions arrayed in an eclectic fire sale. The for-sale list read like a diagnosis of attention deficit disorder: rollerblades next to a paint easel, an ice-cream maker sitting atop empty photo albums, a fishing rod leaning against a croquet set.

'Do you think we're charging enough for the dartboard?' I asked Jules.

'Yes.' She ignored me as she arranged my DVDs, having spent days wrestling me to relinquish my attachment to superfluous inventory. I'd capitulated on everything but my treasured collection of books and my classic Pentax 35mm camera. Now I wasn't so sure.

'But not too much?'

'No.'

Finished with the DVDs, Jules began to construct an attractive tower of beer steins. Early browsers were perusing what we'd dubbed the Apartment Store. That was back when it was funny. It didn't feel funny now. I twitched watching people handle my things. A girl wearing a purple scarf over an orange sweater picked up one of my silver Marc Jacobs peep-toes. I jolted. Oh no. No way. She could *not* have those shoes.

'Maeve!' exclaimed my mother, quick eyes taking in the scene. My father, crowding in behind her, was beaming. When I'd told them over dinner about my plan, they'd been delighted, proud of my sacrificial initiative. In return, they'd been more than generous in discharging my debts. Dad had even given me a gas card with $200 to get me started.

'We've come to help!' bellowed my father. He was never spot-on with volume control. Several people turned to look, but I was too traumatized by my ongoing amputation to be embarrassed as usual.

'Great!' Jules beamed. 'Here – wear this.' She produced a sticker that said 'Ask me for help!' and handed it to my dad. I looked at her suspiciously. Funny that she'd had that lying around. I hadn't been expecting them.

'Okey-doke. Jules can tell you what to do.' My gaze returned to Tacky Girl. She'd slipped on the Marc Jacobs. They fit. I jumped. 'I have to . . .' I started towards her.

'Actually,' my mother looped her arm through mine, redirecting me towards the door, 'your father's going to stay and help so that you and I can spend some mother-daughter time together. We thought you'd need a little break.'

'What a great idea!' Jules' broad smile suggested

39

it was she who was about to get a major break. Dad's grin was equally shit-eating. I eyed them all.

'I don't think . . .'Tacky now had the box tucked under her arm. 'Oh.' I reflexively reached an arm towards the shoes, but my mother was an effervescent defensive back, herding me helplessly towards the door.

'Don't you worry, dear, your dad's happy to help!'

Jules and my father waved like I was off to my first day of school, and just like that I went from a person who had everything, to a girl with a moderate wad of cash and only ten pairs of shoes.

While my ownership of material possessions was being decimated, my mother distracted me with lunch. I never did have a good attention span.

'Your father and I discussed it, and we'd like to give you a parting gift,' she said as we shook out our napkins.

I frowned. 'You've been too generous already.'

'Consider it a gift that keeps on giving. To us, specifically. We've decided to pay for your cell phone until you get to LA and get somewhat settled. I'll feel better knowing we can reach you.'

'You sound like Vi.' I laughed. 'You do know I'm going to the heavily populated American state of California and not to Borneo, right? I doubt I'll be abducted into white slavery.'

'Don't count yourself out. You're a good-looking girl.' She opened her menu as I considered whether

40

she was being facetious. Did I have to add abduction into white slavery to my list of road-trip concerns, between sun poisoning, contaminated drinking water and car problems? With my mother it was hard to tell.

We ordered our salads, and discussed my planned route.

'And Laura's expecting you?' My mother gave me her full attention.

'Oh yes,' I lied, giving my full attention to an imaginary piece of food I pretended to pick off my knife. 'Job and apartment.'

'How remarkably generous, given you haven't seen each other in fifteen years.' I made a non-committal noise.

'We're quite proud of you,' she said. My head jerked up. 'It's very brave to start over like this.'

'Thanks.' My voice was a little choked.

She reached across the table to touch my hand. 'I know it's been tough, Maeve. Would you like to talk about anything?'

I instinctively hunched as I shook my head.

'It's not too late for you to reconsider postponing your departure a few weeks for Cameron's memorial service.' My best friend's birthday was approaching. She would have been twenty-eight.

'I can't,' I said. 'They don't mean it. Seeing me only reminds them. Best to leave it and move forward.'

'Sometimes you have to move through something before you can move forward,' she ventured.

'Mom, I'm leaving soon, and who knows when I'll be able to come back for a visit. Can we make this about me and *not* Cameron?'

A flicker crossed her face, but all she said was, 'Of course. Tell me more about this marathon.'

I lit up. 'It's my first. I'm really excited.'

'All that running you do, I'm sure you'll have no problem.'

'Sprints. This marathon is a challenge.' My tone got a little smug. 'Brick's never run one either.' My brother and I were competitive about track.

My mother rolled her eyes. 'He's never had his period either, but I doubt he wants one just because you have.' My mother discouraged sibling rivalry. It didn't mean that it didn't exist, though. It particularly cut when my baby brother managed to accomplish something I hadn't. Even though he was younger, sometimes I felt like I was chasing to keep up with him. The marathon was mine alone.

The waitress delivered our salads.

'I lived in California for a brief time.' My mother surprised me.

'You did? When?'

A frown creased her forehead. Even though my forehead was smooth, I dragged an involuntary finger across my brow. Connellys were doomed to have divots. 'Well, I don't recall *exactly*,' she began. 'It had to be around 1966, because it was before I met your father. There was this chemistry major at Berkeley, fervent guy . . .'

I was relieved the story didn't end with the revelation that my mother under another name was on the FBI's most-wanted list for revolutionary activities in the sixties. We talked about everything and nothing. The check came, and I reverted to a child, not even pretending I'd contribute.

'I thought we might stop by the mall, pick up any last items you need,' my mother said after she paid.

'I do need film for my camera,' I said. I tended to burn through it. 'And sunscreen.'

'Oh yes. I hope you'll take lots of photos and share your journey with us.'

'Wouldn't be able not to,' I confessed.

'Before we go, I have one last thing for you. A Connelly kind of road map,' She said, extracting a bundle from her bag.

Jules and I were collapsed on folding chairs in my barren living room, Oliver hopping about the apartment in an agitated manner, cataloging empty space. Jules had done a pirate's business, and sold almost everything through a clever series of price reductions as the day went on. Everything left in the apartment would either go home with her (various belts, shoes, cooking pots, and one string of chili-pepper lights that would come in handy for Cinco de Mayo), or be packed in my car bound for Los Angeles. The boxes of dog-eared books were stowed in my parents' attic, though I'd had to fight to convince them I couldn't possibly part with a single volume out of four crates.

'Thanks, Jules. I really mean it.'

'No problem.' She wafted a hand in my direction, 'S'long as you don't change your mind about the Fiorinos. Did you have a good day?'

It *had* been a good day. After being muscled into the car, it'd hit me hard that it would be one of the last times I'd see my mom for a while. I'd felt like an ass for resisting. It's funny how quickly you stop caring about inanimate objects once you're sufficiently parted from them. People are harder to keep, but they matter more and their loss lingers longer.

'It was nice. We spent most of the day talking. You know my mom lived in California once, and she and my dad drove cross-country together before I was born?'

'Hunh-uh. That's cool,' Jules said. 'Beer?'

'Let's get boozy, Suzy.'

She handed me a can of Busch. No point in squandering the profits on the good stuff. We resumed study of eight small statues perched on an empty box in front of us. Oliver danced along the box, approaching then retreating from them, not sure if they were friend or foe.

'So what are they again?' Jules asked.

'My mom made them for my trip.' I was touched that she'd paused work on her current sculpture commission for me. It was a big step. 'She called them kachinas. I'm supposed to leave them along the way.' The eight figures were partially anthro-pomorphized happy, round animal-Buddha-type figures, each about the size of a pool ball. Each incorporated a combination of animals, or animal and human, most pairing selections a mystery to me, given the eclectic workings of my mother's mind.

'What do you mean?'

'I'm supposed to spend time getting to know each one and identifying it with . . . something. Kind of like a Rorschach test – whatever I feel when I contemplate the kachina is its chakra. When that chakra is evoked, either because of how I'm personally feeling or because of how a place makes me feel, I'm supposed to commit the kachina to that place.'

'Sounds complicated.'

'See, like this one, it's a knot of intertwined leaves and stems, like new shoots, and what looks like a hummingbird in there. It makes me think of new growth. So maybe I'd take it to my first day of my new job or leave in the yard of my new apartment or something.'

'And you can't keep them?'

'I think it's a metaphor that I shouldn't regret selling my shoes.' I laughed. 'Even items home-made by one's mother are meant to be left behind, and all that.'

'I don't know,' mused Jules. 'It sounds pretty cool. Letting go of things. You can make them mean anything – fear, loss, a bad guy, a bad time – and then you leave them behind. Because you can't really get attached to something you already know you're going to leave somewhere. So maybe it's more for—'

'Maybe.' I cut her off. I was feeling good and forward-looking. I didn't want to dwell on past missteps. It didn't help that the first kachina was a girl intertwined with a crab, looking backwards. I had a pretty good idea what that one meant. 'I'm supposed to keep the last one.'

'That one?' Jules gestured towards a statue Oliver had decided to befriend.

'Yes.' I'd noticed right away it was a combination of a plump female mother-figure and an owl that resembled my favorite stuffed animal. My protectors.

'I'm glad you get to keep one. They're so pretty it'll be tough to leave them behind.'

'Yeah,' I agreed.

Jules finished her beer, then looked at me. 'Well, I can't have another or I can't get home. And I'm stalling anyway. I guess it's time to say goodbye.'

I nodded.

She unfolded her five foot eleven inches from her chair, and I stood also, two inches shorter. Two modern Amazons without weapons, unsure of what to do next.

'Take care of the bar,' I said. 'I don't want to hear from Billy and Brooks that you've been slacking. And make sure Joe doesn't have a heart attack.' Translation: I'm going to miss you, Joe,

Billy and Brooks but I can't admit it and I refuse to cry.

'You too, girl. Be careful driving, and call me. We're going to miss the hell out of you.' Jules, clearly, was much more in touch with her emotional side.

'You're psyched to be the only hot gal at the bar!' I shifted us back to banter.

'Roger wilco.' She hugged me so hard I thought my ribs would crack. Since she initiated, I let her. More than that, I sank into liquid, let the love pour all over me, and drank it in like a greedy child. Just for a minute. Then I pulled away. We were both blinking.

'You call me, kid.' She didn't look at me as she gathered her bags of my former stuff. We both knew I wouldn't often. It wasn't really my thing. But for her, I would, once in a while.

Jules stopped at the door. 'You know, bad luck isn't really a thing. It's like weather. It happens, but it doesn't follow you around specifically. Sometimes, when you think its bad, it's actually a sign of good luck, like rain on your wedding day.' She looked at me, and recited one of our favorite silly Southern expressions. 'I'm not sayin' . . . I'm just sayin'. There's no such thing as attached bad luck. But frame of mind, now that stays with you for ever.'

We held gazes for a moment. Then she smiled and said, 'Come home soon.' And she was gone. I was breathing fast and shallow, from all the things that wanted to come out of my mouth but couldn't. Seconds ticked by. Then adrenaline and the voice clamoring in my heart won over my inertia. I ran to the back of the room, then whirled to dash after her.

Her car was pulling out when I hit the sidewalk.

'Jules,' I screamed, waving my free arm. 'Jules!' I reached her battered Saturn and battered it some more, willing it to stop with the intensity of my need. She hit the brakes and I ran to the driver's-side window.

'I forgot . . .' I gasped, breathless from my sprint. 'I forgot to give you these.' I offered the box.

Jules looked confused, then understanding. She took the brand new pair of prized red suede boots that didn't hurt my feet even a little bit.

'You didn't have to,' she smiled, 'but I'll take them.'

'I did.' I was still panting. 'I did. I'm sorry,' I said for no clear reason. 'Thank you.'

'Don't ever be sorry and don't ever feel you need to thank people for loving you,' she said. 'I'm your friend. Even when your ass is all the way in California.'

I nodded tightly. Facial control was essential.

'You ready?' she asked. I nodded again.

She smiled. 'Love you.' She paused, then smiled more broadly. 'And I know you love me back.' And she drove off, one hand fluttering out the window.

I waved back, goodbye to my friend, goodbye

to my boots, and goodbye to the small kachina I'd tucked into the box. It was one of an egg intertwined with what looked like a tadpole, and it was the first one I'd had an immediate reaction to. My reaction had been gratitude. To Jules, for putting up with me, for understanding me. And most of all, for being around to say goodbye to me. I was down to nine pairs of shoes. My journey had begun. I went to bed, ready for morning and for my new adventures to arrive.

CHAPTER 5

ROAD TRIP, DON'T FORGET THE BIRD

My first adventure sucked. I stared at Darryl from Okay, Oklahoma, in disbelief.

'You're kidding, right?' I willed him to crack a smile and tell me he was 'jes' joshin''. He didn't.

'Nawp.'

I rubbed a hand over my face, praying it was a dream. When I opened my eyes, I was still staring at a John Deere cap and a mechanic named Darryl. Darryl had a deeply lined tanned face and repeatedly deposited chewing tobacco spit into a can of Dr Pepper. Darryl also had very bad news.

The trip had started out fine. Our routine was set from our first night camped outside Sweet Lips, Tennessee, I in my tent, Oliver cozy in a little birdie fleece-lined Snuggle Hut that hung from a hook at the peak of my tent. We'd followed back roads across North Carolina, Tennessee, and Arkansas, snapping stylish pictures of Elsie in front of landmarks like the sign that proclaimed 'Welcome to Sweet Lips! They're Smilin' 'Cause You're Here!' I ate a lot of boiled eggs. After a few days of pouting silence, Oliver adapted to the new routine and started complimenting me again. Elsie guzzled gas. Our journey had been adventure free. Until today.

We woke in Toad Suck, Arkansas. The day was hot and sunny, and I was eager to keep going. After forcing down a heavily salted egg, we visited Paris, Arkansas before pointing Elsie towards Okay, Oklahoma. Leaving Charlotte farther and farther behind felt miraculous. Like I had superpowers – the power to shake off great weight, the power to give the gift of life, the power to let the day take you where it would. Freedom. Savoring it, my superfoot unconsciously pressed the gas pedal too far, causing Elsie to wobble precariously as she picked up speed. I eased up.

'Sorry, old girl.'

Nothing could shake my optimism. I improved the tan on my left elbow. On either side of the deserted country roads were endless fields of something agricultural. Corn? Soy? Alfalfa? I'd stopped and taken a picture to figure it out later. I couldn't tell you if alfalfa was a tall yellow stalk or a mossy green carpet. Whatever it was, instead of finding the unchanging landscape boring, I found it soothing. As had become my routine, I didn't play music in the first hours of the day, preferring to let my mind wander. Mostly, I let it wander into wholly unrealistic but highly entertaining fantasies of my new life in California.

John Mayer was just bending on one knee to

propose, when Elsie started wobbling in earnest. I frowned at the speed gauge. She shouldn't be wobbling at 45 m.p.h. That usually started at sixty. I tried accelerating all the way to sixty before slowing down, as if to reset her, but the shaking became violent, steering wheel yanking at my hands. I slowed. As long as I held it to 40 m.p.h., there didn't seem to be any problems.

I considered this. I considered Elsie's history of 'surprises.' I considered the endless rows of unidentified plants and complete lack of humans surrounding me. I made a decision. After consulting the map, I decided that Okay was a suitably sized city and I could continue my course. Which brought me to now, here with Darryl at Okay Body.

'How far can I get?' I hoped my desperation didn't show. Never let a mechanic see your fear.

'Fronts could go anytime.' Spit.

'You're telling me I have suicidal front tires?'

'Guess so.' Darryl wasn't big on pronouns.

I closed my eyes. 'How much?'

'Cain't just replace two. Ya gotter change all four.' Spit.

My eyes popped open. 'What's wrong with the back two?'

'Cain't have two new tares and two old tares. Getcher wobblin' that way. An's hell on th' axles. Gotta replace all four.'

'How much?' I repeated, bracing myself. When he said three hundred and twenty dollars, I started breathing very fast and my heart went feral.

'Installation's 'nother two-hunnerd-fitty.' I fought the impulse to break into a run, sprinting wild and free away from Darryl and his numbers. Instead I held up my hand to silence him, pressing the other on my chest to keep my heart inside it. My bad luck curse giggled somewhere.

'Five . . .' I swallowed. So much for not showing my fear. 'Five hundred and seventy total?' I quavered. That was half of what I had left. At $4.02 a gallon, it cost me $80 to fill up Elsie's tank, which I did more than once most days. After four spiffy new tires, I wasn't going to make it very far. I was definitely voting in the next election. Gas was ridiculous.

Darryl's voice brought me back from political fervor. Surprisingly, my evident panic had the opposite effect from what I'd expected, and his eyes softened.

'Got a deal goin' where if ya buy three tares ya get the fourth free. Those tares'll work with yer car. Save ya eighty bucks.'

'Oh.' I exhaled with relief, nodding. It wasn't much, but it was something. 'Let's do that.' I even managed a smile.

"Course, ain't got 'em.'

'What?'

'Gotter order 'em. Take ya three days, mebbe.' Spit.

'Three days.' My look was blank.

'Yep.' He matched it.

Three days in this town. I had a thought. 'If I'm

53

going to be here three days, can you give me some work? I'm really strong – stronger than I look. And I'm a hard worker. And honest. I've never stolen a thing in my life. I can pitch my tent right here, and I can clean, I can work a register . . .' I trailed off as Darryl shook his head.

'Crystal does all that.' He said it as if I was supposed to know who Crystal was. Maybe I was. Maybe she was Miss Mechanic Oklahoma, doing mechanical goodwill all across the state. Maybe she could have an 'accident' that would take her off her feet for a few days . . .

'Place up the road could use some 'sistance,' Darryl interrupted my plotting.

'Really?'

'Rico at the Okay Burrito's always lookin' for day labor.'

My face fell. 'Oh. I can't get around. No car.'

'Reckon ya can borrow the bike. Got left when Okay Spoke went outer business. Can pitch yer tent here if ya want to, too. Get to Rico's, turn left where Nellie's Flowers used to be an' follow on up past Duke's to the light. Hang a right and carry on 'bout two blocks. Be on yer right.' Darryl seemed to think I'd spent a past life in Okay, cavorting with Crystal, Nellie and Duke, but I didn't care. I loved him. I especially loved that he didn't ask me any questions about where I'd come from and how I'd ended up this ill-prepared far from the state that had issued my license plates.

'Thanks.' I beamed. 'Thanks a lot.'

'No worries.' Spit. 'Want them tares, then?'

I set up my tent on a charming piece of asphalt behind the garage, fragrant with diesel. Darryl took a shine to Oliver, so his cage was installed in the Okay Body office. I worried that Oliver would develop a mediocrity complex, but there was no other solution. As I pedaled off on Darryl's bike, Oliver was wooing Crystal with compliments about her hair and figure. If Crystal had ever been Miss Mechanic Oklahoma, it was fifty years ago, so she was charmed right to the roots of her blue rinse. I was assured he was in good hands.

I found Rico's with no problem, because I'd made Darryl draw me a map to supplement his helpful directions. Okay Burrito was a generic-looking place with a big marketing challenge convincing people the food was better than the titular-proclaimed average. It was run by a short Hispanic man sporting the most precise middle part I'd ever seen and a trim mustache. Rico's nervous energy made it seem like he was fluttering even when he was standing still. When I explained why I was there, his face split into a huge grin.

'You start now?'

It was three o'clock. 'Sure.'

'Good, good.' He actually rubbed his hands together. And then he disappeared, leaving me alone in the restaurant. I was startled. I'd at least expected a lesson in how to make a burrito, and maybe an apron, but I shrugged it off. How hard could it be? You throw a bunch of stuff in a tortilla and roll it up. It's not like the customer could see what was inside. I was studying the menu when Rico reappeared.

'Yes, yes. You're just the right size.'

Size? Oh, right. Apron. It wasn't the cleanest thing I'd ever seen. It was actually brown. And sort of . . . furry.

'You can try on in back. I'll stay here.'

And then he handed me a donkey suit.

'What . . .' When I hesitated, he shook it at me.

'You pass out these.' He pointed to a stack of flyers. 'You get customers into the restaurant.'

My mouth dropped open.

He waggled the donkey again. 'You work all day, fifty dollars cash. No tax. And burrito for lunch and dinner.'

I grabbed the donkey suit. It looked like it would fit just fine.

After an all-egg diet, the burritos were heaven on earth. The work was not. The not-too-hot day was gone. Or maybe synthetic donkey suits are endothermic. For whatever reason, I was sweating my ass off. I refused to think of my sweaty predecessors. Instead I smiled at passersby and tried to force flyers they didn't want into their hands. I reminded myself not to take it personally when people crossed the street to avoid me. I did that with perfume squirters at the mall. Though after

56

a few hours as a burro, a spritz wouldn't have hurt me any.

At 9 p.m. Rico locked the front doors and handed me thirty dollars and a burrito.

'You come back tomorrow. You make good donkey.' He fluttered at me. I felt more like an ass when I climbed on the bike to pedal home, donkey hanging around my neck like a bad Hercules impersonation, furry legs waving in the wind.

The shop was closed when I got back. Through the window I could see Oliver sleeping in his cage. I pressed my hand against the glass as if it would bring us closer. It was the safest place for him, but I felt very cut off. My phone was dead – I needed Elsie to charge it – and I was separated from my bird. Both hands on the glass now, I watched Oliver sleep. I resolved never to go to prison. To be permanently separated from what you loved by glass would be horrible. Tears threatened to leak out of the corners of my eyes. Since I'd never been more alone, I could have let them. But with resolute hands I wiped them away and straightened.

'You did good today, kid,' I told myself, and went to get comfortable on my asphalt bed. I hadn't even read a page of my normal nightly reading before I was sound asleep.

'Genie grants a Texan an' a Oklahoman each a wish,' Darryl started his joke. 'Texan says, "I wanna wall so high and thick, nuthin' can get inter or outer Texas. Keep dem Okies out." "Bam," genie says, an' it's done. Oklahoman scratches his head, thinks a bit, an' asks, "So that thar wall is so thick, nuthin' can get inter or outer Texas?" "Yep," says the genie. "Right then," Okie says. "Fill it with water."' Darryl chuckled loudly at his own joke.

I laughed, though I'd heard six variations on the same basic theme in only a few days in Oklahoma. I suspected I'd hear six more variations in Texas, with the states reversed.

Crystal giggled as she fed Oliver sunflower seeds. Oliver had a fan for life in Crystal. Crystal had a fan for life in me. Turns out she and Darryl were sister and brother, and lived around the corner from the garage in a neat clapboard Victorian. The inside of their house looked like a doily factory had exploded. The lace wheels covered every surface, including the toilet seat.

'I like to tat lace,' Crystal said with pride as she showed me around, pausing at every indistinguishable doily. It took over an hour.

I was grateful for the meal, but equally grateful they didn't offer me the guest room. It was creepily filled with shelves of glassy-eyed dolls, all of whom were introduced to me by name: Mary Kate, Angelina, Britney, Farrah, Bo, Victoria and the incongruously named Oprah Bo Peep. I'd have had nightmares.

After my tour we sat down to supper. I was

58

delighted to expand my menu of eggs and burritos with watery beef stroganoff and cherry pie from a box. Crystal said grace, head bowed. 'God bless this meal we are about to receive, and God bless Maeve, Oliver, George W. Bush, Nancy Reagan, and the person who invented watermelon jellybeans.'

After supper, we played gin rummy. 'Let's leave the washing-up and play cards!' Crystal was thrilled to have a new player. After a few deals I could see why. She was remarkable – she won every single hand.

'I practice a lot on the computer,' she demurred when I complimented her. Darryl rolled his eyes.

'Cheats,' he explained, when she went to the bathroom. 'Have a gander.'

I peeked under the card table where he indicated and was astonished to see several royal families and multiple double-digit cards stuck to its underside with chewing gum. Darryl shrugged. 'Winnin' makes her happy. Don't bother me none.'

I'd have to call Brick and explain this form of brotherhood.

I lost interest in cards after that, and was relieved when Crystal realized that we were about to miss the beginning of *Shrek* II and raced to the living room. We followed. It was nice to have a movie night after being on the road. Darryl made popcorn out of real corn kernels in an old-fashioned iron corn-popper with a long handle, and we munched and giggled through the movie, Crystal most of all.

When it was over, I stayed for one more cup of tea, despite the threat of being invited to stay, then Oliver and I wandered back to our Asphalt Sweet Asphalt.

It took five days rather than three to get the tires delivered and installed, but the $280 I earned made it all worthwhile – even the criminal drubbings at gin rummy. And I'd come to care for Darryl, Crystal and Rico. Their quiet kindness reassured me that I could venture out into the world and make a new start, that there'd be help along the way. That and my new business plan.

When we left, the most affected was Crystal, who bid Oliver a tearful goodbye, raining sunflower seeds on him. She pressed a box of bacon-flavored gumballs into my hand.

'To go with all those eggs you eat,' she explained.

Once I hit the gas, we paused only long enough to take the obligatory Elsie picture at the town sign. I felt a twinge of guilt as Okay diminished in my rear-view mirror. The mirror also reflected the ear of a large donkey. Rico was expecting me at work, and instead I'd slunk off in the early-morning light with a newly shod Elsie and his donkey suit. So much for never having stolen a thing in my life. I intended to repay him and return the suit when I was done. I hoped the kachina I'd left on the counter holding down my IOU note made up for it. To him, the little statue resembling a fox and grapes would be an odd form of security deposit. To me, it meant ingenuity.

60

And hopefully the earning ability to never, ever have to resort to the bacon gumballs.

Bonnie Bunn, of Bunn in the Oven, stared at me blankly. 'You want to what?'

I gave her my most engaging smile. 'I have this donkey suit, see.' I displayed it. 'And you sell burritos. I'd attract customers. We'd make you a reputation as the best burrito in town! People would think Bunn, and crave a burrito.' It was a thin argument. Burritos occupied a wafer-thin slice of Bonnie's menu, which was heavier on baked goods than sandwiches, never mind Mexican entrées. I'd had better success at Loco Taco in Loco, Oklahoma, and Bell-A-Burrito in Uncertain, Texas. But Bonnie offered the only burrito in Ding Dong, Texas, so I had to give it a shot. I was a little desperate. Given the distance between west Texas towns, I didn't want to leave Ding Dong without plenty of money stockpiled. It was a long way to Noodle.

Bonnie wasn't convinced. 'You mean like the guy used to walk around in the cell-phone suit in front of Hank's place?'

I was about to launch into an emphatic explanation of why Hank was a brilliant marketer, when I stopped. 'Used to?' I said instead.

'Haven't seen him in a while.'

'Where is Hank's exactly?'

Five days later my guilt as I drove off in the middle of the night with Hank's cell-phone suit was eased by the fact that I'd lured fifty people into his store, and my use of legalese in the IOU approached official. More importantly, I had enough gas money to get to Truth or Consequences, New Mexico, which had both a Mexican restaurant and a cell-phone store.

CHAPTER 6

UNKNOWN *AND* SURPRISE

I tapped my pencil against my teeth as I studied the map. Unknown, Arizona, looked pinprick-tiny. I was seasoned at route-planning now, triangulating desired towns, available camp-grounds and potential burrito, cell-phone and (after Sunshine, New Mexico) chicken restaurants. The small towns were the trickiest. I'd arrived at faded crossroads 'towns' to find they no longer existed, their entire memory reduced to a dot on an outdated map, dependent on lazy fact-checkers for this fragile proof they ever lived. It shook my self-assuredness that something as seemingly substantial as a town could fade just like that. If we couldn't keep a town alive, how vulnerable was something fragile like me? I reapplied SPF70 sunscreen.

I could go the lower Arizona route, entering at Portal and passing through Paradise and Tombstone, to Greaterville before reaching Unknown. Beyond the irresistible Unknown was the equally alluring Why, Arizona, on the Tohono O'odham Indian Reservation.

'Tohono O'odham, Tohono O'odham, Tohono O'odham,' I said three times fast, just to see.

My other option was the northerly route from Eager, through Superior, Carefree, Surprise and Nothing. There was also the appeal of a little town named Brenda near the California border. I wondered if the whole town dressed in dowdy clothes and was secretly resentful of a prettier older-sister town somewhere named Betty.

It was a difficult choice. I called my sister.

'It's early, cruel wench,' Vi mumbled into the phone.

I looked at my watch. Oops. 'Sorry. I've driven across three time zones in two weeks, including states and Native American reservations that don't observe daylight savings. The actual time can ricochet wildly within sixty miles, so my understanding of it has devolved to "diner open" or "diner closed". I'm in a diner.'

'Diners allow birds?' Oliver was talking up a storm, wooing me for some pancake.

'This one does.' 'Diner' was a strong word for the folding chair I occupied in the back of the local Texaco store, but the pancake breakfast #2 Thelma had whipped up for me between register sales was good. It was a $3.99 splurge, but a stomach riot was incipient at the prospect of another hard-boiled egg and I'd had a lucrative cell-phone stop yesterday in Rodeo.

'So what's up?'

I explained my dilemma.

'Brenda is tempting,' she agreed. 'You could see if the residents wear funny outdated hats. But Eager,

64

Superior, Carefree, Surprise and Nothing denote a negative emotional trend from vain purposeless to unanticipated emptiness. It sounds like bad feng shui to me. In contrast, Tombstone, Portal, Paradise, Greaterville, Unknown and Why all tap into the fundamental questions of life, the afterlife and why we're here. You could actually drive through a version of heaven on earth. That sounds much more interesting. Besides, I've been to Surprise, and the surprise is that it's a boring suburb of Phoenix. Nothing to see but Top Shop. Better to go to Surprise, New York, in the Catskills.'

Trust my sister to know about both Surprises. I didn't ask. She had a brain like a sponge.

'Philosophical genius,' I complimented her. 'There's an Eden around there too.'

She laughed. 'Now I want to go with you. Call me if you find the Fountain of Youth.'

It might not be heaven on earth, but the drive from Tombstone toward Unknown was gorgeous. The sky was blue and impossibly large, the road a ribbon of asphalt snaking across the wide golden prairie. In the distance the grasslands met sloping brown hills. I fancied the hills were great slumbering creatures that had dozed off when the earth was young and been gently overgrown with a blanket of grasses and flowers. When they were fully rested, they would wake and stand, rubbing decades of soil from their eyes and shaking off crumbling sod and scrub trees like I dusted off sand from the beach. Then they would lumber gently into the distance to wherever mythical creatures go for a bite to eat after a long nap.

I'd enjoyed my detour to Tombstone, the 'Town Too Tough to Die', site of the most famous shoot-out in the Wild West. I'd visited the very spot where Sheriff Virgil Earp, Wyatt Earp, Morgan Earp and Doc Holliday battled cattle-rustler Ike Clanton and his band at the O.K. Corral on 26 October 1881, followed by a quick lunch and Elsie photo op at Big Nose Kate's Saloon.

As I headed south, the distant hills became more pronounced, pushing upwards to full-fledged mountains and jutting cliffs. I was driving through the cradle between the Santa Rita Mountains to the west and the Huachuaca Mountains and Canelo Hills to the east. Cattle and the occasional cluster of deer roamed the high desert scrublands. I felt like I'd stepped back in time to the cowboy era.

'Howdy, pardner,' I said to Oliver as we cruised past steel windmills and the occasional ranch, with charmingly authentic gates proclaiming Circle Z or Lazy Bar.

'Carrot,' said Oliver.

'Howdy, pardner.' Oliver cocked his head inquisitively. 'Howdy, pardner,' I repeated, waiting for him to catch on.

Silence.

'Howdy, pardner.'

'Carrot. Squaaawk. Are you thinner?'

'Never mind. How about some Death Cab for Cutie?' I named a favorite band.

A few miles ahead, a road traveled off to the east. I consulted the map. It looked to be the turn-off for Unknown. I took it, looking at the sky to assess the time. Not that I had any tracker skills or anything like that. I couldn't tell time from the sun any better than I could put my ear to the dirt and detect the approach of a stagecoach. Still, I'd acquired some road savvy. I'd learned that in small towns people stop at yellow lights and you'd better be ready not to plow into the back of them. I'd learned that beef jerky was popular with truckers but not their intestines so it was best not to use the gas station men's room if the women's room was occupied, no matter how bad you had to pee. And I'd learned that the sun dropped fast in the west. From about four, the sun's rays slanted noticeably, permeating the light with a day-is-ending feeling. When it began to set in earnest, you had about an hour before it dropped like a stone and everything became as dark as ink. At that point you wanted your tent up for the night.

As I was mentally counting my remaining pairs of clean socks, Elsie emitted an ominous clunk and rattle. A horrible grinding noise came from under the hood and the car bucked once before all momentum ceased. At that moment the music ended, and it was to the sound of utter, penetrating silence that we coasted to a stop on an unnamed road in the least populated place I'd ever been.

For a moment I sat there, my mind not grasping our predicament. Stupidly I looked at the gas gauge, but I wasn't out of fuel. I'd filled up in Tombstone. Next most stupidly, I looked at my phone. I hadn't had a signal since Rodeo this morning. Besides, who would I call? Vi, can you magically appear from DC to save your little sister again? Dad, you're helpless to aid me, but in my panic I'll tell you all about this predicament beyond your control so you can have a heart attack worrying from afar? This bad luck curse was getting out of hand.

I unbuckled my seat belt, but hesitated, reluctant to exit the car. If I got out, it became real. If I sat in the car, I could pretend I'd merely pulled over to take a scenic photo. Or check the map. I dug out my camera and cranked down the window. I shot a picture of the stretching yellow grasslands and distant rolling hills. I looked at Oliver. He looked at me.

'Howdy, pardner,' I said.

'Oh shit,' Oliver said.

I opened the door and stepped out. The silence wasn't really silence when you listened. There was the whisper of the slightest breeze and the gentle rustling of blades of grass. Birds chirped. My pulse thumped triple time.

I released Elsie's hood and stared at her mystifying guts, as if the problem came with repair instructions, like one of those guns where you pull the trigger and a sheet of paper rolls out with the word BANG on it. Except my blown gasket or whatever would release detailed instructions that could be completed with water, some extra motor oil, jumper cables and an old T-shirt, because that was pretty much all I had in the way of car repair. I closed the hood.

I looked up the road, stretching without variation to the east. I looked down the road, stretching without variation to the west. I felt the impending presence of bad news, like a long-ago waiting room. Cameron had not been doing well. Her family had asked me to wait outside her room for a bit. A white-coated doctor stepped out. He conferred with a nurse, and she pointed. They both looked at me. He started in my direction, shoulders weighted with news I didn't want. The room pressed around me, and I wanted to escape, to run away from that white coat that was going to ruin things. I looked up the road again, and broke into a run. I sprinted for all I was worth, arms pumping, braids flying, knees lifting higher and faster, inadequate Converse low-top sneakers blurred with motion. I raced against panic, running hard. All thought disintegrated into pounding feet, burning lungs, pouring sweat. I ran until I thought my lungs would burst, then stumbled to a stop, doubled over gasping, sweat dripping from my face. I let out a yell that came from deep within, expelling all my frustration. It felt good, so I did it again, straightening.

'Dirty rotten luck, you won't always win!' I

shouted at a sky that calmly absorbed my rage into its wide, unwavering depths. I shook my fist for dramatic emphasis, which made me feel both silly and satisfyingly cinematic. A butterfly drifting lazily on no particular trajectory briefly lighted on my fist, then floated on. I watched for a minute until its butter-yellow wings got lost among a host of other languidly circling butterflies. Then I turned and jogged slowly back to my life.

Calmer this time, I again looked up the road, and again looked down the road. I absorbed the unchanged setting of nothing but road. I regarded the sun, relentlessly speeding its course towards extinguishing in the ocean somewhere near where I wanted to be. I looked at my trusting bird. They all seemed to be waiting for my decision. I realized I was waiting too, and shook myself. No one else was going to magically take care of this. I had to figure out what to do.

First, ascertain the level of hopelessness. I slid behind the wheel and tried the ignition. Nothing. That, combined with the lack of any BANG under the hood, meant Elsie was out. But she was presumed repairable. Elsie always bounced back. She was older than me. Her determination to live was why I liked her. The last thing I wanted was for her to get plowed under by some semi-truck barreling down the road after dark. I shifted the car into neutral and got out, wishing I'd packed lighter. I angled the wheels, then put my shoulder into it and pushed. It was slow, sweaty, exhausting going, but I eased the car over to the side of the road. Then I dug around in my purse until I found a compact. I opened it and placed it in the back window to hopefully reflect a warning to any approaching headlights. It wasn't much, but it was something. I felt clever for thinking of it, which gave me a needed confidence boost.

Next, I considered Oliver. I hated the idea of leaving him. The sun was setting now, promising cool temperatures, but who knew when I'd get back tomorrow? It could get hot. Roasty, even. I could never live with myself if I returned to find Oliver dead on his perch like a cooked quail. No, there was nothing for it. I'd have to take him with me. Thank God I'd had his wings clipped right before we left. He was so particular about who did his nails and feathers that I'd made sure we went to his favorite birdie spa one last time pre-departure, forestalling the need to break in a new LA groomer as long as possible. Cockatiels don't like change.

'Want to go for a walk, buddy?' I gently extracted him from his cage.

'Road trip. Don't forget the bird!' he chirped happily.

'Yeah, this is all fun and games to you,' I chided as I secured a loop around his right leg that connected by a long cord to a bracelet I secured to my wrist. It was a precaution considering his clipped wings and the improbability that he'd stray far from me, but it made me feel better. I perched him on

71

my shoulder. He promptly clambered up my braid like a rope ladder to settle down on top of my head. I slipped his Snuggle Hut inside my jacket. When it got cold, he could nestle in it.

I removed extra sweaters and socks from my overnight backpack, and replaced them with my sleeping bag, my current book and essentials from my purse. I tied my tent to the bottom loops. I looked longingly at my Thermarest, but there was no room. It would be an uncomfortable night. I tested my headlamp to make sure it had full juice. No telling how far I'd be walking in the dark. Finally I grabbed two large bottles of water and stuck a boiled egg in my pocket.

With a last pat for Elsie, I locked the door and started walking.

'I'm a girl with a bird on her head, destination Unknown,' I said to no one in particular. I amused myself with all variations of heading into the unknown as I kept a slow pace so as not to unsettle Oliver. I didn't want to burn out my own energy either. Fifteen minutes after I set out, the landscape was unchanged and the sun selfishly abandoned me. Soon after, the darkness was impenetrable and I was dependent on my headlamp. I prayed that Unknown still existed. Then I pondered whether the unknown *could* exist in tangible form. My anxious brain spiraled into a loop where I almost convinced myself that I wouldn't find anything there because there was no 'there' there, and to get to Unknown I had to travel within.

That's what walking alone in the dark in the middle of nowhere will do to you.

Frogs and crickets sang a lively chorus. I sat down after a while to rest and put on an extra sweater. Oliver clambered down my arm to my wrist, not liking the cold either. I tucked him into his Snuggle Hut and both into my jacket, and he gave a happy 'tut', comforted by my heart beating beneath his cocoon. I resumed walking. Tree cover over the road was thickening, fracturing the moonlight. I hadn't seen a single car in three hours. It was only around nine but I was getting tired. I figured I'd walk another hour.

After half an hour, the road did something funny. I swept my headlamp from side to side, but the night gobbled its puny effort. I could see little beyond my feet. Still, as far as I could tell, the road split around an island of land. I stepped off the road, anxious not to tumble into a pond or something. The land appeared lawn-like, as far as southern Arizona had lawns. I advanced cautiously, but the path remained clear. After picking my way several hundred yards, my headlamp caught a picnic table. I wilted in relief. It must be some kind of camping or roadside facility. I would stay here. Maybe, come daylight, I'd discover a toilet. Happy thought.

The ground was clear beyond the picnic table. After kicking a few rocks out of the way, I pitched my tent, moving carefully so as not to jostle Oliver. I hung his hideaway from a hook on the tent ceiling so I didn't roll on him in my sleep, and draped a shirt over it for warmth. He was making a contented grinding sound, meaning he was about to fall asleep. I pulled off my Converses, wincing at the shin splints setting in from my impromptu sprint, and undid my braids, combing my fingers through my long hair. I debated shucking my jeans in favor of more comfortable sweats but decided against it. I planned to get up early, and it was cold as ass. The temperature had dropped significantly when the sun had set. I alternated between worrying about Oliver, who was, in fact, snug as a bug in his little birdie glove, and my conviction that my own glands were swelling by the second with the onset of an aggressive sore throat. I would double my Emergen-C intake tomorrow.

I slid tiredly into my sleeping bag, zipping it up to my chin.

'Tomorrow will be a better day, pal,' I murmured to my sleeping bird, before I dropped off myself.

CHAPTER 7

RUBY IN THE ROUGH

I was being abducted by aliens. Bright lights were flooding the tent in a swirl of colors. Some red, some blue, but most of all a penetrating white light I'd seen even with my eyes closed. Eyes cracked open now, the entire tent was illuminated. My sluggish brain struggled to understand. I'd been in the forest in the middle of nowhere. Hadn't I?

A car door slammed. Wait a minute. There was nothing supernatural about that, unless the aliens drove a truck. I heard booted footsteps crunching towards my tent, accompanied by another beam of bobbing light. Fully awake now, alarm dissipated my confusion. Oh God. I was going to be murdered by some isolation-deranged cowboy, cut into small pieces and fed to pigs to destroy the evidence. My family would be tormented the rest of their lives, wondering. I canvassed the tent for potential weapons, but the most lethal thing I had was yesterday's sweaty T-shirt, and I was still wearing it. I debated whether I could run and protect Oliver at the same time. No, too risky. I'd have to fight . . .

'Knock, knock,' drawled a pleasant, twangy voice. 'Care to come on out here, li'l camper?'

I breathed shallowly, not making a sound. Maybe he'd decide no one was here.

'I can see ya in there.' The voice sounded amused.

I remained immobile, frozen with indecision and the irrational hope that maybe this would all stop happening, that I'd wake up, that the lights would go away, when . . .

'Howdy, pardner!' My bird introduced himself.

There was a disembodied chuckle. 'Howdy back atcha, nature-lover. Whadda ya say ya come on out here and make our acquaintance proper like?'

Resigned, I unzipped my bag and crawled out of the safety of my tent. I stood, pushing my hair out of my eyes, blinking at the light shining on my face

'Wall now, ya are a young thing ain't cha?' the amused speaker pronounced. 'And prettier than ya sound.'

Was this some weird kind of hillbilly courtship?

'Road trip, don't forget the bird!' Oliver chirped, anxious at being left alone. This is why people get dogs, I thought. The beam left my face and shone on the tent.

'That a 'tiel in there?' My assailant's question surprised me. 'My ex-wife had one a them. Damn thing never shut up and had a mouth like a sailor. Terrible to be enjoyin' a bite a meat after a long day's work with a foul-mouthed fowl in the back hollering "legs up and open wide, toots" the whole time.'

I squinted, trying to make out my extraordinary visitor while his beam was directed towards Oliver. I could only distinguish impressive height and breadth and something glinting at eye level before the light returned to me. I winced and turned my head.

'Sorry 'bout that.' The light went out. 'Guess you musta been sleepin'.'

I faced him again, but he was backlit by the headlights of what I guessed was a sizeable dual wheel SUV truck, and all I could ascertain was his considerable bulk.

'Care to share your name, missy?' he asked, not unkindly.

I shifted in my sock feet, hair a curtain around my face. Should I tell him?

'Tell you what. Seein' as you mebbe warn't expectin' me, I'll go first. My name's Lawrence Oscar Fenter Ashburn Perry. From a long line of pioneer ladies who married a lot of folks but didn't want to give up the name they had before. I'm the sheriff here in Unknown. People mostly call me Bruce.' The light clicked on again, this time shining at a bronze star on the chest of his brown uniform. The beam then angled up, revealing a face that wasn't scary even with the gruesome flashlight-under-the-chin effect. He had a thick dark mustache, round cheeks and deep eyes surrounded by appealing crinkles. He looked like an amiable Bavarian barber.

The light clicked off. 'An' you?'

'Maeve,' I said. 'Maeve Connelly.' It registered that I might be saved. This man could take me to civilization.

'Wall, Maeve Con'ley, what're you doin' camping in the middle of my town square?' were his astonishing next words. My jaw must have dropped wide open because Lawrence Oscar Fenter Ashburn Perry chuckled. I looked around, and sure enough I could make out faint building outlines in the truck headlights.

'Is it . . .' I hesitated. 'Is it a . . . ghost town?'

His chuckle turned into a guffaw. 'That'd make my job easier. No, Unknown's a full-on thrivin' little town with enough colorful characters for a serial TV show.'

'How many people?' I asked. From what I could tell, it must be like Dellview, North Carolina, the smallest town in North America, population ten. Except here they inhabited shacks set way, way far back from the road.

"Bout eight hundred or so, give or take. Depends on the season. If we have a bad winter, population jumps 'bout nine months later.' Another chuckle.

'But I didn't even know it was there,' I protested. 'There are no lights.'

'Wall now, you're right there. You picked quite a night to visit. Ronnie Two Shoes was being a doofus as usual when trimmin' his old cottonwood, and

78

one of the branches snapped the power lines clean through. It's a miracle he didn't fry hisself up like a chicken nugget. Right at dinnertime too, so good folks couldn't cook up a bite to eat for Sunday dinner or watch *America's Funniest Home Videos*. Which tonight turns out to be the night Henrietta Mankiller finally gets a video on that damn show. Ronnie'll be run out of town. Very least, he'll be eatin' shit at the Guess Who's Coming to Diner for a while, I can tell ya. Pardon my language.'

Timing was clearly not my thing. 'I thought I was in the middle of the woods.'

'A hundred more feet and you'd be bunking in the community center,' he said. 'That your Plymouth Road Runner 'bout ten-twelve miles back?'

I nodded.

'You walk all that way in the dark?' I nodded again. 'With a bird?' Another nod.

'Wall, it's cold as charity out here,' Bruce pronounced. He had that right. 'I can't let ya stay in the square, I'm 'fraid. And I can't put ya in the jail without ya bein' under arrest.' I was pretty sure I was glad on that one, though his regret seemed genuine. 'But I might be able to help. You put on some proper shoes and break down your little campin' site while I make a call.'

I did as he said. I extravagantly squandered a pair of clean socks, putting a second pair on over the first. My feet were two blocks of ice. It was heaven to slip on my sneakers. I made a mental note to finish off all the Emergen-C packets I had tomorrow. I could buy more. I wrapped Oliver's Snuggle Hut in a wool sweater with him inside it. He squawked in protest but I ignored him. I didn't want him getting sick either. He was a bitch when he was sick. I stuffed my tent and sleeping bag by the light of my headlamp and was perched on the picnic table with all my worldly goods in a backpack and a Snuggle Hut when Bruce returned.

'Looks like you're in luck. Follow me. And mind the roots.' He shone his flashlight along the ground. When we got to the truck, it was 'Climb on up.' I was too tired to ask where we were going. I sensed Bruce was a decent man. Besides, what choice did I have? He was dead wrong about my luck.

In the cab of the truck, blessed heat seeped into my bones. Oliver felt it too because he inched out of his cocoon and rested in my lap. I couldn't see a thing out the window. The luxuriously soft seat and the warmth of the car were making me drowsy.

'Lawrence,' I said. 'Why do they call you Bruce?'

'Wall, I reckon it's because I like Monty Python so much,' he answered obligingly, leaving me as mystified as before. 'And it sure as hell beats Larry Perry.' I said nothing more.

After a short trip we pulled up to a long, low adobe house. The truck headlights lit up attractive pink walls and a doorway framed by some kind of flowering tree. Bruce shut off the truck and I clambered ungracefully down. Bruce ignored the front door and followed a path to the left through an archway cut into the long wall. Beyond appeared to be a courtyard garden. I could see candlelight flickering through double glass doors to the right. Bruce went through them, and I followed him into a beautiful and spacious kitchen. The centerpiece was a rectangular wooden table burnished to a rich, warm brown. The floors were ochre tile. A welcoming fire flickered in the hearth dominating an exposed brick wall on the left, and candles on the table guttered in the draft we created. The only sound was the tick-tick-tick of a heating saucepan on a restored antique O'Keefe & Merritt gas stove. Bruce wiped his feet on a colorful rag rug and stepped in, pulling off his sheriff's hat. I remained his dutiful shadow.

'Hello, Bruce. How you doin', Bruce? All right there, Bruce?' squawked a voice from beyond a darkened doorway to the left.

Oliver, on my shoulder now, began hopping agitatedly, lifting one foot then the other, a cockatiel sign of anxiety.

'Lulabell, hush your beak,' said Bruce.

'Quiet, Lulabell. Quiet,' mimicked the squawk.

Oliver raced from my wrist to my shoulder and back again in a fretful loop. On one pass he nipped my ear lobe.

'Ow, Oliver!' I rebuked. He scrambled to my

elbow, canvassing the room for the provoking sound. His crest feather was fully erect, another fear indicator.

'Right, Bruce!' said Lulabell.

It was too much for Oliver. He released a torrent of sounds. 'Squawk. Carrot. Are you thinner? Road trip, don't forget the bird! Howdy, pardner. Oh shit.'

Silence from the other room.

'Yours's just as bad as Lulabell for the potty mouth,' Bruce observed.

'Oh no,' I rushed to assure him. 'He almost never says that.'

'Oh shit,' repeated Oliver.

Sigh. 'That's his only bad word. I have no idea where he got it.' I had a pretty good idea where he got it.

'It won't be for long,' Bruce forebode.

On cue, from the next room Lulabell spoke again. 'Fuck me. Legs up, toots.'

'Oh shit,' Oliver contributed excitedly.

Bruce rolled his eyes. A tiny woman hurried into the room. She wore her graying hair in two long braids and I instantly tumbled in love. 'Don't you mind Lulabell,' she said. 'She spent too much time in the sheriff's office when she was young listening to foul-mouthed criminals and even fouler-mouthed deputies.' Here she shot Bruce a dirty look. He managed to look abashed. It clicked that this was his ex-wife.

It was hard to make out detail by candlelight,

but she was clearly no more than five feet tall. At five foot nine, I towered over her. And Bruce towered over me. What a funny couple they would have been. Her movements were precise, with no inefficient gestures. Three steps to the stove, a glance into the pot. Reach for a mug with one hand, extinguish the gas with the other, pour liquid into the mug with one hand, extract a spoon from the drawer with the other. Turn to the table, simultaneously placing the mug and spoon before one chair and pulling out another. It was like watching an expertly choreographed dance. I didn't realize I was transfixed until she demanded, 'Well, are you two going to sit or am I going to need neck surgery from looking up at you?'

We sat. Bruce cleared his throat.

'Maeve, this here is Ruby. Ruby, this is the gal I was tellin' you about,' he said.

'It would be a remarkable feat if you managed to come up with a substitute stray girl in the fifteen minutes since you called, Lawrence,' Ruby said. She examined me in the candlelight.

'I'm Maeve Connelly,' I said. 'This is Oliver.' Oliver was torn between Ruby's compelling presence and the phantom cockatiel in the next room, swiveling his head from one direction to the other.

'Howdy, pardner.' He focused on Ruby, on his best behavior. He was definitely getting Cheetos tomorrow. They were his favorite, but I usually discouraged saturated fats.

'Howdy yourself.' Ruby returned the greeting seriously. I plummeted even further in love. I casually crossed an ankle over my knee, hitching my jeans cuff to show off my knee socks. I thought Ruby would appreciate the lizard motif.

Her level gaze returned to me. 'I'm Ruby Ransome.' Inelegantly, I sneezed in response. Three times fast.

'Bless you. I understand you've had car trouble.'

It wasn't a question but I answered anyway. 'Yes, ma'am.'

There was another squawk. We all looked confused, because it didn't come from Oliver or Lulabell. It emitted from the vicinity of Bruce's stomach.

'Bruce? Bruce, you there?' It was a walkie-talkie. Bruce fumbled to turn its volume down, shooting a sheepish look at Ruby.

Ruby rose fluidly. 'We've all had a long night. Lawrence, you're needed. Go back to the station. I'll handle it from here. Call me tomorrow at ten o'clock with information on PIGS and Barney's schedule.' I had no idea what she was talking about, but I knew that when she said ten o'clock she didn't mean it like most of us mean it. She meant ten precisely. From Bruce's look, he knew it too. He bent and kissed her cheek.

'You're a good woman, Ruby.' To my surprise, Ruby blushed. To me he said, 'I'll be seein' about your car.' Then he was gone. Suddenly I was too exhausted to think.

'Maeve, you'll sleep in room number 1.' I didn't question her choice to identify her rooms by number rather than function. I just hoped number 1 had a bed in it. I rose tiredly. 'Oliver can bunk with Lulabell,' Ruby finished.

I froze, panic blooming. 'No,' I said, before I could stop myself. Ruby looked at me in surprise. 'I mean, I'm sorry, you've been so nice and all, it's just . . .' My voice trailed away. How to explain that I couldn't be parted from my bird? My life was topsy-turvy. Oliver was the only thing tethering me to myself. I didn't trust him out of my sight. I opened my mouth. Then closed it. I looked at her helplessly, mute. 'He might get scared,' I finally said.

Ruby's eyes told me she knew exactly what I meant. 'I don't want bird poop all over my bedroom,' was her logical position.

'I have this Snuggle Hut, see.' I held it up. 'I can wrap him in it. He won't be roaming free. And he was just clipped,' I pleaded. 'Tomorrow I'll walk back for his cage.' I stopped. I shouldn't talk about tomorrow. Ruby wasn't adopting me. She was putting me up for a night.

'Let's have no foolish talk about walking twelve miles.' Ruby relented. 'We'll deal with tomorrow when it's tomorrow. Your bird can stay with you. Keep him in his tent. Follow me.'

She lifted a candle and stepped in her gifted, precise way through a door opposite, away from Lulabell's roost. A hallway stretched into the shadows.

I followed the dancing candle past a series of darkened openings, and through another glass door, which put us outside, the hallway becoming a covered adobe walk. We stopped in front of a door with a brass numeral affixed. Room number 1. Ruby opened the door.

'I trust you'll be comfortable. There are towels in the bathroom. I'll expect you for breakfast at eight thirty. I know it's early considering your night, but that's when I do business.'

I nodded. She set the candleholder down on a bedside table. As she passed me, she paused. She took my hand and gave it a squeeze. 'Sleep well. Everything will sort itself out. Or we'll get it sorted.' With that she was gone, with the exact number of steps required to reach the door, pass through it and close it behind her with a soundless click.

I sat on the bed, awake only long enough to take off my shoes, secure Oliver in his tent, set the alarm and register that the bed was pillowy soft, before blowing out the candle and sliding under the covers and into sleep for the second time that night.

When the alarm dragged me awake in the morning, the sun was brilliant. I flung out a hand to silence the beeping, and encountered . . . air. I blinked at the bedside table, but it wasn't there. I realized the sound was coming from the *other* side of the bed, then recalled I was not home.

I was in a strange bed, owned by a strange woman, with no clue what I was going to do about my car. I hit the snooze button and fell back into the bed. My eyes drifted shut as I contemplated the depth of my tiredness. I'd rest while I could, I decided, so I'd be equipped to handle whatever was thrown at me today.

Then my eyes flew open and I bolted upright in the sickening way you do when you've had a sudden, horrifying realization. My eyes leapt to the clock. I wilted in relief when I saw it was only eight and I hadn't missed meeting Ruby. The proud owner of a thumping headache, reward for my abrupt blood pressure spike, I rubbed my temples and surveyed the room.

Coral adobe walls met ochre tiles, accented by sage-green window trim. White curtains flanked windows on both sides of the room. My headboard boasted an image of horses cantering across the prairie that you might expect to find painted on velvet rather than inlaid on beautiful wood in an otherwise tasteful room. The walls were decorated with colorful inlaid tiles and hammered metal mirrors. I pushed back thick feather-filled covers and stepped out of bed. My dusty backpack was on an antique dresser that matched a wardrobe and bedside table. Ruby must have brought it in. I retrieved a clean sweater and underwear. After some deliberation I decided on my favorite parrot-adorned knee socks. I hoped Ruby would like them. I stepped into the bathroom, taking advantage of Oliver's silence to shower.

Refreshed and dressed, I collected Oliver and left the room. My door opened to a passage flanking a square courtyard. To my right the corridor passed doors numbered to 6. The courtyard was enclosed by adobe walls, and looked to be a combination of flower garden and vegetable garden. To my left was the door we'd exited last night. I went through it.

Daylight revealed a beautifully decorated house with a Native American motif. Through an arched doorway on the left was a sunken living room, with more doors beyond. On the right I could see a comfortable social room with a number of small tables and a television. I kept walking. Ahead was presumably the front door we'd ignored the night before. Before reaching it, I turned into the kitchen, pulse accelerating out of uncharacteristic nervousness.

Ruby Ransome was sitting at the long table, red reading glasses studded with rhinestones perched on her nose, perusing a paper. She didn't look up when she said, 'There's coffee.'

I helped myself to a cup from the carafe on the sideboard, loading it with milk, and listened absently to the low murmur of talk radio. I avoided a bowl of boiled eggs with a shudder. As I tried to decipher what the program was discussing, I realized that it wasn't the radio, but live voices. Human voices, not Lulabell's uncomprehending mimicry.

The fireplace dominating the far wall was a through and through, another hearth opening into the room opposite. The voices were coming from that room.

I sat across from Ruby, curious. Three minutes passed while she finished reading, then, with meticulous movements, she folded the paper and placed it aside.

'Good morning.' She assessed me. 'Did you sleep well?'

'Yes, ma'am, thank you,' I said.

'No more ma'am,' she said, and I knew it wasn't a 'don't, stop, don't stop' thing. She meant no more ma'am.

'Sure,' I said. There was a burst of laughter from the other room. 'Is this a hotel?' I worried about paying her.

'More of a boarding house. People live here,' she said. 'Tell me your plans.'

More like the great sucking sound of a complete lack of plans, I thought. 'I'm driving to California,' I said. 'Or I was. I drove across from New Mexico yesterday, through Tombstone. I've been on the road a few weeks, but it should only take a few more days now. I'm going to Los Angeles. To start over.' I mentally groaned. Why had I said that last bit?

'What are you starting over from?' Ruby pounced.

'I needed a change,' was all I said. What else was there to say?

She nodded. 'You're going to have some setbacks, I'm afraid. Unknown's mechanic, Barney, is out of

89

town for a bit. You barely missed him. He wasn't supposed to leave until tomorrow, but when that fool Ronnie put the lights out, Barney decided to leave early.'

I nearly laughed out loud. Could my luck have been worse? 'A bit?'

'Yes. You never know how long with Barney and these trips. Sort of depends on his luck at the tables. Simon Bear will drive over from Sierra Vista with the tow truck and bring your car to PIGS in a few days, but Barney could be gone anywhere from a week to a month.'

'PIGS?' I ignored her last statement. No way he'd be gone a month, I denied.

'Politically Incorrect Gas Station.'

'But . . . surely there's someone else.'

Ruby looked at me. 'How many towns did you pass on your way from Tombstone?' she asked.

'One,' I answered, dreadful awareness sinking in. 'If it counted as a town. It was more like an intersection.' I recalled Sonoita.

'It counted. Around here you won't find a stop-light until Nogales.'

My mind raced. There had to be a way out. I was desperate to get to California. The idea of being stalled in the middle of nowhere made me want to scream. Maybe I could rent a car. Or catch the Greyhound. Or . . . As my brain churned, my heart conceded. I wasn't going to abandon Elsie. First of all, I loved her. Second, I couldn't afford a new car. Hell, I had no idea how I was going to pay for the repair . . . A horrifying thought cut through.

'I don't have the money to stay here,' I confessed. 'I just have my tent and enough gas money to get to California. I don't know what to do.' The last was more to myself.

She regarded me some more. It was like she could see everything. 'You seem healthy.' I was, but I felt irrationally guilty and furtive, as if a remainder of every sick day was germinating within me.

'Yes.' My answer was breathless. 'I am.'

'Then I see no reason why we can't work out an arrangement.' She folded her hands, neat on the tabletop. 'For some time I've been chafing at the demands of the boarding house, as I've wanted to spent more time on other pursuits. You can manage those requirements for me, in exchange for room and board. Number 1 is empty. If you like the room, and feel the arrangement is a fair bargain, it's yours.'

I was speechless. She was offering to let me stay in this oasis. I wondered if it was too much charity to accept.

'It isn't charity, mind you.' Ruby read my thoughts. How was it everyone could do that? 'You'll do what's needed when it's supposed to be done, and correct the first time. I won't be paying you, so you'll have to discover other ways to earn the money you need to pay Barney. The schedule here is plenty flexible to allow for that, and I suspect you are a resourceful girl.'

I said the first thing that came to my mind. 'What on earth makes you think I'm a resourceful girl when I'm broke and stranded in the middle of nowhere?'

'Unknown, Maeve. You're in Unknown. Nowhere is in Oklahoma,' Ruby admonished. I almost asked her where, wondering how I'd missed it, but held my tongue. 'A young lady who gets herself this close to California on a shoestring and boiled eggs in a 1970s relic while taking care of her bird is resourceful in my book. Not to mention walking twelve miles in the dark and managing to pitch a tent in the middle of the town square during a blackout.' She broke into a wide smile. 'I can just see Lawrence debating with himself over what to do when he saw that tent.'

I said the only thing there was to say. 'I accept your offer, Ruby. Thanks. Um, how did you know about the eggs?' As of now, I was officially not ruling out supernatural occurrences in Unknown.

'Your things are in the common room. We retrieved the keys from your rucksack and Lawrence brought them by this morning. I took the liberty of discarding the last egg. It looked a little forlorn. And it appears the donkey and the chicken may need a good cleaning. Dry-cleaning would be best.'

I decided not to try to explain.

'Not that eggs are a bad idea. You could stand to gain five pounds,' Ruby added as an afterthought.

She cocked her head, considering. 'Make that eight. You're quite tall. Now follow me.' She stood and eyed Oliver, who had been docilely sitting on my head the whole time. 'I expect it's about time we introduced your young man to Lulabell.'

I followed Ruby through the door to the left of the hearth into a large common room, stretching the length of the house. The room was cozy despite its size. Opposite were windows and paned double French doors opening into the courtyard. A collection of café tables was arrayed in front of them, doubling as dining tables and games or work tables. Two women were having breakfast at one, the source of the chatter I'd heard earlier. Immediately right, in front of the hearth, was a squishy tan leather sofa, flanked by two matching armchairs. In the corner was a kitchenette with a curious family of refrigerators – one large one next to six smaller versions, like a mother duck and her ducklings. A large rolltop desk hugged the far left wall, along with another sofa and armchair grouping centered around a television. Crowded bookshelves filled the space between.

Next to the door was a palatial birdcage that made Oliver's modest house look like a single-wide mobile home. Inside was an inquisitive-looking pearl cockatiel. Oliver came to attention. I scooped him down to my hand as a precaution.

'This is Lulabell,' Ruby pronounced. 'She's very friendly. Normally she's free to wander, but since your man is human-bonded, I thought we'd see how they got on for a bit first.'

Oliver's cage had been set adjacent on the cabinet. I slipped him inside, and we both stepped back to watch. Lulabell didn't move, affecting an uninterested air, though following Oliver's every move with her eyes. Oliver hopped from one perch to another in a constant cycle of movement – alighting millimeters from Lulabell's cage before jumping away – all the while muttering to himself. He didn't seem perturbed, so I stopped worrying.

'Great hair,' he finally squawked. I was impressed at his savvy choice.

Lulabell just eyed him.

'Are you thinner?' Oliver tried again.

Lulabell tilted her head.

'Pretty,' Oliver repeated.

'Show some tits.' Lulabell was won over, and the two of them began madly chirping back and forth.

'Lord knows there'll be no peace now,' growled one of the ladies.

Ruby smiled. 'Maeve, let me introduce you to the Cowbelles.' We walked over to two women who could have been a hundred and looked to have another hundred in them each. 'April War Bonnet.' Ruby gestured to a tiny Native American woman with long, still dark hair, and a brown face as wizened as a crab apple. 'And Busy Parker.' Busy's skin was powdery pale, every wrinkle emanating the essence of smiling, framing snapping blue eyes.

'And who's this?' April's voice was gruff and low.

94

'This is Maeve. She's going to be staying for a while.'

April considered me. Busy stood and embraced me in a cloud of violet perfume. It was so unexpected that tears welled in my eyes. I blinked rapidly to conceal them.

'Welcome, welcome,' Busy fluttered, all bonnets and tea services. 'Don't mind April. That's just her way. She's a total bitch.'

I was surprised into a belt of laughter.

'Better that than a lavender-wearing, stranger-hugging nincompoop,' April retorted in her gravelly voice. She shook my hand in a firm clasp. 'April War Bonnet. You need any bodies buried, you let me know.' I wasn't sure she was kidding.

'Let's go a little easy on Maeve her first day,' Ruby said with equanimity.

'What's a Cowbelle?' I gave in to my curiosity.

'Back in the forties, a group of ranch women organized to foster social interaction among women living on isolated ranches, and called themselves the Cowbelles. April and I are the last founding charter members of the Santa Cruz County Cowbelles,' Busy explained. 'We still have regular meetings.'

'At eight o'clock here for breakfast, at noon over there for lunch, and at five on the sofa for sherry.' Ruby's tone was dry.

'Bite your tongue, Ruby,' April growled. 'Sherry my ass. It's Scotch. And mind we don't run out. The bottle's light.'

'That's Maeve's job now,' Ruby said. 'I'm about to show her the ropes.'

And she did. And just like that, I became a boarding-house manager with a room of my own.

CHAPTER 8

THE GIRL WHO COULD

An hour later, my head was swirling, and I panicked I'd forget everything. Ruby was not a person to disappoint. My job was to clean the common areas and Ruby's kitchen, do dishes, laundry, and keep the cupboards full of clean sheets and towels. I wasn't to go into boarders' rooms. This was unfortunate, as I was fascinated by April War Bonnet. In addition to April and Busy, there was the regional circuit judge who spent one week a month in Unknown, and the occasional random visitor. Ruby provided breakfast supplies and household basics, so I was in charge of stocking those things. I also did Ruby's personal grocery shopping. There'd be supplemental tasks, like helping Ruby in the garden, as needed. It was definitely a good deal, but I had to figure out how to make some cash to pay for the tow and repair of Elsie. I didn't anticipate many costume gigs in Unknown.

I scribbled throat lozenges on the grocery list, as my throat was sore and scratchy after my nocturnal adventures, and stepped outside. I promptly had a sneezing fit. I hoped I wasn't becoming one of those people allergic to sunshine. I followed Ruby's directions from our address on Emerald Street to the center of town. It wasn't far. Unknown consisted of a handful of streets, named after the rainbow. No stoplight. There was a center square, on which I'd pitched my tent. It hosted the community center, housing the town hall, sheriff's office and jail. All of the commerce existed on Main Street and Red Road, which flanked the center square. It was an eclectic mix. There were several local artisan craft stores, the Guess Who's Coming To Diner, and two clothing stores. You wouldn't lack for hand-crafted jewelry in Unknown, but if you wanted a video, better sign up for Netflix. The Wagon Wheel Saloon boasted that it was Unknown's original cowboy bar, serving cold beer and pool. The Velvet Elvis offered pizza, several doors down from a shuttered PIGS, sign proclaiming 'Back in a few'. The smiley face dotting the 'i' didn't soothe me but seemed well intentioned. Gathering Grounds had an appealing coffee-shop allure. Up Market was your only bet for groceries and sundries.

'So it's fancy stuff, then?' I'd asked Ruby.

Her look was quizzical. 'No, it's quite normal. It's owned by Patrick and Jenny Up.'

I was heading in that direction when I was arrested by a store called The Little Read Book. The sign featured a grass-skirted Hawaiian dancer and Chairman Mao both reading red tomes as they swayed to the hula. Unable to resist a bookstore,

I pushed open the door and was greeted with the heady smell of many volumes gathered in one place. It was perfect. The hardwood floors creaked just right. The sun slanted through the front windows, perfectly highlighting floating dust motes. There was a table for staff picks and favorites, and the best-sellers were displayed on a front-facing bookshelf. Comfy chairs and couches occupied sunny nooks, and café tables invited people to linger over coffee. The sound of grinding beans drew me to a small café within the store, where a beautiful woman worked an espresso machine. She was exotically unique, with almond eyes and long dark hair.

'Aloha!' A beatific smile accompanied her greeting. 'What can I do for you?'

I developed an enormous girl crush. My second in two days. Her wide smile made you want to know her.

'I'm Maeve,' I said.

'Tuesday,' she said, in response to my non-answer, smile widening.

I frowned. It was Thursday, I was pretty sure.

'Coffee in five days?' I asked.

She giggled as if I'd told the funniest joke in the world. 'No, silly. Tuesday's my name. You're funny.' I had the urge to say something hilarious. She had that kind of laugh.

'I just got here,' was my inane response.

'Cool.' Her nod supported my decision. 'I live on Purple Street. My car is the one with the

99

bumper sticker saying "I'd Rather Be Doing the Hula".'

'Mine is the one sitting outside PIGS waiting for Barney to get back in town and fix it.'

'Ah. A compulsory visit.' Tuesday laughed.

'Kind of,' I admitted. 'That's why I came in. I'm looking for work.'

'Oh yay!' Tuesday beamed at me, giving a little hop. 'I need more time off.'

My heart burst. I'd found a job. In a bookstore! 'I love your shop,' I gushed.

'Yeah, it's good. But it isn't mine. I teach hula and dance. I only help out when Noah's in a bind.'

'Noah?'

'Grouchy owner extraordinaire.'

'Want to be my best friend?'

'Sure!' Her laugh was rich. 'Where are you staying?'

'Ruby Ransome's boarding house.'

'Oooohhh, I love Ruby. Lulabell is the bomb.'

'I have a bird. He's learning dirty words from Lulabell as we speak.'

'Uh-oh. So you want to work here?' A wrinkle appeared. She leaned closer. 'Listen, new best friend, Noah's not really that grouchy, but maybe you could come back tomorrow morning? Today isn't the best—'

'Tuesday!' A bellow interrupted her. 'Tuesday!'

She sighed and gave a shrug. 'Here comes Cranky McCranky Pants. Guess you'll meet the man himself now.'

100

She turned to the disembodied voice. 'In the coffee bar.'

A man appeared from around a bookshelf. He was tall, very tall, maybe six four, with dark brown hair and startling green eyes. And a frown. I'd never allow a furrow that depth on my forehead.

'Did you see where I put the receipts from the Decatur Book Festival?' As he spoke, he sighted me and did an unexplained double-take, before refocusing on Tuesday. He peeked at me sideways more than once.

'Nope,' she said with a wide smile. I waited for him to yell again, but he didn't. He looked perplexed.

'I swear I put them somewhere special.'

'I'll bet you did!' Tuesday chirped. 'Remember the Monkey Flower special orders? You put them on the top shelf of the cookbook section.' She winked at me. 'We found them two years later.' Noah's forehead remained creased.

'But I never lose things.' More divot. My hands itched to rub it out.

'Only when you put them in special places.' Tuesday agreed.

'Helen came in,' Noah explained. 'Looking for a copy of *The Book of Murder.*'

'Ah.' Apparently this made sense to Tuesday, as she nodded. 'You'll find them. You always do. You're the most organized person I know.'

'Apparently not.' He gave a rueful laugh, then turned distractedly to me, extending a hand.

'Sorry. I'm Noah. Glad to have you here. Traveling in the area? Anything I can help you find?'

I took his hand. It was strong and knew how to shake properly. In fact, all of him was fit. Long and lean, with defined features. I'm a sucker for killer cheekbones, and Noah had them like razors. Plus all the rest.

'Maeve Connelly.' I felt a little fluttery. 'In town temporarily.'

'Nice socks,' he said. 'I like socks with birds on them.' I gripped the coffee bar counter to keep upright. His attention returned to Tuesday. 'Well crap,' he said. 'So I've lost them.' I got the impression that for him it was more like misplacing a kidney than an expense sheet.

'Um. Maybe. We found the Monkey Flower special orders.' She tried to sound a ray of hope.

'I'm very organized,' I piped up. They both looked at me. 'I keep great track of things.' It was true. I might not always deal with my paperwork, but the stacks were meticulous.

'That's an excellent quality.' Noah maintained a polite demeanor.

'Noah, Maeve's looking for work,' Tuesday said. I thrilled that my new bestie remembered my name. 'She wants to help out in the store.'

Noah assessed me, then turned away. 'I'm sorry. We're not hiring.'

'What?' Tuesday and I yelped in unison. I was so in love with the store and its one employee, I'd moved in, in my mind. I had to get this job.

'Noah, I need help!' Tuesday wailed.

Noah's green eyes evaluated. 'Do you have bookstore experience?'

I hated answering. 'No.'

'And you're looking for a temp position?'

I wanted to lie, but it was true, so I nodded.

He shook his head. 'I'm sorry. This is a bookstore, not a summer job fair. My staff have to be knowledgeable about books, and intend to stick around more than three weeks.'

'I've spent legions of time in bookstores, as an avid customer,' I protested. 'I know more than some college kid who worked in his uncle's bookshop one summer.'

'I'm sorry. We're the only bookseller in a fifty-mile radius, and people come here because we know literature. You look more like a . . . a . . . model, or something, than a book geek.'

'Hey!' Tuesday objected.

He looked uncomfortable, and it was probably common sense not to hire anyone who wandered in off the street, but he was pissing me off. 'You don't look like a creepy evil child-toucher, but I'm reserving judgment. The neighbors always say you'd never have guessed.'

'Don't take it the wrong way.' He held up his hands. 'I take matching people to books seriously.' Pause. Frown. 'And I'm not a child-molester.'

'Well, not a good one, at any rate,' I snorted. 'You don't have any kind of children's section to speak of.' I pointed. 'If you had a genius like me working here, I'd shift those shelves over and turn that corner into a kid-friendly section called The Little Read Picture Book or The Little Little Read Book, and offer Saturday story time.'

'Noah.' Tuesday's eyes widened at my suggestions. 'She isn't Gina.' I caught her eye and she mouthed, 'Tell you later.' To Noah, she said, 'Ruby trusts her. She gave her a room.'

'It wouldn't be responsible to hire an unqualified person off the street,' Noah resisted.

'Test me before you decide I'm unqualified.' I faced him, hands on hips.

He held up his. 'I've hired walk-ins before. It doesn't work – even if they have charming braids and funky knee socks. I'm being realistic.'

'Try me.' I repeated my challenge.

'Try you?'

'You're the customer, I work here. Test me. Ask me a literary question I can't answer. If I can answer five toughies, I get the job.' I crossed mental fingers. I'd read a lot of books, but I was no Seamus Heaney.

Tuesday's eyes jumped between us like she was watching a tennis match.

'What are you reading now?'

Easy. '*The Bean Trees*, Barbara Kingsolver. I'm being regional.' *The Bean Trees* was set in Tucson.

'Who wrote *Dubliners*?'

I fought back my eye-roll. This was almost insulting. 'James Augustine Aloysius Joyce. Who also wrote *Ulysses, A Portrait of the Artist as a Young*

Man, *Finnegans Wake*, and some mediocre poetry. My favorite short story from *Dubliners* is "The Dead".'

'His middle name was Aloysius?' Tuesday giggled.

'Okay.' Noah squinted. I knew it was going to get harder. 'I like the classics. I've read most of them. I'm looking for something I haven't yet discovered. What do you recommend?'

Tuesday snorted. 'Like *that's* ever been a real question. Who reads all of the classics?'

We ignored her. I racked my brains. '*I Capture the Castle* by Dodie Smith or *Good Behaviour* by Molly Keane are excellent choices.'

He shifted his feet. 'I like thrillers but don't want garbage. What's an intelligent new release?'

'Oh come on,' said Tuesday. 'I work here and I don't know that.'

'I think the new Jack Reacher novel by Lee Child is at the top of the chart,' I said. I'd spied it on the best-seller shelf when I'd walked in. Noah's furrow indicated my answer was sound. I made a mental note to buy a copy.

'I'd like something for my son,' Noah persisted. 'He's thirteen.'

I paused. I didn't want to give the obvious Harry Potter answer. I pondered a moment, then nailed it. '*The Boy Who Could Fly*,' I announced. 'It's not that well known but it's a wonderful book, where a boy who loses his father escapes into his imagination as a superhero while he struggles to take care of his mother and sibling.'

'You are *so* hired.' Tuesday burst out laughing.

Noah looked uncomfortable. And oddly distressed. Too bad.

He caught Tuesday's eye. Then, 'Ruby took you in?' Clipped.

'Uh-huh.'

They exchanged glances, communicated something I didn't understand. She nodded.

Finally, 'Fine.' His tone was terse. 'You can help out a few days a week. Come Monday at ten. Tuesday, you'll train.'

'Sure.' Tuesday's head bobbed.

Noah walked away, then paused. 'But we don't recommend *The Boy Who Could Fly* around here,' he said before disappearing through a door at the back of the room.

I was confused, especially as Tuesday's giggles amplified. I looked at her questioningly.

'Oh,' she said. 'He wrote it. He wrote the whole series. He's N.E. Case.'

And my jaw hit the floor just like that.

CHAPTER 9

A-MUSE-ING

I was bubbling over when I talked to Oliver as I tidied the breakfast area.

'And I met the guy who wrote *The Boy Who Could Fly*, and *The Boy Who Could Walk Through Walls*, and *The Boy Who Could Stop Time*. All of them – he's not that much older than me, but he's written this whole series. The actual guy! He's my new boss!'

'Nice tits!' said Oliver. I seriously had to move his cage away from Lulabell.

'And I have a new best friend,' I said. 'Well, besides you. Her name is Tuesday. She's half Hawaiian, half Chinese. We have a date.'

After Noah had conceded to hiring me, I'd spent the afternoon hanging around Tuesday like a teenage sycophant at a lifeguard stand, and she'd explained his odd behavior.

'You're blonde and she was brunette, but otherwise, the resemblance is strong. Gina wore long braids and had this great smile. The problem was that she was a *criminal*.'

'What'd she do?' I marveled.

'Destroyed Noah's trust in mankind,' she

107

exaggerated. 'We'd always had good luck with short-termers, and for a small store it can be a perfect arrangement. Then Gina came along. She told Noah she wanted temp work to be near a grandmother who'd broken a hip, so of course he couldn't say no. He's a big old softie. We were glad for the help. It gave me more time to teach dance and him more time to write.' I nodded.

'She was fine at first. Smart, fun to be around. You could overlook the occasional butt-flossing cut-offs. After a few weeks, I went to Tucson at the same time Noah flew to New York for a meeting and we left her in charge. When we got back, the store was dark, and the register had been cleaned out. She even stole some knick knacks from Noah's office.'

'She was a con artist?' I was shocked. Who would rob an independent bookstore?

'Totally. She had a party girl habit and wanted the money for clothes and an extravagant nightlife. Noah was heartbroken. It wasn't the financial loss – he makes his money from the books. He was wounded to the core that a person could be so calculating and callous. Plus she pinched his favorite stuffed monkey.' I didn't ask. Tuesday sighed. 'He feels things too deeply. He hasn't hired anyone since – it's like he had a bad break-up and can't date again.'

'That's awful!'

'It doesn't excuse him being harsh to you, though I'm impressed he had it in him. He could never accuse anyone of being a criminal, much less a potential criminal, even after it was proven. That's why he grilled you on books. He was desperate for an objective excuse to send you away.'

'I forgive,' I joked. The incident had been eclipsed. I had a job, and I was far too thrilled with the movie and dinner date I'd planned with Tuesday. We'd agreed that after my first day of work, we'd order pizza and watch *Juno*, which she'd gotten on Netflix.

A violent sneezing fit yanked me back to the present. It could have been caused by the organic Seventh Generation cleaning liquid I'd just blasted at the café table, but the ferocity of the attack alarmed me. I'd been sneezing quite a bit since arriving in Unknown, and my sore throat hadn't improved dramatically. With my luck it wasn't just a cold. I recalled an article I'd seen on incurable spore infections in the rural southwest. Allergic rhinitis onset could occur at any age. Come to think of it, my lungs had felt swollen all morning.

'Oh my God,' I said to Oliver. 'I have pneumonitis.' It had to be my run the day before. I'd done twelve miles along lanes through the fields. I recalled my deep, raggedy inhales. Or it could be just a cold from my night on the ground without my Thermarest, but why take risks? I was a big believer in medicine, and the bigger you painted the problem, the better stuff you were likely to get. If I could get the A-bomb of antibiotics, I'd take it.

'Better go see Dr Samuel Looking Horse,' growled April War Bonnet. I jumped. She'd been silent, her diminutive frame completely concealed by the large armchair she occupied. She appeared to be reading a coupon circular.

'What?'

'Dr Looking Horse, over at the clinic on Blue Street. He'll put you right.' April's eyes had a gleam, and I wondered if she was setting me up for trouble. My few days' acquaintance had taught me caution. I'd already endured a near heart attack over the dried llama fetus she'd left on my bed, a good-luck token from a Bolivian witch doctor, and had wasted half a day looking for my cupcake and lightning-bolt knee socks before I realized the café tables were 'wearing' them.

'Is he a real doctor? Not like your witch-doctor friend.' I hadn't been able to get rid of my 'lucky charm' fast enough. I'd rather stay cursed.

'Phffft. Natives Americans can be real doctors, you know.'

Horrified, I protested, 'I didn't—'

She cut me off, enjoying herself. 'He is. Plus, he's the only doctor in town.' That sealed it. I was going.

'And when you go, steal the lobby magazines for me.' Ah. That explained the gleam. Up Market only carried a few out-of-date periodicals.

★   ★   ★

An hour later, I was sitting in a paper gown, my backpack stuffed with clinic magazines. My life of crime was getting out of control, but the alternative of disappointing April promised retribution, probably in the form of my makeup glued to the counter. I'd been delighted to find a cheery little health center, rather than a larger, impersonal hospital. I didn't like hospitals. The clinic's smell of oranges was a pleasant change from disinfectant masking funk. Waiting for Dr Samuel Looking Horse, I envisioned a kindly, wizened old Native American, like the guy who cried in the pollution commercials, or Graham Greene. That's not who walked in.

'Somebody needs a spanking,' I muttered.

'I'm sorry?' Dr Looking Horse gave me a curious look.

'I'm sorry?' I parroted, with my best Innocent Look.

'Did you say something?' Quizzical.

'What?' Innocent Look.

'Did you . . .' He paused. 'Uh, never mind.'

Dr Looking Horse was in his early thirties, well over six feet tall, and chiseled like the dusky-skinned shirtless lothario sweeping up a feisty beauty on the cover of a book called something like *Savage Native Love*. In this case, he wore a white lab coat and his gleaming black hair was pulled into a ponytail. April's twinkle became understandable. I was ready for my exam.

'I have my charts.' I handed him a sheaf of folders.

'You carry your charts around?'

'Mmm-hmmm.' I was non-committal. It was a time-saving measure.

His eyes met mine after he scanned the first file. 'I had a sneezing fit, and my lungs feel a little swollen. Oh, and there's the tenderness in my armpit.' I waggled my elbow like a chicken. The new symptom joined my swollen lungs as a competing illness. The exam would need to be thorough.

'A sneezing fit?' Bemused this time.

'It could be spores.' I was earnest. 'I'm new to the area. Not adapted.'

'I see.' I suspected I wasn't being taken seriously. Still, he was a professional. 'Let's have a look. Cough for me.' He placed his stethoscope to my chest. Coughing had never been so fun.

It took less than twenty minutes for Dr Looking Horse to pronounce me perfectly healthy. 'There's absolutely nothing wrong with you.'

'Well isn't that sweet.' I gave him my most charming smile.

A hint of a blush stained his calm expression. He turned away. 'I'll write you a prescription for a multivitamin if that will make you feel better about acclimatizing to our spores.'

I squinted at him. 'Uh, no thanks, I have loads.'

He faced me again, expression serious. 'Ms Connelly, there's no reason for a woman of your health to worry about such minor discomforts. It's very unlikely—'

'Are there things a newcomer to the area would

need to be concerned about?' I persisted, this time with a new agenda. Why take home a prescription if you could take home the doctor? 'Spores, contaminants in the water, poison oak? Maybe you should give me a primer. Over dinner.'

'I . . .'

The door opened and a nurse with violent pink lipstick popped her head in. 'Dr Looking Horse? Liz Goldberg is here – it's an emergency. Tommy fell out of a tree and broke his arm.'

'I'm sorry,' he said to me. His regret looked genuine. 'I must go.' Then he smiled. 'I imagine you'll survive any Unknown hazards just fine.' And with that he was gone, and I had to decide on my own whether he was being intentionally funny.

On Monday morning, I bounced down Red Road to The Little Read Book, eager to embrace my new job. Whether from nervousness or excitement, I hadn't been able to sleep a wink after 6 a.m., so I'd already done my chores for Ruby and gone for my run.

No one was in the shop when I entered, all the lights off.

'Hello,' I called, walking to the register. A note on the counter read:

IOU. I got that book. Ronnie Two Shoes.

'Hello?' I repeated. 'Cujo?' I wondered if there was another power outage, but when I flipped the lights they came on. I walked toward where Noah had disappeared on my first visit. I'd spent a fair amount of last week hanging around Tuesday, giggling over the attractive doctor and Oliver's new words. But I'd never ventured into the back, and hadn't seen Noah. I found him in his office, but hesitated in the doorway.

N.E. Case was playing with his dolls. Specifically, he was sitting on the floor, swimming an action figure through a tub of water, muttering to himself. That, and the way his hair stood straight up, decided me not to interrupt. I backed away, but my movement caught his eye. He looked up, confused, a thousand-mile stare.

'I'm Maeve,' I reminded. 'I'm starting work today?' It came out as a question, but he couldn't have forgotten so quickly.

'Oh.' He looked distressed. 'I don't have time to train. Is Tuesday here?' He seemed torn between the toys and me.

'Nice dolls.' I couldn't resist.

His expression became haughty. 'They are *not* dolls. They are creative visualization devices. They help me when I'm blocked.'

'I hear there's a sale on Scuba Steve down at the five and dime.'

Green eyes squinted at me. 'My sister had that Wonder Woman T-shirt too. When she was *eleven*.'

Score one to Noah for jabbing back when he was caught swimming his action figure.

I lost his attention. 'Anyway, I'm sorry I can't train you, I need—'

'You need a shower, no more coffee and some sleep.' Tuesday bustled in, and cut him off with authority. Noah looked back at his tub.

'I'm close. I think. I mean . . .'

'I didn't see your car all weekend, which means you've been here and are probably sugar-deprived, which makes you cranky, which makes me cranky. It is therefore in my self-interest to feed you and send you home. Up, up, up.' Her hands under his armpits were firm as she lifted him to his feet and propelled him out into the café. I trailed after them. 'I know you hate to take time away when you're on a roll, but you need a break.'

'I have to finish ten chapters of *The Boy Who Could Breathe Underwater* by Friday,' he protested. Then he reverted to muttering. 'How does he get back? Does he . . .'

'Noah, you were playing with your toys, which means you're stumped. I'm making you breakfast then sending you home. You're banned until tomorrow.'

He blinked her into focus, and frowned. 'They are *not* toys. They are creative visualization devices. They are professional tools. Like Rorschach tests. Or . . . or . . . something.'

'Visualize this: you eating breakfast and going home. The store will stay standing one day without you.'

He capitulated. 'I could use some sleep. Will you be okay?'

'Yes.'

'The reorder is due today.'

'I'll be fine,' she assured him, walking to the coffee bar. 'I've got Maeve.'

'Sorry.' Noah looked at me, tugging a hand through his nest of hair. 'Not much of a welcome. I've been working all weekend.'

'When I have a hard time focusing, I find that picking the right socks can help.' He looked dubious, so I rushed on. 'I mean, not *literally*, like the socks themselves do anything, but organizing your thoughts to choose the right pair can put you in the proper mindset.' I hitched my jeans and showed him my favorite bookworm socks. 'I wore these to start my new job.'

'I appreciate the effort,' he said. 'Those are nice socks. But I'm not sure they would help.' He sighed.

'Eat this.' Tuesday dropped a plate of scrambled eggs and a sliced tomato in front of Noah. 'Then go home. Maeve, let's get this place operational. Can you please fire up the register, while I try to figure out which book Ronnie Two Shoes walked off with?'

Fascinated, I didn't want to leave Noah, but I obeyed. When I turned again, there was only an empty plate in the café.

I didn't see Noah until the next day. I showed up promptly at 9.45 a.m., key in my hot little hand.

Tuesday had a performance in Tucson, so she wasn't coming in for two days. I'd gotten up early to run, eager to start work on time. I hoped I remembered everything she'd showed me. I knew she'd had to cajole Noah into trusting me alone in the front, and he'd only conceded because of his deadline. I wasn't supposed to know that, but I'm expert at translating hushed voices.

'When Noah's on deadline, he doesn't do anything but write,' Tuesday had explained to me. 'And I mean anything – he can forget to eat, sleep, change clothes. Forget about helping you in the store. Sharp as a tack the rest of the time, but not the last mile. You'll probably want to bring him a sandwich around lunch. It might seem like the secretary fetching coffee, but trust me, low blood sugar equals cranky equals not fun. It's in your best interest.' I could relate. I was a bitch when my blood sugar bottomed out.

I was feeling confident. It was pretty basic register operation and sandwich-making, nothing I hadn't done in past jobs. Traffic was light. Yesterday we'd only had a few browsers and a handful of coffee-seekers. I put out inventory, kept track of what needed reorder or restock, kept the store tidy, ran the register, and made coffee and sandwiches in the café. Today was no different. In the absence of customers, I busied myself dusting the front table. Then I busied myself changing it. No one was going to buy *War and Peace* unless they already intended to, no matter how prominently it was displayed. It was a waste of prime real estate. I replaced it with *Eat, Pray, Love* by Elizabeth Gilbert. Similarly, *Run* by Ann Patchett and *Then We Came to the End* by Joshua Ferris replaced *Madame Bovary* and *Moby Dick*. Time for some fresh voices.

At 11.38 exactly, I could resist no longer. It was *almost* noon. I sidled into Noah's office.

He was sitting at a large cherry desk staring into space and drumming his fingers. He looked less demented. And very attractive.

'Knock, knock, J. Alfred Prufrock,' I called.

He looked up, surprised. 'Oh, hello.' Back to drumming.

'I was wondering if there's anything you don't like on your sandwich?'

'Hmmm?' Absently. 'Oh, whatever.' Then he came to himself. 'Oh, you don't have to do that. I can make my own lunch.' He didn't move.

'It's no problem,' I assured him. I hesitated. 'What's got you blocked?'

His head swung back toward me, body following as he rotated his leather office chair. A far cry from the Gin Mill office, this one was tasteful wood and leather; only the numerous 'creative visualization devices' belied the perfect image of a gentleman's study. A polar bear, a male action figure and what looked like Nemo the fish lay on the desk. I bit my lip.

'I don't know how to balance underwater time and land time,' he said.

I pondered. 'Maybe he can breathe both water and air, but to preserve his ability, he has to return to an aquatic environment at various intervals. It would add a race-against-the-clock element. And show his ingenuity – like the length of time he can spend on land can be prolonged if he goes somewhere with lots of humidity.' My Southern roots inspired me.

Noah's jaw dropped. He turned his back without a word and started typing madly into his laptop. I slipped out to fix the most delicious sandwich ever. When I slid it on to the desk, he didn't look up from his rapid key-pounding. He was still doing it when I left for the day, locking him inside at six o'clock.

Shortly before closing the next day, I surveyed the new arrangement of shelves in the rear left corner, wiping my brow. I was reconfiguring the area to put the chairs where there was the most light. A voice in my ear made me jump out of my skin.

'The boy has universal consciousness of, and can communicate with, all sea life. How would it apply to animals that spend time on land *and* water, like sea lions and polar bears?'

I thought. He waited, stare intense.

'Can he push his telepathic powers to the higher land creatures by finding that element of their brain that dates to their ancestors' time in the ocean? Whether you believe in the Bible or Darwin or Native legends, at one point the earth was entirely covered in water and our genetic origin was aquatic.'

'I like it. It's a good way to slip in some science to educate my readers as well.' He turned toward the office. I was buoyant. He paused. 'What do your socks look like today?' was his surprising question.

I hesitated, embarrassed to expose my fascination, but tugged my jeans to show him the fishes, sea horses and aquatic creatures decorating my favorite undersea knee socks.

'Interesting.' He gave a thoughtful smile, then was gone.

I was humming, brewing coffee, when Tuesday came in the next morning.

'You're early! How'd it go yesterday?'

'It was divine.' I glowed. Tuesday did a double-take.

'I rearranged the Religion section,' I covered. I didn't want to disappoint her yet that soon I'd be spending all my time huddled in the back office collaborating with Noah about a boy who could overcome any obstacles, inspiring and educating kids everywhere. 'How was the show?'

'It was good, but I wish I'd had someone take pictures. People kept asking me.'

'I'm pretty handy with a camera,' I offered. It was the one hobby I'd stuck with. I loved the permanence of pinning something as fleeting as an expression or a shadow to paper.

The bells on the door sounded before Tuesday could answer. Her expression plummeted. 'Auwe! Gotta run. Back in a sec.' She disappeared.

I looked up to see a human bollard. The woman's short stature combined with her grey wool coat created the impression of a cement postbox. It also begged the question of why she was wearing a grey wool coat when it was seventy degrees. Perhaps to match the curls hugging her scalp like an ironwool Brillo pad.

She marched over to me. 'Helen Rausch. I need a book on poisons.'

'Oh. OK. I'm Maeve.'

'I'm uninterested. Poisons?'

I blinked. 'Sure. Do you want a history of poisons, an encyclopedia of poisons, an Agatha Christie novel . . .'

'I want to know how to cause death by poison.'

Use your face, I thought. What I said was, 'Plants, then? Or pests?'

'Liz Goldberg.'

Two blinks this time. 'Um.'

'Are you developmentally challenged? I. Want. To. Poison. Liz. Goldberg.'

'Helen, how lovely you're looking today.' Noah, at my side, was the epitome of gallant. 'Did you just set your curls? They're perfection.'

'Noah. Not bankrupt yet?'

'Open until six today.'

'Writing atheistic tales to corrupt the souls of our youth must pay well.'

'If I come across such a writer, I will enquire about his earnings prior to conveying your outrage. Now, I understand you're looking for a book.' He placed a hand on her shoulder and guided her to the gardening section, head bent.

'Is she gone?' Tuesday hissed from where she was crouched below the counter. I nodded. 'Thank God. Helen Rausch. Trundling proof that not everyone in Unknown is likeable. Sorry I had to dash, but Noah has strict orders that he handle Helen. She's too awful to inflict on the staff, and she does ask for the most awkward things. What did she want?'

'To poison Liz Goldberg,' I marveled. I admired the way Noah deftly rang up a Thai cookbook for Helen only ten minutes later, and saw her out before returning to his office.

Tuesday snorted. 'Those two have been feuding since a ranch boundary dispute between their great-great-great-granddads. Liz keeps threatening to shoot Helen. I wish she would. Oh!' She bounced back to me, hopping up and down and clapping. 'Can you really shoot my student recital Thursday?'

'If I shoot your student recital I'll end up in jail and Michael Moore will make a sad documentary about me,' I said, starting the coffee.

'Silly.' Tuesday swatted me, giggling. 'Take pictures. If you do it, Uncle Frank and I will treat you to dinner.'

'Will do, cockatoo. Who's Uncle Frank?'

She patted her stomach. 'It's my little belly. I call it Uncle Frank – the unwelcome relative who moves in and will never leave.'

I didn't see any belly, but didn't comment. I was impatient for the coffee to brew. I'd take Noah a cup and see if he needed any help. I was surprised he hadn't stopped by after Helen left. 'How does Noah take his coffee?' I was casual.

'Hmm?' Tuesday glanced up from her order forms. 'I dunno. Oh, ask Beth.'

A tall, blonde woman entered the store, having just stepped from the Lacoste advertisement where she lived. I'd never seen a more perfect embodiment of pink-cheeked Midwestern beauty. The only thing keeping her out of the Colgate toothpaste annex to her Izod home was the lack of smile.

'Hey, Beth,' Tuesday greeted her.

'Is he here?' Beth dispensed with hello.

'Yeah, you know.'

Beth rolled her eyes. Apparently she did know, and wasn't charmed. 'He left the sink running when he left this morning.' She turned to me. 'Hi, I'm Beth Watson, Noah's girlfriend.'

I shot the coffee pot I was gripping out of its cradle and hot liquid ran down the back of my hand. 'Shit!' I jerked my burned appendage out of harm's way. 'Sorry!' I apologized to Beth. 'My language! Too much time with Lulabell. I'm Maeve.'

'Are you OK?' asked Beth, as Tuesday exclaimed, 'Oh, honey!'

123

'Sure, sure. It barely got me.' My hand was throbbing. 'I'm so clumsy!' I blew out my bangs and shrugged my shoulders, as if commiserating about a third person.

'Listen.' Beth turned to Tuesday. 'Can you remind Noah that I'm going up to Tucson for work? I'll be back Friday. Oh, and remind him we have dinner with my brother and his wife Saturday, and I don't care what his deadline is, he better be there physically *and* mentally.'

'I'll try!' Tuesday's cheerful reply sounded forced.

Beth turned back to me. 'You should be more careful. I think there's aloe vera cream in the bathroom for that burn. Noah wouldn't like it if you claimed workman's comp as a result of your own clumsiness.' And with that, Becky Thatcher's doppelgänger left to do whatever it was perfect blondes did in their spare time.

I didn't know why I was disappointed. Had I really thought I'd become writing partners with Noah and spend the rest of my life in Unknown, Arizona? Hell, no. I was on my way to Los Angeles to drive golf carts around movie sets. It didn't affect me that he had a girlfriend. I'd barely have time to get to know him before I left.

'I think Beth is right.' Tuesday pulled me from my thoughts, with a sly grin. 'You should do something about that hand.' I looked at it. It was angry red and hurt like hell. 'But I don't think aloe vera's

124

gonna do it.' She winked. 'You'd better see a doctor.'

'You know,' I responded with a broad smile, 'I think you may be right.'

CHAPTER 10

WHAT THE DOCTOR ORDERED

I looked around the Velvet Elvis pizzeria. It didn't disappoint – in addition to velvet Elvises at every stage of his career, there was no shortage of poker-playing dogs.

'Early Elvis or late Elvis?' I asked my companion.

Samuel looked thoughtful a moment. 'Early Elvis. As a doctor, I can't condone how he abused his body at the end.' He flashed his white grin. 'Plus I'm a sucker for "Hound Dog".'

'Uh oh,' I said. 'I'm late Elvis all the way. I love the idea of the comeback. And "A Little Less Conversation".'

'We'll have to see if we can overcome this seemingly insurmountable obstacle,' Samuel said. His off-duty hair was down, a shiny curtain. I didn't think we'd have a problem.

'Thanks for fixing me up this afternoon.' I waggled my bandaged hand.

'Yes, well, before you continue a course of self-injury, you should tell April that she's perfectly able to subscribe to magazines herself. I had to put out my medical journals after your last visit, and self-diagnostic hysteria skyrocketed. Everyone thought they had lupus.'

I blushed. 'You noticed.'

'Don't worry. Happens every time Busy comes in for her heart medication.' His smile was warm. It was hard to imagine him being angry with anyone.

'Well, this burn was nothing . . .' I waved my hand again.

'I know.' White teeth.

I ignored the tease. Despite the mildness of my injury, Samuel had tended it as gently and thoroughly as if it'd been a gunshot. 'The time I stapled myself to the bulletin board at Gin Mill, *that* hurt. And the time I tried to deliver pizza on roller skates. I wore that cast for three months.' I shook my head sadly. 'I had to pay for the pizzas too.'

'I can see you'll keep me employed.' Samuel laughed. 'But in this case, *I'm* paying for the pizza.'

Samuel was a charming and attentive companion. I was fascinated by his stories from the reservation.

'I'd love to see it sometime. I really like Arizona,' I said. 'It's the opposite of anything I've known. North Carolina is lush and verdant. Maybe that's why I find the barrenness of the desert so striking. Life fighting to survive and making it. It's completely alien. When I get my car back,' a wistful pause for Elsie, 'I'd like to photograph more of it.'

'You like photography?'

'Yep. I'm covering a recital for Tuesday on Thursday.' It sounded silly, so I giggled. Samuel grinned. 'The Bitty Bees Touch Their Knees? I'll be there too. Last year Celia Sweet danced right off the bandstand, so now we have a doctor on call just in case.' He was thoughtful. 'My *ama' sa' ni* – that means grandmother – turns ninety next week. What do you think about coming to the party and taking pictures? You're a lot alike. You both have a bright light.'

I caught my breath. 'I'd love to.'

He nodded. 'It should be quite a party. No one cooks like my *ama' sa' ni* and her sisters. There are eleven Nizhoni sisters. None of them ever left the res.'

'Did you grow up there?'

'Yes and no. My family home was there, but I went to an off-reservation boarding school. Not one of the "Americanization" schools of the nineteenth century that were intended to brain-wash you into being white, but one where I could get a solid education. In my area, schools were ill-equipped, unfunded and understaffed. My mother went to Brown, and she was determined for us to attend the best schools possible.'

'We?'

'My brother Javier and I. He's five years younger than me and lives in San Francisco. Computer geek. He didn't like rural life.'

'You do?'

'I lived in Albuquerque for med school but didn't

128

love it. I always wanted to be either a doctor or a veterinarian. I didn't get into vet school, but someone slipped up at the University of New Mexico medical school, so doctor it was.' He flashed a grin.

'Yeah, I struggled between advanced sub-particle physics and sandwich-making myself. Did you ever think of moving back?'

'Not really. Health care on the res is terribly underfunded. Under the terms of the Treaty of 1868, the US government provides free health care, but the pay for providers isn't lucrative. I struggled with a sense of obligation to go back, but ultimately I had to pay off my med-school loans. My compromise was a split – private practice here, and one day a week I provide non-emergency medical services at an Indian Health Services Clinic on the res. I like being close enough to go back when I choose. Mostly I treat diabetes management. Long-time residents aren't made to process the high-concentrated-sugar foods introduced from the outside. Speaking of sweets,' he asked, 'would you like dessert?'

What was sweet was when he covered my hand as we shared a sundae.

He kept the hand as we strolled through the crisp night back to Ruby's.

'Well, thanks for walking me home,' I babbled when we got to her door, suddenly shy. 'You really need to come back in the daylight and see the garden. Ruby's bougainvillea is beautiful. And you can meet Oliver. His language skills have significantly expanded since he met Lulabell. Though it's not *really*—'

Samuel interrupted, leaning close. 'Maeve. How about a little less conversation?'

'Hound dog,' I whispered, before I shut up and did something else with my mouth.

'Well?' demanded Tuesday when I danced into work. I swooned against the counter and sighed dramatically.

'Dr Samuel has *excellent* bedside manners.'

'Ay-yi-yi! Can you spell future-baby-daddy! I'm so jealous.' Tuesday swooned next to me. 'He is soooo hot.'

'I know,' I said smugly. 'We're going to your recital together tonight and out to dinner tomorrow.' My face grew warm and I shivered at the memory of Samuel's kisses. There was nothing shy about his skills in that department.

'You should treat yourself to a new pair of socks. Go remind Noah he has to write you a check tomorrow.'

'Don't you have to remind him to pay you too?'

'Nope. I live in the studio above his garage rent free, in exchange for helping out.' She slapped my butt. 'Hop to it, 'cause I'm gonna leave – I have to make a ridonculous number of paper rosettes for tonight.'

I found Noah leaning back in his chair, crossed

ankles propped on his desk, bouncing a ball against the wall.

'Howdy,' I said.

He turned and broke into a wide smile. He'd shaved. 'Hello, little muse!'

I had to stop from shuffling my feet and saying 'aw, shucks' like a country bumpkin. 'Did my hourly wage go up? Tuesday says to remind you to pay me.'

'I sent ten chapters to my editor, so I've rejoined the living,' he announced with satisfaction. 'I'll write your check now.' He frowned. 'If I could just find my pen.'

'Um . . .' I started to point out the one tucked behind his ear when he gave a rich laugh.

'Gotcha!' He retrieved the pen with dramatic flourish, wiggling his eyebrows. 'Not *all* writer stereotypes are true. Check it out.' He hitched up his pant legs to reveal bright blue socks covered in polar bears. My laughter satisfied him. He swung his legs to the ground and wrote the check.

He stood, but when I reached for my salary, he held it beyond my grasp.

'First you have to agree to put *Grapes of Wrath* back on the front table.'

He'd noticed. Tuesday was right – the non-writing Noah was transformed into an active manager. I groaned. 'It's so *depressing.*'

'It's also the book-club selection this month.'

I jumped to reach my paycheck, but he held it over his head. 'It'll take more than a month to read that book. It's six hundred and eight pages.' I remembered every one from the bitter summer it'd been assigned as vacation reading.

'Promise,' Noah demanded.

'Fine,' I grumbled. 'But only for the month. Then I'm replacing it with *The Coroner's Lunch*.'

'To higher learning.' He held up his hand for a high five. I jumped to slap his palm, and toppled on to him.

'If you wanted to dance, you only had to ask,' he teased as he caught me. He spun me in a twirl.

'A dance will cost you a quarter,' I joked.

'As it happens, I've got payment right here.' He waved my check, then swung me into his arms. I was astonished at his rock-solid frame, considering he typed for a living. The man had a chest. He led me in a little waltz around the office. Then, arms pointing, we tangoed cheek-to-cheek out into the store, where he dipped me dramatically.

'Are you fond of dancing?' He looked down at me dangling over his arm.

What I wanted to know was how men always sensed you were getting action. Was I emitting a pheromone? It never failed that when I was the object of one guy's attention, others came out of the woodwork. What I said was, 'Where do you go dancing?'

'Bitty Bees Touch Their Knees.' He righted me. 'Tuesday's having a recital tonight.'

His enthusiasm was infectious. I didn't want to kill the buzz.

132

'I'm already going.' I opted for vague. 'I'm taking pictures for Tuesday.'

'Great! We can go together and get something to eat after.'

'Um. Actually, I'm going with Samuel. Dr Looking Horse. He's picking me up here.'

Noah's smile vanished. 'Ah. That was fast work.'

I started to get mad. Who was he to judge? Men with girlfriends shouldn't be waltzing other girls around their store anyway.

'I'd invite you *and Beth* to join us, but it doesn't sound like you and Samuel get along.' My tone was sharp.

Noah turned away. 'Samuel's a great guy. I like him. I'm not sure about Beth tonight.' I was pretty sure he meant that literally. He didn't know where Beth was.

'She's in Tucson,' I said. 'For work. She said to remind you that you're having dinner with her brother Saturday.'

'Oh, right. Well, here's your check. I'll see you at the community center later.' With that he disappeared, leaving me in a mood far removed from the one I'd come in with.

CHAPTER 11

GETTING INCORPORATED

I refused to let him ruin my humor.

'And closed out the café register?'

'Yes.'

'And did the order sheets?'

'Yes.'

'And put *The Grapes of Wrath* on the front table?'

'Yes. *And* I managed to run fifteen miles before work.' I got a little saucy.

'Fine.' Noah frowned. The bell on the front door jangled, and from the way his right eyebrow drew down, which was his 'tell', I didn't need to look. 'Samuel.' He nodded. The two men shook hands. Samuel turned to me with a smile.

'Ready?'

I nodded. He was breathtaking. I hesitated. 'Do you want to walk with us?'

Noah shook his head. 'No, you go on. I'll see you there.'

I wondered if it was unprofessional to hold hands in front of my boss, but it felt good when Samuel took mine, so I didn't really care. When we stepped outside, Samuel pulled me close for a kiss.

'I've been waiting to do that again,' he said, then reclaimed my hand.

We headed to the town square. The site of my aborted campout was a pleasant rectangle flanked by Main Street and Red Street, filled with trees, picnic benches and an expansive lawn. At one end was the community center, and at the other a bandstand evoking the innocence of Dick Van Dyke musicals. Weather permitting, at least once a week there was a community event, like a dance, concert, potluck picnic, outdoor film screening or kickball game. Tonight, the bandstand was decorated with fairy lights, a rainbow of paper rosettes and a makeshift purple curtain, and was surrounded by rows of folding chairs.

The park was crowded. The whole town turned out. News of my arrival preceded me, and I was surprised at people's eagerness to get acquainted, and their warm reception. It made me a little shy, but that didn't deter anyone.

'It's the most tasty salad – basically green beans and peas,' Liz Goldberg said, as she scribbled the recipe for me on a crumbled receipt.

'Great, thanks. I'm planning to introduce more vegetarian items on to the lunch menu at the bookstore.'

Bruce got an alarmed look on his face. 'Yer not gonna make everything all oatmeal bread and sprouts, are you?'

'No,' I assured him. 'Your roast beef belly-buster,

135

double the meat, double the cheese, add hot peppers and mayonnaise, will still be there.'

'So will your high blood pressure and elevated cholesterol,' sniffed Ruby.

'In fact, when I update the menu, I thought I'd rename that sandwich The Lawrence,' I said. 'Maybe I'll call your salad The Liz.'

'Maybe you should ask the boss,' said Noah.

'Maybe I'll call the turkey sandwich The Noah,' I said.

The arrival of a pert blonde about my age prevented his retort. 'Sandy Irwin from the nail salon,' she introduced herself. Her nails were a vision, an Arizona state flag gracing each one. 'You have to come to the Wagon Wheel for a beer sometime. A bunch of us girls are meeting on Friday for happy hour.' She scribbled her number and the details on to the back of the nail salon's card. As soon as Sandy moved on, an elegantly coiffed woman glided into her place.

'Poppy Tarquin; my husband runs the nursery. Listen,' her tone was conspiratorial, 'for a proper manicure you must go to Nogales. Sandy is a sweet girl, but she can't do gels for shit.' I was startled at the profanity coming from such an elegant creature. 'I have a girl. I'll give you her number.' She scribbled a note.

'Where'd Samuel go?' April demanded. I looked around. He'd vanished.

'I can't imagine,' Ruby's eyes twinkled, 'what could drive him off like that.'

'Hunh,' grunted April. She shoved a piece of paper at me. 'Give him that. It's a list of magazines the waiting room should carry.' I was beginning to look like a Japanese temple, scraps of paper everywhere.

Jenny Up wandered over next and struck up a 'casual' conversation about the sanitary (read: unsanitary) nature of pet birds visiting grocery stores. Samuel had quickly reappeared after April walked off, but faded a second time after ten minutes of Jenny's speculation on the number and nature of diseases a pet, for instance a cockatiel, might introduce into the environment.

It was almost a relief when Helen Rausch approached, with muttered invective that I'd best watch out before eating anything Liz Goldberg recommended because 'that hussy is pure poison'.

When the music cued, Helen rushed to get the middle seat of the first row before one of those sneaky Goldbergs did, and Samuel went to claim our seats. I lurked around the bandstand as unobtrusively as possible, snapping shot after shot. The show was an unintended work of comic genius, as Tuesday tried to shepherd the children of Unknown through various routines, like herding cats. Little Bloom Tarquin stomped on Frieda Watson's foot when Frieda stepped upstage of her. Frieda ran off in tears, Tuesday scurrying after her, as Bloom pirouetted prettily alone center stage, other dancers staying cautiously back. The Nez twins froze like deer in the headlights when they stepped on stage and didn't move until Tuesday skipped out and danced with them. But it was Patrick Up Jr. who stole the show when his lederhosen broke and the short pants fell to his ankles, revealing Spiderman Underoos.

I burned through film, but I was nervous, feeling like each moment once gone could never be recaptured. It'd been a long time since anyone depended on me. I didn't want to let Tuesday down.

Even after Celia Sweet had danced (safely) offstage after the last number, I continued to shoot. Liz Goldberg with Tommy (in a sling) telling the story of his fall to Jenny Up, with elaborate hand gestures. Helen scowling at them. Bruce towering over Ruby but looking half her size as he nervously offered her pink lemonade. Noah lifting Frieda Watson in her tutu on to his shoulders. Click. Click. I loved the sound the shutter made as I stole this part of Unknown. The permanence of photography left me in awe. Nothing alive was that enduring. It felt powerful to control it. Click. Tuesday flushing with pleasure as she accepted accolades. Click. Ronnie Two Shoes, thumbs hooked into belt loops, chatting up Sandy. Click. The setting sun highlighting the planes of Samuel's throat as he laughed. Click. Samuel turning towards me. Click. Samuel reaching to tug the camera away from my eye.

'Hi, shutterbug. You hungry?' Samuel's goal in life seemed to be making sure I ate enough.

'Hey.' Happiness poured out of my smile. 'Getting there. What a great night.'

'Aloha? Where are my people?' I heard Tuesday demand. 'I need my people! Maeve, Samuel! Let's go eat!' She waved us over, and it was my turn to flush. I was her people. I happily fell in with the crowd bound for dinner.

Later, stuffed with chile rellenos, Samuel and I meandered back to Ruby's. We'd dawdled to allow Bruce to escort Ruby home in private. Inside, I noticed that Oliver had taken up residence with Lulabell. They were snuggled on her perch, and he was making his happy grinding noise.

'Look,' I whispered to Samuel. 'They're in the same cage.' But Samuel wasn't looking at them.

'What an excellent idea,' he murmured. And without another word, I took his hand and led him to number 1.

'You need to see Child,' April rumbled. We were contemplating the pile of film on the table.

'My goodness, you took a lot of photos,' Busy fluttered.

I was worried about the cost of developing. My checks from Noah were minimum wage, and I was still paying off Simon Bear for towing Elsie. I wondered how I could barter. 'What child is that?' I asked absently.

'Child Sugar. He develops the pictures here. In the back of the print shop.'

'The octagonal building?' I was interested. I'd seen it on my runs.

'Yep.'

'Oh, you'll like Child,' Busy said. 'He's a lovely man.'

'You think everyone is lovely,' growled April.

'No I don't!' Busy protested. 'I think you're a skanky ho.'

A picture-perfect model for cardigan sweaters looked up when I walked into the print shop an hour later. When he saw me, he smiled, white teeth brilliant against his ebony skin. He reminded me of Cook from *The Shining*.

'I'm guessing you're Maeve Connelly,' boomed a rich bass.

'How did you know?' We'd never met.

'Ruby mentioned that a young lady wearing knee socks might be by today, most likely with a barter scheme at the ready.'

'She's very good,' I nodded, 'at knowing things.'

'She is indeed.'

I laid the eleven rolls of film on the counter. We eyed them.

'Will Noah let you work for me Mondays from four to eight o'clock in the evening? Mondays are my late night – everyone wants his or her weekend images ten minutes ago – however, I dislike missing *NewsHour with Jim Lehrer*. I'll instruct you in the operation of the machines. You may develop your own film after the paying customer orders are complete. You will only be required to compensate me for the cost of the paper if you rely on your own labor.'

'Absolutely,' I said, with no idea what Noah would think.

'Let us be civilized.' Child gestured to two armchairs and I sat. He pressed a button on an electric kettle, and in less than a minute loose tea was steeping in an Aurora Royal Patrician bone-china teapot, matching fragile cups at the ready. I truly had been expected. Child settled in his chair. 'Tell me about yourself, Maeve.'

I froze. Child was the first person to ask me about my past. Most of the time, I peppered people with questions, got them to talk instead. I preferred it that way.

'Not much to tell, really. My car broke down and I'm earning the money to fix her up. Are you originally from Unknown?'

'My family comes from Pittsburgh. Ruby did mention your situation. I am sorry for your car misfortunes. Where is your family?' He poured the tea through a silver strainer.

'North Carolina. How long have you lived here?'

'I moved to Unknown in 1988. Did you attend university in North Carolina?' Most people can be conversationally diverted with ease. You ask them something about themselves. Child was unshakeable.

'Mmmm hmmm. I bet Unknown hasn't changed

much. Is it pretty much the same as when you arrived?'

'They offer an excellent book on the history of Unknown at Piece of Work, the artisan shop on Red Road. What did you study in school?' It was like fencing.

'Oh, lots of things. How did you get into prints?' The walls were hung with beautifully framed antique maps, old posters from something called the Monkey Flower Festival, and intricate line drawings. The shop felt like a Victorian parlor except for the photo-processing machines behind the oak table serving as a counter.

'I studied art history at Carnegie Mellon. What did you do after college?' Riposte.

'This and that. I haven't really decided on a career.' Parry.

'When did you complete your studies?' His gaze was level.

'December. When did you open the shop?'

'Ten years ago. So you must have taken some time off school. You're what, twenty-four, twenty-five?'

'A lady never tells,' I demurred. He was sharp. And undeterred.

'So photography is a career interest for you?' Redoublement.

'Career? I don't know. I like taking pictures.' I decided to give him something. Retraite.

'Tell me what you like about it.'

'Capturing people as they really are. What do you like about framing prints?'

142

'Putting things in their best light. Is photography what you did during your time off from the university?'

'Nope. Prison,' I joked. I didn't want to talk about my time off. 'My goodness, is that the time?' Feint. 'I have to get to work.' I didn't have to do any such thing. It was my day off, but I was anxious to escape Child's inquisition. I gave him a rueful smile. 'It wouldn't do to be late the day you ask your boss for Mondays off!'

'No indeed.' Child smiled back.

After agreeing to meet on Monday, I fled. I resolved to have a better plan next time. I'd pepper him with questions. There'd be no opportunity to talk about me. The encounter left me unsettled, a feeling that stayed long after I was sprinting between grassy meadows. I ran hard, breathing the smell of sage, sunshine resting like a hand on my head, but I couldn't run off the feeling that something was following me.

'These are incredible Maeve! A million mahalos!'

We were looking at the photos from Tuesday's recital. 'This one of Bloom Tarquin is precious!' I'd caught her mid-pirouette, tongue at the corner of her lip in concentration, light haloing her blonde curls. I was anxious for Tuesday's approval. Child had carefully tutored me in operating the sensitive developing machines, but it'd taken more than a couple of rolls to get a feel for them. My first set of prints came out completely black.

My second split images over two sheets. With the third I managed to center the images and produce a roll where Bruce's camping photos were only slightly orange.

'I'm sorry, Child.' I'd pushed back sweaty bangs, hot with frustration. 'I'll pay for these.'

'Don't be silly. Training is a cost of business. These machines are highly calibrated, sensitive creatures, easily thrown into bad behavior. Rather like chefs. You'll get the hang of it.'

And eventually I did. It was 3.30 in the morning and Child had long since gone home and finished his sherry nightcap when Bruce's image of a flushed pheasant taking wing emerged crisp and clear, blue sky and gold meadow vibrant in color. No one was there to hear me whooping, but Child must have known, because when I showed up unscheduled at closing time on Tuesday, he didn't seem surprised.

By Friday all he said was, 'Remember to lock up.' He'd given me keys when it became apparent that my nocturnal fervor showed no sign of stopping. When Samuel hunted me down with a basket picnic, I could barely sit still, eager to continue creating prints, ushering him out the door with a hasty kiss.

It was worth it. After mastering the machines, I'd cleared the backlog of customer orders (and learned a few things about Ronnie Two Shoes), and had turned to my own film. My pile of rolls had grown as I continued to take images of

Unknown and its citizens. Like Sisyphus, when my task seemed met, it multiplied.

'I can totally use these for promotional cards.' Tuesday fanned out pictures of herself dancing, and hugged me.

'What are those?' Noah pointed to another folder.

'Oh.' I shrugged, embarrassed. 'Nothing.'

I reached for it but he was quicker, flipping it open and spreading the candid photos. Tuesday doing the hula behind the coffee bar when she thought no one was watching. Child snoozing in his armchair. April War Bonnet whispering new dirty words to Lulabell. I worried that they looked invasive. These subjects didn't know they were being captured.

'Maeve, these are amazing.' Tuesday's voice was hushed.

Noah paused at one of himself. Beth was talking to him, but he wasn't listening, he was looking past her, directly at the camera. He looked at me again now.

'You've captured the town well.'

I liked that he used my word, *capture*. I was grabbing moments. 'You can keep things from disappearing,' I said.

'But you're not in any of them.'

'What?'

'Where are the pictures of you and Tuesday gossiping when you should be working? Or you running down the back roads, braids flying?' I was embarrassed at his awareness. I preferred to stay below the radar. He tapped a photo of Ruby, Bruce, Samuel and Tuesday walking over to the Wagon Wheel saloon. 'You should be in this.'

'How can I take the picture if I'm in it, silly?'

He gave me a look. 'That's exactly it. Why were you behind taking the picture and not walking with everyone else?'

'I was catching up.'

'Or hanging back?'

I had the same uncomfortable feeling I'd had with Child. Like being rebuked, but I wasn't sure what for. 'I'm a tourist here,' I said breezily. 'Strictly observer status.'

'Don't remind me.' Tuesday groaned. 'It feels like you've always been here. You belong in Unknown. I hate the idea that you'll leave.'

Anxious tickle. California waited. Unknown was a temporary trick of bad luck.

Noah considered me, then said, 'We'll display your pictures in the store. You can sell prints for Elsie.'

'No one'll want to *buy* my pictures,' I protested.

'I think you'll be surprised. How much for this one?' He tapped a shot of him and Beth walking, heads bent together. For some reason it made me irritated.

'Five dollars unframed.' I named a ridiculous price.

'Fine.'

'Kill me for vanity, but I'll take these two.'

Tuesday waved two pictures of herself dancing. I felt guilty for overcharging.

They both handed me money, and just like that I was Maeve Incorporated.

CHAPTER 12

SNAPPING

It was my bad luck that Jenny Up decided to buy new cook-books as soon as the store opened. Some days we sold nothing but lunch, but the day I was late, we had customers at the unlocking of the door. It figured.

Noah smiled pleasantly at Jenny as he rang her up, but his right eyebrow was drawn down so I knew he was steaming. I stepped between him and the register and completed the sale, but he didn't return to his office. Instead, he loomed until the door closed behind her.

'You're late.'

'I'm sorry.' I was still breathless. I really was late.

'How am I supposed to finish ten chapters on time if I'm tending customers while you loll about in bed? God help us if someone needs a doctor.'

I was offended. 'I was not lolling in bed! I was in the darkroom.' Truth was, I'd barely seen Samuel all week, except for our daily lunches. And I'd completely neglected my marathon training. I frowned. I had to fix both of those deficiencies.

Last Monday, Child did not pass me on his way out, as usual, but was waiting.

'Come with me.' He led me out the front door and around to the back of the octagonal building. There was a separate entrance, which he unlocked to reveal a small room painted black, counters covered in trays, machines, filters and bottles.

'This is my darkroom. The photographs you've been taking are wasted on automated printing. How would you like to learn to develop negatives and print by hand?'

'I'd love to.' I breathed in a chemical smell that wasn't offensive.

Clipped to a clothesline were 8" by 10" black-and-white prints of pueblo life. They were flawless, capturing snapping eyes in a wrinkled face, a profile half in shadow, colorfully garbed dancers, a raptor seizing a snake.

'Did you take these?'

'My wife.' His voice was heavy with sadness. I remembered that Child was a widower.

Loss makes you selfish enough to think that you alone know what it feels like. You don't. Child had reminded me what we shared. 'My best friend died,' I surprised myself by offering. 'She loved to draw. The last picture she gave me means the world to me now.'

Child gave a brief nod. I was relieved he didn't ask *how* Cameron had died. I hated recalling my last images of her, stretched gaunt by an illness that didn't understand the rule that the young don't die. I hadn't taken any photos then. I didn't want to preserve the disease.

Her drawings were better. I said, 'Show me how it works.'

Time disappeared as Child taught me to thread negatives on to a spool in the pitch black, operating by feel. Light would expose them. I thought it ironic that blindness was essential to creating visual images. Once the spools were in the tank, the film steeped in carefully mixed chemicals, the minutes were measured by a faint glow-in-the-dark timer. Developed negatives were hung to dry like snakes in a Taiwanese alley, the dull color a contrast to the vivid pictures they contained.

'Everything about the process camouflages how visual the end result will be,' I said.

'Until this part.' Child smiled, switching on the enlarger. We were now working by the glow of an amber safe light. He cut a strip of dried negatives into smaller sections, and edged one on to the machine like a slide on to a microscope. A sharp black-and-white image of a flower appeared close up, and Child introduced me to the world of filters, dodging, edging and burning the image on to photographic paper. Once exposed, the paper went through a series of three chemical baths to fix the image. First the image is 'stopped' in a stop bath. Next it is 'fixed' to make it permanent and remove the paper's sensitivity to light. Child told me that the process extracted silver from the paper.

'After a year of prints, you might be able to scrape enough silver for a stud.' He laughed.

Finally the print went into a water bath to rinse the chemicals, before being hung to dry.

Images fixed, lights on, I studied the five black-and-white prints we'd produced. 'How different a single image can look depending on how you print it,' I marveled.

'It is an art,' Child agreed. 'Now down there is black-and-white film. I suggest you collect some rolls and explore your own artistry.' He pressed a key into my hand.

For a week, I'd spent every free moment in the darkroom, and the rest of the time in a semi-daze, smelling faintly of chemicals. I didn't *look* at things anymore; I snapped them with my eyes. I saw everything through the frame of the lens. I couldn't admire sunset without itching to photograph leafy shadows. If an image escaped, the loss was palpable. People became subjects. I started to view Samuel as a collection of planes and angles, smooth brown skin a canvas to capture the play of light. I was obsessed with capturing the essence of Tuesday, hinted at in her wide smile, but ephemeral. I wanted a still image to portray Ruby's precise way of moving. Or Ruby's precise way of informing me that the bareness of the linen cupboard, breakfast bar *and* refrigerator yesterday was unacceptable.

Which brought me back to my present predicament.

Noah looked mollified to learn I hadn't been late because of morning delights with Samuel, but not defused. 'It is completely unacceptable that you're over an hour late. I have a deadline *today*.'

I had to laugh.

'You think that's funny?' His expression devolved to thunderous. I decided not to explain my thing with timing. I had an unpleasant flashback to Joe at the Gin Mill. But this was different. I'd been *working*. I'd popped into the darkroom to drop off film, but the need to see my dawn photo shoot had been too great. Then, I couldn't leave until the negatives were done.

'I'm sorry, Noah. I really am.' I wasn't. The man could ring his own register once in a while. I was doing important work. People *valued* it.

'We ran out of John Grisham. He's number one on the best-sellers list and we ran out because you didn't order more. Part of your job is filing weekly orders.'

'I . . .'

'We ran out of *napkins*. I had to put paper towels in the café. Beth called us the Little Redneck Truck Stop.' That was kind of funny, but my smile was the wrong answer.

'Stock hasn't been put out, sales reports never got generated last week, and you put peanuts in the salad instead of walnuts. We're lucky no one went into anaphylactic shock.'

'You're not an infant, you know,' I snapped. 'You own the shop. The buck does not stop with your minimum-wage slave. It stops with you. Your shop, your buck. Stopping.' It wasn't poetry, but I was angry.

'Yes, and I'm the one *paying you* to work for me. Forget the basics – this place is a wreck with your half-finished projects. We have shelves in disarray for some imaginary future children's nook. We have half a vegetarian menu. And now we have only half the best-sellers in stock, and only half the stock on the floor!'

'And the store is half again as appealing as it used to be. I've worked hard,' I shouted over the little voice that said he was right.

'Until you lost interest.'

'My career has no value?' I elevated my hobby on the spot. His jab went to my anxious place. 'I'm supposed to tiptoe around your creative brilliance and not do anything for myself?'

'Interacting with humans wouldn't be a bad idea. It beats running away from everyone or hiding in a darkroom.'

'Working in the darkroom is *art*! It takes time. I'm doing hired *jobs*, I'll have you know. I am not *hiding*.' My protest felt oddly like a lie.

'Right. You're so focused on your *career* that you don't replace sold prints? There aren't any left. My store is naked.'

That stopped me. 'We sold them all?' I hadn't noticed. The bookcases now sported only forlorn nails. I felt a pang of guilt.

He was yelling now. 'You aren't doing even the basics of your job. You show up for film money and it's my privilege to pay you for coming in late and leaving early. You've become unreliable, and customers don't want to shop where staff radiate desire to be elsewhere.' His arm flung wide.

My bravado left me. He couldn't see me as that girl. I wasn't careless Maeve. I was reliable Maeve. Talented Maeve. Desirable Maeve. New Maeve. I needed Noah to see that.

'I . . .'

At my expression, he stopped, his own face becoming stricken. He plowed a hand through his hair and dropped into a chair.

'Damn, I'm sorry. I should not be taking my stress out on you.' He rested his forehead in his hands. He looked exhausted.

I fidgeted, but he didn't say anything. 'Have you eaten?' was the closest I could come to 'sorry'.

'Forgetting my morning coffee is no excuse to be rude. I'm a grown man. It's not your job to fill my bottle.'

'We could both use some.' I set about making a pot.

'I like having you around the shop,' he said as he watched me. 'And you have good ideas.' I felt awful.

'You have good ideas too,' I said.

'I live in Arizona.' His smile was rueful. 'What do I know about humidity?'

'I *am* sorry.' This time it was easier to use the word. I meant it. 'I like being here too. I'm not sure why I got so obsessed with the photography. Maybe it's because I never had a passion before.'

'No punk rock or poetry phase in college?' he joked. I made a non-committal noise. He raked his hair again. 'Who am I to talk? You've seen me work. A lot of being able to create is stepping out of your life into someone else's. I love it, but I'm no good at straddling two worlds. When I'm in the not-real one, it makes me dependent. You make it easy to count on you.'

'You *should* count on me,' I protested. 'As long as this is my job, I should be doing what I'm paid for.'

'Your photography is beautiful, Maeve. I don't want you to stop that.'

I squelched my flush of pride. The admiration had been like a drug, my darkroom mania the actions of a junkie.

I poured two cups of coffee and pulled up a chair. 'Been playing with your toys?'

He rose to my bait. 'They are *not* toys. They're—'

'I know, I know, "creative visualization devices",' I teased, glad to have redirected. 'What's the problem?'

He sighed. 'I think it's wrong to have an environment where everyone co-exists happily. That doesn't happen. My setting is bordering on Disney, full of joyful frolicking sea creatures. There needs to be threat within the society. I don't want to be Uncle Remus, bluefish singing on my shoulder.'

'Make an evil sea creature.' The answer seemed logical.

'It's not that simple. I'm afraid to characterize anything as a bad element. You should see the angry letters I received from third-graders when I painted warthogs in a negative light.' He grinned. 'One offended reader demanded an apology, but informed me that I was not to reply in cursive because he couldn't read it yet.'

'Crayon hate mail?' I laughed.

'My editor stopped forwarding the letters when I tried to respond to every one with long-winded justifications and apologies at a *See Jane Run* language level. I was so upset. It was worse than the time someone called me a bigot on Amazon because I made a joke about Frenchmen fleeing a battle. I hate to offend anyone.'

I thought a minute. 'How about jellyfish? No one likes jellyfish. The Boy can't communicate with them because they're non-thinking creatures. They drift without cerebral activity, and harm whatever they touch.'

We talked until the lunch crowd arrived. Afterwards I spent the afternoon catching up on my paperwork, surreptitiously slipping to Up Market to buy the toilet paper I'd also forgotten (paper towels would *not* do), and diagramming how I wanted Bruce to rearrange the tall shelves, currently in disarray from my insufficient efforts. I was shamed when I saw how much I'd let slide. I had to put limits on my darkroom time.

When Helen came in, I decided not to disturb Noah, and was able to deflect her interest in torture devices of the Middle Ages to a nice history of Charlemagne.

'You're looking fatter,' she grunted, as I rang her up.

'Hey, thanks!' I looked up with a smile. Samuel's attention to my diet must be working. My genuine pleasure took her aback. And disappointed her. She trundled out without another word.

I felt good about what I'd accomplished in a day, and was humming as I flipped the sign to closed. When I went to say good night, I saw Noah framed, head in hands, in the semi-dark, screen saver dancing. I took a mental picture. I appreciated how he'd opened up earlier. It occurred to me that he had no idea how many mistakes I made in the darkroom, the discarded prints the world would never see, the number of times I consulted Child for advice. It wasn't only writers who struggled for perfect tone and content.

I made a decision.

'Hey,' I said.

He looked up.

'Want to come to the darkroom and see what I do?'

CHAPTER 13

EXPENSE

'Still no Barney?' Vi asked.

'No.' I nibbled on a bowl of pistachios. Ostensibly for customers, I'd mowed through most of them.

'How long has it been?'

'I don't know. A little while.' I considered two pictures featuring Ruby dancing with Bruce, and Ruby laughing with the Cowbelles. It was Ruby's birthday.

'A little while? It's been over two months!' Vi's exclamation recaptured my attention.

'Really?' Surely it hadn't.

'How can you not notice? You're stuck in the sticks! Aren't you climbing the walls?'

'There's a lot going on,' I defended. 'I'm training for the marathon, taking hula lessons, and Tuesday and I started a book club. And I spend lots of time in the darkroom.' But still. Where had two months gone?

'The pictures you sent are amazing, Maeve.' The sincere admiration in my sister's voice took my breath away.

'It's hard to take a bad photo here.' I went

for casual. 'I've been getting lots of jobs. I've got my first wedding in two weeks. And we sell framed candids at the store.' My attention strayed back to the prints of Ruby. Child had helped me frame them with rich red wood and a pewter-glaze inner frame, with double mattes. The materials had been heart-stoppingly expensive, but the finished product was beautiful.

'I'm impressed.' Vi said. 'How's Samuel?'

'He's like a male version of you – he watches what I eat, he slathers me with sunscreen, he makes sure I don't train every day, he turns on a light when I read, he keeps me from stepping into traffic when I walk and talk at the same time. He takes good care of me.'

'I like to hear that!' She said. After a pause, she ventured, 'Why don't you stay?'

I frowned at the phone. I couldn't stay in Unknown. 'Because I'm going to California,' I insisted.

'Plans change.'

'I'm not giving up my plan because of car trouble!' I was tougher than that.

'What makes it giving up?' Vi asked.

'Stopping halfway would definitely qualify as flaky,' I protested. It occurred to me that I hadn't emailed Laura in over a week. We had been in regular contact, but recently I'd let the correspondence lapse.

'It's not like you saw something shiny and got distracted,' Vi countered. 'You can change what you want to do.'

'No,' I insisted. 'I can't. I want to go to California. I'm making the best of a bad situation.'

'Really?' said Vi. 'Because it sounds to me like you're having the time of your life.'

Her words left me unsettled, a feeling that was amplified when Beth walked in. Despite my best efforts, I was unable to warm to her. I did have to admire the perfection of her manicure. On the rare occasions I could sit still long enough to get one, it never made it out of the salon unblemished.

'Hey, Beth.' I waved.

'Working hard?' Her tone set me on the back foot.

'That was my sister.' I didn't know why I was giving her an explanation. The store was empty.

'Comparing your latest *Cosmo* quiz results?'

'I don't read *Cosmo*.' My defense was automatic.

'No? How ever did you learn to giggle and flip your braids and coo so that Bruce or Ronnie come running to carry the heavy boxes?' Her tone was arch. Was she joking? She shook her head, looking at me. 'It's like the women's movement never happened. Did you misunderstand and think they were talking about a Tampax product when they said feminism came about because women shed blood for the right to vote?'

She didn't have manicured nails. She had raptor's talons. My mouth was so unhinged I could have unhooked my jaw and swallowed a wombat.

This new Becky-Thatcher-turned-Ms-Snide kept going. It occurred to me this was the first time we'd ever been alone. 'Don't think Noah isn't on to you. He hired you because Tuesday begged him. You're not up to his standards, which I believe he told you to your face when you started. He was hoping you'd find something more suitable once he'd given you a leg up.' She paused for effect and a cold smile. 'That's just an expression, by the way. Noah is too nice to bring it up again, but fortunately, he's got me. You should consider your long-term plans. I'm sure there's a Hooters hiring somewhere.'

She strode to Noah's office, leaving me an odd combination of fury at my silence and anxiety over the truth of what she had said. Even the sight of Samuel crossing the square to join me for lunch didn't cheer me as it usually did.

Noah emerged with the weekly sales report and a frown.

'Is this right?' He gestured at the sheet, and I remembered.

'Oh, no!' I used my brightest voice. 'My mistake. It doesn't include the French Impressionist coffee-table book.' I nudged the oversized tome completely out of sight under the counter with my toe. It was the store's albatross. We were *never* going to sell it. 'We sold it yesterday!'

It'd cost me a lot to fake the sale, but seeing his worry lines ease was worth it. He smiled. 'That's good news. Last week would've been in the red otherwise.'

'Mmmmm hmm,' I agreed. 'Big sale.'

'I'm surprised. It's been hanging around like an unwanted in-law for over a year. I don't know what Beth was thinking ordering it. Who wants to spend three hundred and fifty dollars on a book? We're not a glossy art book kind of town, no matter what she'd like.'

'Tourists.' I pretended to share his bemusement. I'd faked the purchase to slip extra money in the register. I couldn't bear Noah's distress when the store underperformed. When sales were poor, he mourned the books not being read. This week we'd only sold two paperbacks. I also didn't want to risk him closing the shop. He made plenty of money from his *Boy* books.

'One more and we're out of stock,' I said. I'd slip the book back on the shelf later. Maybe someone would be crazy enough in the brains to buy it for real.

'We only had the one.' He looked confused.

'Nope! I found another buried in the stockroom.' I gave a shrug. I didn't want to keep the thing. It weighed three hundred pounds.

'I'm sure there weren't two.' His frown deepened.

I began to sweat. Noah didn't let a trick get by him with inventory. 'All evidence to the contrary!' I sang, then froze when I realized I was doing a pretty good imitation of braid-flipping. I hated Beth with a passion that burned white hot.

'Hmm.' He didn't look convinced. 'Well, June will be a better month.'

I barely heard him. Was Beth right? Was Noah

cueing me to move on? 'Who knows if I'll be here?' I snapped. 'Me and my flipping braids might be on our merry way.' Noah looked taken aback. I was surprised at my vehemence, but I'd already been on edge about Vi's presumption that I'd be so easily sidetracked. It was the opposite of what I was trying to show my family. Yet here I was, financially no closer to ransoming Elsie than when I'd arrived. It *was* like I'd gotten distracted by something shiny.

'I *am* capable of following through with my plans,' I persisted. 'I have the marathon.'

'I never meant to suggest otherwise,' Noah appeased. 'For the record, I have never once seen you flip your braids. May I? It sounds dramatic.' He was teasing me. I ignored him.

'In fact, I'm going for a run now.' I stepped from behind the counter. I wanted to think about things, make a plan of action. 'If you recall, we agreed that I could take breaks for my training?'

'Of course,' Noah continued to placate. 'I'll mind the front.'

'Good.' I paused. 'You can handle the new menu items?'

'I'm sure I'll manage.'

Another hesitation. 'Bruce will be by to help rearrange the shelves.'

'Okey-doke.'

'Just follow the diagram,' I instructed. 'Don't change anything. It's all there.'

'Yes, ma'am.' Amused now.

'Fine.' I walked to the door. 'I'll have my cell phone. Just in case.'

'Right-o. Better hustle, braids, before the midday sun.'

'Right,' I said.

Later, as I pounded down the familiar curves of Emerald to Purple to the country lane between the Goldbergs' fields, I was blind to the beauty around me. I was concentrating on California. I decided to research studio jobs involving photography, but my thoughts kept getting interrupted as I worried whether Bruce would be able to read my chart and move the shelves just right.

CHAPTER 14

CROSSING A BORDER

I was seething.

'I couldn't resist,' Beth had exclaimed. 'So I bought them. Aren't they great?'

They were four framed prints depicting pastel scenes of Victorian children playing on beaches or with tops or hoops or whatever stupid thing Victorian boys dressed up like girls used to do. They were *not* great. They were tacky and ugly and just being near them diluted my own exceptional good taste.

'They'll be *perfect* in the children's nook,' her narcissistic rant had continued. She'd paused and given me an assessing look. 'It's just that, Maeve, well, with your taste . . .' She'd let the thought trail off, and had given me a rueful 'I get that we can't all be as lovely as me' shrug. Her gaze had swept from my Converse low-tops to my *That's How I Roll* T-shirt. 'You're what, Maeve? Thirty? Thirty-one?'

'Twenty-six,' I'd ground out.

'Oh.' Delicate brows had arched, bow lips had formed a perfect 'o'. With a bemused shake of her head, she'd walked out, French manicure smoothing a blonde tress, lavender Theory suit perfectly hugging her perfect bottom. Which I wanted to bury my foot in.

I tried to conceal my fuming, but couldn't help thumping books down harder than necessary as I muttered.

'The Little Read Picture Book is *mine*.' Thump, thump. '*I'm* the one who came up with the idea. *I'm* the one who dragged those heavy-ass shelves all over, and lost brain cells painting them rainbow colors. I nearly *died* making The Little Read Picture Book.' This was almost true. I'd accidentally tipped over a bookshelf and trapped myself in the space under where it hit the wall. I'd been there for two hours until Bruce came in for lunch.

'Who does she think she is, foisting ugly-ass mass-produced art on me?' Thump. The cheap prints were a far cry from the classic children's book covers I'd planned to frame. 'It's a *children's book* nook. The art should be about *books*.' Slam.

'Hey, easy on the furniture.' Noah appeared behind me after I banged the cabinet.

'Sorry,' I mumbled. I wasn't in the mood. I retreated to the café and was clunking coffee mugs on to the counter when I broke one.

Noah had followed. 'Cease fire!' He held up his hands. 'I didn't think I'd pissed you off yet today. What's up?' His eye fell on the pictures. 'And what in God's name are those awful things?'

My mood lightened a tad. I told him.

166

'Oh no. No. Those things are not hanging in my store. They give me cavities.'

I blew out my bangs in relief. 'I thought we could use children's book covers. You know, framing the books in shadow boxes.'

'Sure. You can grab some from the back.' He was distracted by the pictures. 'Is that boy wearing a dress?'

'I thought maybe used copies with the original cover art. I've been finding them on the Internet.' I reached under the counter and pulled out the vintage copies. 'I have a stack of them.' Noah returned his attention to me.

'How long have you been doing this?' He lifted an old copy of the first volume of the Hardy Boys series almost reverently. I couldn't read his look.

'A while. It's tough because Amazon.com doesn't always post a photo so I can't be sure of the book's condition. I've had to send some back.'

'Why didn't you go down to the used-book store in Nogales?'

His question sparked my ire over another sensitive subject. I turned my back on him. Slam. Thump.

'I. Can't. Go. To. Nogales. Because. You. Don't. Give. Me. The. Six. Days. Off. I'd. Need. To. Walk. There.' I bit out my words. Considering my luck, I had it pretty good in Unknown. Since Vi's call, I'd been chafing at my utter inability to leave its confines. Tuesday went to Tucson at least once a week and returned with exotic groceries like

167

saffron, havarti and *Us Weekly*, and weaving tales of stadium-seating movie theaters and dance clubs. The most exotic I could get on foot in Unknown was Fu King Chinese.

'Get your purse,' Noah said.

'What?' I turned.

'You've been here what, two months? And you haven't been out of town? You must be going stir crazy. Let's go. Road trip.'

'Don't forget the bird,' I said automatically.

'What?'

'Never mind. We can't just go, in the middle of the day,' I protested.

'Despite the way you fan about the place, last I checked, I still own it. Which gives me the authority to close it. Even in the middle of the day.'

I was already halfway to the door.

Ten minutes later we were heading south to Nogales, my head hanging out the window like a Labrador. I was so excited to be riding in a car, to be going somewhere, I didn't care that the wind was tangling my loose hair. I was amazed when only half an hour later we pulled into the good-sized city of Nogales, on the border of Arizona and Mexico. It was bustling with traffic and humans and had at least twenty stoplights and a McDonald's.

'Lunch first, or bookstore?' Noah asked.

After the sleepy tempo of Unknown, I was a little overwhelmed by the activity. Pedestrians hurrying between shops and life-threatening street crossings, trucks and cars honking, people zipping through traffic on bikes. 'Um . . .'

Noah read my face. 'Lunch,' he pronounced. 'With beer. Let's go to Mexico.' He turned left and I shrieked.

'Noah!' The sign over our lane declared 'Border Xing Mexico Only'. I was terrified we were trapped on a course that would drain us into Mexico. I didn't know much about South of the Border, but I'd read *All The Pretty Horses* by Cormac McCarthy and didn't like it. Noah laughed, then parked in an ordinary parking lot overshadowed by the intimidating-looking government checkpoint.

'Very funny.' I blew out my bangs and got out of the car.

'I'm serious.' He led me towards the imposing fence and a sign that proclaimed 'International US-Mexico Border'. 'Let's go to Mexico for lunch. A friend of mine has a place.'

I hung back. 'I can't go to Mexico.'

'Why not?'

'Because the gate's scary as hell' didn't seem like a good answer. 'I don't have a passport, sport.'

'You don't need one. Got a driver's license?'

'Ye-es. Are you sure?' I found the idea of casually strolling to another country for lunch unsettling. It should be more complicated. The high walls and dangerous-looking fencing supported this.

'We could go over to Morley Avenue and take the underground drug tunnel if you prefer.' He grinned.

'Don't even joke like that,' I hissed, looking for Border Patrol and DEA agents to swoop down. Vi would not welcome the phone call from a Mexican prison. Did Mexican prisons allow phone calls?

'Maeve, I do this all the time.' He took my hand, and tugged me. I felt a tingle shoot up my arm. Then I got mad at myself. Why was I breathless around Noah? Samuel was a marvelous boyfriend and no slouch in the bedroom. I was satisfied.

Noah's voice recalled me to the scary-looking chute we were poised to enter. 'Let's see your license.'

I handed it to him without thinking, eyeing the border crossing. Perhaps I should ask the guard, just to make sure. The area seemed weirdly abandoned. The few men in white shirts, apparently US Border Patrol, looked anything but militant.

'Nice do,' Noah teased. 'Rocking the Sinead look?'

I snatched my license back from him. I was completely bald in the picture. 'It was an ill-judged impulse. My stylist assured me I had a "shapely skull".' I laughed it off. 'But my sister was right. My shaved head looked like the villain Gargamel from the Smurfs cartoon. I wore a lot of hats. But they don't let you wear anything on your head at the DMV.' Oh, the fight I'd gotten into that day, already irritable after an exhausting hour in line.

'I prefer it this way.' He tugged a tress and smiled at me. 'I'm getting attached to those

170

braids of yours.' I was going to make a smart comment about how he'd initially rejected my braids and funky socks, but I didn't. For a moment we held like that, eyes locked. When he tugged my hand again and said, 'The taqueria awaits,' it felt like I could safely follow him anywhere. And just like that, I became an international traveler for the first time.

'I have enough to decorate the whole nook now,' I gloated as I hugged my bag. 'That place was the mother lode!'

'I'm glad you liked it.' Noah smiled. 'I'm happy you included the Spanish version of *Cucú*.' He named the Mexican children's book I'd bought. I flushed with pleasure.

'It's such a part of the culture down here. It'd be wrong not to,' I said.

'Ah ha.' He laughed. 'A convert!' It was true; he had practically had to drag me back across the border. I *loved* Nogales, Sonora. Stepping through the gate had literally been a portal to another world. My mind was aswirl with the chaos and color of the town. I'd run out of film. I'd insisted on exploring every turning, chasing pictures up alleys, until Noah had commanded that I stop or we'd be placing that phone call to Vi for bail or hostage money. Not every part of Nogales was suited to tourists. But the center teemed with friendly people, colorful goods and joyful noise. In addition to my books, I boasted a fabulous turquoise ring, a carved wooden day-of-the-dead skull, a brightly woven belt for Tuesday, a pottery bowl decorated with chilies for Ruby, a deliciously full stomach and a slightly sunburned nose.

I squinted in the sunlight. I was having a perfect day. I didn't want to go home.

'I don't want to go home,' Noah said. 'I'm having too much fun.' He slung a casual arm over my shoulders.

'What's in mind, partner in crime?' I masked my over-delight with a bland tone.

He looked around. 'How about we get inked?' he said. For a moment I thought he'd said 'naked' and my pulse shot into my mouth, pounding madly. Then I spied the tattoo parlor next door and felt like an idiot. The sun was definitely getting to me. We looked in the window. A bald man was getting eyeballs tattooed on the back of his head.

'Got any?' Noah asked playfully. He pulled on my jeans belt loop and pretended to peek down my backside. 'Anywhere interesting?'

'No.' I giggled, swatting him. 'You?'

'I think it's time. Today's the day. Let's get you a tramp stamp.'

'Where's yours?'

'My treat, baby. Whatever you want.'

'You avoided the question. Again.'

'How about a butterfly? I'll pick the location. And I'll supervise closely, to make sure they don't make a mistake.' He wiggled his eyebrows suggestively.

'Stop changing the subject. Have you got one?'

172

He contemplated me. 'No, not a butterfly. How about a jolly roger?'

I faced him, hands on hips. 'You're the Roger Dodger. You totally have a tattoo. Confess.'

He looked away. 'I have one. I got it a long time ago.'

'Really? What is it? Where is it? Where were you when you got it? What made you decide to get one?' I was fascinated that relatively straight Noah had this racy secret.

His look was superior. 'That's very personal. A gentleman never tattoos and tells.'

I felt oddly cheated that Noah had a tattoo and I didn't. 'I always wanted one.' I was serious. I turned back to look through the window. 'I still do.'

'Why haven't you gotten one? Afraid of the needle?'

'Lord, no. I couldn't decide what to get. It's so permanent. What would I love enough to live with for the rest of my life? I'm not exactly great with commitment.' Noah knew enough of my history.

A tiny frown line appeared on his forehead. I put a finger on it. 'Watch that,' I warned. 'You'll get a dent. Not a tattoo I'd want for ever.' I didn't want to talk about tattoos anymore. My desire to have one paired with my inability to pick a design made me fretful.

'So what *would* you want for ever?' he persisted. I had an uneasy feeling the conversation wasn't about tattoos anymore. I didn't want to go there.

'What's next?' I changed the topic.

'We could get something to eat.' Noah caved in.

I rubbed my belly. 'I'm not sure I could. I'm still full of Rosa's delicious tacos.' We'd stuffed ourselves in Nogales, me surprising myself with my lack of concern about the ingredients or sanitary conditions. Being in another country was like having a holiday from my neuroses.

'You sure put 'em away.' His tone was admiring. 'I figured you needed the strength to finish your inquisition.'

I'd been fascinated by Noah's friend and peppered Rosa with questions about her life, her family and the taqueria. She hadn't been able to squeeze in a single question. I shrugged. 'I like to get to know people.'

'Thank God she ran out of Jarritos guava soda or we'd be there still, hearing about Cesar's son Juan's daughter Ana's boy Hector—'

'Let's go there,' I interrupted, spying a place across the street.

'Uh, Maeve . . .' Noah called after me as I headed towards the decidedly seedy bar. Nothing could stop me today. I was Maeve the Intrepid Explorer. I was a Force. Noah had a way of making me feel competent.

'It'll be fun.' I pushed open the door, paper covering the small round window, and blinked at the interior darkness just as I'd blinked coming out of the bookstore into the sun. The cowboy-hatted bartender stopped polishing glasses, and

174

weather-beaten men with bulging forearms and faces like leather swiveled on their stools. Beer posters curled off cheap brown siding, and plaid with a side of Merit cigarettes was the name of the game. I slid on to cracked red vinyl. Noah hastened to the stool next to mine.

'Two Sol,' I ordered, feeling ultra-Mexican. The bartender grunted. He put two bottles in front of me. 'Got limes?' Surprisingly, he did. They were produced, I instructed Noah in proper lime-procedure, and we clinked. 'Cheers, big ears. Thanks for a great day.'

'The pleasure was mine.' His look made it the truth. 'If I thought I had to crowbar you out of Mexico, that was nothing compared to the book-store. Considering you work in mine, I was a little offended they had to close to get you out of there.'

'Books are my friends. A bookstore is kind of like a reunion for me.' His look was dubious, eyebrow cocked like a Sherlock Homes actor. 'It's true! I had a hermit period. I dropped out of school and didn't know what to do with myself. Books were better than people.'

'I know what you mean.' He became serious. 'For me it was writing. After my dad died, things were tough. Mom worried all the time. It was like she was eroding before my eyes. I was sure she'd disappear. So I took care of my kid sister, and escaped into stories about a boy who could do everything.'

'Weren't you one?' I asked.

'What?'

'A kid. Weren't you one too? You call your sister a kid like she was the only one that needed taking care of. Who took care of you?'

He considered me. 'I took care of myself.' I opened my mouth, but he beat me. 'So who were your best friends? Of the bound page variety?'

I yielded. 'I don't think you can have a favorite book. Different ones suit different moods. Sometimes when I'm sad, I want to be more sad – like the catharsis of taking it to the limit will burn it up more quickly. Other sad times, I want to laugh hysterically.'

'If you were stranded on a desert island,' he persisted, 'what three would you take?'

I mused. '*Pride and Prejudice*, because it's the greatest romance ever written. *Catch-22*, because its satire gives you perspective on what's really crazy. And *A Bear Called Paddington*, because no matter how many times I read it, it makes me laugh every time.' I grew wistful. 'There's something about children's books that releases you back to the freedom of being a kid.'

Noah waited, but I was done talking about books. Instead, I launched into one of my favorite games. 'Would you rather only drink water for the rest of your life, or never see the ocean again?'

'Would you rather . . .' lasted us through two more beers and the drive home. I was deciding whether I wanted to eat only hamburgers for the

176

rest of my life or live for ten fewer years when we pulled up to Ruby's.

'Really?' Noah demanded. 'Ten fewer years?'

'Of course! I love food. Imagine never eating Rosa's tacos again. Living for ever is overrated. Why cling to life when you can't eat or enjoy yourself?' I thought of how hard Cameron fought to live when she couldn't do either, and got flustered. Fortunately Noah was getting out of the car and didn't notice. It took me a second to realize he was walking around to open my door. Samuel did it all the time, so I don't know why I was surprised. I slid out of the truck and looked up at him. His head blocked the porch light, giving him a halo and obscuring his features. He leaned toward me.

'Maeve.' Ruby's voice cut the tableau. Noah stepped back and I turned, refusing to wonder what he'd intended.

'Ruby! I went to Mexico! I got you a bowl!' I babbled.

'How thoughtful. I have good news.' Her perfect posture indicated nothing out of the ordinary. I felt silly for thinking something had been. Ruby continued. 'Barney has returned. Unlucky at craps, it would seem, and eager for work. He will look at your car tomorrow.'

'Oh.' The news I'd been waiting for didn't feel like I'd thought it would.

'I can see you're pleased,' Ruby said. I squinted at her unreadable expression. 'Noah, Beth was looking for you. Something about tickets to the ballet. Maeve, come along. It's high time we discussed the Monkey Flower Festival. October is nigh upon us.'

'I'm off,' Noah said with a casual wave. 'See you tomorrow, Maeve.'

'Right.' I matched him. 'Hey, Ruby, wait until you see my skull. Can I hang it in the common room? What's the Monkey Flower Festival? We're in June, right? Isn't today still in June? I didn't miss a month, did I?' I followed her neat steps into the house, shutting the door firmly behind me.

CHAPTER 15

NOTÍCIA MÁ
(*PORTUGUESE*: BAD NEWS)

'N ice ass!'
If a bird could holler, that's what Oliver did. I'd brought him along to separate him from Lulabell, but so far Project Wash Your Mouth wasn't going well. The ass that was facing us stilled, then slowly backed up, extracting its attached person from under Elsie's hood.

'Hi! You must be Barney. I'm Maeve.' I stuck out a hand.

He shook with a filthy paw. 'Barney.' He was a bear of a man, in denim overalls, with bushy red facial hair.

'*Quero otra bebida alcolica por favor*. I'd like another alcoholic drink, please,' requested a soothing female voice. If you lived in a computer-simulated home, she would greet you each day and warm your bathroom floors. Her name would be something gentle, like Sharon. A hydraulic pump sipping Kir Royale. I spotted a dusty cassette player on Elsie's roof.

'Learnin' Portuguese,' Barney explained.

'*Bueno*,' I said, disappointed. No drunken drill bits.

'*Como que posso pagar por isso?* How would you like me to pay for that?' Sharon wanted to know.

'Quite a car you got here.' Barney patted Elsie. I warmed to him. He had good taste.

'*Onde fica o putalheiro?* Where is the nearest brothel?' asked Sharon's dulcet tones.

Barney hastened to stop the tape player. I declined to ask what part of Brazil he planned to visit.

'Legs up and give me some, toots,' Oliver chimed in.

Equally shamed, Barney and I focused on Elsie. He started speaking. It might as well have been Portuguese. I extracted the salient double whammy from his explanation.

'How much?' My inner masochist asked him to repeat the sum. I had a flashback to Darryl in Okay, Oklahoma, but this time I didn't worry about showing my fear. I was approaching paralysis.

'If'n I get that part, be around two thousand seven hundred dollars. If'n I don't, you'd need a whole new engine. At that price, be better to get a new car.'

'Oh shit. Carrots!' said Oliver.

'That's a lot of carrots,' I agreed. I decided not to torture myself with minimum-wage calculations yet. 'Can you get the part? And do you have a paper bag handy?' Just in case. Untreated hyperventilation can cause an exploded lung.

'There's a bunch of things your gal needs, but your main problem is your trans won't engage due to broken 1–2 band. To fix that, you need a new band, and these two parts that go 'long with it. Miss Elsie here's no spring chicken, so those parts aren't just laying around like one-legged beggars.' I winced. Politically Incorrect Gas Station was right. 'It's gonna be hard to find, and it'll cost you.'

'But you can find one?'

'If'n anyone can it's Carla. She's my parts gal over at Tucson Auto. She can find cocaine in a snowstorm.' I hoped he was praising her tracking skills, not her drug addiction. 'Here's the thing. If she finds one, she won't order till it's paid for. I got no credit with her on account of some bad luck with the dice, and maybe some lag time on paying for parts. It's cash and carry. And PIGS ain't got that kind of cash.' Along with his colorful analogies, Barney was unabashed about his vices. 'I'll do what I can here, replace the muffler, change the filters, swap out some fuses, freshen up your juices, and you can pay me when you can. But to get them main parts, you'll need cash up front.'

'If she finds them, how much time will I have?' It was a lot of money.

'You don't want me to guess. Way my luck's going, I'd bet wrong.' He pulled a face.

Normally I'd commiserate, but despite the magnitude of Barney's bad news, the prospect of more time in Unknown was not as distressing as it should have been. Still, I cursed myself for the

181

money I'd blown on children's books, pizza with Tuesday and photo paper. I'd forgotten my agenda. What on earth was I doing on a committee for the town festival the same month as my marathon? I needed to get back on plan. It could take me weeks to order the part, pay Barney and have enough to get to LA. With that thought, I hurried back to work, the sound of Sharon asking if something was legal ('*Isso e legal aqui?*') fading into the background.

I was surprised to find Ruby at the café when I arrived. I'd contemplated asking Tuesday to stay while I ran to the clinic to see Samuel. He was expert at addressing my health concerns. The fluttering in my chest hadn't subsided and I was worried it could develop into a myocardial infarction. Shock can do that.

'I sent Tuesday on her way and brought you some lunch,' Ruby said. Bruce waved from a table set for three with chicken salad, fruit and iced tea.

'Wow, thanks, Ruby. You didn't have to do that.'

'Life isn't about "have to", Maeve. I suspected you might have received bad news.'

My shoulders slumped even as my heart warmed. 'It's going to be a lot of money.'

'Howdy, gal!' beamed Bruce as we joined him.

'All right there, Bruce?' Oliver mimicked Lulabell. Bruce ignored him.

'I hear you're going to chair the publicity committee for the Monkey Flower Festival.'

'Oh.' The fluttering accelerated. 'I . . . I . . .' The

182

festival was four months away. The marathon was four months away.

'Lawrence.' Ruby shot him a look. 'Maeve has a lot on her plate. We don't want to overwhelm her.' She patted my hand. 'We're grateful for whatever help you can give while you're here. With your talents, you can make some lovely posters before you go.'

I relaxed. I visualized LA in October, but couldn't conjure the sandy beaches as clearly as I used to. I could see a perfect meadow shot that would work for a Monkey Flower poster. 'Tell me more about the festival,' I asked. Last night was the first anyone had spoken to me about participating.

'Wall, it's 'bout the biggest thing that happens in Unknown all year. There's a parade and booths sellin' food and art, a stage for singin' and performances, and fireworks at night. Folks come from all around. There's drinkin' and dancin' too. Someone always ends up in the tank.' Bruce smiled across the table at his ex-wife. 'You should see Miss Ruby here on the dance floor. She has the lightest step in town.'

Ruby accepted his courting as calmly as ever. 'It commemorates the first bloom of a flower the Tohono O'odham and Navajo have relied upon for many purposes. The tradition of celebrating its arrival has continued for years.'

'Actually, it's not just one flower. There are hundreds of monkey flower varieties,' Noah chimed in from behind me. My pulse jumped.

183

'Ruby, is that your famous chicken salad? Who's sick?' Noah pinched some chicken from my plate and winked.

'There's plenty, Noah, so pull up a chair and plate and dine like an adult. No one's sick. I thought perhaps Maeve could use some cheering after seeing Barney this morning.'

'How did it go?' Noah pulled his chair close to mine.

I blew out my bangs. I couldn't very well do my ostrich routine with bad news if these people kept asking me about it. 'It's going to cost a ton, and it may take ages to find the parts.'

Noah face lightened. 'Bummer,' he said cheerfully, loading chicken salad on his plate.

'Too bad you sent that burro costume back where it came from,' Bruce lamented. 'Woulda been better than Ronnie's piñata head for the parade.'

'We do events here at the store,' Noah said. 'You know, the festival would be a great time to inaugurate The Little Read Picture Book. We could hold story hour, and have April or Henrietta Mankiller tell Native stories about monkey flower legends and uses.'

'I could teach the hula!' Tuesday swooped down. 'Ruby, is that your famous chicken salad? What's the occasion?'

'Maeve's stuck here,' Noah announced. 'The car repair will take for ever and cost a ton!' He made it sound like I'd won the lottery.

'Yay!' Tuesday pulled up a chair. 'I always do a performance at the festival. This year the Cowbelles want me to teach them to do something as well.'

'Oh shit,' said Oliver.

'Oh lord,' said Bruce.

'As long as they don't dance off the stage and hurt themselves,' said Samuel. He dropped a light kiss on my mouth. 'I came to feed you lunch and to hear what Barney said, but it looks like you're having a party. Ruby, is that your chicken salad?' He tugged my nose and smiled. 'You must be pretty special.'

'Scooch over, Noah,' Tuesday ordered. Noah scowled but did as he was told, and Samuel pulled a chair next to me.

'The Monkey Flower Festival is important to my people. You'll see some amazing dancing and storytelling performances from the elders.'

'I'll get some great pictures!' I said, then remembered I'd be in LA. I pushed the thought away. I could always come back.

'Maeve, you have to help me with the Bitty Bees float,' Tuesday said. 'You saw how hopeless my paper flowers were at the recital.'

'I see I missed the invitation to the party.' If she was teasing, Beth didn't quite pull it off. The mood at the table dimmed from rollicking pizza commercial to a sober investment-banking ad. 'Tuesday, you don't have to make paper flowers. You can buy them off the Internet.'

185

Tuesday looked chastened, and murmured, 'You're right, I guess. It's just not as fun.'

'Beth, would you like some chicken salad?' Ruby offered.

'Oh no. I don't eat mayonnaise.' Beth wrinkled her nose in distaste.

'Twat,' said Oliver.

For some reason I found this hysterically funny and erupted into laughter. Within seconds the entire table was roaring, whether because they found it hilarious too, or because I snorted loudly as I laughed, I'll never know. I couldn't remember when I'd been happier.

CHAPTER 16

THE L WORD

The sun slanted through the front window, highlighting the planes of Noah's face and the bulge of his forearm muscles below rolled-up sleeves. Forearms that were crossed in anger as he glared at me.

'Maeve, The Little Read Book is not that kind of store. We are a *book*store. We sell *books*. We do *not* sell trash.'

My arms were folded too as I returned his glare.

'It's about reading, and getting people to read more. Not whether something has a dusty leather cover.'

'My store is not dusty.' His pitch rose. 'And I don't sell this crap. My goal is not to make my customers dumber.'

'That's the *Economist*.' I pointed at the brand-new magazine rack at the front of the store, the cause of Noah's ire. 'It makes you smarter.'

'This is *Us Weekly*.' He shook it at me. 'I'm less intelligent just for holding it.'

My stance was mulish. 'It's not as if I've stocked *Playboy*.'

'I can't believe you did this behind my back. I

take one day off, and this is what happens. We are a *book*store not a news stand. We do *not* sell magazines!'

'You've actually been selling them like crazy,' Tuesday interrupted mildly from where she was arranging the staff picks.

We both stopped and looked at her.

'In one day Barney bought *Popular Mechanic* and *Sports Illustrated*, Ruby bought *Traveler*, and Bruce bought *Cooking Light*. April War Bonnet picked up copies of *Oprah, Newsweek, Glamour, Cosmo, Self, Ebony, Golf Digest, GQ, Road and Track, Men's Health* and *Forbes*. She requested that next week you get in *Mad Magazine* and *Garden & Gun*.'

We continued to stare. She shrugged.

'I didn't ask. In contrast, you only sold one book yesterday. Liz Goldberg bought the latest R.L. Stine *Goosebumps* for Tommy.'

Noah's brown wrinkled. 'We don't carry *Goosebumps*. Kids Tommy's age should be reading R.L. Stevenson, not R.L. Stine.'

I looked away guiltily, to see Samuel coming through the door. I welcomed the distraction. Noah, for some reason, looked even more peeved.

'Samuel!' I smiled and waved. He gave me a harried look as he hurried over.

'And what is this emergency that requires me to leave the clinic and run over here while actually sick patients are waiting for me?' His cross words were tempered by the fact that Samuel couldn't be abrupt if he tried. Underneath his skeptical look was concern that something might truly be wrong.

I remembered the rash I'd discovered that morning. 'Oh, see, look.' I worriedly lifted my shirt and showed him the outbreak along my abdomen. He stared in disbelief. I started to feel a little foolish. Perhaps I had overreacted. 'Um, it could be Omenn syndrome or Rickettsialpox or Malassezia furfur,' I said. 'Possibly discoid lupus erythematosus. That's indicative of a serious . . .' My voice trailed off. Noah and Tuesday busied themselves stacking books and pretending not to eavesdrop. I got the impression that Noah was enjoying my discomfiture.

'Maeve,' Samuel chided me. 'This has got to stop.'

I felt hot and defensive. 'It was worse this morning.'

'Maeve.' Samuel looked at me kindly. 'You don't have lupus. Or Omenn's. And I doubt you've been bitten by mice mites.' That was how you got Rickettsialpox.

'Well I'm not a doctor,' I snapped. 'How would I know? With my bad luck, if there was just one mite in the whole state of Arizona it would be me that got bitten!'

'Maeve.' He looked deep into my eyes, and cupped my face with his hands. 'It's not bad luck. And it's not the leukemia. You're in remission. You're healthy now.'

I felt like I'd been punched. I couldn't breathe. My eyes filled, and I couldn't see either.

Tuesday gasped, then silence hit the room like a bomb. I stared at the blurry outline of Samuel, aghast. How could he? He'd said the L word out loud. No one did that around me. It was forbidden.

'What the hell?' said Noah. 'Maeve?'

I blinked hard. The room spun. Nothing would go into my lungs. There was no air and I was dying. I felt Noah staring, mouth hanging open, while Tuesday gnawed at her lip. I felt dizzy and hot. The room was pressing in. The white coat was walking down the corridor toward me. Cameron was in a box. I was . . . I was . . .

'Maeve,' Samuel beseeched. I shook my head and backed away. He reached for me, but I turned and dashed out the door, ignoring him as he called my name. I broke into a run, temporarily blinded by the sunlight. I ran as if my life depended on it, sneakers pounding the pavement. I ran unseeingly past the post office, past the market and up the hill. I ran beyond the paved part of the road, stumbling on the rough dirt track. I ran and ran even after my side was stabbing with pain. Now that the word had been spoken, it permeated the air and I might breathe it in. It could catch me unless I stayed ahead of it. I kept running, until a stone caused me to roll my ankle, and took me down hard. The earth felt wonderfully solid and strong underneath me, like something that could protect me. I lay gasping, face pressed into the warm grass at the side of the road, until my gasps turned to sobs.

190

I'd pretended to leave it behind. It was part of college. It was part of Charlotte. It was part of the past. But it wasn't. Leukemia was part of me and it was constantly lurking, waiting for me to let my guard down. I was bawling uncontrollably now, the grass making little cuts on my forehead, fingers digging into the soft dirt.

The first time I lost a clump of hair, it'd been a good day. The chemo had been gentle on my body that week and I felt well. Vi was taking me out for pizza to celebrate. I would only manage a fraction of a bland slice of cheese, but it would feel good to be partaking in such a normal activity – a couple of gals going out for pizza on Friday night. I only spent time with my family at that point, my one experiment of telling a friend having gone badly. Susan had withdrawn as if a touch might infect her. After a few forced calls, I'd stopped answering, and she, after time, had stopped calling. Teenagers aren't ready for cancer. I couldn't visit the university where I was in school because my old dorm was off limits. There was construction across the street and the air, infected with molds and funguses, was potentially toxic. I decided that it was better to simply fade away rather than explain. Maybe my classmates knew, and maybe they didn't. I hadn't really cared. The germ-fest of a college campus was out of the question, and everything connected to it seemed remote.

That day, though, I was feeling good as I brushed

some color across my cheeks. Too much was garish against my wan skin, but just a shimmer improved the hollows carving deeper each week. That would change when steroids bloated my features like a sumo wrestler, but in the beginning I was modeling the Skeletor look. On the days when I felt good and had a little energy, I didn't feel ugly. Satisfied, I surveyed my reflection as I ran a hand through my long blonde hair. A thick clump of strands came along with it, tangled among my fingers.

I stared, breathless with shock. I'd been bracing myself for the loss every time I brushed my hair, but this day I'd been distracted, guard not in place. It was a sharp kick to the gullet. A reminder that even on the days I felt good, the cancer was still winning. It was 22 April. I was eighteen years old.

Strong hands on my shoulders brought me back to the present. Samuel rolled me over and eased me up against his solid shoulder, brushing the tangled hair from my face.

'It's going to be OK, Maeve.' He wiped the dirt and tears from my cheeks with a cool handkerchief. He placed a soft kiss on my forehead, then slid his arms under my knees and shoulders, carrying me to where Noah was waiting in his truck. I could only sniffle. I didn't even care that I looked a wreck. Now that everyone knew I was rotten on the inside, what did it matter what I looked like?

Samuel settled me on to his lap in the front seat. Noah looked concerned. He started the truck, and turned around on the dirt road, pausing once to encircle my ankle for a squeeze so brief and private I might have imagined it. Then he put the truck into drive and took us home.

CHAPTER 17

MONSTER IN THE CLOSET

Ruby was waiting at the door, and led us to my room with her precise steps. I buried my face in Samuel's neck, ignoring everyone. He started to speak, but Ruby gave a shake of her head. He nodded, and after laying me down, gave me a gentle kiss and left the room. Noah hovered uncertainly in the doorway, but with everyone ignoring him, he followed Samuel. When we were alone, Ruby poured water into an ewer and gently washed my face with a cold, wet washcloth. It felt stupendous. Then she brushed my hair.

'You'll sleep now.' Her voice didn't invite contradiction. I blinked at her. Maybe I could, maybe I couldn't. But if Ruby thought it was the thing to do, I'd try. She pulled the shades on the unaffected afternoon sun, then faced me in the gloom. 'A closet isn't scary in the daytime, Maeve. It holds clothes, not monsters. Whatever is scaring you, bring it into the light. Its strength will fade.'

My first reaction was that she didn't know how strong cancer was. Then I stopped, because how did I know? One thing you learned when you were sick was how to hide it, like vodka bottles in the basement. You'd see people heaving in treatment rooms, then exiting the hospital with bright smiles and the best wigs money could buy. Many pulled it off, though it required distancing yourself from people. But that happened anyway.

I figured Ruby wasn't talking about cancer itself being my monster in the closet, but its memory. It was a nice idea, but almost three years later, I still looked over my shoulder, fearful. Ruby pressed her palm gently on my forehead and held my eyes with hers. As if she'd drawn something out of me, I relaxed, lashes fluttering down, and sighed. Perhaps I could sleep, just for a bit.

When I woke, it was full dark. For a moment I was confused. Then memory flooded back. I tensed. Then, slowly, relaxed. A part of me was relieved. It'd been getting harder and harder to hide my secrets.

At home, people knew I'd been sick, but by my dictate no one talked about it. We'd all go back to normal and eventually I'd be normal too. Once my hair grew back, we'd forget it ever happened. Of course no one forgot, but we pretended pretty well. We pretended I ate normally. We pretended everyone took nine million vitamins. We pretended that eight years of college was about average.

In Unknown, no one knew better. I'd refused to spoil their untainted image with the truth. I couldn't bear the pity creeping back into my life.

But it had begun to chafe. How could I make new friends if I couldn't trust them enough to be myself? Samuel was like heaven. I'd cut him short when he'd tried to discuss my medical records, but he knew everything all the same. Maybe because he was a doctor, or maybe just because he was Samuel, he'd been perfect. God, it was nice to have, to *want*, sex once more. Samuel made me feel human again. It was the sweetest drug, and I craved more.

'Cancer' is a word like 'rape'. You can never say it comfortably. It's irretrievably tainted, and I dreaded becoming an untouchable in Unknown. I knew how people changed towards you. You even change towards yourself.

Being told you have cancer alters everything. Before you feel sick, before you lose your hair, before people have to hide their pity, before the first cold sore. Just that word, lingering like a rapacious specter after it's verbalized, transforms you for ever. I used to think my body and I were partners, together against the world. We acted in synch. We were a team.

With that word, our relationship broke. Suddenly I was going to bed with a stranger. Who was this body, full of rabid cells, out to destroy me? This would change, of course, as my body and I forged an uneasy truce to unite in our battle against a shared enemy. But it was never the same after that. We became two separate things, me and my body. I'd catch myself staring at an alien-looking hand or knee, thinking, who do you belong to? We paired up for specific ventures, but became untethered easily. I resented the secrets it kept from me. How was it that I didn't know what was happening before my diagnosis? We just didn't talk anymore. Even now, I distrusted it. I could discipline it, and make it run, but I always worried what it was doing behind my back.

In the dim light, I saw that Ruby had laid clean jeans, a T-shirt and my favorite Rainbow Brite striped knee socks on the chair by the bed. I was fairly certain those socks had been in the dirty laundry this morning. I pushed back the bedcovers and sat up. My secret was out now, so no help for it but to face them. And maybe . . . I looked at the clean socks. Well, just maybe. I smiled as I pulled them on.

Tuesday was sitting with Ruby at the kitchen table, talking over mugs of tea. I tensed walking in, but for once, the conversation didn't stop, replaced by guilty looks and fake, over-broad smiles, when I entered the room. Instead, Tuesday said, 'Hey there, sleeping beauty.'

Ruby rose, stepped to the stove. 'Ah, Maeve. Excellent timing. You can help us settle the matter of whether Tuesday should allow Ronnie Two Shoes to join the hula class she is offering to the Cowbelles at the senior center. He claims he needs the exercise, but we suspect he just wants to watch the belles shaking their booties.'

I laughed. 'I don't know. I might shake my booty if it meant I got to see Ronnie in a grass skirt.'

'Fair point.' Ruby nodded, turned on the kettle. I joined Tuesday at the table.

'I brought over Season Three of *Bones*,' said Tuesday. I remembered it was date night, and felt guilty for assuming she was there to cluck over me. 'I'll cook 'cause you've had a rough day,' she continued matter-of-factly. 'Do you want cereal, salad in a bag or frozen pizza? Uncle Frank doesn't care.' I laughed at my choices.

'Don't you want to hear about the cancer first?' I surprised myself by saying. No one gasped, no glasses shattered as they slipped from startled fingers.

'If you want,' said Tuesday. 'There's time.' Her response astonished me more than my offer. *There's time*, so nonchalantly. The presumption that you could get to something later was novel. I turned it over in my mind. Could you be happy doing half a trail because you could go back and do the rest another time? The idea was like a green shoot poking through the dirt. The kettle whistled, and Ruby prepared tea the way I like it, half teaspoon of sugar, no milk, setting it before me as she sat.

'You're good now?' Tuesday met my eyes straight on. It was alarming but pleasing.

'I like the way you ask. The first time someone asked if I was "in remission yet" it took the wind out of my sails, like if I said no I'd somehow failed. But I am – about two and a half years.'

Tuesday nodded. 'That's excellent.'

I stuck to the facts. I wasn't good with specu-lation. 'I was diagnosed with acute lymphocytic leukemia spring semester of my freshman year of college. I had chemo and radiation treatment for two years. I dropped out of school and moved home. I was pretty sick most of the time.' I'd never spoken about it to someone who didn't already know. I wasn't sure where to go. Tuesday sensed I was a little lost. She was too, but she did her best.

'Did you lose your hair?'

'Every strand. That wasn't the worst, though. It's the things you aren't expecting that get you the most,' I said. 'I knew my hair would fall out. Anyone who's ever watched TV knew my hair would fall out. I was prepared.' After that first day, I'd stoically watched clumps of hair swirl down the drain during each shower – a brief, lukewarm affair, devoid of the fancy products I'd once delighted in, to protect my chemo-dehydrated skin. 'My sister Vi and I bought hats and scarves and pretended it was fun. And when the time came, I bore up just right, going through the typical Girl-Exuding-Strength cycle of bob to pixie to shaved head. I learned how to wrap an African scarf and pretended I felt stylish.'

They both sat quietly, listening. It felt obscene and ungrateful to say what I was saying, consider-ing I'd lived when so many hadn't. But I couldn't stop now that I'd started.

'It was when the hair fell off my arms that I lost it. It was an inconsequential thing – I can honestly say that prior to its absence, I'd never appreciated arm hair to any degree. But when it was gone, I felt like I couldn't live without it.' Both Tuesday and Ruby contemplated their forearms. I did too, covered now in fine blonde hair.

I remembered the day sharply. I'd felt the loss so keenly I'd slid boneless to the bathroom floor. All my sorrow over the chapped lips and cold sores and baldness, all the stuff you were supposed to be brave and stoical about because that was a part of having cancer, had poured into my naked arms, and I had sobbed and sobbed. I'd felt as exposed as a writhing grub without that thin blonde pelt. After a while, I'd pulled it together and finished moisturizing so I would be ready for the next day's chemo. I hadn't had much of a choice. Later, when I'd lost my pubic hair, I'd been prepared. But I didn't tell them that. Some things the healthy don't need to know.

'But the treatment worked,' I said. 'After two years, I was in remission. My hair grew back, I returned to school. I was fine for a while.' No point in being suspenseful about the hard part. I reflexively rubbed at the furrow on my forehead. 'I relapsed a year and a half later.' I hadn't felt sick at all. I'd been planning to shop after my appointment. It had been five days before Christmas.

'That must have been hard,' Tuesday said.

There is absolutely no way to tell someone how

it feels to be racing the clock to get to your sister because if you're alone when realization sinks in you'll drive your car at maximum velocity into a wall. That instant when choosing your own death seems better than it taking you against your will.

'Mm-hmm.' I avoided eye contact. 'It was tough for my family. They warn you that it's easy to get caught up in your own drama and overlook your family's pain, but that's wrong. When I relapsed, I dreaded telling them more than being sick again. I couldn't bear the fear returning to my father's eyes.'

'Is it different when you relapse?' Tuesday asked.

'The second time, we caught it early. The treatment was nowhere near as bad. They'd made a lot of advances, and I needed a much less severe regimen. The side effects weren't as bad.' Except the dry skin, cold sores, nausea, fatigue. The distancing of people wasn't so bad the second time either, as I hadn't replaced the ones I'd lost the first time around. 'I knew what to expect.'

'Does that make it worse?' Ruby asked. 'Piling dread of anticipation on top?'

'You'd think so, but no. The scariest thing about being sick is the complete lack of information. I spent my first months obsessively researching medicine. If I could throw around words like lymphocytic, anthracyclene, intrathecal or nanotechnology and understand what they meant, I could have some control. I had flash cards for the drug names. I still remember them – L-asparaginase, vincristine, dexamethasone, daunorubicin, methotrexate, 6-mercaptopurine. It helps, knowing. Walking around in a strange room in the dark is a lot harder than walking around it with the light on.'

We were quiet for a moment. Then Tuesday said, 'Well from now on I'll remember not to tug your braids so hard in case they fall off. So what do you want to eat? Uncle Frank is starving.' And I snorted tea out of my nose, I was laughing so hard.

When Samuel came over later, we didn't talk.

'I'm sorry,' he whispered, as he settled me against him in bed.

'I'm sorry too,' I said, 'for putting you in that position for so long. And I promise we can talk about it. But not now, OK?' I was worn out from talking. I felt rather than saw him nod. He held me close, stroking my hair until I fell asleep.

CHAPTER 18

THE GIRL WHO COULD, PART II

It was the most ordinary day. I was in the hospital and we were waiting, because that's what you did. Even though it was Wednesday, everyone was there, blue paper booties on their shoes.

'Another game of Uno?' asked Vi.

'No.' I was sullen. I flicked a stray card from my bed to the floor. Green six. The doctor was late.

She picked up *Us Weekly*. 'Britney Spears is going back on tour.'

'I'm sure my treatment includes an auditorium full of breathing, coughing tweenies.'

'Brit-Brit would love the blue booties. Mine make me feel fancy and beautiful.'

'I feel like I got ready in the employee bathroom of an Abra-Kababra after my day shift cleaning grout with Pete Doherty's old toothbrush.'

It was sunny outside. I wanted to feel it so badly.

'Leonardo DiCaprio and Kate Winslet are doing another movie.' Vi tried again.

'Maybe they'll both drown this time.' I was too tired even to be crabby properly.

My dad looked up from his Sudoku. 'Don't worry, Maeve. I'm sure you'll be able to come home today.'

'You're sure? Really? How sure? Medium sure? Supersize sure? Sure like Johnny-Depp-is-a-hot-piece sure? Or more pork-bellies-are-the-way-to-go sure?' The words lashed out, trying to fill the space of my impotence with their vigor. Everyone froze. I wilted. 'Sorry,' I muttered.

'How about some iced tea? Lemonade?' My dad stood carefully, expression controlled. I didn't want to think what his face would turn into out of my sight. 'We could all use some refreshment.' I didn't answer. The mere thought of lemonade made my ulcers sting.

'Maeve? Want anything?'

'A pony.'

'I'll have half unsweetened iced tea, half Diet Dr Pepper,' interrupted my mother. 'And a kiwi if they have any.'

'I'll take a beer,' said my brother.

My dad thumped him. 'Call me when you're twenty-one, kiddo.'

There was one of those shock freeze moments in the room where the air went still and everyone's heart stopped for a beat. A single, unacknowledged stutter of time. Casual references to events far in the future were to be avoided. Ba-boom. One beat. Shimmer. Then life resumed.

'Be right back.' My father escaped.

'You know what? I want something after all.' Vi

straightened once my dad was out the door. 'Let me grab him.'

She hurried out. She was gone longer than a drink order. I could only imagine what was being said. The repairs that were needed.

'Having cancer doesn't make you noble,' I said to my mother. In the movies they don't show you too fretful for another stupid game of Uno or being rude to your sister.

'It doesn't make you excused either,' my mother said.

I was silent. She took pity. 'What do you think of my execution?' She held up her Etch A Sketch.

'I'm all for it.'

Brick snorted a laugh. My mother went back to her sketching. '*I* like it.'

'It's hard,' I whined. I wanted her attention back.

'Anyone who would debate that is an imbecile.' She didn't look up.

'You win.' My smart mouth wouldn't stop.

She put down the Etch A Sketch. 'Would it hurt to be nice?'

'Depends on your pain threshold.' I plucked at my blanket.

'I'm taking that repartee book away.'

'Don't,' said Brick. 'Quoting has improved her normal conversation.'

'There's so much *waiting*. If I'm not vomiting, I'm waiting,' I complained. It wasn't fair. They could go home whenever they wanted. 'If they really think the treatment isn't working, shouldn't there be frenetic activity?' I demanded. 'Bells and flashing lights? White-coated people thundering down the hall-way? Zach Braff interior monologues?' Being faced with death is supposed to be dramatic, not weird pockets of nothing to do.

My mother leveled me with her look. 'We're waiting too.'

And with that I felt their pain. Shame washed over me. They were there for me and I was being a bitch. I resolved to be better.

It didn't last long.

Brick tossed down his magazine, and started playing with my new wig. 'You know, baldy, you almost look like a man.'

'So do you.'

He held up the wig. 'Who does your hair?'

'How would I know? I'm not there when it's done.'

He played with strands and affected a snooty French accent. 'And 'ow do you want ze hair done today?'

'In silence.'

He tossed the wig at me, and looked at his watch. 'Unfortunately, you got it. I gotta go. I missed track practice yesterday so I have to go today. Sorry, kid.' I hated the unspoken accusation. The relief he was hiding behind the *sorry*. I thought of my brother running free and far away, and when he kissed me goodbye, I couldn't help thinking, 'You asshole, I could do that, if only . . .'

I got to go home that day.

★   ★   ★

When the knock came, I turned off the safe light and admitted Child to the darkroom. I hadn't been printing. I'd been staring at drying images in the amber glow, wondering how I might have fit into the pictures if I'd never gotten cancer. Would I have had the self-absorbed confidence of Beth? Would I have dared Sandy's short hair? Would I have had the fearless ability to scatter love and dance like Tuesday? If I knew, I'd do it.

'I thought I might find you here,' Child said. No surprise there. For days I hadn't been anywhere else.

'I gave myself the week off work,' I said.

'I'm beginning to better understand Noah's good-luck wishes when I hired you,' he joked.

I snorted. 'Noah's an example of why smoking crack while pregnant is not a good thing.'

Child examined the hanging prints. 'Nice work.'

'I'm not in any of them,' I said. It wasn't self-pity, it was a question. I remembered Noah's earlier comment. How could I be expected to be in the picture if I was taking it? Was it strange to love being behind the camera? It didn't mean I didn't want to be with people too.

Child didn't answer right away. 'I think you're in all of them,' he said finally. 'Your eye, your world, how you see things. Anyone looking at these is closer to you than to the subjects.'

He tapped a picture of Samuel sitting alone, eyes closed, meditating. 'This is how you look at someone with affection.' Then he tapped a picture of Bruce with Ruby. 'This is how you look at someone with love.'

I frowned.

'And this.' He chuckled. 'Well, don't let Beth see this.'

'What do you mean?' It was just a picture of Beth sitting in the Wagon Wheel, looking like . . . Beth.

'Trust me.' Again the chuckle. 'I was thinking you could assist me in developing some prints. It's just one roll.'

'Sure.' I didn't know Child took photos.

He turned out the lights. 'Hand me a spool.'

I heard him pop the film canister open on the counter and pull the film.

'The night my wife died wasn't special.' Child's disembodied voice prompted a jolt of adrenaline. 'I'd cooked a pot roast. Janie did most of the cooking, but I chipped in where I could. It wasn't a dramatic event, table romantically set, me waiting into the night as candles guttered lower. It was the ordinary plates in the kitchen.'

I recalled the ordinary days. Waiting, and *Jeopardy*. Getting the right answer, getting down a whole serving of Jello, getting the news that the boy next door had died. I knew what he meant. 'Her name was Janie?'

'Janie Sugar, sweet as candy. I ate my dinner and put the rest away. I figured she'd got caught up in Tucson and could reheat something when she got home. I was watching *Prime Suspect* when the state trooper arrived. She loved that show.'

'What happened?'

'She hit a deer. They gave me a box of her things. Everything sparkled from the dusting of glass. At her funeral, I almost expected Janie to glitter too. In a way, I wish she had, so I could remember it. All I really remember about that day was almost choking to death on a miniature mushroom quiche because I didn't have enough saliva in my mouth to swallow it down.'

I swallowed reflexively.

'It was a long time before I could face her closet. Her sweaters smelled like Tea Rose. Every time I tried to box them up, the smell would drive me right out of the house, and restart the fantasy that it was all a terrible mistake and any second she'd walk in the door and want to know why in the name of the good lord I'd packed her favorite twinset with foul smelling mothballs. In the end, I gave in and let the ladies take care of it. Twelve hours and everything was gone. Except her camera. That was the only thing that mattered to me. She never went anywhere without it. The lens was shattered in the crash, but the film was safe.'

I knew it didn't take Child this long to thread negatives. 'What was on it?'

'We're about to find out.'

I took in a breath. 'Child, when did Janie die?'

'Six years ago. I was afraid to know the last thing she saw. What if she'd spent her last day immersed

209

in disappointment or injustice? You never knew what Janie would shoot. I wasn't ready for her final impressions of the world.'

'Why now?'

'For six years no one's used this room, or stepped into Janie's shoes. I think folks didn't want to offend me. They hauled their children to the Sears in Tucson for their Christmas card.'

'But all the film . . .' I was busy on Mondays.

'Three times as much as before you came. You unfroze things, Maeve. It's like we all got pulled in the wake of your forward motion when you run. Watching you work images reminded me that no matter what's on this film, Janie loved her craft.'

We were quiet. 'No one talked to you about it?' I asked.

'Some of the widows tried, but I wasn't interested. I didn't want to be defined by being a widower.'

'When I had leukemia,' I said, then paused. I tried to recollect how many times I'd spoken those words. Not many. 'I met this girl, Cameron. We were on the same treatment schedule. We became best friends, comparing radiation tattoos and bragging about who had more side effects – you get oddly competitive about symptoms. It was stupendous to have someone who understood. But then she got sicker, and I felt guilty because treatments working for me were failing her. We both had to fight resentment. I got scared too. My "treatment twin" faded and died in front of me. At the funeral, being alive felt like a brand – my family a bubble of toxic happiness among her family's pain. After that, I put space between myself and other patients.'

'Seems to me you keep the healthy world at arm's length as well.'

'I didn't start out secretive, but no matter who you were before, once you tell people, they change towards you. A guy I was dating broke up with me because he thought I might be contagious. Can you believe that? It's hard to imagine in this day and age that anyone would think cancer was contagious, but I can assure you that many of our comfortable assumptions get shattered when we go to the other side.' I shook my head.

'Most people don't appreciate how lucky they are until they aren't.'

'My cousin told me I was unfairly lucky, because she'd been dieting for years and I lost tons of weight just like that. She said I looked like I'd been in a famine like it was a good thing. I told her she looked like she'd caused one. There should be a Miss Manners for cancer. Though I don't think Miss Manners would've approved when I put hair remover in my cousin's shampoo. But hey, if you want the cancer look, who am I to deny you?'

Child chuckled. 'They need Miss Manners for loss, too. I had a fellow tell me I was lucky to be able to date again, that he was stuck with his old lady for the rest of his life. I remember thinking

I'd trade half of my remaining days to have Janie back, and the other half to shove the guy into a sack and stow him on a plane to Uzbekistan.'

'I detest the hijackers that turn your diagnosis into their drama. One friend was so overcome with my news that she had an asthma attack, fell over, and had to be rushed to the emergency room. I had cancer cells coursing through my body and I was breathing just fine.'

'I recall a widow that wanted to hold hands and weep together over our loss. I wanted to stuff her in a sack bound for Uzbekistan too.'

'Some people, no matter what I say, they're visualizing the chisel on my tombstone.'

'It's real nice to have you talk with me, Maeve.'

'People make it hard to keep to yourself here,' I said. 'Folks want to talk about stuff. I'm surprised they left you alone.' Maybe it was different when you were old.

'Even widows run out of steam eventually. Though if I never see another casserole with Fritos on top it'll be too soon.' Child chuckled.

'I hate cut flowers,' I said. This time my mind spun away.

'Look at what you got,' Maria sang, as she brought a gorgeous arrangement of lilies and hydrangea into the room. My mother and I were sitting quietly, reading. Well, my mother was reading *Wesley the Owl: The Remarkable Love Story of an Owl and His Girl.* I was reading the back of my eyelids.

Transfusions made me tired. For that matter, my mother may have been reading her eyelids too. Donating her platelets to me wore her out.

Maria had the body of a sand-filled balloon tied about the middle with a rubber band, and favored teddy bears on her scrubs. Her clogs squeaked in a perfect note of high B flat when she walked, she called me sugar, her hugs were squishy and her smile never wavered. I loved her.

'They're beautiful!' my mother exclaimed. 'Who are they from?'

'A florist,' I said.

'Sugar, you crack me up!' Maria's laugh sounded like bells. When she laughed and walked at the same time, it was a symphony. She read the card. 'It looks like it's from your Aunt Leigh.'

'I'm astonished it's not an ugly sweater,' my mother murmured. Aunt Leigh worked at J. Jill. Her sweaters to our family were a Christmas staple, and regularly brought joy to at least five people at Goodwill around 26 December. There was nothing wrong with J. Jill. There was everything wrong with Aunt Leigh's taste in sweaters.

'It says "Happy Birthday, Maeve".' Maria looked at me over the card. 'Maeve! Did you have a birthday?'

'At least once,' I said.

'Last week.' My mother swatted my legs under the blanket.

'She only remembers,' I pretended to whisper an aside to Maria, 'because the epidural wore off.

Doctor did all the work but she takes all the credit.'

'Un-hunh. See, now, here it's the other way 'round. *We* do all the work and they get all the credit.' Maria's laugh rippled. 'But how'd I miss your birthday, sugar?'

'It was your day off, Maria. Cecile was here,' my mother explained.

'Don't tell me that lazy tart didn't set you up with a party.' Hands on her hips. Cecile and Marie were best friends. 'What did you do?'

'I took a Demerol nap,' I announced.

'We didn't do much. Maeve was worn out.' With a spiking fever ruining my sleep for days, we'd *all* been exhausted.

'I'm bringing you a balloon and a cupcake later,' Maria said.

'Can I have a red tricycle and a Bald is Beautiful Barbie?' I asked.

'You can have anything but bad news,' Maria answered.

'I'll settle for some white blood cells and a hug.'

'Couldn't avoid it, sugar. I'd do it now, but . . .' She hefted the flower arrangement. It really was gorgeous. We admired them a moment. I was thinking ahead to Maria's next question.

'So where shall we send them?' Flowers aren't allowed in cancer wards. Patients are too sensitive to smell.

'I sent the last ones to the maternity ward, right?'

'I think so.'

'Can you find someone elderly? Someone who doesn't get visitors? Tell them it's a secret admirer,' I instructed. 'But pull out one of those hydrangeas for Mr Naveen.' Mr Naveen worked in the gift shop.

Maria beamed at me. 'That's why you're one of my favorites.' She headed for the door.

'Maria, when you come back, can I get some of your magic mouthwash?'

She gave the closest approximation of a frown that was possible with Maria. 'Is your throat bothering you again, sugar?'

I nodded. Please God, let it be a sore throat and not mucositis.

'I'll take a look when I get back. What did you get on your last test results?'

'Nail polish,' I said.

She belted peals of laughter.

'Remember to use your inside voice, Maria,' I called after her.

'Sweet girl,' she called back to me.

I didn't feel sweet as I watched the flowers depart. I loved Maria but I didn't really want to be a hospital favorite. I wanted to go home and be someone no one ever thought about sending flowers to.

'We'll have to write Leigh a thank-you note,' my mother said. 'That was very kind of her.' It was. People meant well. It was also an innocent blunder that reminded you how disassociated you were from normal.

'Mom? Can I tell her not to send more? Can we tell them all?' It was a sincere question. I really wanted to know if that would be OK. We looked at each other in silence. Because we honestly didn't know.

'I think I'm ready.' Child brought me back. 'Let's see what we've got, shall we?'

Janie's pictures were beautiful. She'd stumbled on a community picnic. Her camera caught women sharing mangos covered in hot sauce, children chasing one another, men squinting through cigar smoke. Each one drew you into Janie's eye, and I understood what Child had meant earlier when he said he could see me in my photos. I was relieved. There was nothing to dread here.

We finished printing and hung the glossy wet images next to my prints, now curling into dryness. An image of Noah caught my eye. It was a weekend picnic, the group gathered in ordered chaos, young people looking anywhere but the camera, except Noah. He looked directly into the lens, expression neutral, as if asking, 'But for what happened, who would *I* have been?'

Child interrupted my thoughts. 'You're not responsible for other people's happiness, Maeve, just as I wasn't responsible for Janie's last day. Let yourself believe that. Figure out what makes you tick. Don't wait as long as I have.'

'I'm trying, I guess. It's like a split path. I used

to love chasing a curved trail, and now I'm stuck at a fork no Frost poem can solve. My *it'll never happen to me* is gone for ever. I can't go back, but I'm unsure how to go forward.'

'My life would be a lot easier if I could get my selves to agree on anything,' he commiserated. 'All I can assure you is that nothing will happen if you spend your time alone in a darkroom. Or in front of *NewsHour with Jim Lehrer*. The sun is shining, Maeve. Let's go outside and share some lemonade. I love the taste of cold lemonade.'

'If you'll let me give you something,' I said. The third kachina was the organic twining of leaves, new shoots rising around the hummingbird with its strong heart. Healing.

'It seems a fair bargain.'

And so we did.

'Child?' I asked as we stepped into the light. 'Why do you dislike Uzbekistan so much?'

When I got home, I slipped through the yard to avoid April and Busy and the home shopping channel in the common room, Oliver and Lulabell chattering madly. I reached my door undetected with relief. April's ears were as sharp as cricket hairs. I'd been doing so much face time in the last few days you'd think my new album was about to drop. I felt the need to burrow into a book.

My foot kicked something as I stepped into my shaded room. There was a large envelope with my name on it on the floor. I settled on to the bed to open it, expecting Ruby's shopping list. It wasn't.

I extracted a slim volume, heavy pages bound between beautiful hand-made covers. I turned it over gently. It was a children's picture book, each page framing its words in beautiful watercolor drawings filled with a boy, a girl, a bird, and lots of tall trees. It was inscribed to me. I began to read.

THE GIRL WHO COULD
for M.

Once upon a time there lived a Boy and a Girl. They were about that age where they were curious and just starting to understand things – a little older than you and a little younger than me.

The best way to see curious things was to climb very high. The Girl was an excellent tree-climber. The trees were very tall. The Girl wore knee socks to protect herself.

The Boy did not like to climb. He was afraid of heights. He would stay at the bottom and write down what the Girl saw. He had excellent penmanship.

Together they climbed a great many trees and wrote a great many things down.

One day a branch the Girl was sitting on broke. It wasn't her fault but she fell a long way. Even though she was wearing knee socks, she got a bad cut on her knee.

The Girl went to the best doctor and she gave her a special bandage. Lots of time went by, but she refused to take off the bandage.

'Does it hurt?' asked her mother.
    'No,' said the Girl.
    'Are you bleeding?' asked her father.
    'No,' said the Girl.
    'Are you infected?' asked the doctor.
    'No,' said the Girl.
    'Why won't you take the bandage off?' they asked.
    'I'm afraid,' said the Girl. 'The bandage stays.'

The Girl decided to go where there were no trees. She walked a long way and came to a fence. On the other side was a vast open space with no trees. She went through the gate and walked to the middle. It was a very large space indeed.

'How large do you think this space is?' the Girl asked. No one answered her because she was alone. The Girl thought about writing it down, but she had forgotten a pencil. It didn't matter. No one could read her handwriting anyway.

★   ★   ★

The Girl sat down. 'I'll be safe here.' She sat for a long time. Nothing happened. She began to fidget. There wasn't much to look at.

The Girl decided to go home. It wasn't any fun with no one to talk to. When she got to the fence, the gate was locked. The Girl could see her house beyond the fence. She looked to the left. The fence stretched waaay into the distance. She looked to the right. The fence stretched waaay into the distance.

The Girl sat down. The moon kept her company all night, even when the lights went out in the town.

In the morning, the Boy walked up to the gate. 'What are you doing?' he asked.
'I'm stuck on this side of the gate,' she answered.
'Why don't you climb over?' he asked.
'I can't,' she said. 'I might get hurt.' The Boy went away.

The next day the Boy brought the Girl a cheese sandwich. 'I don't have anything to write,' he said.
'I'm sorry,' she said. 'I can't get over this gate.' She was getting lonely, though, with no one but the moon for company at night.

The next day the Boy brought the Girl a cheese sandwich and something else. 'I brought you some knee socks,' he said.

'I wore my knee socks and I still got hurt,' she said.

'These are special knee socks,' he said.

She took the socks.

'Well?' asked the Boy.

'I'm thinking about it,' said the Girl. She was getting tired of the vast open space with no trees. She was also getting tired of cheese sandwiches.

'Maybe I'll try the knee socks on,' she said. She put on the right sock. It fit perfectly. She put on the left sock. It wouldn't fit over her bandage, no matter how hard she tugged.

'Take off the bandage,' said the Boy.

The Girl wanted to wear the knee socks. She liked spaghetti better than cheese sandwiches. She liked curious things better than vast open spaces. She took off the bandage.

They both looked at her knee. There was nothing there. Not even when they looked really close.

'I guess you can climb over now,' said the Boy.

'I guess so,' said the Girl.

And she did.

The next day, the Girl woke the Boy up early. They found a very tall tree.

'What do you see?' called the Boy. He didn't hear anything. 'Have you made a discovery?' asked the Boy. There was no answer. 'How can I know what's there if you don't tell me?' shouted the Boy.

Something floated down from the tree. It was a knee sock. A second one followed the first.

The Boy paced back and forth. Then he sat. Then he paced some more. There wasn't much to look at down there.

Maybe I'll just try the socks on, the Boy thought.

And just like that, the Boy and the Girl were sitting side by side on the highest branch, admiring the view.

When I got to the part about the knee, I unconsciously rubbed the scar on my abdomen where my port had been. It was a hard ridge, like I'd been chipped for Darwinian tracking. Only the healthy allowed on ships to repopulate when we relocate from a dying planet. Still, I consoled myself, if you got left behind, you got to keep all the stuff. That's a lot of Jenga. I kept reading.

When Ruby knocked on my door, I'd read the book three times, and my cheeks were wet. I wasn't sure why, but the emotion wasn't unwelcome. I could use the practice. I could also use a tuna sandwich.

'Maeve? Are you joining us for lunch?' My return had not gone unnoticed after all. I wiped my face and opened the door.

'No thanks, Ruby. I'll grab something at the café. I have to get back to work.'

Ruby put relish in her tuna. Yech.

Noah looked surprised when I walked into The Little Read Book. I was suddenly shy.

'Hi,' I said.

'Hi,' he said. 'That dress looks pretty on you.' I was wearing a lilac dress that floated when I twirled.

'Thanks.'

We ran out of ideas. Silence stretched. I broke it. 'I needed tuna.'

He nodded. 'I get that way about spaghetti.'

I laughed. 'Better than cheese sandwiches. I love my book.'

'I'm glad.' He walked to a table and held out a chair. I sat. He sat.

Without a word, he reached out and grasped my hand, hard. We looked at each other, his hand crushing mine. I smiled, and his grip relaxed. But he didn't let go.

'You could have told me.'

'When did I sign up for a reality show?' I tried to tug my hand back.

'Hey,' he said.

I stopped struggling. 'You could have told me you own a Fall Out Boy CD,' I retorted. 'I would have seriously reconsidered working here.'

'I like to know what the kids are up to.'

A minute passed. I fidgeted. He looked awkward. 'A lot of having cancer,' I forced out the word, 'is worrying about the people around you. There's an overwhelming need to take care of the recipient of your bad news. People cry on your shoulder, like you've triggered their own death awareness. It's weird and exhausting.'

He nodded, holding my eyes.

Silence fell again, neither of us knowing what to say.

The door tinkled, and I realized we were still holding hands. Embarrassed, I withdrew. Beth's arrival made me more flustered, though she was always civil in front of Noah. When she spotted me, she became equally ill at ease.

'Oh. Hello, Maeve!' Her volume was for the hard-of-hearing. 'How. Are. You. Doing?' She spoke slowly and over-enunciated. Did she think my illness had rendered me deaf and slow? Noah's frown matched mine.

'Fine.' I stood. 'Getting back to work. Things have piled up.'

'Good! Good!' Beth shouted, as she dug in her purse for her Purell hand sanitizer. 'Glad you're not tired!'

Apparently having cancer took the bullseye off my forehead. Oliver was right. She *was* a twat.

'I just came by to drop these off, honey. You

224

left them on the counter.' She handed Noah his sunglasses. 'Gotta run.' She bolted from the store.

I frowned. Noah mistook the cause.

'You're not going back to work. Let's get out of here,' he commanded.

'Nogales?' I perked up.

'Wagon Wheel. I'm buying you a beer.' He strode to the front, flipping the sign to Closed as he held the door for me. Twenty minutes later, we were the only patrons at the bar at one in the afternoon on a weekday. Imagine that.

'You from around here?' I teased, with the hackneyed pick-up line.

'I grew up on the Gulf coast of Florida.'

'Really?' Noah didn't strike me as a beach-volleyball type.

'Yep. First bookstore I worked in had a defibrillator on hand, in case any of the elderly clientele got too excited about the new releases. Of course, just *getting* to the bookstore was a lifethreatening challenge because Florida drivers are so bad. I did like the clowns, though.'

'Clowns?'

'It was the winter training ground for the Ringling Brothers Circus. Growing up, we were forbidden to hang around the circus people, so naturally every kid in the neighborhood spent every waking minute watching them practice.'

I was fascinated. 'Were they creepy? Do they wear makeup when they practice? How do they all fit in that little car? How come they all carry bicycle horns? Can you juggle?'

He held up his hands in surrender. 'I stopped following the clowns when I was eleven. I can't tell you the tricks of the trade.' He winked. 'But I *can* juggle.'

'Show me.'

'Hey, Vic, throw me a couple of limes,' Noah called. Vic complied, and Noah expertly tossed the fruit.

I applauded when he was done. 'All I can juggle is credit-card debt.'

'You're falling behind.' Noah indicated the full pint stacked up behind my half-finished one. I drained my glass and clutched the full one.

'Don't hug the glass!' Noah chided. 'It's the first sign of alcoholism.'

'I have a reputation for abuse.' I laughed. 'Half my college dorm thought I was on drugs. I was pale, not eating, losing weight, skipping class and sleeping all the time. One day, a classmate walked in as I was about to shoot up an injection to help me produce white blood cells. I hid the needle and yanked down my sleeve, but it didn't look good.'

'You stayed in school when you were sick?' He seemed more comfortable talking in the casual setting. I did too. Or it could've been the beer.

'Not long. I was the loser who moved back in with my parents to sleep under my old Michael Jackson posters.'

'Prince Charles lives with his mom. I think he has Burt Bacharach posters, though.'

'The Menendez brothers lived with their folks too. Until they killed them.'

'There's legal aid for your defense. I looked into it when my sister Lily was thirteen. Thirteen is a trying year.'

'Good thing my parents didn't know about the legal aid. They put everything on hold to take care of me, and I acted like a petulant teenager.'

He squinted at me. 'I'm trying to imagine you whispering down the phone, listening to N'Sync and telling your dad to mind his own beeswax.'

'Oh, I can tell you to mind your own beeswax with the best, buster. I've perfected fifty inflections of sneer in English *and* Spanish.' I did my best impression of a snotty teenager. '"Where are you going?" "Out." "Out where?" "Out*side*."'

'Scarily accurate.'

'That's probably why the hospital sent me home.'

'I've seen too many movies. I have an image of you, brave and bald in a hospital bed.'

'Unless you're really sick, they prefer you to go home – it's cleaner and safer. And the nurses like an empty room to sneak into to watch *General Hospital*. If you ever want to know all the ways that *General Hospital* isn't realistic, by the way, ask a nurse. Make sure you have a few hours.'

'I'll remember that if I misplace the hammer I use to bang myself on the head repeatedly,' he said. He signaled the bartender. 'Vic! Two more.' I opened my mouth to protest, but he hopped up. 'Have to hit the men's room. Be right back.' His triumphant grin indicated awareness that he'd silenced my protest. I closed my eyes to check if my head was spinning. Not bad. Only mild spin. I could still walk.

'I don't see why I have to wait,' I moaned. 'I'm perfectly capable of walking.'

'Hospital rules.' Jean didn't look up from her *Good Housekeeping*. 'You have to ride the wheelchair. He's on his way.'

I hated being in the hospital. 'It's ridiculous. Leo can be doing other things. Like wheeling around people with broken legs or emerging baby friends. I don't need him.'

She ignored me. She was so intent on her magazine, I hoped it was teaching her how to shellac the shelf that would change the world.

'I've been waiting nine thousand hours.' I tried again. The X-ray had only taken six minutes. The waiting area was tiny, and in my desperation I'd already finished the battered *Parents* magazine from 1997. There was no one to talk to. The only other person was a little kid sleeping on a stretcher by the door.

'If only I had a *Good Housekeeping* or something . . .' I was musing in a very loud voice, when Jean sneezed. Twice. Without covering her mouth. I felt the adrenaline shot. I wheeled backward as fast as I could without looking like a wild animal. As I got closer to the kid, I smelled something horrendous. The poor little guy was covered in vomit. I opened my mouth to say something, and Jean wiped her hand across her nose. And didn't use the Purell hand sanitizer conveniently everywhere in the hospital. I closed my mouth. I rolled closer to the kid and covered my nose.

'Maeve?' Noah snapped his fingers in front of my face. 'Where'd you go?'

'Sorry.' I jumped. 'That Lucky Spencer from *General Hospital* puts me in a trance every time.'

Vic delivered our beers. And two shots. 'Upgrade,' he said.

I was dubious.

Noah tossed back his shot. 'Chicken?'

Not a chance. 'Prost!' I downed mine, and slammed the glass upside down. My enthusiastic gesture tipped me off the stool and on to Noah, pinning his beer between us. 'Don't hug the glass,' I sputtered.

'I'm too busy hugging you.' He didn't hurry to put me aright. I didn't rush to pull myself off. When I did, our eyes caught.

Confused, I shoved my face in my beer. 'How come you left Florida?'

'I don't like to talk about it.' He looked away.

I was about to snort at the irony when I had an idea. I kicked off my shoes and pulled off my favorite rainbow-striped knee socks. I straightened and put one on each hand. My sock puppets faced each other as I used a falsetto voice. 'Hello! I'm a visualization facilitator!' said the right hand. 'I'm a creative visualization device!' said the left hand. I turned them both to face Noah's laughing face. 'Maybe we can help!'

'OK, OK.' He held up his hands in defeat. 'But please don't make me put my hands in your dirty socks.'

'My socks are *not* dirty,' I said in a haughty tone, thankful I'd put on a fresh pair right before work. But I put the socks back on. My feet were cold.

Noah finished his beer, and waved at Vic. 'My dad died in a plane crash. His Cessna went down in the Gulf during a storm. They never found a body. After that, I detested the sight of the ocean. I couldn't stop thinking my dad was still out there, rolling around. As soon as my sister started college, I moved to the desert. That's why I picked the University of Arizona.'

'When I started having nightmares, my doctor told me cancer patients often suffer post-traumatic stress disorder. They used to think only combat veterans suffered from it, but now they say any traumatic event can cause it. One of the characteristics is wanting to avoid places that remind you of your trauma.'

'Dr Connelly, did you just diagnose me with PTSD?'

'I have PTSD from working for you.'

'I'd hardly compare my stresses to those of war soldiers.'

I shrugged. 'I used to feel guilty about that, but I think Dr Gerber was right. I was definitely in shock at the way my body had treated me.'

'It looks pretty nice to me.' His smile was suggestive.

I rolled my eyes. 'How old were you when your dad died?'

'Eleven.'

I thought of something. 'Your first book was about a boy who could fly.'

'My sister Lily was only eight when Dad died. Mom was working all the time and Lily started getting in trouble, fights at school. She was sending boys to the school nurse for stitches!' He sounded proud. 'I made up stories to keep her in line. She wouldn't get to hear the next chapter if she didn't behave. I wrote about a boy who could fly because I wanted her to know that just because something bad happened to Dad didn't mean that it would happen to everyone. It was rotten luck.'

'Now you're writing about a boy who can survive underwater.'

He shrugged, uncomfortable with the scrutiny. 'Just because I occasionally escape into stories doesn't mean I don't try to tackle my demons.'

'Just because I run doesn't mean I always run away,' I offered. We smiled at each other.

Noah struck a theatrical pose and intoned, 'Now is the water of our discontent made glorious desert with this sun above. Friends, Romans, Vic! Send me more beers!'

'Noah!'

'The lady doth protest too much, methinks.' Noah and Vic ignored me. More beers arrived. Noah toasted. 'Be not afraid of wastedness: some are born wasted, some achieve wastedness and some have wastedness thrust upon them.'

'To pee or not to pee. That is the question.' I hopped off the stool.

'Is that a stagger I see before me?' Noah called after me as I wobbled to the bathroom.

When I got back, I struggled to remember what we'd been talking about.

'Your sister. Where is she now?'

'If you can believe it, Lily flies mail planes in Alaska.'

'Guess your stories worked.'

'She's the one that sent *The Boy Who Could Fly* to an agent. It never occurred to me.'

'I think it's great that you do what you love.' I was a little envious.

'What about you? What do you want?' Noah's smile was naughty.

'All I want is a warm bed, a kind word, unlimited power and world domination.'

'It's good to have goals.'

'It's good to have beers!' I toasted. 'And to know you're capable of lightening up.'

'I don't know what you're implying.' His tone was lofty. 'I'm a party animal.'

I snorted. 'More of a party mineral.'

'Right. That's it. It's game time. BarOlympics are *on.*'

'BarOlympics?'

'We're going to play some games.'

'What's in a game? That which we call rainbow socks by any other name would smell like feet.' I recited.

Half an hour later, we were clutching the bar and laughing hysterically.

'A hundred thousand sperm and *you* were the fastest?' I gasped.

'I beat you,' he reminded me, panting. We'd been doing sprints between the bar and the jukebox.

'I need to see the instant replay.'

'It doesn't matter whether you win or lose. What matters is whether *I* win or lose.'

We'd competed in a decathlon of sprints, long jump, speed-drinking, quarter hockey, breath-holding, thumb-wrestling, hopping on one foot and handstands. Vic had nixed the mustard toss. The final game was bar football.

'She shoots! She scores!' I flicked the folded paper football through the goalpost Noah had created with his hands.

'Damn!'

'I won! I won!' I bounced up and down.

'Beginner's luck,' he dismissed.

'Mad skills,' I corrected.

'How're you guys doin'?' Vic called.

'No more.' I shook my head. 'I'm done. I'm

Drunky Drunk, the Mayor of Drunkville. This little athlete is retiring.'

'We are in violent agreement.' Noah nodded. 'Except I'm Drinky McDrinky Pants.' He tossed Vic a credit card, and waved off my effort to contribute. 'The boss can pay for the company meeting.'

I was surprised when we tumbled out of the Wagon Wheel into bright sunshine. It wasn't usually the case when I left a bar after hours of serious drinking. We lingered, looking at each other. Noah had just opened his mouth, when I ripped a loud hiccup. I fell apart into giggles.

'Good night, good night! Parting is such sweet sorrow,' Noah said with a grin. 'Now get thee to a nunnery.'

'To sleep, perchance to eat ice cream,' I responded as I turned away. I carried his smile with me as I staggered home. I needed a serious nap to sleep it off before my date with Samuel.

'Ready?' Samuel asked several hours later. I hadn't shared my afternoon's escapade, but that wasn't what he was asking about. Tonight was my first public appearance post-Cancergate. I didn't feel anxious, though. I felt floaty and happy.

'Yeppers.' I giggled. He gave me an odd look. I wiped off my smile. Proper ladies didn't go boozing in the middle of the day. I concentrated on walking a straight line to the door.

'What should I say? If people ask.'

'What do you want to say?'

'None of your beeswax, Jack?' I pronounced with relish.

He laughed. 'How about "I tried leukemia for a while but it didn't fit me, so I moved on."'

'Ooh, that's good.' I was impressed. I'd spent a long time trying to come up with just the right language and cadence. I'd have to remember that.

'I've had some practice.' He grinned. I was pulled out of myself for a second into a flash of the pain and loss Samuel must face on a regular basis as a doctor. I flung my arms around him and gave him a spontaneous squeeze. He was surprised, but recovered to hug me back. I squeezed harder, and within seconds I found myself dangling as he easily bent backward, hauling me into the air. I staggered when he put me on my feet, but he set me right. I took his hand to aid my steadiness, and we headed out.

'What's the movie, groovy?' I asked.

He gave me another look. 'Same as it was when you asked twenty minutes ago. *The Thin Man*. One of my favorites.'

'Mine too!' I gave a little hop. 'I tried to match the main characters, Nick and Nora, drink for drink once watching it and was on the floor halfway through. Never again.'

He laughed. 'Three drinks puts you on the floor! I'm surprised you made it to the twenty-minute mark.'

I decided not to tell him I had more than three in me already. Thank God I'd managed a nap and a shower. I adopted a lofty tone. 'I used to put them away like anybody else,' I informed him. 'You're looking at my high school's spring break downhill funnel women's champion. I only stopped drinking after I got sick.' Right after remission, I hadn't wanted the vulnerability that went with intoxication. I giggled again. Today had gone just fine.

'I'm not complaining. Being a lightweight makes you a cheap date.' He leered at me. 'And easy. Did I mention I brought wine?'

Uh-oh. I swatted him as we rounded the corner of Main Street. 'Like you have to work that hard.'

He stopped and kissed me, and we spent a few minutes in that pleasurable pursuit before resuming our walk. The square was a checker-board of blankets on which picnics were being consumed or prepared. We saw Tuesday waving and headed in her direction. We weaved our way through the patchwork of quilts.

'Oh Samuel,' Liz called. 'Tommy got into the poison oak. I was wondering . . .'

Samuel was already extracting a bag from his pocket. 'Ruby mentioned it,' he said. 'I brought some samples. If this doesn't work, come see me.' She accepted the package gratefully.

'And Maeve, thanks so much for agreeing to babysit next week.' Liz looked so appreciative, I hid my wince. Minding Tommy was like caring for ten Ritalin-deprived demons.

'No problem,' I lied.

'I imagine watching him will make cancer seem

like a walk in the park.' Her smile was rueful. I started, then appreciated the casual acknowledgment.

'Don't be so sure,' I joked. 'Except that when I'm watching Tommy, I'm still gorgeous.'

We moved on as Samuel whispered, 'Don't touch him with your bare hands. Poison oak sucks.'

'Maeve, I finished fixing the belts and caps on Elsie. She's looking right sexy on the inside, except for that missing piece. I even gave her a hot wax.' Barney was stretched out on a plaid blanket with a woman who was the embodiment of Ellie Mae Clampett from *The Beverly Hillbillies*, right down to the handkerchief halter and platinum-blonde curls. The three-inch press-on nails with crystal chips were her own individual touch.

'Can you say that in Portuguese?' I kidded.

Barney screwed up his face. 'Only the last bit, and only in the form of a question,' he said seriously. We navigated on to the sound of him muttering, '*Posso eu ter uma cera quente?*'

'It's polite to arrive no later than six so that you don't trample over more considerate people's blankets,' Helen sniped as we passed.

'But then you would have trampled on ours,' was my logical retort. My tongue had a mind of its own.

'Don't think that just because you were sick you get special treatment, missy. You don't. I've been plenty sick in my lifetime, I can assure you.'

237

'She's never been sick a day in her life,' Samuel muttered in my ear as he hustled me on.

We were almost at our destination when we reached a seamless row of blankets. There was no way across without stepping on one. The dirtiest one, next to April and Busy's blanket, was unoccupied. I was hopping gingerly toward the middle to vault to the other side, when I tumbled into a heap.

April's braying laugh called the attention of the whole town. She was doubled over in fits. Busy's breathy giggles accompanied her. Samuel reached down and helped me stand. I staggered up and dusted myself off, red-faced. I'd stepped into a hole, covered by the blanket.

'Haw, haw, haw.' April's deep honk sounded over and over as she delighted in the success of her trap. It was her Sistine Chapel.

'Sleep with one eye open.' I managed my threat through gritted teeth.

'Haw, haw—' Her laugh stopped abruptly as her eyes widened and her face froze. 'I think I just peed myself.'

We reached the safety of Tuesday's blanket as April reassembled her joke. Bruce hadn't arrived yet, so he was a prime target.

'Yay!' Tuesday smiled and wiggled when we arrived. 'I got here super-early so I could get all our blankets together. It's perfect!'

'Mahalo,' I said. I was ready to sit. I was starting to feel a headache coming on, and I was famished.

'Ruby, is that your chicken salad?'

She passed me a plate, while Samuel poured us wine and Tuesday spread out dips and crackers. I was scouting a place to discreetly dump some of my wine when April's guffaw sounded again, accompanied by an enraged shriek. We looked over to see Beth, hair askew, panties flashing, taking an unexpected tumble. She flailed as she struggled to right herself, making the exposure worse. It'd been a while since laundry day, from what I could see. Noah and Bruce skirted the trap and reached to help.

'Goddammit, April,' Beth screeched. 'You're more cow than Cowbelle! I could have been seriously injured. Quit grabbing me.' She turned on Noah and Bruce, slapping their hands. As she tugged down her pink linen pencil skirt and teetered for balance on matching heels, Tuesday muttered, 'Who wears that to a picnic?'

April was still guffawing. Her Sistine Chapel had become her Taj Mahal.

'All right now, April, that's enough.' Bruce tried to silence her mirth.

'Noah, *do something*.' Beth's pitch was glass-shattering.

Noah looked at her in disbelief. 'Like what? You want me to fight April?'

'No! Yes! Aaargh! You are so passive! It's like dating goddamn Gandhi!' She grabbed Noah's arm and hauled herself upright. 'Drunk in the middle of the afternoon Gandhi, that is.' I flushed at that. I felt furtive and illicit about our afternoon's secret escapade.

'I'm going home,' Beth announced, and stomped out of the square, not caring whose blanket she trampled.

'Beth . . .'

Noah started after her, but stopped when she snarled, 'Don't follow me! I strongly suggest you give me some space for a good while.' And off she went.

'She's always had a temper, that one,' Ruby observed. 'Chicken salad, anyone? Lawrence, I've saved you a seat.' Bruce packed April's blanket into the hole and joined Ruby.

Noah looked unsure.

'Don't worry, Noah,' I said. 'You're not smart enough to be Gandhi.'

He made a face at me.

'And you don't wear dresses like Gandhi, either,' seconded Ronnie Two Shoes.

Tuesday groaned. 'Ronnie, those weren't *dresses*, they were *robes* . . .' I tuned out the ensuing debate as Noah sat on the blanket next to ours.

'She's a handful,' Samuel said.

'She prefers it when I say "piece of work",' Noah joked. 'She thinks I mean masterpiece.'

Dark clattered down in a Monty Python instant, the way it did in southern Arizona, and we looked towards the screen set up against the back of the community center. I settled against Samuel's chest, ready to enjoy myself. I'd faced the town and it hadn't been bad at all. They knew I'd had cancer and it didn't change a thing. I smiled at the opening scene of the thin man's silhouette on a wall. I did not think at all about the man alone on his blanket next to me. It was hard, though, because we laughed at exactly the same bits.

CHAPTER 19

BELL PEPPER

Eating a fresh cold bell pepper on a hot, sunny Sunday afternoon is like a religious experience. Since I didn't go to church, it was as close as I was going to get, at any rate. I'd spotted the smooth, golden vegetable in Ruby's fridge when I was putting away her groceries, and even though it was her only one, I couldn't resist its organic curves. I fondled it, then stole it. I felt bad for taking it – yellow peppers weren't cheap – but more in a William Carlos Williams way than truly penitent.

> This is just to say,
> I have eaten
> Your pepper
> Which was in
> The icebox
> And which
> You were probably
> Saving
> For supper.

I paraphrased.

Forgive me
It was so crisp
So tempting
And so cold.
And I decided
To try
An experiment.

I settled on to the edge of the picnic table, legs dangling, thinking Noah would have appreciated my poem. I *had* decided to try an experiment. I tore off the top of the pepper and gutted the seeds. Then I crunched into it, loving the cool crispness exploding like juicy bubblewrap in my mouth, feeling the hot sun, the dusty planks under my butt. I was a girl sitting in the sun, enjoying a pepper. I took another bite.

'I remember this,' rejoiced the inner voice that did the movie narration for my life. I caught my breath. This was the sort of thing I didn't think. 'I remember this,' the rogue thought repeated, firmly. I forced myself to relax. This was the experiment, after all.

'Yes,' I said out loud. 'I remember this. I liked this. I *like* this.' I felt a scary delight in articulating the words, a thrill of panic accompanying my daring, as if acknowledging my pleasure would alert someone to take it away from me. I took another bite.

'I wonder what else I can remember,' I challenged the empty yard. The yard didn't do anything. It just sat there, gnats flying lazy circles over the yellowing grass.

'Well, if no one is going to stop me . . .' I wondered if I hoped someone was going to stop me. But of course no one did. No one ever had. Only me.

'Honeycomb cereal,' I pronounced. 'Eating an entire watermelon with a knife while reading a trashy novel. Watching a dog chase sticks into the waves. Finding money I didn't know I had in my pocket. The smell of bergamot . . .'

After a while I stopped speaking aloud. I let my mind wander wherever it wanted for a change, reacquainting itself with forsaken memories, lost friends regained. Funnel cake. The way your stomach drops when you spin the Tilt-A-Whirl fast enough. The way the two sometimes don't mix. I surveyed all the simple pleasures I'd walled off because to admit they mattered would be to suffer if I lost them, and apprehension slowly, slowly let go its talons. It was hard to fear the reaper snatching flavor from your mouth when you were bathed in mellow afternoon sunshine in a sleepy yard, after all.

Holding hands. First dates. Clean sheets. Realizing you had another hour to sleep. As my thoughts roamed, I lightly held the kachina of the girl entwined with the crab, Cancer, warming it with my hands. I knew my mother had made it for the moment when I decided to let it go. In some ways, I hadn't been in the grip of bad luck,

244

but had myself been the crab, clutching the past tight with my claws. I rose and settled the fourth statue among the raspberry bushes. I sat back down to continue my musings, a fraction lighter. Inner tubes on the river. The pull-through parking spot. Relaxing outside on a sunny day.

I sat there a long time. A girl, just like any other girl. Enjoying her pepper. Only when the sun set and it began to get chilly did I go inside to get ready for dinner with Samuel.

I woke gasping for air. I was captured in tar, fighting to sit upright. The blindness, protective in the darkroom, was now menacing. My disoriented mind struggled. My last memory was the beast sidling outside my periphery, angling to burrow back in, scuttling claws poised for damage.

'A leukemia cell is a blood cell that transforms into a malignant cell capable of uncontrolled growth,' my doctor had explained. My imagination saw a dark, evasive creature, not dissimilar from its crablike namesake. The slightest brush would pervert a normal cell. Once infiltrated, it would multiply in the marrow, shredding healthy cells as it went, my very bones hosting their own destruction. I put a hand on my chest to feel red blood turning inky. But there was nothing. Just my rapid heartbeat.

The nightmare loosened. The sound I'd attributed to dragging claws became Samuel's deep, easy breathing. I lay back, shaken. My experiment earlier in the day had had consequences. *Everything* I'd blocked for so long was flooding back, good and bad alike.

'It's like school,' my mother said. I wondered what *her* school had been like. Young Jane Eyre attended, apparently.

'Sort of.' Dr Gerber played along. 'A two-year course of radiation and chemotherapy is automatic for your type of leukemia. We'll do a regular rotation of three weeks on, two weeks off. We like to follow the same schedule every week, but of course we adjust for specific conflicts.'

'See,' my mother said. 'Like a class schedule.'

'I quit school and I still have a regimen?' I joked. 'English 101 and Intro to Sociology replaced by Induction, Consolidation and Maintenance? No fair. I thought I was going to get to smoke pot and write bad poetry.'

'Maeve!' my mother chided.

'Okay, okay. No pot. Do I get Cliffs Notes before the exam?'

'That's what I'm for.' Dr Gerber smiled. 'Induction is the first step, reducing the cancer and evaluating reaction to treatment; consolidation is the intense phase, to eliminate all leukemic cells; and maintenance delivers lower doses over a longer period to destroy strays and outliers.'

'Spring break?'

'Between consolidation and maintenance.' He had the grace not to say '*if* you pass'.

I liked the pre-set regimen. It spared me the worry on adult patients' faces as they dissected the meaning of adjusting treatment schedules. I didn't have to decipher the import of every radiation session. Radiation meant it was Thursday. Thursday happened every week.

'We like Thursday so you can have the weekend to recover,' Dr Gerber explained. What he meant was you had the weekend to collapse.

'No different from Thursdays now – I usually need the weekend to recover from quarter beer night. Instead of quarter beers, I get quarts in here,' I joked. 'And I don't have to pay. Thanks, Blue Cross! I'm no cheap date.'

'But you'll take your clothes off every time.' Dr Gerber smiled. My mother looked horrified. That's when he became the Gerberator.

Back in bed in Arizona in the dark, my heart rate slowed to normal. I had expelled cancer from my blood, but it continued its grip on my mind. When was it over? When did 'remission' become 'normal'? I thought about looking at pictures in the dark-room. What 'normal' would I go back to? I didn't know who cancer-free Maeve would have been. She didn't exist.

Except.

Except we both liked bell peppers. We both laughed until we tinkled a little at David Sedaris. We both fought a constant battle of wanting to stay slim and wanting to eat every single package of Rondele garlic and herb spread in the grocery store. And . . .

'Samuel,' I whispered, shaking him. 'Samuel, wake up.' There was something else that we both liked.

CHAPTER 20

FLIGHT

'Congratulations, graduations!' I sang to my brother.

'Thanks,' Brick's voice was gruff, pleased, but too cool to admit it.

'I'm proud of you.'

'Hey, I didn't do anything you didn't do.'

I snorted. 'Except in half the time.'

'Yeah but . . .' We let the thought trail off, still in the habit of not talking about it.

'Know what you're going to do this last summer before the rest of your life?' I filled the space.

'I haven't decided. I'll either deal drugs to housewives out of an ice cream truck, or get a job at the Avis rent-a-car in Myrtle Beach. I figure that would make me the first guy to meet the girls coming to town. Snap 'em up fresh off the plane.'

'It's good to have goals. So you're going back to Arthur's Deli?' I guessed.

'Until I find a real job.'

'Let me know how that "real job" thing works.'

'Right. Haven't you taken over a bookstore or something?'

'Not quite yet,' I laughed. 'I'm sorry I'm going to miss your graduation ceremony.'

'Mom and Dad said they'd pay for the ticket if you want to fly back.' He reminded me.

'I . . .' I couldn't find the right words.

'I understand.' He cut me off. 'You're not ready to come back yet.'

'No,' I admitted.

'Aaah, it's just a bunch of guys wearing dresses and funny hats giving long-winded speeches. You're not missing anything.' There was another pause. I'd missed my own ceremony, quietly leaving school with my diploma in December. I hadn't felt connected enough to want fanfare.

'Thanks for understanding.' I said. 'Try to soothe the wounded souls of your frat brothers when they realize I won't be there.'

'I'll make them grilled cheese sandwiches and tomato soup.' He named our favorite comfort foods. 'I'm glad you're staying out there, kid. I like seeing you go for it like this. You're gonna knock it out of the park.'

'You too, Mr *summa cum laude*,' I said. 'I love you.'

After I hung up, I sat for a moment looking at the kachina in my hands. It was the fifth one, a ring of small creatures, maybe squirrels, maybe possum, maybe bear cubs. They were a team, whatever they were, the cluster supporting each other and a rounded roof above their heads. It made me think of my family, and their support.

Even as my brother approved my decision not to return for his graduation, I wanted him to know that all the family's attention wasn't sucked up by me. We'd join forces to hold protection over him his whole life, too. It was time to pass the mantle of being the baby of the family back to my little brother. The comforting statue was hard to part with, but my decision was sure. I carefully packaged the kachina for its trip to the post office, and beyond, to my brother on his big day.

'Maeve, sweetheart, would you be a dear and pick up some sherry for me? You know I like a little nip before bed,' Busy intercepted me on my way out.

I did indeed. Her 'little nip' amounted to two or three bottles a week.

'I don't know how you can drink that crap,' came April's predictable growl. 'Scotch. Now that's a real woman's drink.'

'It's so I can tolerate you. I prefer the Oloroso, dear. Preferably Lustau.' As if I didn't know.

'Okey-dokey, smokey. April?'

'Copy of *Family Handyman Magazine*.' I stopped and faced her, hands on hips. No way was I putting ammunition for mayhem into her hands.

She glared, then huffed. 'All right, all right. I promise not to tape the sink sprayer.' She confessed to the prank that had soaked me and Oliver, causing him to skyrocket and bonk himself woozy on the ceiling. I kept staring. She threw up her hands.

'How was I supposed to know the bird would be on your shoulder? I'm sorry he hit his head. Jumpy creature . . .'

I didn't move. She sighed. 'And I won't put bouillon cubes in the shower head again.' I'd smelled like beef broth for days after my unexpected soup shower, feral cats hounding my steps. Samuel had developed an intense work schedule, refusing to stay over until Sandy treated my hair with strawberry deep conditioner. I wasn't falling for any more of April's practical jokes.

I relented. 'I'll get you a nice gardening magazine. I could use some help out there.'

'I'm not doing any damn gardening until it's my turn to take a dirt nap. It's a hobby for death's door,' she grumbled. Then her face contracted in horror. 'Maeve . . .'

'Life's a garden, April,' I said. 'Dig it.'

'Frou-frou hippy bullshit,' she groused.

'Hey, April, what did the Zen monk say when he wanted a hot dog?'

She snorted.

'Make me one with everything. And if you untie the lines around my desktop items by the time I get back, I might even get you some colored Sharpies.' I'd been poised to pull out the chair when I'd spotted the fishing line strung between the legs and my desk set, prepared to tumble it all to the floor when the seat was pulled out. April's face fell as the sound of Busy's giggles followed me to the kitchen.

Oliver and Lulabell were in her cage on the table.

'Nice hair,' said Oliver. Sadly, I didn't think his compliment was directed at me.

'It's starting to look like the Romantic Palace in there,' I commented.

'Legs up and give me some,' said Lulabell.

'Make that the Playboy Mansion,' I revised. 'I'm off to the post office and the store.'

'Road trip! Don't forget the bird!' said Oliver.

I paused. I hadn't really had much Oliver time. He preferred Lulabell to my shoulder these days. 'You want to come, buddy?' Jenny didn't really like it when he came to Up Market, but she'd get over it. Oliver hopped on to my finger, and I settled him on my shoulder. He ran up and down, excitedly tugging hair out of my braids.

'Carrots! Howdy, pardner.' He looked expectantly at Lulabell. 'Nice hair!'

Lulabell mirrored Oliver's movements back and forth across her perch, crest feather up and down. 'Howdy there! Howdy!'

'You want to come, Lulabell?' I'd never taken her on an outing before, but I didn't see the harm. I was getting Jenny's dirty looks anyway. She couldn't make them dirtier. Lulabell hopped on to my open hand, and I settled her on my other shoulder. I grabbed the recycled grocery bags and Ruby's list and headed out the door. I walked toward the square, considering whether to stop by Barney's first. So far, he hadn't made any real progress on Elsie. We were still in limbo, waiting for that one missing part. His Portuguese was improving, though. He could ask for seven different kinds of pharmacologicals now.

It was when Oliver bit my ear that I noticed the clouds. They were coming in fast. One thing I continued to marvel at about Arizona was the rapidity with which the weather changed. What had been a sunny day looked to be a humdinger of a storm. I knew enough to realize that I'd better get inside. Oliver didn't like storms. I had no idea how Lulabell would react.

I picked up the pace. I didn't have time to get home, so I'd hole up in the bookstore until it passed. Oliver was pressed so close to my neck that he was practically in my ear. Lulabell was rocking anxiously. As I stepped into the square, thunder sounded like a crack, making me jump. And Lulabell flew away.

My jaw dropped. Lulabell could fly. Cockatiels were clipped not to fly, but Lulabell could fly, and I had taken her outside. Did I have the worst luck on the planet?

'Lulabell!' I called, frantic. I scanned the tree-tops but didn't see her. Thunder cracked again, and I saw the flutter of a terrified bird. She was thrashing among the branches and I was petrified she would hurt herself. I was also horror-struck at the possibility that she would fly away. Ruby would kill me.

'Lulabell!' I cried again, but my voice was drowned out by the commencement of falling hail.

I started shaking. My bird was freaking out, and Lulabell was flying farther and farther away. Never taking my eyes off her in case I lost her, I cupped Oliver in my hands. Think. How did you get a free-flight bird down from a fifty-foot tree in a hail storm? And what was wrong with me that I assumed Lulabell couldn't fly just because I'd never seen her do it? Hail beat on my head, as I stood helpless.

'Maeve, what's the matter with you? I've been calling. Get inside!'

I didn't even look at Noah. 'Take Oliver.' I held out my hands cupping the bird, eyes still on Lulabell.

'Are you crazy? Come inside!'

I chanced a quick look. 'I can't.' My voice cracked. 'Please. Look after my bird.'

He stared. Without a word, he took Oliver and hurried back to the store. Within minutes he was back, shaking a jacket over my shoulders. Rain mixed with the hail.

'What is it?'

'Lulabell.' I pointed. 'I . . . I . . . It's all my fault.' I fought tears.

His mouth was grim. 'What do we do?'

'Give me your phone,' I ordered.

Noah handed it to me and I dialed. 'Bruce? I have an emergency and I need you to do something.' I forced my voice to be calm.

After giving him instructions, I hung up and focused on the bird. Lulabell fluttered agitatedly from branch to branch. I made clucking and calling noises. I even propositioned her. Anything to keep her close.

When Bruce arrived fifteen minutes later, Noah and I were both soaked to the bone. He'd brought what I'd requested, and Noah unloaded the ladder and rope, while Bruce extracted Lulabell's cage. I kept my eyes glued to the bird. When Noah started to climb the ladder, I shouted, 'No!'

He stopped. 'Maeve, it's wet and slippery. Be reasonable.'

'I'm going.' No way was anyone else going to get hurt because of me. 'She knows me better.'

'You can't manage the cage . . .'

Without a word, I tied one end of the rope around the cage handle, and the other into a thick knot. 'Once I'm up there, throw me the knotted end of rope.' I was already on the ladder.

Bruce started to object, but I gave them both a look. They shut up.

I climbed past the top of the ladder into the branches, then turned to catch the rope. I caught it on the first try, then hefted the cage. I balanced it on a branch, and began pulling myself branch to branch, lugging the cage after me. When I'd climbed as high as I thought I could go, I found a good branch and hung the cage, door open.

'Lulabell,' I called to get her attention. I backed down a bit and sat on a branch to wait. I almost wet my pants in relief when the panic-stricken bird flew to the safety of her haven as soon as she saw it. Cockatiels are homebodies. I closed her inside and made more soothing noises. Shivering in what was now a cold spring rain, Lulabell didn't look comforted. I carefully reversed my course out of the tree.

When I handed the cage down to Bruce and Lulabell was safe, I started shaking. I had to pause at the top of the ladder for some deep breaths before I climbed all the way down. Noah was hovering anxiously. So was Bruce, but for different reasons.

He shut Lulabell in the truck, and squinted at the sky. 'I don't like this storm. Too much rain too fast.'

'I'll bring Oliver home,' said Noah. 'Ride with Bruce. Go get dry.'

I shook my head. 'I'd like to walk,' I said. The rain had all but stopped, and the five-minute walk made more sense than ruining Bruce's lovely leather seats. Plus, I wanted to collect my thoughts.

'Don't tarry,' Bruce advised. 'Rain could start again any time. Hard to say what this storm's got left in it.'

I nodded, and set off on foot. My pace was rapid as I berated myself down Main Street, up Orange Street and along Emerald Street, one eye on the sky. I tried to prepare words for Ruby. I dreaded the look in her eyes. I hated looks more than words. I tried not to remember eyes above a surgical mask, the look when she thought I wasn't aware. I tried not to think about what I'd temporarily forgotten, that I was a girl who stung those close to her, even when I tried to do the right thing. I was too tired. Bad luck had won. All I wanted to do was give up and go to sleep.

CHAPTER 21

PRACTICE

I gathered my courage at the doorstep, then stepped into the kitchen to face Ruby. Her back was to me, as she packed a bag at the kitchen table at a greater speed than her normal high efficiency. She sensed me enter and turned.

'There's been an accident. We'll need your help. Please gather as many extra blankets as you can find in the hall closet. Hurry now.'

I shut my mouth and did as I was told without a word. I changed into a dry sweatshirt and rain jacket, and grabbed all the blankets I could carry. When I returned, she was loading her Volvo wagon with Thermoses and jackets. I added the blankets. She collected and tested an enormous flashlight, with a radio and siren built in. It was still early, and light enough despite the grey sky, but I held my tongue. She would tell me in good time. We got into the car, and she turned north.

'Where are April and Busy?' I asked.

'The rain this afternoon flooded Harshaw Creek and weakened the banks at the bridge. The seniors were returning from a trip to Sonoita in their bus when one of the banks gave out and the bridge collapsed, likely from the vehicle's weight. The bus is in danger of falling into the flooded water.' Ruby's white knuckles on the steering wheel belied her even tone. 'I don't know more than that. April, Busy, Helen Rausch, Elsa Morrow, Diane Wall, Lupe Ortiz and Henrietta Mankiller are trapped on the bus, along with Liz, who was driving.'

A shiver ran down my spine as icy as floodwater. I couldn't bear the image of Busy being swept away by roiling brown mud. My knuckles were as white as Ruby's when we pulled up to the collection of flashing lights and vehicles clustered at the south end of the bridge.

It was a disaster scene in miniature. The creek wasn't wide, maybe twenty feet across, but it was wider than the bus. The bridge had failed on the north side, bank crumbled, and now angled from the south bank straight into the water. The bus was tilted, tail in the water, nose pointing up at a hypotenuse angle. The fierce current of the swollen creek was tugging at the tail and the west-facing side of the bus. The immediate threat was obvious. The south bank sustaining the bridge, and the bus, looked dangerously unstable as currents buffeted the saturated mud and the dangling concrete.

Ruby hurried over to where Samuel stood, a few feet back from the bank.

'Everyone is still on the bus, and they seem unharmed aside from bumps and bruises.' He answered her unspoken question, as he settled his jacket around my shoulders over my thin one. 'But Helen . . .' He pointed. I squinted. There were six frightened faces that I could see, sitting very still in the first two rows of the bus, and Liz in the driver's seat, but no Helen. I looked at Samuel.

'At the back.' His mouth was grim.

I spotted her. Helen was tumbled at the bottom of the bus, clinging to one of the bench seats. From her knees down she was submerged in the filthy water swirling around the rear door.

'The impact with the side of the bridge must have jarred open the door.' Ruby's voice was tight. Samuel gave a sharp nod. 'But how did Helen end up there?'

Samuel met Ruby's eyes. 'Liz was driving the bus . . .'

'. . . so Helen sat in the back row,' Ruby finished with a shake of her head. 'Can we get blankets down to them?'

'Too risky,' Samuel said. 'We don't want Liz to open the door in case the water rises. Also, we can't risk adding any weight or getting too close to the edge of the bank until Barney secures the tow rope to the front of the bus.

Bruce and Barney were deep in conversation. Barney was shaking his head.

'The weight is likely to cause the whole bank to collapse. I'm afraid to get too close.'

'Can we come at it from the other side?' asked Bruce.

'I called Simon Bear. He's driving in from the north with John Buell, but it'll take them twenty minutes to get here. Even then, it'll be a trick trying to attach the tow rope. That water's fierce even for those guys and the tail of the bus is farther from the bank.' Barney's prognosis was not cheering.

'What about the ladder from the extension fire truck over at County? Can we stretch it out over the bus and harness them ladies to safety? Forget the bus.'

'Mebbe. Still worry about weight on the bank. Fire truck can be farther back, but it's heavier. Could collapse this side jes' like the other. That'd be bad.'

'Work with me, Barney. We've got to do something.' Bruce begged.

Rain started to fall again as Noah and Tuesday pulled up. Right behind them came an ambulance and the county ladder truck. Bruce hurried to stop the vehicles well back from the edge of the creek. More people arrived as word spread through town, a crowd of locals forming a ring, prepared to help however they could.

'What can we do?' panted Tuesday. Ruby raised her hands helplessly.

'This is bad.' Noah looked up at the rain.

Barney took off his cap and smoothed his hair, then replaced it. 'Mebbe we could extend the tow cable and get Ronnie to climb down. He's pretty nimble. Not ideal with the tow back that far, but lower risk of stressin' the bank.'

Bruce frowned. 'That's askin' a lot of Ronnie.'

'He's the lightest.' Samuel agreed with Barney.

'I'll do it, Chief,' Ronnie said.

'Can we secure him to something?' Noah asked.

'There are life jackets on the ladder truck,' Ruby said. 'Can you make a harness out of one with a rope? Then he's attached, and has a life preserver on, just in case.'

'Good idea, Ruby,' Samuel agreed, as Bruce nodded. 'I'd like to send down jackets for the ladies on the bus too, if Ronnie can safely secure the tow cable on the front axle.'

'The thing is going to be speed,' Bruce said. Once we start, we got to do this as fast as safely possible.'

I didn't have much to contribute. Samuel and Noah worked together to fashion a harness for Ronnie, while Bruce and Barney peered over the bank and debated how close they dared back up to the creek bank. Tuesday stood close and rubbed my shoulders to help us both stay warm. We watched Barney back the tow truck within ten feet of the bank. We held our breath as Ronnie struggled with the tow cable towards the lip of the creek, clambering across the riven concrete. He attained the front of the bus and rolled on to his back to hook the cable around the axle.

'I need more cable,' he yelled.

Bruce and Barney locked worried eyes, and Bruce nodded. Barney put the truck in reverse and backed up inch by cautious inch.

'I got it!' Ronnie shouted, and everyone started to cheer, when there was a horrible grinding sound. A section on our side of the bank gave way, and the near right lip of the bridge shuddered and slipped a foot, tilting precariously and causing the rear of the bus to fishtail downstream. Barney put his truck in drive, wheels spinning without traction. Under increased pressure, the collapsed cement piling on the far upstream side crumbled further. Without its support, the bottom of the bridge sank another three feet into the relentless current, steepening the bus's angle.

The back door of the bus was torn open completely, and Helen Rausch lost her grip and washed out, arms flailing against the torrents sweeping her away.

'Get the truck!'

'Get the ambulance!'

'Throw a life preserver!'

Voices cried all around me, but I knew there was no hope for that. Helen was bobbing away quickly. The fields were too rutted for any vehicle, and the nearest crossover road was miles down the creek. I wasn't good at much. I couldn't even take care of a pet bird. But there was one thing I could do, and that was run. I grabbed a life preserver off the pile and started sprinting. I could sense people running after me, but I quickly outpaced them, Samuel's jacket fluttering from my shoulders back toward them. Weeks of practice made me sure-footed on the uneven ground. I never knew how fast I was, because I'd never run *toward* anything before. I kept my eyes glued to Helen. My feet ate the ground, and soon I overtook her. I looked ahead to a bend in the creek, and sited my target entry. There was an S-curve in the creek that even the floodwater hadn't conquered, leaving a shallow beach and protected spit on the far side. I clocked Helen's progress, her eyes rolling with fear, and judged my timing. I launched over the lip of the bank, grabbing an over-hanging tree branch with one hand and dangling above the water. For once, luck was on my side, and Helen passed the curved spit of land close enough for me to grab hold of her.

The weight of her body combined with the pressure of the water almost snapped my wrist. The one clutching the tree strained as well. I was strong, but both the water and Helen were fighting me.

'Stop thrashing!' I yelled, but she was like a wild animal. I wasn't going to be able to hold her with one hand. I let go of the branch. The freezing water took my breath away, but I didn't have time for shock. If I went into deeper water with Helen, we didn't stand a chance. The little peninsula was providing a limited barrier against the churning water. I thrust my feet into the silty bottom for traction and used both hands to haul Helen to my chest. Her flailing elbow connected solidly with my eye and starbursts exploded. My grip loosened from pain and surprise and she started to slide away. I recovered my hold and concentrated on hauling us back towards the beach. The life jacket was more hindrance than help, and my frozen hands scrabbled to grasp the surprisingly strong woman. Inch by inch I used the creek bed, branches, anything I could, to leverage us further into the lee of the spit. At last the water released its suction and I heaved us on to the beach. I lay gasping for air on my back, Helen crushed against me.

'Over here!'

People descended. Several hands rolled Helen from my chest. The scene was chaos.

'Bring the stretcher!'

'We need blankets!'

'Are you insane?' Noah shouted. 'You could have killed yourself!'

'Noah, hush. She saved Helen's life,' Ruby chided. To me, 'That was something, Maeve.' She reached for my hand to help me up, and I cried out. Samuel was there in an instant.

'Let me see.' His gentle fingers probed my wrist, while Ruby helped me sit up. Someone wrapped a jacket around my shoulders.

'I'm fine.' I used my other hand to push myself to my feet.

'Stretcher!' Samuel and Noah shouted at the same time.

'No,' I protested. For once I didn't need the reassurance of Samuel's care. 'I can walk.' I couldn't stop beaming. 'I can *run*!'

'You sure can.' Bruce voiced admiration.

My smile faded. 'The bus . . .'

'It's secure on the cable. Firemen are getting everyone off. They're facing a lot less risk than you did,' Bruce said.

'Let's get back.' Noah's tone was impatient. 'You'll catch your death.'

He took my elbow, and Samuel stepped close to my other side. I shook them off.

'I can walk by myself.' In fact, I felt great.

We crossed the field back towards the road behind EMTs porting Helen on a stretcher.

'Samuel,' I said. 'You need to go.'

He shook his head. 'Her vitals are stable. They'll take her to the hospital and keep her overnight to be sure. There's nothing for me to do. I need to get you to the clinic and X-ray that wrist.'

I wanted to protest, but common sense dictated that my wrist needed seeing to. And I was thrilled to be going to the clinic, and not to the hospital with Helen. We reached the road in time to see a fireman handing a cable-clipped Liz from the bus to a waiting fireman on the safety of the road. The rest of the seniors were bundled in blankets, clutching Thermoses. Everyone looked shaken but unharmed.

'I think you're going to have to take them all in,' Ruby said.

Samuel nodded. 'Sorry,' he said to me. 'Looks like this won't be a speedy stop.'

'I don't mind. I'd rather make sure everyone is OK.'

We piled into various wagons and trucks to be chauffeured to the clinic. Despite Samuel's objections, I made him see the seniors first. They were being stoical, but I could tell Lupe and Busy were exhausted. Other than bruises and Busy's elevated blood pressure, my hairline wrist fracture was the only injury of note. Samuel wrapped it tightly. When he was done, we headed for the door. I was starving. To my surprise, the waiting area was packed with people. Everyone was there. They stood when they saw me, and began to clap and cheer. Blood rushed to my cheeks and I hung back, but Samuel shoved me forward to accept the attention. Immediately I was surrounded by well-wishers, congratulating me and patting me on the back.

As one creature, we migrated out of the clinic and down to the Wagon Wheel. Tuesday had gone ahead to warn them, and tables had been pulled together. Within minutes, plates of potato skins and pitchers of beer appeared. Everyone chattered excitedly, relishing the retelling now that the danger had passed. Tuesday handed me a beer, and cried, 'To Maeve!'

'Hear! Hear!' everyone shouted, even Liz Goldberg.

I couldn't stop smiling. I went to the bar and ordered a cheeseburger. 'Make it the size of my head,' I instructed. I was ravenous.

'That's on me.' Noah appeared at my elbow.

'Naw, man, it's on the house,' said Vic, the bartender.

Noah looked me over. 'Are you really OK?'

I nodded, grinning.

'You've had quite a day. *Two* rescues.' It was hard to believe only hours had passed since Lulabell flew off.

'Three,' I corrected. 'I rescued my desktop items from an April prank.'

'The fishing line? Good catch.'

'I'm on my game,' I said.

'You're a mess.' He smiled back. I was. Ruby had brought a change of clothes to the clinic, but my hair was all over the place and I smelled like wet soil. 'I'm sorry I yelled,' he apologized. 'I thought I was going to have a heart attack when you jumped into the river. Breathing underwater is only for made-up people.'

'It was the only way.' I shrugged.

'Try not to do it again,' he begged.

'Try to take better care of your seniors,' I countered.

'Excuse me,' a voice interrupted. I turned to a man with Jerry Orbach hair and Danny De Vito stature. 'Chuck Hall.' He introduced himself. 'Are you Maeve Connelly?' At my nod, he said, 'I'm with the *Daily Dispatch*.' He named the regional paper. 'We'd like an interview, if you're up for it. We want to do a feature on the rescue.'

'Me?' I giggled.

'Not every day we get a local hero. Is it true that after the bridge collapsed, you yanked an old lady from a raging flood?'

'She rescued an escaped pet cockatiel from the storm earlier in the day, too. Sort of a town mascot,' Noah informed him.

'Fantastic. You catch criminals too?'

'The only thing she's going to catch is a cold, if she doesn't call it a night soon.' Samuel nudged me. He'd been hovering protectively since we'd walked over from the clinic.

'I haven't had my burger.' I laughed.

'Me neither,' said Chuck Hall. 'I'll have what she's having,' he told Vic. When the burgers arrived, we sat at the table surrounded by everyone, and tucked in. I answered the reporter's questions, frequently interrupted or corrected by other witnesses participating in the interview, amplifying my daring.

When we were done, he said, 'We'll need a picture. Didn't have time to bring someone down with me. You got a local guy?'

'Oh. It's me, I guess,' I said.

'I can do it!' Tuesday trilled. 'Who's got camera?' Someone handed her a digital camera. She beamed at me. 'What do I push?'

Chuck had me pose surrounded by everyone raising his and her beers. Tuesday snapped the shot and promised to email it to Chuck.

A wave of tiredness hit me. Samuel saw it happen, and stood. 'All right, folks. Time to get Wonder Woman home.'

'Spoilsport,' I managed around my yawn.

'Who looked the other way when you chased the painkiller I gave you with beer?' he teased.

He insisted on driving me home, and I didn't protest. Though it was only a few blocks, he had to shake me awake when we arrived. 'I'll let you sleep,' he said, giving me a kiss at the door before walking back to his car. 'I'll check on Helen at the hospital in the morning and come by the bookstore with a report.' I nodded sleepily. He paused. 'What you did today took courage,' he said. 'Not many people would have done it.'

I blew him a kiss and headed to my room. I registered as I passed that Lulabell seemed no worse for the wear, and Oliver had been returned and was sharing the safety of her cage.

When I woke, I was sore all over. I groaned and swallowed two painkillers as soon as I was upright. I debated changing into pajamas, since I'd fallen asleep in my clothes. It didn't seem right to go from clothes to clothes. I settled on my favorite Kalyx yoga pants as a happy compromise. Then I headed to the bookstore. It was early, but I couldn't wait to see the paper.

April called after me on my way out. 'Hold up, Atalanta. We're coming too.' She, Ruby and Busy fell in. We walked at a good clip. I couldn't help but marvel at the bright blue of the sky and the strength of the sun. It was like the storm never happened.

But I felt transformed by the events of the day before.

We arrived to find Bruce, Liz and little Tommy chatting on the step.

'Wall, there she is,' said Bruce. 'Thought I'd come for coffee, wait for the paper.'

'Look, Tommy,' Liz said. 'Maeve has a wrap on her wrist, like you.'

'Did you fall out of a tree?' Tommy asked.

'Maeve was very brave,' Liz explained. 'She saved Helen Rausch from drowning in the river yesterday.'

Tommy looked baffled. 'Why?'

By 9.30 there was a crowd sipping coffee. Pavlov would have been proud. Every time the bells sounded, we looked up expectantly, but it was always another customer to have coffee and wait for the paper. When it seemed like everyone in town was crammed into the store, we turned once more in response to the bells, only to groan collectively as Helen walked in with Samuel, who bore a rare look of irritation.

She marched up to the counter. 'Half caf, half decaf vanilla cappuccino with two percent skim milk, and I want that milk piping hot.' She looked around at everyone staring. 'What?' She swung back towards me. 'If you think you get some kind of special treatment or thank you from me, you've got another think coming,' she snapped. 'So? Do you work here or not? My cappuccino?' Brushes with death do not, apparently, have the same effect on everyone.

The entrance tinkled again. The newspaper deliveryman was not expecting a stampede, and dropped the bundle of papers on his foot in alarm when the crowd surged towards him. He staggered out in a hurry, leaving it to Bruce to cut the ties and disseminate papers.

Noah waved off bills. 'On the house today,' he said, grinning.

Tuesday brought me a copy, and we scanned for the article. It wasn't hard to find. Right on the front page was the headline 'Local Girl Saves Unknown Woman'.

I cut out a copy of the article and mailed it to my family. It was a good thing there was a caption with my name below the photo, though, as the picture was too blurry to recognize my face.

Ruby was in the kitchen having tea that night when I got home from work. Without a word she stood and switched on the kettle when I walked in.

I sat down. She set home-made coffee cake before me.

'Maeve, I owe you an apology. In all the excitement yesterday I never acknowledged it.'

My mouth dropped as she beat me to the words I'd been forming. Didn't *I owe her* the apology?

'I should have attended to clipping Lulabell's wings some time ago. She is not accustomed to free flight. I overlooked the proper care of my bird as I pursued my attempt at playwriting.'

273

'You're writing a play?' It was the first I'd heard of it.

'One of the projects I've been able to undertake with your assistance around the house. It turns out, however, that I do not have a talent for it. The world shall live in wonder over the founding mothers of Unknown.'

I didn't know what to say to that. It was hard to imagine Ruby not accomplishing whatever she set her mind to in a fluid manner. Unnerving, in fact. She was like my opposite, her competence a necessary offset to my calamity.

'Ruby, do you believe in luck?'

Ruby didn't speak as she prepared my tea, one hand squeezing the honey bear, the other pouring water, one hand reaching for a spoon, the other dipping the tea bag. If she'd had the arms of Shiva or Vishnu, imagine what she could accomplish. The cup didn't make a sound as she set it precisely on the table.

'I believe that birds fly away because their wings have not been clipped, not because they are in the company of someone afflicted with bad luck. I also believe it is reasonable that young girls who have had bad things happen through no fault of their own might believe in bad luck.'

I looked off. 'When I first got sick, I walked in a cloud of anger with a chance of rage. I'd see people smoking cigarettes or eating fried eggs on cheeseburgers and couldn't understand it. Axe-murderers and rapists were perfectly healthy and I, who had never done anything to anyone, was fighting for my life. What had I done to deserve it?'

'You could conjure a variety of explanations where you internalize responsibility for becoming ill, but they would all be incorrect. Our own worst enemy is often ourselves. I would hope that yesterday demonstrated to you your own capabilities.'

'I'm good at one thing, at least,' I said. 'I can run.'

'We all have the potential to be good at anything we choose. Have you heard of deliberate practice?' Ruby asked.

I shook my head.

'It's a way of thinking about achievement. Researchers suggest we've historically been incorrect in our belief that talent is integral to success. It's not that talent doesn't exist, but rather, that it may be irrelevant. Studies of accomplished musicians, athletes, artists and thinkers reveal no early indication of future potential before intensive training.'

'What about Bill Gates?'

'He may have written his first software at age thirteen, but his story doesn't suggest extraordinary abilities. It was a tic-tac-toe program. Many young boys were fascinated with computers at that time. The real question is why did Bill Gates rise to the top?'

'You don't believe in natural talent?'

'The premise can be insidious. If we find that something doesn't come naturally, we might conclude we have no talent for it and abandon the pursuit, even if it's to our detriment.'

'So what causes success?'

'If you believe in deliberate practice, carefully designed hard work and always stretching beyond your abilities. It's not as simple as "practice makes perfect". It's continually focusing on your weakest elements and trying to improve them. Those who persevere are high achievers.'

'So I'm not born a violin prodigy?'

'I believe you could become a violin prodigy without innate talent if you wanted it badly enough. The key lies in knowing what you deeply want. The more you want something, the easier it is to sweat through the deliberate practice.'

'So you can make your own luck?' I considered my quest for the Maeve that could have been. It was pretty clear there was no 'parallel me' I could jump to and pick up the trail mid-stride. I liked the idea that if I figured out what I *wanted* to be, I didn't have to settle for the mess I had.

'Why not?'

'So what you're saying is, if I don't have any talent for play-writing, but engaged in deliberate practice of the craft, my community might be able to see the story of our founding mothers performed at the Monkey Flower Festival?' I said, smile sly.

Ruby looked surprised, then laughed. 'I suppose I am.'

'You'll glue them to their seats,' I predicted.

'How clever of you to think of that.' And with that she got to her feet, folded the newspaper, collected the coffee cake and retrieved my empty cup as if she had six hands.

CHAPTER 22

RELATIONSHIPS ARE HARD

The phone rang so many times I thought she might not answer. Part of me was relieved. I'd struggled with my preference to send an email, but it wasn't right. Deliberate practice.

'Hello?'

'Jules! Happy birthday!'

'Who's this?'

'It's me. Maeve!'

There was quiet. Then, 'You're shitting me. Damn, girl, I haven't heard from you in forever,' said my closest friend in Charlotte.

'I'm sorry I haven't called.' I meant it.

'I left you, like, seventy-eleven messages. I thought maybe . . .'

'No,' I said. 'I'm fine. I really am. Great, in fact. I'm just an asshole for not calling.'

'How's LA?'

I laughed. 'I don't know. Elsie broke down in this place called Unknown, Arizona.'

'All this time? That's crazy!'

'The funny thing is, I kind of like it here. It's like *Northern Exposure* in Arizona. *Southern Overexposure*, SPF 90 required.'

'So you're gonna stay?'

I puckered my brow, then rubbed out the dent. 'Of course not. I'm going to LA as soon as Elsie's operational.'

'Well, good, because I'm still planning to come and visit. Though you might have to make room for two . . .' She giggled.

'Tell me.' She radiated new-love euphoria that was dying to talk about it.

'He's awesome. His name is David. He's this sexy cowboy with crazy sideburns and he drives a motorcycle and plays the sax.'

'Sounds hot, fembot.'

'I'm nuts about him. You know that feeling when you've been out a coupla times and it zings into your soul that this could actually be a person you spend the rest of your life with?' I did know that feeling. Unbidden, an image popped into my mind, but it wasn't Samuel. I frowned again, then rubbed irritably at my forehead. Jules continued gushing.

'It gets better the more time I spend with him. He's funny, smart, sexy, and he makes *me* feel funny, smart and sexy. I swear the other night we were falling asleep and I knew without a doubt that I'd never been happier in my whole life. Of course I told him, and you know what he said? He said it would be better if we were falling asleep on a big pile of money . . .'

I let Jules ramble. I was thinking. Really, I should be interrupting, talking over her to share my own passion for Samuel, but I didn't. I couldn't match her exuberance.

'I'm really happy for you, Jules,' I said at last.

'Thanks for remembering my birthday, pal. And thanks for that little doll you put in the shoebox. That was really cool.'

'I . . .'

'I know.'

'I'm working on being better.'

'Don't be too tough on yourself, kid. You're better than you realize.'

'Really?'

She laughed. 'Not really. But I get you.'

'Thanks, Jules.'

'Love you, babe.'

'Love you back.' I was surprised at how easily it came. Maybe I *was* getting better.

'But if you wait until next year to call me again, you can suck it.'

The candlelight played on the planes of Samuel's face, his eyes warm chocolate. We were back at the Velvet Elvis. We'd made a special date to talk. We hadn't yet discussed what had happened. I'd needed a little time. Now I was feeling ready.

'I like your hair down.' He smiled. My hair was down in smooth waves. I'd brushed it a hundred strokes, like I used to do when I was young. After I stopped chemo and radiation, I'd been surprised at how strong and fast my hair grew back. I had refused to cut it, in case it was a fluke, but it had gotten in the way when I ran, sticking to my sweaty face and neck. That was when I began my habit of wearing braids.

I tucked a strand behind my ear. 'I'm trying to let it all hang out a little more.'

'I'm sorry, Maeve.' He repeated his apology. 'It wasn't my place to tell people.'

'It's OK.' I meant it. 'Part of me was relieved.'

'It was torture watching you torment yourself.'

'I always wonder if politicians feel relieved when their skeletons are sprung from the closet. If they're thankful when the mistress is finally revealed once they are securely in office, so the dread goes away.'

'What held you back?'

'A mean and hurtful third-grade teacher,' I quipped. He gave me a look that let me know what he thought of my joke. I answered his question seriously. 'I guess I thought I didn't get an election day. No "safety point" after which people can't change their minds about you and stop being your friend.'

'Either you own up to all that makes you who you are, or you're forever in hiding.'

'How'd you get so smart?'

'Native American. We're born mystical and shit.' He grinned.

'Watch one episode of *Antiques Road Show* and your powers will be neutralized. It's ethnic kryptonite – strictly white-people stuff.'

'The old folks say you can't kill emotion. You

might squash it flat, but it doesn't lose mass – it will spread wide, seep through the cracks, find a way.'

'Turn into rashes on my tummy?'

He smiled. 'You're my favorite hypochondriac.'

'Maybe I was trying to get face time with the hot doctor.'

'You didn't have to work that hard. Is there anything you want to ask me? Other than how the great spirit gave maize to my people?'

'No. Yes. Maybe.' I hesitated. I'd asked the Gerberator all the questions back in the day. *Am I going to die? Will it keep coming back? Will I be able to have children? Why me?* But there *was* one thing. The risk was if I didn't like the answer.

'Do I . . .' I stopped. Count to three. Try again. 'Does it feel *different* when we . . . ? You know, my body. Can you tell I was sick?'

'No.' He answered like he'd been expecting the question.

'Not at all?'

'I'd say "absolutely not, that's the silliest question ever", but I'm afraid you'd throw a breadstick at me.'

I threw a breadstick at him, looking away to hide my relief. During chemo, I'd fought a macabre battle between the demand of my hyper-dry skin to remain hydrated, and the resulting torment of using the bathroom.

'The most rapidly dying and regenerating cells are the ones most impacted by chemotherapy,' my doctor had explained. 'That's why you're getting sores in your mouth. Vaginal skin is like that too. Think of it as another mouth,' he had suggested.

But it wasn't another mouth. I'd stopped feeling desirable or female. There were times I thought I'd never want sex again. Until Samuel, who knew everything and wanted me just the same.

He grabbed my hand now, grinning. 'There is nothing about your body that isn't perfect.'

'There are the scars.' I tugged my hand, flustered.

He refused to let go. It seemed to be a habit with the men in Unknown. 'Scars are cool.'

'Ugh. They remind me of the creepy little aliens that lived in my arm and side.'

'Those aliens were perfectly innocent ports that delivered life-saving medicine.'

'When I was in remission, everyone asked if I was excited. I wasn't anything. I didn't feel invincible. I didn't feel depressed. I'd come to the end of my to-do list and didn't know what to do next. I sort of panicked. The routine had grounded mc, and I didn't know what I was going to do without it.'

'That's common.'

'My body and I didn't belong to each other anymore, so we couldn't celebrate being better or chart a course of what to do next.'

'Maeve, your body *does* belong to you. And it's beautiful. Inside and out. Ah, perfect timing!' He looked up to see the waitress approaching with a cake and candles. Behind her were three others. When they reached the table, they broke into a chorus of 'Happy Birthday'. Soon the entire pizza joint was singing.

I let them serenade me, blushing and sending Samuel filthy looks across the table.

'Thank you! Thank you!' I waved to everyone as the entire restaurant clapped, and blew out my candle. 'Just so you know,' I hissed, 'I wished for you to wake up and realize you are naked in a room full of hundreds of colleagues taking the medical board recertification exams.'

'You only have to take the boards once.' He grinned. 'I'm safe. But I like you thinking of me naked.' He wiggled his eyebrows.

'Samuel! It's *not* my birthday!'

'It is for part of you. Healthy cells are being born by the hundreds as we speak. Today is *their* birthday. Instead of pretending nothing happened, why don't we celebrate what *did* happen. In many ways you're a miracle.' His look got earnest. 'Today could be your *re*birth day.'

'You're not going to make me go through some weird ceremony where I crawl out of a pair of pantyhose in a turtle-shaped baby pool filled with jelly, are you?'

'No. I'm going to give you this.' He reached down and pulled out a thick folder and two oblong packages wrapped in bright paper.

'What is it?' I was curious.

'It's a rebirthday gift. It has three parts. This

284

first.' He flipped open the folder. 'Here. This is a study about cancer recidivism. And see here, these are your last blood-test results. Now do you see how when you were twenty and you relapsed . . .'

I stared in wonder as Samuel patiently and carefully showed me just how healthy I was, with charts and diagrams and medical records. My heart constricted.

'So you see,' he said at last, 'there is no reason you won't live a long and healthy life. At this point you're no different than anyone else.' He smiled. 'Except your cells are younger and sexier.'

'Are you getting fresh with my plasma?'

'Beauty is only skin deep.'

'That's deep enough for me.'

'Open it.' He pushed the first present toward me. I did. It was a beautifully framed image.

'Your last scan,' he explained. 'I had it framed so you won't forget.' It was oddly beautiful, the radioactive tracer injected in my veins lit up to provide a color-coded picture of my body. 'Now this one.' He pushed over the second gift. It was a beautiful leather-bound Harrison's medical dictionary, like the ones in his office. This one was inscribed. It read: *A book full of things that don't apply to you. Trust me, I'm a doctor. Samuel.*

'Every day you're supposed to look up something you don't have. Go on, try it.'

I flipped to a page near the beginning. 'Ankylosing spondylitis. A form of chronic inflammation of the spine and the sacroiliac joints.'

'Excellent choice.' He beamed at me. 'Swollen sacroiliac joints are less sexy than hairy moles.'

This was fun. 'Can I do another?' I asked.

'I don't know,' he answered. 'There are only so many entries in the book and you have a lot of mornings left. Maybe you want to go slow.'

I looked at the voluminous tome and thought about having more days than it had entries. What would I do with them all? It was a little terrifying. In that, I was no different from anyone else.

I looked across the table at Samuel, blinking back tears. His thoughtfulness was overwhelming. I felt warmth. And affection. And that was all.

'Samuel,' I said.

He met my gaze, and nodded. Then he covered my hands.

'It's just . . .'

'We're friends.' His eyes were sad.

That was it exactly. 'I think you're wonderful.'

'I think you're pretty wonderful yourself.'

'Thanks for taking such good care of me.'

His smile was rueful. 'I did too good a job, I'm afraid. I don't think you want someone taking care of you anymore.'

'But I want more for both of us. Passion, crazy climbing-all-over-you need and joy. And we're . . . we're like a warm bath.'

'I know.'

'Really?' Irrationally, I was upset. I didn't want *him* to not want *me*.

'I'm glad you said something first.' Technically I hadn't. But wait. This was what I wanted.

'Thank you,' I said. 'For being you.'

He squeezed my hand and grinned. 'Break-up sex?'

'Check, please!' I smiled back.

CHAPTER 23

THE CURSE OF THE ALIEN HAND

Alien Hand Syndrome. A neurological illness in which a sufferer's hand acts independently of the other and of the patient's wishes. Alien hands can do complex tasks, often the opposite of the normal hand: unbuttoning a shirt buttoned by the other hand, or pulling down trousers the other has pulled up. The hand may become aggressive, pinching or slapping the patient. In at least one case, it tried to strangle its owner.

After my morning run, I hurried into The Little Read Book, anxious to be there before Noah. I wanted to see his face when he came in. He'd flown to New York for a meeting with his publisher, and Tuesday, Bruce and I had worked around the clock to finish the children's nook in his absence. The book-shelves were painted bright primary colors to match the new area carpet, there were kid-sized chairs and tables I'd been hiding in the stockroom, and the café now offered juice boxes. I'd stayed until 2 a.m. to hang shadow box frames displaying our collection of classic children's books. It was perfect.

By the time he walked in at 12.47, I was vibrating with impatience. The sight of him sent a jolt through my system. I was going to have to ask Samuel for a sedative later.

'Oh, are you back already?' The most erect posture of my life belied my casual tone. Noah gave me an amused look.

'My flight was delayed.' He smiled. 'Careful, or I'm going to think you missed me.'

'Cha. Name one person in the history of time who misses the boss when he's away.'

'Monica Lewinsky. You're wearing your favorite rainbow socks.' He had me there. I was wearing my most happy socks.

I was about to retort when he said, 'I missed you.' And there I was, mouth hanging open like a fish. He laughed, eyes holding mine for ten eternal seconds.

'I . . .' I started.

'Did I miss it? Am I late? Rats!' Tuesday's bracelets jangled more than the doorbell as she bounded in. 'Poppy Tarquin completely forgot to pick up Bloom after dance lessons so I was stuck at the studio until she remembered she had a child. I swear, what am I, a free babysitter? And now I'm late to meet the Cowbelles. Well?' She turned a shining face toward Noah.

'What?' He looked confused.

'Oh goody! I'm not too late!' Tuesday clapped. 'Well, for *this*, anyway.'

'Close your eyes.' I smiled. He did as he was told. I led him to face the corner nook. 'OK, open.'

He did. I waited. He didn't say anything. For a long, long time. I felt an anxious wiggle. Did he hate it? Was it too unserious? Noah was very serious about books.

He looked at me, tone controlled. 'You did this?'

Oh God. He was upset. He hated it. I hesitated. Should I give Tuesday and Bruce credit for their hard work, or take all the blame? I blinked so he couldn't see I was fighting not to cry. I battled an urge to run, feet twitchy. How had I gotten it wrong? I managed a nod, looking down.

'This is . . . by far . . . the most . . .' I peeked up and noticed he was blinking too. Kind of like me. And his eyebrow wasn't drawn down like it did when he was upset. He was staring at the mural on the far wall. 'Is that . . . ?'

'Tuesday did it.' I relaxed. He was looking at a large painted image of a girl with long braids and a boy wearing knee socks sitting in a treetop. Tuesday had rendered an excellent copy. 'There's even a shelf for your toys.' I pointed. '*If* you feel like sharing.'

'They are not toys,' came his lofty refrain. 'They are visualization facilitators. Grown men do not play with toys.' He looked at me. He ventured further in. 'It's amazing. Everything is so little.'

'Everything is cuter in miniature,' I said.

'And the undersea corner?'

'I figured it'd be hard to have kids fly or walk through walls, but maybe they could breathe underwater. There's a treetop corner too.'

His smile was huge. He tugged a braid. 'You're right. I like being one of the kids. I could get used to you being around.'

I took an involuntary step backward. Part of me wanted to take care of Noah so badly I dreamed of snatching him under my arm and running far away to shove him in a warm nest and feed him soup. But with my luck, I'd trip and drop him into poison ivy, where he'd break an arm. I was still too unsure of myself. Noah had had enough bad luck himself.

'Hey, man, don't cry or anything. It's just a shop.' I looked around for Tuesday, but she'd vanished. It was a trick she perfected when Noah and I bickered.

He caught my shoulder and turned me back. 'It's not just a shop. It's perfect. Thank you, Maeve.' He hugged me tight. I stiffened, then sagged like a sad sack, absorbing his support. I didn't want him to let go. Then I got anxious. This was exactly the problem. I was trying to be a new girl. One who could take care of herself. Certainly not one who over-hugged another girl's boyfriend.

I pulled back.

'It's amazing how well we fit,' he said.

'What?' I said, startled.

'Your little bookstore in mine,' he mused. Suddenly

I felt the weight of a thousand books and magazines. Was I responsible for the store? For the first
time, I was relieved to see Beth walk in.

She was beaming. 'Hello!' she sang. 'Welcome
back!' She flung her arms around Noah, and I
became considerably less happy about her arrival.

The smile he returned seemed forced.

'Have you got anything to say to me?' Her tone
was coy.

His 'Of course' was clipped, so I was surprised
when he followed it with 'Happy anniversary.'

'You didn't forget!' She kissed him on the
mouth. Air left my lungs.

'I did not,' he said. 'We're going to Bella Mia in
Nogales. And I have a spa gift certificate for you.'

My blood pressure shot like mercury in a ther-
morneter, spiking so fast I feared a plasma geyser
might burst through the top of my head. I realized I was staring, and bolted for the café. What
was the matter with me? I'd seen them kiss before.
Samuel and I kissed in the store all the time. Or
we had, I corrected. I shook my head to clear it.
I hadn't had so many emotions in succession since
I was fifteen and gotten my first kiss from Jack
Jost, only to find him kissing my friend Alison ten
minutes later. Never mind that spinning a bottle
was involved.

My instinct was to call my sister, but I resisted. I
couldn't forever dial her up to get my head straight.
Besides, there was nowhere private, and whispering
furiously behind a cupped hand in the stockroom

was ludicrous. What could she tell me that I didn't know? I was overreacting.

I shoved napkins in the dispenser in irritation. As if I'd conjured him, Noah appeared. I registered Beth dancing out of the store. Noah sat at a café table and gestured to the chair opposite.

'So, tell me what happened while I was gone.' His smile was genuine.

'Not much.' I shrugged, remaining behind the counter. I didn't mention my break-up. It struck me how pathetic it might look, if he mistook my motive in fixing up the store. 'We had a good week in the café.'

'The store stayed open, then?' he teased. 'You didn't float off to take pictures of air motes or something?'

My blood pressure pounded again. How could he take a frosted tart like Beth seriously and treat me like a piece of fluff? Watching them together made me want to hurl. I tossed my rag down and flung an arm toward the nook. 'How much time do you think I took off, Noah?' I demanded. 'You were only gone for three days. You think that Little Read Picture Book sign, the murals and the shelves all painted themselves?'

He looked startled. 'Maeve, I . . .'

'And considering you forgot to pay me before you left, technically I've been working for free, so if I wanted to take off and photograph naked baby bottoms, I'd be perfectly entitled!'

His face was stricken. 'I'm sorry. I'll pay you

right now. I didn't mean . . . Getting ready to leave . . . I was distracted . . . I just . . .'

'Forget it,' I snapped. 'Include it in next week's check. But try not to forget that most people don't have their jobs for kicks. And for the record, taking care of you is a lot more work than you think.' I turned my back, hating myself but unable to stop my mouth. I sensed rather than saw him disappear into the office. I was relieved when he didn't come right back. After a while, I felt safe enough to sit on the floor of the café and rest my forehead against the cool refrigerator door.

It was when I was in remission and eased back into school that I started running in earnest. I felt most in control of the wayward vehicle when I was running. In class, I floated around the edges. Former classmates, seniors now, would squint with vague recognition but quickly lose interest as I didn't respond and recollection failed to come. I was the oldest in my classes. I made good grades. I didn't date.

Ten days before Christmas, I stopped by the Gerberator's office a week after my regular blood tests to pick up some antibiotics. The flu had been going around, and I didn't want to take any chances. I was impatient in the waiting room. Vi and I were going Christmas shopping, and I couldn't wait. I'd detested shopping before I got sick, but afterwards it was like a balm. I loved the cool, controlled climate of the mall, appreciated the cash-for-object exchange, bound myself to things. Sales transactions were discreet and tidy. You knew the outcome in advance.

It didn't register when the nurse led me to the Gerberator's office instead of handing me a prescription. When he started talking, I frowned. I needed to decide whether to get my mother new clogs or gardening tools for Christmas.

'You mean I have the flu?' I asked stupidly.

'Your white blood cell count is thirty-eight thousand.' He waited.

My needle went off the record. 'No,' was all I said. 'No.'

'I'm sorry, Maeve. We need to begin treatment right away. I'd like to admit you.'

I stood. I sat. I stood again. 'May I have the flu shot?' I didn't want to get the flu.

He shook his head sadly. 'You know you can't. We'll run some tests and determine a course of treatment.'

It was the first Christmas I'd had to spend in the hospital.

Twenty minutes past closing time, I hadn't moved to lock the doors. The store was empty. I sat on a sofa watching the light change. Part of me hoped Noah wouldn't come out, while part of me desperately wished he would. It seemed to be how I felt about everything lately. Slapping outstretched hands. When Noah did approach, his step was tentative.

'Maeve?' Hesitant.

I turned my head. He held out a check.

'My New York trip went really well. So that's a little more. I mean, it's a raise. I'm giving you a raise. You deserve it.' He looked away. 'I know I'm a little difficult.'

'No.' I shook my head. 'I don't know why I said that.'

'Is everything OK?' He sat down next to me.

'It will be.' I said the truth. 'I think it just takes time. Sometimes I feel like I'm learning how to be friends with adults, because I'm not sure I am one myself.' I picked at a button on the sofa cushion, then forced myself to look at him.

'You're an adult.' His eyes jumped guiltily away from my boobs. If I'd been less miserable, I'd have laughed.

'In years, maybe. Anyway, it wasn't you.'

He shoved his hands in his pockets and cleared his throat. 'What *was* it, Maeve? Why did we fight today? Did I do something wrong?' His earnest face made me want to cry.

I felt sick as I recalled the Gerberator saying, 'People with posttraumatic stress disorder may act like they are under threat, becoming suddenly irritable or explosive even when not provoked.'

'No,' I said. 'You didn't. You're a good man, Noah. And an excellent friend. I'm grateful you put up with me. I can be a moody, bossy creature!' I forced a laugh.

His relief was evident. 'I'm glad. I really value

our friendship.' He looked at his watch. 'Are you OK to close up? I have to get Beth. You know women and these anniversary things.'

I laughed. 'Go. I'll see you Monday.'

'Is Samuel picking you up?'

'Not today.'

He unfolded his tall body. He gave my shoulder a quick squeeze. 'It's nice to be home.' The word sprung a fence between us – one of us was home and one of us was not. 'And I love the nook. Every time I turn around, things get better here because of you.'

I watched him walk out, reflecting that it was unfair that a man's legs could look that long and sexy in jeans, and knowing two things. I was in love with Noah Case, and I had to get the hell out of town because of it. It would kill me to moon over him from a distance, and I never, ever wanted to make him look that vulnerable again.

CHAPTER 24

CLAPP YOUR HANDS AND SAY YEAH

Chagas Disease (Portuguese: *Doença de Chagas*). A tropical parasitic disease commonly transmitted to humans from birds by an insect vector, the blood-sucking assassin bugs of the *Reduviidae* subfamily *Triatominae*. Symptoms include sustained high fevers, occasional delusions and obsessive behavior.

'Clapp Cement.'

'May I please speak with Clem Clapp?' It felt like asking for a venereal disease.

'You got him.' The voice was brusque. I hoped I hadn't guessed wrong. I looked at the website. No, this was my guy. I was sure of it.

'Is this *the* Clem Clapp, editor and CEO of *Plymouth Road Runner: The (Good) Times*?' I poured all the admiration I could into my question.

His voiced warmed. 'That'd be me. Who am I speaking to?'

'Sir, it is an honor. You are speaking to Maeve Connelly, 1970 Plymouth Road Runner N96 Air

Grabber Coupe, 727 auto transmission, yellow black stripes.'

'That's a rare beauty, that one. I have one of those myself, Moulin Rouge, no wheel covers.' Satisfaction radiated from his voice.

'383 CID rated at 335 b.h.p. and 425 torque?' I carefully read Barney's notes.

'426 CID Hemi rated at 425 b.h.p. – that's 317 kW – and 490 torque. Can run the quarter-mile in 13.4 seconds at 105 m.p.h.' Perfect. It was engine-compatible.

'Beep, beep.' I mimicked the car horn's signature Road Runner beep.

'Beep, beep,' he responded with the reverence of a secret handshake.

'Is it true, Mr Clapp, that you have *six* Plymouth Road Runners, sir?' Awe.

'Call me Clem. There's no better vehicle than the Road Runner. It's a personal privilege to ensure these American icons never become extinct. What would the road be without them?' Bingo.

'Six cars.' I whistled. 'How do you ever decide which one to drive? It's a shame you can't drive them all at once.'

'That's the God's honest truth. I don't have a system, just go with my gut. The roof leaks on Angie so I don't drive her in the rain, and Vicki doesn't like the cold none too much. Sylvie has extra tinting, so she's great for summer days. The seats clean easiest on Becky, so she's best for driving the offspring to school. Dorothy – that's Dottie – gets the best gas mileage, and Tootsie, well, she was my first. I have a soft spot for Tootsie. You get to know your girls, and you know which one's raring to be driven any given day.'

I assumed that by girls he was referring to his cars, all lovingly mentioned by name, whereas his progeny was anonymously lumped together as 'offspring'. 'How *is* the weather in Boise?' I worked on camaraderie.

'Just the ticket for fishin', drivin' and sellin' cement.' He chuckled. 'And how can I help you, Miss Connelly?'

'Call me Maeve. Clem, I couldn't help but be impressed at *Plymouth Road Runner: The (Good) Times*. That's quite a publication for a man as busy as yourself.' I had the latest issue up on the Internet. It looked like a third-grade newsletter. You could almost smell the Elmer's glue.

'It's a labor of love.'

'I loved your piece on the Duster with adjustable spoilers. I never knew that about side-to-side yaw.' I owed April for that one.

'Well thank you kindly.' He sounded chuffed. Time to go for the kill.

'I noticed you don't publish on a regular schedule. I found myself so eager for more after reading the last issue that I wanted to find out when the next edition will be available.'

'That's a good question. My wife doesn't quite share my passion so I'm on my own for the newsletter. There are quite a few members of Plymouth Road Runner: An American Fan Club – of which I'm founder and president – but I do most of the work myself. With running a company, my time is limited. There's only so much one man can do.'

'Too bad there aren't any photos. I'd love to see your girls.'

'I'm not the most computer-minded guy on the planet. My talents run to bills of sale. But I'll learn. I plan to turn this baby into a first-class publication.'

'Clem, I might be able to help you out.' I started to talk. He became excited.

'Maeve, your dedication to the Road Runner does you credit. I like the way you think. But that's a lot of work you're proposing to take on. Now tell me, if you do this for me, what can I do for you? Need cement?'

I couldn't hold back my smile. 'Actually . . .' I laid out my proposal.

'So he went for it?' Vi asked.

'Uh-huh.' I crunched a celery stick.

'And what exactly do you have to do?'

'When I told him how Elsie and I got to Unknown, he was laughing so hard I was afraid he'd have a heart attack. I promised to help him modernize the newsletter and to write a regular column called "Road Runner: A Tough Love Story". He has a thing for colons. It'll be about my various road trips, and feature pictures of Elsie in all the small towns I've visited, the car troubles we've had, and how we fixed them. Car-enthusiast stuff.'

'That sounds like a pretty sweet deal.'

'Not exactly.' Clem hadn't been a total mark. 'I also have to help him with his company newsletter, *Cement Times: Solid Facts*.' I was racking my brains for photo ops for that one. 'My first piece is going to be "Step on a Crack, Break Your Mother's Back: Does It Give Cement a Bad Name?".'

'In return you get the part.'

'Yep. Vicki will be Elsie's organ donor while both Clem and I keep looking for replacements. If Barney finds one first, I send Clem back his parts. If Clem finds one first, I help him out with his various newsletters until I've worked off my debt.'

'But his car won't work in the meantime.'

'He can still polish it. And he has five others. Clem believes the more Road Runners out there, the better for the emotional psyche of our nation. He'd rather I got Elsie back on the road, even if it means taking Vicki out of circulation. It helps that he's a nice person who genuinely wants to help.'

'You found the perfect donor.'

'I couldn't wait around for Barney anymore. There weren't any available parts. So I started thinking of alternatives – if there weren't available parts, I'd try unavailable parts. I narrowed it down to unavailable parts that could be made available.

Someone with more than one car. Someone who'd care about fixing another person's vintage car. Someone who might want something I had to offer. From there, it was easy.'

'Ingenious. Given how clever you've become, wouldn't it be easier to buy the part off Clem and avoid the newsletter business?'

I cleared my throat, with slight shame. 'I don't think I could afford it.'

'But you've been working for ages! And selling your pictures!'

'Yeah, well, there were things . . .'

'What kinds of things?'

'Oh, I put some money into projects for the store. And it was Ruby's birthday. Then there was the DVD player for the house, some hula skirts for Tuesday, a yoga mat for Samuel, some rabbit ears for my in-room TV, new running shoes. You know, *things*.'

Vi was quiet. 'Maeve, has it ever occurred to you that maybe you don't want to leave Unknown? It took you less than two weeks to get the money to leave Charlotte, and five days to get a new set of tires in Oklahoma. Maybe there's a reason you're not saving more efficiently. I know how determined you are when you set your mind to something.'

'I'm determined,' I said firmly. Whether she was right was irrelevant. I had to go.

'Why so suddenly unwavering?'

I opened my mouth. I closed it. I tried. 'Have

you ever stayed up all night picturing someone who wasn't there?'

She sighed. 'Noah?' Somehow she knew I was nodding over the phone. 'Are you sure it's hopeless?'

'Yes.'

'Are you sure it's hopeless because he has a girlfriend or because you don't think you're good enough?'

Her words were a shock. At my silence she went on. 'I don't know if I'll say this just right, because it was awful when you were sick, but in some ways your cancer was one of the best things that ever happened to me. I learned to appreciate the day. Because you got a second chance, I can tell you that you've only brought me good things.'

'That guy dumped you because you didn't go to his sister's wedding. Because you were with me.' My throat hurt saying it.

'Lucky break I got out early, I say. Don't get me wrong. It wasn't always easy. But in the end, we all won. The thing about second chances, though, is that they aren't worth beans if you don't do anything about them.'

'But . . .'

'Get out of your own way, Maeve.'

After we hung up, I had an impulse to run. My feet twitched to sprint through fields. I ignored them. Instead, I stood, and went to the kitchen to meet Bruce and Ruby for a cup of tea and see how her play was coming.

CHAPTER 25

HOW WE DANCED

Hula-hoop Intestine. An affliction where excessive or strenuous hula-hooping may result in persistent loin pain. In severe cases, patient may present traumatic rupture of the abdominal muscle, twisted intestine or acute spinal subdural hematoma.

'Ay-yi, I can't believe you're leaving us!' Tuesday wailed.

True to his word, Clem had delivered the parts to PIGS, and Barney was performing the transplant. I was giving notice at the book-store.

Noah's face was expressionless. 'When do you expect to leave?'

'Next week.' I had enough to pay Barney for his time and get to Los Angeles. As soon as Elsie had proven she wouldn't reject Vicki's guts, we were ready to go. *Nós partimos.*

'Noooooo . . .' Tuesday wailed. She ran around the counter and flung her arms around my neck.

'You can have my rabbit ears,' I said.

'Really? Cool!' She beamed. Then her face fell. 'But who'll take my pictures?'

'I'm going to LA, not Fiji!' I laughed, then hesitated as I caught Noah's look. 'Or Child can fill in.' I shouldn't be misleading.

'But you'll be back for the Festival?'

'We'll see, Tuesday,' I demurred. I didn't want to make promises I couldn't keep. For all I knew, once I got to Los Angeles I'd never want to leave. Work might be demanding.

Noah hadn't spoken. Now he cut in. 'I don't suppose you can be any more specific than "next week", can you?'

I turned to face him, figuring that was the end of Tuesday. She had a knack for conflict avoidance.

'It's not very professional notice, is it?' he continued.

I might've laughed, if it wasn't so sad. Even Noah's Angry Eyebrow (fully on display now) was dear to me. Not to mention there wasn't much about how we ran the store that constituted standard business practices: closing shop to go to Nogales, opening at 10 p.m. to let Liz in when Tommy forgot he had a book report due, me going running when I lost my temper.

'I'm leaving Monday,' I said gently. 'Barney will be finished Friday. Sunday night Ruby's having a farewell dinner for me. I hope you'll both be there.' Surprisingly, Tuesday hadn't fled. I was touched.

'You bet I will! I'm going to call Ruby right now.

We'll send you off with a *mino'aka* – that's a smile.' She twirled, dance infusing her movements. 'We'll need fairy lights and paper flowers, and some floating candles. Oooh, and sparklers! Maybe I can find some leis . . .' She talked to herself all the way out the door, ticking off thoughts on her fingertips as she went, forgetting it was my day off and she was scheduled to work.

I turned back to Noah, *mino'aka* playing on my mouth as I pulled off my jacket. Looked like I was staying. The smile faded at his expression.

'Well?'

I was ready. 'I've filled out the café and stock-room order forms for the next four weeks. They tend to be predictable. All you have to do is fax them in on Mondays. You'll have the books and food you need. I've also asked Beth to come by and help out for the next few Thursday mornings until you get into the new routine. She can put out the stock.'

'Beth?' He frowned. 'I wish you hadn't done that.'

I was taken aback. 'Why not?'

'The last book Beth read, the title began with *Cliffs Notes*. She has no idea . . . That ridiculous art book . . . and . . . Well . . . never mind.' He looked uncomfortable.

'No problem,' I soothed. 'We'll ask Ruby. It only entails putting out new stock. I ordered the titles. Anyone can do it.'

'So you're just anyone?' His anger dissipated.

'No. I'm the girl who's spent the last seven years of her life in neutral, who needs to get back on course.'

Noah sat heavily on the couch we'd shared earlier. I joined him.

'Careful,' I mimicked. 'Or I'll think you're going to miss me.'

He stood abruptly. 'I'm sorry, but I need to go through the office so I can prepare for this rather abrupt departure and make sure that you cover all the bases before Friday. It being only three days away.' He wasn't going to make this easy. He headed toward the back. 'Oh, just curious.' He turned, tone caustic. 'What socks are you wearing today?'

We both looked at my naked toes in flip-flops for a moment, nails gleaming coral, and then he strode to his office and shut the door without a word.

Ruby was so quiet in her approach that I jumped when she laid hands on my shoulders.

'Come along. Everyone is here.'

'Everyone?' I tried to sound casual. I hadn't seen Noah since I'd told him I was leaving.

Ruby sensed my question, but she also sensed I didn't want it acknowledged. 'I'm sure there'll be stragglers,' she reassured. 'But at the moment, your farewell party has quite a crowd already.'

'It just goes to show you, if you give the people what they want, they'll show up,' I joked. I don't know which was more shocking – fifteen people gathered waiting for me, or the stab I felt in unguarded moments when I remembered I was leaving them. I followed Ruby to the yard. It was an enchanted place. There were lights strung along the walls and trees, and even the edges of the long table spanning the yard. What Tuesday lacked in paper-flower expertise, she redeemed in fairy lights. Though the paper flowers were there too. The table bore a celebration of candles and an array of red and copper-colored stones, and vegetables from the garden. I'd pretended not to see Child earlier dispatching Tuesday with the cut flowers that had graced the table.

When I walked out, Tuesday grabbed me and squeezed. 'Took you long enough. Do you like?' Her beaming face was impossible to deny. Not to mention the perfection of the garden.

Bruce, Child, Barney and Ronnie Two Shoes were at the grill, preparing kebabs. Male imperative. April and Busy were tippling and bickering about sherry versus Scotch. I had a vision of transporting Busy to bed later. Ruby was laying silverware down in precise settings, as Tuesday was cluttering the table with scattered napkins. Sandy and Liz prepared a salad, while Patrick and Jenny Up laid out pies.

Samuel pressed a brown paper bag into my hands.

'Samuel! You can't keep giving me gifts!' I took the bag eagerly.

'Don't get excited. It's vitamin samples. Obscure ones like bilberry extract and selenium.'

I hugged him. He was a gift I'd miss.

When the kebabs were ready, we gathered for chicken, pineapple, onion and tomato treats on sticks.

'More foods should be served on sticks,' said Ronnie Two Shoes.

'Tuesday, give us an interpretational dance about how you feel about food on sticks,' I demanded, not caring that her kebab would get cold. As I'd known she would, without a thought, she did, leaping up and dancing in the yard in movements that reminded me of the way my mother described sculpture. It got better when Busy told Tuesday she'd got the pineapple wrong and jumped up to do her own version.

Candlelight lit the faces of those who'd gathered. I laughed along as Samuel exaggerated stories of his top ten favorite Maeve Hypochondriac Moments. Clearly they were exaggerated. April brayed a little *too* loud at some. But I'd already unscrewed the top of the saltshaker closest to her. April liked salt on prickly pear pie, which we happened to be having for dessert. Heh.

I didn't dwell on the fact that Noah didn't appear. Beth didn't either. Presumably they were at the ballet or her brother's or perusing bad Victorian drawings of children. I didn't care. It would have complicated things to have him there. Even I, in my limited experience, had learned a thing or two. I wanted to enjoy my own party, and Noah would have strained things. It was better that he didn't come. Even at the end, when we went late and he probably could have still stopped by for a minute. I took what he'd told me about missing me and put it in my vault. If he'd been there I'd have been conscious of nothing but how much I wanted something I couldn't have.

We ate and laughed and drank for hours. April and I carried Busy to bed at midnight. Liz and Sandy, Patrick and Jenny faded away shortly after. Ronnie Two Shoes was hot after Sandy, so he left within minutes to belatedly escort her home. Lulabell and Oliver cooed, 'Legs up, toots' to each other in the Playbird Mansion.

Soon, it was down to the hardest. Child clasped my hands.

'Maeve, it would be a privilege if you would continue to share your images.'

'I owe them all to you, Child. I promise to send you some banal ones,' I teased. He hugged me. When he pulled away at the natural conclusion of the embrace, it was me that still clung.

'I'll treasure my carved memory,' he whispered about the kachina I'd given him, 'though it won't replace the giver.' With that he was gone. It was like saying goodbye to Jules times ten. I had more than a million words caught in my throat. I said nothing.

I was grabbed and squeezed tightly. 'I can't,' said Tuesday. It was the most distress I'd seen her demonstrate. 'Breakfast?'

'Breakfast,' I agreed. 'Wagon Wheel?'

'No. I can't bear a public farewell. I'll cook.'

I laughed. 'Salad in a bag?'

'*I'll* cook,' growled April. We all looked at her in fear.

'No, *I'll* cook.' Ruby rescued us. Everyone exhaled.

Tuesday sniffed. 'Ruby, the dishes tonight . . . I can't . . . I go . . .' She hugged me fiercely and fled.

To me April growled, 'Sleep with one eye open,' and departed. The salt trick had worked. I'd howled at her face when the contents of the shaker emptied on to her pie. I tried not to contemplate the repercussions.

'You look after yourself, gel,' Bruce gave me a bear hug. 'No camping next to town hall in LA.' Then he and Ruby followed April inside.

'Don't touch the dishes,' Ruby ordered, as she left. 'They'll be there in the morning.'

That left Samuel and me. We held hands companionably as we walked to the gate. Even broken up, he was one of the best humans I knew.

'I'll miss you,' he said.

'I'll miss you too,' I said. 'But if you don't date Primrose Tarquin after I leave, you're a nincompoop,' I teased, naming Poppy's attractive and single younger sister.

'We'll see.' From his blush, I could tell it was possibly already in the works.

As we approached the adobe wall gateway,

Samuel swung me close, holding my head to his chest and hugging me tight. He kissed the top of my head.

'Be good, Maeve. Believe in your capacity. You're not going to get sick again.'

'Thank you, Samuel.' I held on to his comfort. 'You're the best thing that happened to me here.' Even as I said it, my mind was a cheater.

Something caught my eye in the dark and I fantasized it was Noah's shadow in the door archway. I squinted, but there was nothing.

Samuel cupped my face in his hands. 'It's been a pleasure.'

'I'll stay in touch,' I said, hoping I would.

With an amicable hug, we said goodbye. And if I was weepy when I went to bed, it wasn't because I hadn't had the perfect parting from my friends. I had. It was because of the one that hadn't happened. Noah hadn't come at all.

CHAPTER 26

WHAT YOU TAKE TO A DESERT ISLAND

Takotsubo Cardiomyopathy. A type of non-ischemic cardiomyopathy in which there is a sudden temporary weakening of the myocardium (the muscle of the heart). Because this weakening can be triggered by emotional stress, the condition is also known as broken heart syndrome.

'So you're really going?' he asked.

'No, I thought I'd load all my things into Elsie and then unload them for fun.' I was being glib, but I was afraid if I looked at him I'd break down and cry or beg him to leave Beth or something equally foolish. Plus I was still angry he'd blown off my goingaway dinner. I busied myself arranging things that didn't need arranging.

When I peeked, his face looked grim.

'Well, that's about it.' My brightness was forced as I backed out of the car. That *was* about it. We were packed. Oliver was sulking in his cage. I squashed my guilt over separating him from Lulabell. I'd said goodbye to Tuesday over breakfast. She was too emotional to watch me drive off. The last stop was for my final paycheck. I'd be in LA the day after tomorrow.

Noah crossed his arms. 'Do you know where you're going? You haven't been out of Unknown.'

'I managed to get here, I guess I'll manage to get out.' I hated being snarky, but if he was kind I'd come unstuck. My throat was tight as it was. I'd already bawled once this morning when I realized April had glued my shoes to the floor.

'Why this sudden rush to leave?'

'Elsie's ready, my debts are repaid. Why would I stay?' I didn't know if I was pushing his buttons or if I hoped he'd give me a reason.

'What about The Little Read Picture Book? Forgetting your plans for story time and book events for kids? You were going to be this apostle of literature, and poof, now you've conveniently forgotten all about it. And the Monkey Flower Festival events?'

'It offends you that I'm pursuing my own projects rather than spending all my energy on yours?'

His eyes narrowed. 'That's a load of crap, and you know it. *You* begged *me* for your job.'

'I'm releasing you from the burden of your charity.'

'Are you being deliberately difficult?' He raked a hand through his hair, leaving it in tangled disarray.

'Are you? Buy some more knee socks – you won't even miss me.'

'It's not about me, it's about you! You're always

running. You're going to end up exhausted. What's there in LA for you?'

'What's there for me in this no-stoplight village?'

He flinched. 'And how long before it's off to the next place? Are you capable of settling down?'

My blood pressure spiked. 'Yes, I am!' I yelled. 'But I'm not settling for less. You're a self-absorbed, high-strung prima donna who expects he can drop out of life whenever he wants and have a cadre of women cater to his every whim. I'm not interested in being a water-carrier.'

'At least I finish what I start,' he thundered, hitting my tender spot.

'I *am* finishing what I started. My trip to LA. I'm finishing it *right now*!' I yanked open Elsie's door to climb in.

Before I could, Noah grabbed my shoulders and turned me to face him. His expression was contrite. 'Wait, Maeve. I'm sorry. I'm sorry. I shouldn't have yelled.'

I stepped away from his touch. He noticed. He dropped his hands.

'I'm sorry I missed the party last night. I thought I'd be back from Tucson in time.'

'Oh? Weren't you there?'

'I have something for you.' Abrupt. 'It's the reason I went to Tucson. It wasn't ready, so I had to wait. By the time I stopped by Ruby's last night, it was too late.' He looked off. 'It was always too late.' I frowned, not understanding. When had he come to Ruby's?

'Here.' He handed me a small box. 'You didn't give me much notice.' I opened it. Inside was a chain and round silver locket. Affixed to the front was a miniature silver Paddington Bear, in his duffle coat and hat, holding his suitcase. On the back was etched, *Please look after this bear*. I opened it, and was confused.

'It's microfiche.' Noah explained the negatives inside. 'I had *A Bear Called Paddington* scanned on to microfiche, so if you ever get trapped on that desert island, you'll have it with you.'

My throat closed entirely, my mouth forming a perfect 'O'. This was no match for the sixth kachina I'd hidden on his office shelf among the 'toys'. It was an ascending swirl of birds taking flight, a thing to lift your heart. To me it meant potential, attaining great heights. Noah's heights would not include me, but it meant a lot to know that a part of me remained with him, a potentially undiscovered talisman. But it didn't hold a candle to the talisman he'd just given me.

I struggled to make a sound, and failed. What could I say when all I wanted was for him to grab me, to kiss me. I wanted it badly.

'Maeve . . .' His voice was low, and he reached towards me.

Do it, I willed him. *Just do it. Say it's me you want*. I couldn't take my eyes off his mouth. I could almost feel his lips on mine. I swayed ever so slightly. Then a burst of light caught my eye. We both glanced as Beth's silver BMW pulled onto Main, sunlight flashing off her windshield as she headed south. I remembered their anniversary kiss in front of me in the store. I remembered her cutting words about me playing up to Noah, about his embarrassment. In truth, he'd never acted other than amicably toward me. Anything more was my imagination. Shame and humiliation washed over me. What the hell was I doing? It *wasn't* me that he wanted.

'Take lots of pictures of the Monkey Flower Festival.' I stepped back. I had to get away. Now.

His right eyebrow creased down and his look darkened. '*You* should be taking the pictures.'

'Hollywood calls.' I affected a careless air.

'So this means nothing to you?' Angry voice now, the sweep of his arm encompassing the sleepy town. 'You don't care about Unknown or people here counting on you?'

'Of course I care! But you knew I never intended to stay,' I defended. He wasn't being fair. 'What do you want from me?'

'I want you to tell me why you're leaving.' His dark green eyes penetrated mine.

So I don't die inside when I see you look at Beth with those eyes, I thought. 'Because I'd rather be there than here.' I broke what was left of us with my answer. 'I have to go.'

This time he didn't try to stop me as I clambered into Elsie, blindly jamming the key in the ignition. I accelerated hard, kicking up a cloud of dust that surrounded the man standing in the middle of the road in the rear-view mirror until I was too far away to see. When I was safely out of town, I pulled over, put my head on the steering wheel and sobbed until even Oliver took pity and told me I was a hot fuck.

CHAPTER 27

TIE HALF FULL OR HALF EMPTY?

Stendhal Syndrome. A psychosomatic illness that causes rapid heartbeat, dizziness, stomach pains, confusion and even hallucinations when an individual is exposed to great works of art. Named after a nineteenth-century novelist overwhelmed in Florence. Particularly upsetting are Michelangelo's statue of David, Caravaggio's painting of Bacchus, and the concentric circles of the Duomo cupola.

It wasn't until I was staring directly into the sun that it hit me I was in Los Angeles. The standstill traffic on I-10 should have been a clue, but it was the perfect round ball heading toward the sea that signified my arrival. The jittery feeling I'd had since leaving Unknown abated for the first time, replaced by a blossoming euphoria. And disbelief. How had I, Maeve Connelly, gotten myself this far? I forgot about kachinas and donkey suits and a bookstore blocked from my mind, and sat in wonder. I'd *done* something.

'We're in LA, bud!' I exclaimed to Oliver.

Oliver raised and lowered his crest feather as he considered the endless stretch of taillights. 'Twat,' he pronounced, then burrowed into his Snuggle Hut, where he'd spent most of his time since leaving Lulabell. Unsatisfying response.

I called my mother. 'Guess what I'm looking at?'

'I couldn't possibly know, dear. A cow's butt?'

'A bumper. Lots of them! This one says "I'll never live east of the 405" and "Give Peas a Chance".'

Silence. Then, 'Well, that's just—'

'I'm in LA, Mom! I made it!' I was actually teary.

Silence again. 'I'm so happy for you, Maeve.' Her voice was tender. I waited, aching with my need. She delivered. 'We never doubted you for a minute. Your father and I are so proud. I've always been in awe of your strength.'

Her statement took my breath away. *My* strength?

'But I—'

'Maeve, cancer isn't a punishment. You didn't earn it by bad behavior or inferior ingredients. It was random. It's how you respond that defines you. I'm not talking about how your body responds to treatment. Cameron wasn't a better or a worse person, she was just sicker. I'm talking about your tenacity. I honestly don't know if I could have endured what you did.'

'I don't feel like I've done anything,' I admitted.

'I never knew how to talk about it with you. In some ways your experience has put you beyond me.'

321

She sighed. 'Maeve, you dug deep for resources many of us never need. I thank God every day you had enough. After it was over, perhaps your fields needed to lie fallow for a while. Now it's time to start using all the wealth you possess again.'

'Thanks, Mom.' I blinked back tears, thankful for the standstill traffic.

'If I could give you one gift, Maeve, it would be to see yourself as I see you. And if you could give me one gift, it would be a chunk of George's Clooney's lawn. But don't get arrested.'

I hung up, images of verdant fields, sunny beaches and palm trees swirling in a kaleidoscope of color behind my eyes.

I'd made good time from my Joshua Tree camp. It was four in the afternoon and Laura wasn't expecting me until eight. We'd planned to meet at her place, but I knew she was at work. She'd described an important shoot, and couldn't leave early. She wasn't answering her phone. I decided to head to Fox studios. I was dying to see it, so why wait? I knew she worked in Building 100, so I figured I could track her down. If the shoot was really demanding, maybe I could help. It might make getting a job easier if I could dive right in. My trip had proven that an ability to sell on my feet worked. My mother's words buoyed me with a new kind of confidence.

After consulting my map, I eased off the 10 and headed north on La Cienega, turning left on Pico. I knew I couldn't drive right up – Laura had complained often enough about the hassles of demanding stars trying to park on the lot – but my map-trained eye spotted a public park across the street. The weather was perfect – Oliver would be fine. In the rear-view mirror I glimpsed the box filled with crimson paper flowers Tuesday had given me to decorate my new home, and smiled. It would do nicely.

'I'm sorry, girl, I don' see your name,' the guard apologized. Distracted by the fact that his eyebrows were shaved into lightning bolts, I almost dropped my ruse to ask about them.

'Well hell's bells.' I recovered. 'What'm I supposed to do with five hundred paper flowers?' I find a Southern accent useful from time to time. I blew out my bangs for effect.

'You say Laura Mills? That the gal, with, you know, the *clothes*?'

'Sure is,' I agreed, having no idea. He had two lightning-shaped earrings to match his eyebrows, and his carefully manicured pinkies sported miniature bolts. Man had an identity.

He gave a conspiratorial giggle. 'Lord, I don' know how that girl keep her job. You know what I'm sayin'?' Hunh. I rolled my eyes and shook my box of flowers in response.

'Help me out here, Shazam,' I begged. 'There's a sad luau scene waiting.'

'Shazam! I like that!' He grinned. 'Tell you what. I don' want that girl to lose her job a cause a me.

This ain't the first time she done forgot to send someone's name up.' He tapped his keyboard and a badge spit out of his printer. 'Don' be stealin' no golf carts, hear?'

'Thanks, man.' I stuck the badge on my Rainbows Make Me Happy T-shirt.

'Shazam!' I heard him chuckling as I walked away. 'That good.'

I consulted the map he'd given me. Building 100 was easy to find. I saw that Stage 5 was closer. I decided to try there first. She was likely to be on set.

Stage 5 was an enormous pink stucco building with no windows, stretching half a city block. The street out front was cluttered with haphazardly parked golf carts, a coffee cart, a semitruck stuffed with costumes, and a scattering of trailers. Teamsters, grips and electrics lounged in open equipment truck beds smoking cigarettes. Double doors into the lobby reminded me of a darkroom entrance, devoid of anything but a serious-looking red light bulb to indicate when filming was in progress. I bypassed the lobby in favor of the enormous bay doors beyond, stepping carefully to avoid wires and cables. Shooting must've been on a break, because the doors were open, and people wearing heavier utility belts than cable repairmen scurried about the cavernous space speaking urgently into headsets. Others stood around drinking coffee and grazing a buffet.

I was a little overwhelmed by the frenetic activity

after the slow pace of Unknown, but I shook it off. This was my new life. I observed a moment, then approached a bear of a man more at home as a roadie for Social Distortion than on a Hollywood set His belt had more colored rolls of duct tape, notebooks and tools than the others.

'Hey there,' I chirped.

He broke off talking into his headset and looked at my box of flowers. 'What are those?'

'Um, not sure. I'm supposed to find Laura Mills.'

His confusion increased. 'Laura Mills?'

'She works here?' My certainty wavered. But Shazam had known her. I must've picked the wrong mark. Guy was probably an animal handler.

'Aaron!' he bellowed. 'You know a Laura Mills?'

'Never heard of her,' floated back a reply.

'I think she's that Lola girl,' said a grungy guy in a Queens of the Stone Age T-shirt and low-tops, shoveling a hot dog into his mouth. He wiggled his eyebrows at Bear. 'You know, with the *clothes.*'

Bear's face lightened. 'Ohhhhhh. *That* Laura.' Confusion returned. 'Why would she be ordering anything?' he asked me.

Crap. I didn't want him to take Tuesday's flowers. 'Personal, I think.' I gave my best 'who knows' shrug, tightening my grip on the box.

'Figures,' Bear grumbled. 'Well you won't find her here. She'll be in Building 100.'

'Rock it, Mr Socket.' I was beginning to get a

bad feeling about Laura's illustrious career. I followed the map to Building 100, distracted along the way by signs for *House, Bones, The Simpsons* and *24*. All Fox productions. It occurred to me to wonder why Laura had been driving Katherine Heigl around. Wasn't Heigl's show on ABC? Maybe she was making a movie. I recognized some building signs for 'coming soon' movies. I also convinced myself that Jack Nicholson whizzed by on a golf cart. It probably wasn't true, but it made a better story to tell Vi and Brick later than Any Guy in a baseball cap almost ran over my foot.

Building 100 was a squat white building, identical to Building 101 and Building 102. Its sign proclaimed *Black Angus*. Laura either worked for the show, or served steak. The unattended reception was standard – industrial grey carpeting, unnatural orange sofa and dusty fake aspidistra in the corner. It fed into a horizontal hallway. I could hear activity. My choices were right or left. I hovered. The door opened and a Greek god walked in.

No, really. Colin Cantell had played a Greek god in *Athens*. And here he was, larger than life (at least his chest), three feet away. Sadly not in a toga. I vaguely remembered that he played a detective on a TV show.

'Hi.' He looked harried. I worked on keeping my jaw hinged, and managed a small squawk. He didn't notice. Must happen a lot. He hurried off to the right. Decision made, I followed, keeping a restraining-order-safe distance behind him and wishing I wasn't carrying a box of paper flowers in case I wanted to casually show off my favorite rainbow knee socks.

'Joel!' he called in a surprisingly high-pitched whine. 'I need to talk to you!'

'Oh joy.' The disgruntled answering voice indicated this was not a shared need. 'What now?' Colin Cantell followed the voice, and I almost trailed him right into the producer's office until I realized it and stopped short.

'It's the script. The part where Kate discovers that the stamp on the confession letter is a rare and valuable Mauritius Post Office that leads to the killer.' He named his co-star. 'Angus would already have known that. He's a philatelist.'

There was a long pause. Then, 'A hard-bitten, streetwise detective with a shady mafia past has an expertise in rare stamps?' The tone was weary.

'Uh-huh.'

'See, that's funny. Because I invented your character and I don't remember that.'

'The script needs to be rewritten. All those scenes need to be taken away from Kate and given to Angus. The show is called *Black Angus*.'

'That's because you insisted we change the name from *Two Sense*. As in *two* people.'

'Like on page sixty-seven . . .'

'Hold on. Hold the fuck on. Where's my script? Why the fuck isn't the script ever where it's supposed to be?' His voice became a roar. 'Lola! Lola!'

I stepped out of sight. A second later Laura Mills tottered down the hall looking tense. And looking like Cyndi Lauper and Posh Spice got into a fight and both lost. The tottering was due to bizarre heel-less platform boots, requiring her to balance on the ball of her foot. These accompanied mesh tights and an extremely short pleated kilt. Her smooth coif from the Facebook photos was now a haywire tangle around a peculiar feather ornament, perhaps to match the fingerless gloves. Only the schoolmarm-style white blouse offered relief for the eyes. She didn't notice me as she wobbled into the office. She looked almost green when she wobbled out. If someone had directed that language toward me, I'd be green too. The only non-invective was the word 'intern', which amplified my bad feeling.

The voices in the office dropped to murmurs. I tiptoed after Laura. The hallway drained into a large room filled with desks. Laura was nowhere to be seen.

'Excuse me,' I asked that-guy-who-tries-too-hard-with-the-skinny-tie. 'Did you see where Laura went?'

'Laura-Lola, Fashion Icon?' His signature was sarcasm, naturally.

'That's the one.'

'Copy machine.' He snickered at the paper flowers. 'Those all the flowers you could afford?'

'That all the tie you could afford?' I followed the sound of the copier.

Laura was muttering over the machine, collecting pink sheets as it spit them out. 'White isn't right. Blue is two. Green is no. Pink is go. Or is pink no? Shit. God, please let the final be pink.'

'Hey, Laura,' I ventured.

'For the last time, it's *LOLA*,' she snarled as she turned. Then her mouth dropped open. 'What are *you* doing here?'

'Surprise!' My announcement was weak. 'I got in early.'

A big smile replaced her shocked look, and she gave a theatrical shriek before hugging me, box and all. 'Maeve! Wow! How'd you find me?' She sounded genuinely glad. I relaxed.

'From your emails.'

'Wow,' she repeated. She gave a little hop, then regained her balance. 'You're here! How fun! Yay! We're going to have all *kinds* of—'

'*Scriiiiipt!!!*' A bellow reverberated down the hall. Laura jumped again, different cause.

'Shit. Hang on a sec.' She grabbed the sheaf of pink pages and lurched off. I stayed where I was and studied the chart above the machine that indicated that all final scripts were to be printed on green paper.

Laura returned shortly. Joel was either color blind or just happy to have a script. She led me to an impossibly cluttered desk.

She made a face. 'I have to share with the other in— I mean another staffer.' Her voice dropped. 'She uses oil in her hair so it smells funny. It's not *me*.' She rolled her eyes and returned to normal voice.

'What does a first AD do?' I asked.

Laura looked shifty. 'This and that,' she hedged. 'I won't bore you with details.' Then you could almost see the light bulb pop over her head. She adopted a superior tone. 'So much is *confidential*.' Her voice dropped. I felt like a one-woman audience for the Laura Mills show. 'But I'm *so* outta here. I've got a connection with this new cop drama, *Badge Attitude*. He's totally going to hook me up as soon as the show's picked up. I'll have my own office and everything.' I was pretty sure I heard a snort from Skinny Tie.

Laura seemed to recall the golden halo she'd painted over her current job. 'Not that this place is *bad*. I mean, I've learned *a lot* and I'm *grateful* for that. But I've grown as much as I can here and it's time to move on.' Another snort. I was starting to forgive him. 'I mean *really*, a tough male/strait-laced female crime-solving duo? It's sooooo formulaic.' I had the feeling she was repeating a conversation she'd overheard on the parking shuttle, and couldn't define formulaic if asked. '*Badge Attitude* is totally going to be groundbreaking. They're tough cops, but they don't have guns. Just *badges* and *attitudes*.' She opened her eyes really wide at me.

330

'Oh,' I said. A tiny frown appeared. '*Amazing.*' I ramped it up. She smiled, satisfied.

'It's gonna be *awesome*. Hey.' She frowned again. 'How'd you get in here?' She wasn't interested in the months it took me to get to Los Angeles, just my presence in her building.

'I charmed the guard at the front gate.' I was smug.

She wrinkled her nose. 'The weirdo with the eyebrows? He's serial killer creepy.' I was silent. Her interest reverted back to Laura. 'But if you got past him, you might be useful at some clubs . . .' She tapped her teeth, thoughtful.

'Where's the intern?' a female voice called from an office somewhere out of sight. 'Colin needs a ride back to Stage 16. And I need my dry-cleaning before six.'

Laura gave an exaggerated sigh and addressed me in a martyred tone. 'Oh, *I'll* do it. Colin and I are *so* close. He won't *say* it, but he prefers me to drive him.' She flipped what hair wasn't occupied strangling her head feather. 'Then I've really got to focus on *my* work.' A little laugh. 'So much to do! I'll see you tonight around nine?' It was a dismissal.

'Sure. Is there a trick with the keys or an alarm or anything?'

'Keys?'

'To the house?'

'I need the keys so I can drive home, silly.' Her tone was impatient.

'You could separate the house key,' I pointed out. 'I'll wait there.'

'Hmm, yeah . . . I suppose. Listen, there's a café near my place called the Sidewalk Café. They'll let you sit there for hours. They don't mind. I'll call when I'm on my way home, 'kay?' She bounced up, dispatch complete. 'See ya.' Twiddled fingers, teetering walk.

I watched her wobbly departure, trying to check my disbelief. My excitement about LA threatened to come crashing down. A miniature, weepy me was inside my head somewhere, curled up in a ball, homesick for Unknown and— but I shut her down. That girl was pathetic. This one wasn't. I pulled myself up, clutching my box.

As I passed Skinny Tie, I paused. 'Can you define formulaic?'

'Adjective. An idea the nature of which is expressed in an unoriginal concept wholly reliant on previous models.'

'That tie's not so bad,' I said.

He smiled. 'Would you like to watch them film the show for a bit?'

I smiled back. 'An answer in the affirmative. A positive response. Assent.'

Twenty minutes later I was settled discreetly out of the way in a director's chair, clutching the 'sides', which was a collection of the script pages they'd be shooting that day. I'd read it twice. Detective Angus was confronting the Chief. I frowned as I read.

Chief: Damn it, Angus! If you're gonna keep breaking the rules, then I'm gonna have to put you behind bars with the rest of the trash.

Angus: It was a good collar and you know it. It may not be our serial killer, but he was scum nonetheless. The streets are safer now.

Chief: I can't have a rogue detective.

Angus: The only thing rogue around here is the idea that you can solve this case without me!

Chief: I've been solving cases without you since before you were born.

Angus: This time it's different. This time it's personal. This time you need a man with a badge and the mind of a killer. A man who knows the rules, breaks the rules, and doesn't look back at the pieces. Only a man like me is going to catch the Butterfly Killer.

Chief: Now he's the 'Butterfly Killer'?

Angus: He signs his victims 'Dragonfly' . . . but calling him 'Butterfly' is gonna piss him off . . . make him sloppy. He makes one mistake, I'll be waiting.

Skinny Tie, whose name was actually Clark, handed me a headset. 'You need this comtech to hear the actors.'

'I'm having trouble with the formulaic concept,' I said. 'Can you give me an example?'

'Don't judge. Before this I worked on *Passions*.'

'I handed out burrito leaflets dressed as a donkey,' I conceded. 'Clark? What's a first AD?'

'An assistant director. She preps the episode, oversees the shooting schedule, and runs the set, coordinating cast and crew. She's the director's right hand.' He pointed to a pretty blonde with a walkie-talkie, a crowd around her, and the biggest tool belt of all. 'Nina's our first AD. She basically busts everyone's balls.'

I must have looked confused, because he winked and said, 'In some cases, as it applies to *interns*, for example, it can mean Abysmally Dim.'

'Actuality Deficit?' I grinned.

'Absolute Diarrhea,' he agreed. 'Speaking of, I'd better get back, or Appalling Disaster will mix Wite-Out with toner ink and blow up the office. Joel would be displeased.' He patted my shoulder. 'She's not a bad egg. She merely occupies a . . . unique state of reality.' He handed me a card. 'If you need anything.'

My vision of waltzing on to the lot and heroically pulling the Nikon lens free from the legendary stone in which it was embedded, fulfilling the prophecy to become the Chosen Image Taker, was ludicrous. Los Angeles wasn't Unknown. If I took a candy bar from the cafeteria and promised to pay another day, I'd be hauled off in cuffs. I wouldn't be talking my way into a job here.

'Thanks, Clark. You'll be able to afford the whole tie someday.'

'Elvis Costello spurns you.' He left with a wave.

I slipped on the comtech and settled in to admire

Colin Cantell's chest. It heaved with intensity as he declared, 'Oh, I'll deliver. And it won't be pepperoni pizza!' I winced.

After the scene was done, the director called, 'Cut,' and the crew jumped. Chairs were returned to their starting position, extras reversed their steps, picture frames swept off the desk in righteous anger were righted, and hair and makeup people swarmed Colin Cantell. Three minutes and the scene was completely reset. Two more, and the director called, 'Action.' Colin Cantell strode into the Chief's office for take two.

'What's your damage, Chief?'

'Cut!' called the actor playing the Chief. 'That's not the line, Colin.'

The director sighed. 'Warren!'

I clamped my mouth shut to keep from saying the line. This was not challenging dialogue. Presumably Warren's voice called: 'What's this I hear about that cockroach going free?'

'Right!' Colin's face lightened. He ambled back to his starting position. We began again.

They got to the third line before a voice cut across the comtech. 'I've got static.'

'Cut!' shouted the director. A sound guy darted out and fiddled with a line threaded down the Chief's shirt. The actors discussed preseason football. It wasn't interesting.

Next take, they didn't make it through the first line before the cinematographer said, 'I see cables in the lower right frame.'

'Cut!' shouted the AD. Someone removed the offending cables.

On take seven there was a loud clattering offstage as some unlucky person tripped over what sounded like a tower of pots and pans. I could almost see steam coming out of the director's ears. The AD shouted, 'NO MOVEMENT ON THE STAGE!' I'd been considering sneaking out. I changed my mind.

According to the guy clapping the slate, shouting, 'Scene twenty, take eleven' (mildly satisfying), they did fifteen takes (unsatisfying). After an eternity, the director announced, 'We got it.' I was anxious to see the female co-star, in the next scene. The crew scurried, moving cameras and shifting cables. I wished I had something to read. After twenty minutes, the AD called, 'First team!' To my astonishment, Colin and the Chief resumed their positions.

'I thought we were done?' I whispered to a hair person.

'We're done with the establishing shot. We still have the medium shots, the close shots, and the extreme close-ups of Colin.' His tone was bored.

'For the same scene?' That could be over forty repeats.

'Different camera, lighting and sound positioning for each.'

'How long will it take?'

He shrugged. 'Depends on Colin getting his lines right, the equipment working and the director being happy.' His eyes never left his iPhone. 'I'd settle in.'

I did, wondering if Clark had been getting me back for the tie thing after all.

CHAPTER 28

WELCOME TO YOUR WATER STAIN

Narcolepsy. A neurological condition most characterized by Excessive Daytime Sleepiness (EDS), in which a person experiences extreme tiredness, possibly culminating in falling asleep during the day at inappropriate times, such as at work or school or public places.

I t was 9.30 when Laura found me drooping into my tea. Waiters had begun to give me the side eye. I'd dozed off several times, like in math class, starting back awake. I'd left *Black Angus* after two tedious hours, not getting close to the next scene. Filming was *not* what I'd envisioned. A Monopoly tournament was more gripping. Cooling my heels at the Sidewalk Café waiting for Laura was no thrill ride either. I'd drunk endless cups of herbal tea, wearing the carpet thin to the bathroom. I was desperate to put my head down somewhere designed for sleep. I missed Oliver, silent treatment and all.

Laura looked frazzled. It might have been the head feather, though.

'What a day!' She plopped down. 'You're lucky, you've been kicking back.'

I blinked at her. I'd gotten up at six to break camp. 'Let's go lay like vegetables on the couch.' I voiced my wish. The idea was heaven on earth.

'Hmmm? Yeah, for a minute. Minka's coming at ten.'

'Minka?'

She looked at her watch. 'Oh Gawd! I barely have time to change!' She jumped up.

'Change?' I left a generous tip to redeem squatting. Laura was halfway out the door.

'I can't wear this, silly!' She smiled over her shoulder, as if I'd said something hilarious.

'Wear that where?' I trailed after her.

'It's Wednesday!' She looked at me with her big eyes. I struggled to recall the import of Wednesdays. She looked disappointed. ' Wednesdays are Buffalo Club.'

'A club?' My mind struggled. I was dead on my feet. Laura kept up a good clip. 'Wait . . . my car,' I remembered.

'We'll get it tomorrow.' She didn't pause.

'But I have to get Oliver.'

'Oliver?' That stopped her.

'My bird,' I reminded her.

'You brought your bird?'

I frowned. 'Of course. What else would I do with him?'

'Oh. I dunno. Leave it or give it away.' My mouth dropped open. She registered it. 'OK, OK, we'll get your car.' She followed me to where I was parked, muttering, 'Minka's gonna be pissed if I'm not ready . . .'

We drove down an alley in Venice Beach and parked by a dilapidated entrance to a more dilapidated unit in a dirty stucco building. It didn't look promising. Laura hurried in and disappeared into another room. I would learn it was 'the' other room. The apartment was filthy. A biscuit-sized living room held a battered mustard sofa, an ancient TV with tinfoil-encased rabbit ears sitting on a cement block, and a scarred coffee table piled high with *Us Weekly, Star*, OK*!* and *In Touch* magazines. April would have loved it. I couldn't blame Laura for the volcanoes of clothing and pizza boxes everywhere, because they obscured the dismal putty-colored carpeting. The adjacent kitchen was stocked with appliances from 1952. I could cross both rooms in eight strides. I peeked through the only doorway to see Laura's back half sticking out of a closet in an even smaller bedroom. I looked back at the sofa and decided I was going to become quite acquainted with the water stain on the ceiling above it. I hoped the pile of books replacing the missing leg would hold. I recalled the 'awesome beachfront pad' from Facebook. The depths of Laura's imagination were becoming apparent. I blocked an image of Ruby's downy bedspread. This wouldn't be for long.

I returned after retrieving Oliver and my suitcase from the car to find Laura decked out in a tulle-swathed costume rejected by *Swan Lake* but embraced by Björk. She was considering an array of gaudy beads when an equally exquisite vision pranced in. Her dress looked like a belted garbage bag designed by Spock, but a garbage bag would have been longer.

'Oooh, I *love* the turquoise belt,' Laura squealed.

'Those pink go-go boots are *darling*.' The Minka creature stuck to script. Formulaic was a good word to know in Los Angeles. 'It's soooo *Lola*! Perez Hilton is gonna love them!'

'Do you think so?' Laura squealed again. Oliver squawked in protest. This brought their attention to me. Silence fell. 'You can't wear that.' Laura spoke first.

'Oh.' I regarded my perfectly normal jeans and T-shirt. Then saw my easy out. 'I *know*. I'm *soooo bummed*. Everything I have is all packed and wrinkled. I *can't* go like *this*.' My formula was Devastated Martyr. I suspected it was a personal favorite of Laura's. 'You guys go ahead. I'll be OK.' Big sigh. Sad face.

'You could wear something of mine,' Laura offered reluctantly. I panicked.

'That's so sweet! But you're such a pencil! I'd never fit!' Her expression approved my words. 'Really – you guys go. I'll be ready next week!'

'Next week?' Minka giggled. 'Tomorrow is Villa!' With that and twiddled fingers they were gone and I was left with blessed calm. I was so happy to be alone I didn't mind the musty apartment.

341

I opened the fridge and found a sad jar of expired mayonnaise, some withered carrot sticks and half a lemon. Instead of stacks of frozen pizza, the freezer held a dozen Lion bars, two bottles of vodka and the aura of an eating disorder.

I took a Lion bar. Laura hadn't given me a key, so a food foray was out. I gave Oliver a wilted carrot.

'At least we can get some sleep,' I said.

'Fuck me.' He turned his beak up at the limp vegetable. Too tired to argue, I shook out my sleeping bag. I didn't want direct contact with the couch. I tried not to think about mold spores. I was digging for my sweats when my fingers brushed something familiar. A wave washed over me. My hand jumped to my sweats and I began to chatter.

'We're Los Angelinos now, Oliver. I'm going to have to get you some shades. Ray-vian Bans maybe? Guess I have to change my name to something hipper. What do you think? Mimosa? Sparkle Snowflake?' I stopped babbling long enough to brush my teeth in the pocket-sized bathroom. 'I think I can touch both walls with my elbows,' I called to Oliver.

I returned to the living room and settled on the sofa. I flipped through a magazine but couldn't generate interest in singing brothers or emaciated actresses. My eyes strayed to my pack. I tried the magazine again. I was wrong every time I guessed which celebrity wore the same dress better. I gave up. I rooted in my pack, and gently withdrew the story. *My* story. I curled against the cushions, already soothed as I started to read about a girl who loved to climb trees.

CHAPTER 29

AT THE WATERCOOLER

Coprolalia. An involuntary swearing or utterance of obscene words or socially inappropriate and derogatory remarks. Coprolalia encompasses words and phrases that are culturally taboo or generally unsuitable for acceptable social use, when used out of context.

Within two weeks, life in LA had settled into a pattern. Naturally, the studio job offers that Laura had promised would fall like golden rain never materialized. After a few conversations that felt like trying to capture mist in a box, I gave up pressing her. Clark set me straight. No past experience, no rich uncle, no dice. He'd keep an eye out, but I wasn't hopeful.

Unworried, I'd hit Main Street, starting with the Italian restaurant closest to Laura's place. You could always get a job waiting tables. Except, apparently, in LA. The manager coolly informed me that the shortest-timer on their staff had been with them fifteen years. At Enterprise Fish Co.

they asked for my résumé. After I created one at the public library, fluffing up my donkey-suit leaflet-passing into 'food service manager of public relations', I was informed that they could not consider any candidate lacking experience in a Zagat-rated establishment. The manager at Urth Café directed me to a central screening agency. Zanzibar required a bartending school certificate. Even the Coffee Bean had a waiting list. In a town teeming with aspiring actors, service jobs were gold. I wandered into a trendy clothing store, but left without a word after intercepting the clerk's disapproving appraisal.

Surprisingly, Laura was unconcerned. 'Don't sweat it,' she said. 'It took me a while too.' Living with her wasn't terrible, though the outfits were hard on the eyes. For a while, she and Minka dragged me around the party circuit, where we were invariably turned away from the first venue we attempted, ending up in the back corner of a second-choice joint, with Minka and Laura whispering how much better it was than the first, which was generally agreed to be 'last season', 'pretentious' and 'beastly hot'. They didn't look at each other when they talked, heads on constant swivel for celebrities, of which there were none (presumably enjoying the beastly hot, pretentious venue that wouldn't let us in). I mostly sat mute until I could beg off and go home. Occasionally some fellow would offer to buy me a drink, driving Laura mad when I declined. I wasn't up for forced conversation or dating. After a while, Laura stopped protesting when I elected to stay in, and I spent most of my nights reading or watching movies.

In the mornings I would feign sleep while Laura pulled herself together for work. Because she overslept and Red Bull was an easy breakfast to prepare, it passed quickly, and she was gone in a tacky whirlwind. Then I would rise, release Oliver, and start my day of rejection at local restaurants and cafés. When I spiraled into the inevitable panic, I would stave off hyperventilation by going for longer and longer runs.

The marathon was going to be a snap. It was pretty along the boardwalk, but unchanging. The sky was blue, the sun shone, the sand was white and the waves rolled. Even the boardwalk characters were predictable: the roller-skating electric-guitar player, the bodybuilder in the red, white and blue thong, the bowler-hat-wearing mime, the Jamaican tumbling crew, the man with no legs and only one arm scooting himself along on a skateboard. We'd nod in recognition as we passed, day after day, the same except my socks. In Unknown, the meadows were constantly changing. One day full of butterflies and varied buntings floating through still air, the next a frenzy of breeze-whipped grasses or surprising new blooms.

The only variation in the California scenery was whether I ran north towards Malibu or south towards Manhattan Beach. Either way, I clocked the end of my run by the same landmarks – the giant predator metal statue, the pizza-by-the-slice sign, the cluster of smokers outside the community center, the hookah café. I would slow to a walk in front of my favorite tattoo parlor, Do You Tattoo, and study the tattoos through the window, feeling further from permanence than ever, a dandelion fluff with no home, no job, no tattoo. If I ran and never stopped, it wouldn't matter to anyone but Oliver. I considered getting a tattoo of Oliver but discarded the idea as pathetic, like the old lady with a hundred cats.

'You can't get a tattoo through the glass.' A voice made me jump one day.

'Christ! You scared me!' I accused. The speaker was a tattoo-covered Mr Clean in a sleeveless Hannah Montana T-shirt – intricately inked designs on his bulging forearms a stark contrast to the tween queen.

He shrugged. 'No scarier than watching you lurk outside every morning.' He looked at his watch. 'I'm guessing about sixteen to eighteen miles today?' My mouth dropped open. He laughed, and tapped the window. 'It's glass. You can see in, we can see out.'

In my solitude, I sometimes forgot I was visible.

'C'mon in. I'll make tea.'

I followed him. The shop was empty but for a Gothic-pale skinny man in black jeans and a black T-shirt with a Lite-Brite skull on it. He squealed when he looked up. 'The little chicken came in!'

'Be nice, Jacob,' Mr Clean said. To me, he said, 'This is Jacob. I'm Marion.'

'Maeve,' I said. 'Are you hiring?'

'Nope. But there's no charge for hanging out.' And just like that my routine expanded to include Marion and Jacob. I still had no job, but now I had something to do in the afternoons, drinking tea and pestering them to let me try my hand at tattooing.

Friday night I was stir crazy, so I joined Laura and Minka, preferring their chatter to isolation. We were at a dive called the Dime, having been turned away from Hyde (again). I was at the bar buying drinks for Laura and Minka, who were swiveling and whispering in the corner. Despite my dwindling reserves, I bought a lot of drinks. Freeloader's guilt. It also let me escape from the minutiae of revisiting every word expelled by gossip blogger Perez Hilton, Laura's personal barometer for where to go (and be turned away), what to wear (clearly misinterpreted), and who to stalk (Score: Laura – o; celebrities – infinity). Laura was one step away from posting a grainy online sex video taken during a DUI arrest in her efforts to become a celebrity.

'Did you invite all these people? I thought it was going to be just the two of us,' a voice said. I turned to face an attractive blond man.

'Did the voices in your head tell you to come and talk to me?'

'My friend over there sent me. He wants to know if you think I'm cute.' He grinned.

I did. His roguish smile was appealing. I didn't think too hard about why I liked it, of whom he reminded me. I decided to work on my people skills. 'Maeve.' I stuck out a hand. His smile widened.

'Bill.' His touch was lingering.

'So, Bill, are you somebody?' I leaned on the bar facing him.

He laughed, blue eyes bright. 'I'm an accountant.' There went my stereotypes about accountants. 'And you?'

'Female impersonator.'

He laughed again. 'I'd say you're *definitely* somebody.'

'New in town,' I said. 'The possibilities are endless.'

He settled himself more comfortably against the bar. 'I'm all ears.'

Where to begin? 'I'm sort of on a trip of self-discovery,' I said. 'It figures that the year I decide to pack up all my stuff and my bird and drive across country to change my life, the nation would be in the middle of the worst gas crisis I've known since an illchosen entrée at Chi-Chi's, but what can you do? I've always had rotten luck. See, I had cancer in college, and I sort of froze, you know? Just when I was finding my independence and growing up, wham! Perpetual adolescence. Other people did all my thinking and I showed up on time. Kind of like a stereotypical 1950s housewife – smile at everyone, do what you're told, worry about nuclear annihilation, buy Forever Fuchsia lip-gloss from the Avon lady. Except for the Avon lady. Makeup on a cancer patient looks as garish as earrings on a monkey. Obviously I made *some* decisions. Like what movies to rent – anything with Julia Roberts, I don't know why, but I always liked Julia Roberts . . . and that hot Tom Cavanagh who used to be on that show *Ed* – or not to buy the red Guess peeptoes even though I really liked them because they were narrow width and those never stretch.' I was word-vomiting, and Bill's smile was long gone. I tried to reclaim my point. 'But I didn't make any decisions about my future. I mean, if you might not have one, what's the point? Better living through denial, I always say! I try to have a positive attitude about my destructive habits.' The words spewed faster, tripping over each other as they poured out of my mouth. 'So I just floated along, everyone's favorite medical pincushion, and then wham again – that's a lot of whams! – I was twenty-six and hadn't made a single choice about what to do with my life. And I need to because I'm totally healthy . . . I mean, healthy like a normal person, I get coughs and colds of course . . . but anyway, I have to do something. So I drove across country in Elsie – that's my car – do you like old cars? I like old cars. Elsie's a 1978 Plymouth Road Runner . . . with the stripes . . .

350

And I love the desert . . . and . . . am I rambling? I'm rambling. So here I am . . . ready for adventure . . . a new LA girl.' I smiled brightly. 'Maeve Somebody, work in progress.'

Bill had straightened, looking past me towards his buddies, alarm stamped on his face. I'd misstepped.

'So, who is Bill Somebody?' I tried. 'Did you ever want to be a lion tamer?'

It was a no-go. 'Hey, listen, I'm really sorry about the cancer,' he said, like apologizing for dirty dishes in the sink. 'But you look great now! Um, that's my buddy waving. I'd better get back. Have a great night!' With a cheery wave and a fake smile, he stepped away faster than you could say 'contagious', leaving only the memory of an attraction.

I ducked into the bathroom. I rested my forehead on the mirror, cheeks burning. Idiot. He didn't want to hear about cancer. No one did. It was like being an ex-felon. If you didn't tell, you were lying by omission, but if you did tell, you freaked people out. Where was the balance? And why the hell didn't I know it by now?

I called Vi.

'It's two a.m.,' she mumbled.

'Shit, sorry. I forgot the time difference.'

'Where are you?'

'In the bathroom at a bar.'

'Tell me.'

I did.

'I'm proud of you,' she said. 'It's a big step.'

351

'He ran faster than drug-store pantyhose,' I protested.

'Forget about him. He's some guy in a bar. What's important is that you shared.'

'But . . .'

'It was the first time. Of course you overdid it. It's like a first date after a break-up. It's a cardinal rule that you don't talk about your ex, but it's all you can think about, and you're word-vomiting before you know it. Then you never hear from the guy again. Everyone does it. The problem isn't the sharing. The problem is being emotionally slutty – too much, too soon. It's no different from sex, really. You have to figure out when the time is right.'

'So you're saying I shouldn't have given Bill an emotional blow-job during our first conversation?' I was feeling better.

She laughed. 'I'm not a hundred percent sure about cancer chats around the water cooler. You may have to defuse some kinds of assumptions. Ease into it. Telling someone you're a survivor, or that you detest broth because you overdosed during treatment is first-base kind of stuff. Busting out with your struggle to come to terms with a fear of death is more home-plate material.'

When I returned from the bathroom, Bill was chatting up a pretty brunette. I heard her saying, '. . . so I said, "My house is right up the road," and just like that the whole band packed up and we headed to my place at three in the morning for quesadillas and late-night dance party . . .'

Sounded to me like she was telling a third-base-level story, but Bill was listening avidly. The rules were different for funny stories, apparently. I sighed. There was a lot to learn about this communication business. No wondered I'd avoided it for so long.

'It was a disaster,' I moaned. 'Can you tattoo a verbal diarrhea shock collar on to a person? Otherwise I'll never meet Mr Right.'

'I read something once that said love isn't about finding the right person, but about finding the right wrong person.' Marion was concentrating on the design he was drawing.

'Is this the beginning of an Abbott and Costello routine?'

'Why don't you listen instead of talking for a change and you might learn something.'

I listened.

'The idea is, we're all different flavors of wrong . . .'

'Can I be Rainbow Sherbet Wrong?' I giggled.

'I want to be Triple Pistachio Wrong,' Jacob called from his perch near the cash register. Marion pinned us each with the look the real Mr Clean gave shower scum. I shut up in a hurry. The shower scum always lost.

'Cranky Monkey Wrong is your flavor,' Jacob muttered. I suppressed my smile. Marion returned to his drawing and his story.

I couldn't resist. 'I think that line should be curvier.'

Marion ignored my brilliance and said, 'By the time we're mature enough to have a relationship, it's because we're all a little wrong. We've done some livin', got our quirks and issues and know what they are. That's essential for a real connection. If you haven't faced up to your crap, you don't know yourself. If you don't know yourself, you don't know what works with you. It's when you've figured out *how* you're wrong that you can best find a mate who complements that.'

'I thought you were supposed to end up with the person who thinks you're perfect.'

'Sounds exhausting and impossible to me. Can't change what you are, and you can't go back to who you were before life stamped some problems on you. It's like a tattoo – once you got it, you got it. Even if you remove it, there's a different kind of mark.'

'Know thy scars?' I was intrigued.

'Doesn't that sound better than trying to undo what's done?'

'So we're looking for someone who fits nicely against our unsolvable problems?'

'Zactly. I got a cadre of persistent demons who like the real estate in my brain and plan to stay. If I ignore them,' a look at me, 'then I don't know my true shape . . .'

'Try barrel-shaped, with an accent of pear,' Jacob called.

'. . . and I can't find the wrong shape that fits with me. Though if I look for a string-bean-shaped num-num-head in a tiresome eighties Goth T-shirt, I might be close.'

It made sense to me. I was pretty wrong. It was easier to contemplate working with my flaws than trying to magically become perfect. The thought felt like a band releasing. 'I'm looking for Mr Wrong.'

'Not just any Mr Wrong. The one you look at with love and think, "This is the problem I want to have for the rest of my life, that I want to be my first and last problem of every day."'

'I'm touched,' Jacob said. 'And I mean that in a very salt-touching-my-open-wound kind of way.'

'I suppose the problem I want to live with for the rest of my life will be a little more compli-cated than not being able to find the remote,' I conceded.

Marion shot an affectionate look toward Jacob. 'I'll say.'

'Hey, Marion. Who's on first?'

'What?'

'Gotcha.' Heh.

Marion and I were wandering around Costco when it happened. I'd begged him to take me along. I loved Costco. You could dine on a buffet of samples, and return home with giant blocks of cheese, tubs of spinach dip and supersized vitamin bottles. Marion had been lured into the clothing section by a giant pack-o-undies. I didn't want the visual of Marion in his underwear, so I wandered to the

355

vitamins. I was out of flax oil, vitamin B and dandelion root. I'd gotten slack on my regimen in Unknown. My health seemed to be holding just fine, but I thought I'd replenish. Laura's apartment was a breeding ground if I ever saw one.

I rounded the aisle, and froze. In front of vitamin C bottles bigger than my head stood a fragile creature, scarf poorly concealing her baldness. She was probably in her late thirties, arms folded to her chest like useless baby bird wings. I fought an urge to bolt.

The woman had the vulnerability of a newborn – a flightless baby bird. It's the perception of cradling yourself. She was rubbing her clavicle. Her port, probably. I took in her careful movements, her pallor, her fatigue. I guessed today was treatment day, and she'd steeled herself to stop on the way home to collect what she needed before losing all her remaining energy. I'd never had to do that alone.

I walked up.

'I like the Nature Made.' I nodded toward the vitamin C. 'It bothers me less when I take it on an empty stomach.'

She looked up, too tired to be surprised.

I smiled. 'Today's Thursday, huh?'

Comprehension flashed. I was a member of the club. 'You?' she asked.

'A long time ago.' I raised my hands and smiled, shrugging. 'I got better.' I wasn't sure how she'd react.

She nodded. 'I'm glad.'

I put my hand on her shoulder and gave a little squeeze. 'Can I help you?'

She nodded again. I knew that exhaustion. I took her basket, and said, 'I'm Maeve.' And it was true. Not Old Maeve or New Maeve. Just one Maeve, as wrong as she was.

CHAPTER 30

HILTON LOWS TO LOEWS HIGH

Charles Bonnet Syndrome (CBS). A syndrome characterized by visual hallucinations, defined as 'persistent or recurrent visual pseudohallucinatory phenomena of a pleasant or neutral nature in a clear state of consciousness'. CBS patients most often report seeing people, animals, buildings and scenery that are not there. Subjects may react positively or negatively to their visual hallucinations.

I was irritable as I jogged back to Laura-Lola's (as I now thought of her) place. My run had been very unsatisfactory. My heart had jerked alarmingly no fewer than three times, adrenaline shooting through my system as the corner of my eye saw one man with a back identical to Noah's working out on the rings, another with Noah's stride crossing the boardwalk to the Waterfront Café, and a third pulling Noah's truck into the Reed and Ocean parking lot. I'd never gotten into a rhythm, distracted by fool's gold sightings and the irregular heartbeats they prompted.

'This is ridiculous,' I cursed, blowing out my bangs. 'Why am I obsessing about someone six hundred miles away who drives me mad?' It'd been over a month. I tried to recapture the outrage I'd felt pulling out of Unknown, but it eluded me. I couldn't even remember the reason I'd been angry, which, of course, made me angry. I'd worked myself into an excellent state by the time I walked in the door.

Laura-Lola, it seemed, had too. Hers appeared to be one of exuberance. She was hopping excitedly around the living room to Britney Spears, which meant she was in her Happy Place.

'What's up, duck?' I asked her curiously, forcing the Grouch back into his trashcan.

She squealed excitedly. 'You're not going to believe it!' Oliver chirped irritably at Laura-Lola's decibel level. Or in protest to Britney. Who knew? Laura-Lola didn't speak bird so she sailed past the insult, working in an extra happy hop to her 'I'm a Slave' dance.

Hope flared briefly. Had she managed to get me a job? Her next words, and my recollection that Laura-Lola never did anything that didn't directly benefit Laura-Lola, squelched such fancy.

'I just found out that Perez Hilton is going to be at the Lisa Kline spring-line launch party tonight at her store on Robinson, *and I'm going to be there too!* Minka got on the list through her uncle!' She beamed at me expectantly. Minka's real name was Miriam.

'Oh.' I struggled for a response. Laura-Lola's brow began knitting together. '*Wow.*' I upped my tone.

'*I know*!' Good humor restored, her pitch elicited another avian rebuke. 'Gawd, it's *so excitin'*.' Her detested Texas twang sneaked out when she was too overwrought to adopt her Gwyn-nthiation, as I dubbed her affected pronunciations. 'It's gonna be *perfect*.' She clapped her hands. 'I need your help, Maeve. You're good with style.' Her lips involuntarily twitched downward before she recovered them. It was wrong in Laura-Lola's eyes that people complimented my style over her (garish) selections. I was a hick from North Carolina who hadn't bought a thing on Robinson *or* Melrose. It affronted her devout commitment to the church of LA. Apparently self-interest overcame injustice. 'My outfit has to be *perfect*. Sexy and stylish. We'll use my clothes, of course, but you can tell me what you think. Something attention-getting, yet . . . classy.'

I surveyed the assorted litter of feather boas, fishnet stockings, vinyl miniskirts and platform shoes. Classy wasn't what leapt to mind. Clothes were strewn everywhere, including an eyelet sweater draped over Oliver's cage that he was happily pulling apart. My bed was barely visible under a pile of garments in season-inappropriate colors, reminding me that it wasn't my bed, but

360

her futon, and I needed to make Laura-Lola happy.

'Sure.' I slid over to Oliver's cage, casually lifting away the sweater. Oliver squawked in indignation. Laura-Lola was thankfully oblivious.

'Maeve, this is it. I know Perez and I are meant to be.' She sighed, her eyes in a far-off place I hadn't seen since she'd been on hold with KROQ to win front-row concert tickets to Justin Timberlake. I'd had to leave the house when she'd found out she wasn't the fifteenth caller. We'd bought a new phone at Costco the next day. 'Once we meet, Perez will instantly recognize the depth of our connection. It's going to be beautiful.'

I boggled over Laura-Lola's disconnect with reality. Perez Hilton was so openly gay that Elton John was jealous. 'You're talking about Perez Hilton, the *Queen* of Media,' I explored. It's true. Even I read his blog.

'Yes. He is so *insightful* about celebrities and how they really feel. He only insults the ones who are shallow and mean or on drugs. And he helps a lot of people. He features undiscovered bands on his website all the time. And they get popular, because so many people listen to Perez.' She was earnest.

'Mmm-hmm. Doesn't he out a lot of gay actors as well? I think he's pretty friendly with Lance Bass.' I tried a more direct tack.

'He's committed to honesty in the industry.' Laura-Lola sounded reverent. Perez was her Obama.

Recognizing that I wasn't getting anywhere with reality, I wavered between begging to go with her to see the comedy unfold, and trying to get her dressed and out the door as soon as possible so I could settle down to the Food Network. I settled for the latter.

'Let's get you ready, Betty. You've got a big night out.' I scanned the floor.

'Oh, yeah, about that,' Laura-Lola said, without any real concern. 'You need to find someplace else to crash tonight. I don't know Perez's situation so we could end up coming back here.'

I boggled again. 'Are you serious?'

She frowned. 'Of course I'm serious. It's *my* house, isn't it?

'House' was a stretch. But even on the dangerous fringes of her temper, I couldn't help arguing, driven by a balloon of panic.

'I've got nowhere to go.' Desperation tinged my tone.

'Can't you go visit Madelynn or whoever?' Her tone was uninterested as she sifted through a pile of clothes.

'It's Marion, and I can't just show up asking to stay!'

'Why not?' She threw over her shoulder the genuinely surprised look of the sublimely selfish. In Laura-Lola's world, everything revolves around her, so supporting actors like Marion don't spring to life until she enters their space, ergo they should be happy, no, *grateful* if she turns up demanding service. Unfortunately, it didn't work that way in Maeve's world.

'Laura, Perez Hilton is gay,' I yelled.

Laura-Lola's back to me froze. Slowly she turned, face like a raptor.

'My . . . name . . . is . . . *Lola*,' she pinched out. 'And I would expect better from you than petty jealousy and character slurs, Maeve. Perez is a catch admittedly out of your league, but there is no need to cast aspirations on his character.'

I swallowed a hysterical giggle blending disbelief over her delusions, laughter at her malapropism and panic over where I'd spend the night.

'Lola, I'm sorry. But please. I have nowhere to go. I'll sleep in the bathtub!' I begged.

'I think you should leave now. I'll dress myself. I won't expect you back tonight. In fact, since you can't be nice about Perez, I think you need to leave your key. There's no telling how long he'll stay and I can't risk you being rude to him tomorrow. You can come back tomorrow night. I'll leave an update on the door. If Perez is still here, I expect you to act with civility. He's going to be my boyfriend after all, so you'll have to learn to get along.' She gave me a 'steely and strong' look stolen from your pick of Jodie Foster movies.

'Road trip, don't forget the bird,' said Oliver, the tension in the room making him anxious. My personal alarm multiplied when I thought about my bird.

Laura-Lola sensed my near hysteria and rolled her

eyes. 'Oliver can stay.' She gave a let's-be-pals-again half-laugh. 'Don't worry about your bird. I kind of like him. He's always telling me I look thinner.'

'Are you thinner?' Oliver dutifully mimicked, and Laura-Lola laughed.

My agitation subsided. I silently thanked Oliver for his uncanny ability to say the right thing. His well-being was paramount. Since I'd left Unknown, he was the only family I had. Wait . . . I shook myself. I didn't have *family* in Unknown. What a weird thought. *Anyway*, Oliver's safety being settled, my temporary homelessness didn't seem like that big a deal. I didn't want to push it with Laura-Lola. The truth was she was letting me stay even though I wasn't yet pulling my weight. One night adrift was better than being totally kicked out. I'd slept in Elsie before. And odds were I could come back later, because Perez Hilton sure as shit wasn't going to spend the night unless Laura brought David Beckham as bait.

'OK,' I sighed. 'Let me grab a duffle and my sleeping bag. And a shower.' I was still stinky from my run.

She gave a terse nod, and returned to her perusal of some mesh panties and a tuxedo dickie.

I left before the horror of Laura-Lola's outfit materialized, stowing my camping gear in Elsie just in case. It was after six when I hit the board-walk and the sun was staring to slant lower in the sky in that way that makes everyone attractive and golden. My mood had lifted as sunshine can make it do no matter the odds. That and watching a little skate-dancing on the circle. The rollerblade guy in a Speedo was my favorite. He really jived to Kool and the Band. My step was light as I wandered down to Do You Tattoo to see Marion. Maybe today I might be able to convince him to give me a tattoo lesson – after all, in Maeve's New World, bad luck should be balanced by good, right? But I skipped up to a dark store and a dismissive 'Closed. We Went Camping' sign.

I sucked in a breath. Despite my protestations to Laura-Lola, I *had* been going to see if I could inveigle a sleepover invitation from Marion and Jacob. I'd had visions of the three of us staying up late watching a *Queer As Folk* marathon and sharing popcorn on the couch. I was all bravado about sleeping in Elsie. I didn't want to. There were lots of weird people who lurked around Venice Beach. I felt stung by Marion's defection, as if it was personal.

'What if today was the day I decided to get my tattoo?' I demanded churlishly of the locked door. 'This could have been the *one* day.' The door was impervious to my censure.

'Fine.' I turned away, stalking off to . . . where? I didn't know. Somehow being homeless on the boardwalk made me feel too close to the seedy people with goat-shit dreads who lived in old VW vans filled with newspaper stacks, the exterior of which had been transformed into nonsensical anti-establishment rants in cramped script

365

spreading from bumper to wheel, mirror to running board. The only deviance from the rant was the occasional peace sign, daisy or anti-Bush bumper sticker. I wasn't up for the alternatives of livid self-righteous liberals or smelly pot-smoking slackers. I turned east towards Main Street.

I didn't know where I was going when I passed O'Brien's Pub. The patio was rollicking with happy, lively people in groups of three and five. They annoyed me. My party of one kept walking. The World Café, Joe's Diner, even the Coffee Bean were hopping. The Library Alehouse seemed less packed so I braved my way in. There were cluster groups of four and six at the door, but I spotted one lonely stool at the bar. I elbowed through and grabbed it.

'Waiting for someone?' gleamed the resident bartender-actor, or 'bactor'.

'Johnny Depp will be here any minute.' I pasted on a fake smile. 'Can I have the Racer 5 IPA?' I ordered my favorite beer.

He winked good-naturedly and turned to get my drink, making me feel like a jerk. LA people were really happy. Maybe it wasn't the place for me.

'Aren't people in LA so fucking happy you can't stand it?' said the guy next to me.

I tensed, on the defensive against a pervert or time-sucking dweeb, and checked him out. He was about my height, skinny, and had a face you liked. Open brown eyes and a grin that said: 'I get it and I was about to make the same joke.'

'To tell the truth, it sort of makes me feel

366

inadequate that I'm not happy all the time. What are *they* drinking?' I demanded.

'Well, it sure as hell doesn't have calories or taste like this.' He raised his pint of beer. On cue, Smiley-Muscles-Bactor-Man returned with mine. I clinked my new friend.

'I'm Judd Wooten.' He wiped foam from his mustache/beard and held out a hand. I figured it was like a spit oath, and we'd be fast friends after. I grasped his paw firmly.

'I'm Maeve. My delusional roommate kicked me out for the night because *she* thinks *she's* going to seduce Perez Hilton at the Lisa Kline spring launch party.'

Judd let out a guffaw. 'New to LA?'

'A month,' I admitted.

'In town for good?'

'I expect to be here a while, but I'm not generally that good.'

'God, I'm glad you're sitting next to me.' He clinked my glass again. 'Does she seriously think she's going to pull Perez Hilton?'

'Dude, she seriously thinks he's going to fall in love with her.'

'Ah, the myopia of young dreams,' Judd sighed, signaling Smiley. 'TJ, another Alaskan Amber for me, and whatever the lady is drinking.'

'I'm still full,' I protested, gesturing to my beer.

'I'm not going anywhere, and you've got nowhere to go.' Judd dismissed my protest. 'Do a jaded veteran a favor, stay, breathe fresh air over me.'

'I'm from North Carolina,' I said, as if it was a liability I needed to disclose.

Judd looked thoughtful. 'After ten years in LA, you really aren't from anywhere else anymore. But I used to be from upstate New York. I don't even remember it. Why did you come here?'

'I had cancer.' The words came out. 'I had leukemia when I was in college. It surprised everyone when I beat it.' I savored the special note of pride in my voice when I said 'beat it'. Practice *was* helping. 'I thought it'd be easier to start over somewhere far away.'

Judd assessed me. 'Your hair is long.'

I ducked my head in shame. 'Yeah, I'm not at all heroic. I took a long time.' Was this word-vomiting?

He tapped my chin, just enough to make me look at him again but not enough to be pervy. 'Kudos to you, kid,' he said seriously. 'I lost my dad to cancer.' He vaulted into the club. 'It's nice to meet a survivor.'

'I'm not sure when you become a survivor.' I believed this. 'I don't think you're there if your scars keep you from doing what you want to do.'

'How long have you been in remission?' He voiced the benchmark between life and death, over a beer.

'Two years, seven months,' I whispered. Judd's face split into a wide smile. 'You're cured!'

'No.' I shook him off. 'Not quite. Five years is just a number. I've been part dead since the day I accepted that I might die.'

'That's not true.' Judd was all confidence. Then he looked sad. 'My dad's remission was for a year and eleven months before it came back. The two-year benchmark means a lot.'

I was having this conversation in a bar after evading survivors' groups for so long. Judd signaled Smiley for his check and I felt anticipatory loss for my new-found friend.

'So what do you do, Maeve?'

I slouched. 'Nothing. I thought I had a job when I got here, but it fell through. At the moment, I run on the beach, take pictures and try to figure out what the hell I'm going to do.'

'What kind of pictures?' Judd looked interested.

'Oh, you know, just people doing what they do. That's what I used to do in Unknown. Only there I got paid for it.' It felt cool to say it like that, like it was a career or something.

'And you're looking for work now?'

'Yeah.' I sighed. 'Starbucks is looking better and better.'

Judd signed his credit card receipt. 'You like shooting?'

'What?' Laura-Lola earlier, maybe, but I was a non-violent person.

'Pictures. You like taking pictures?'

'I love it.' I was getting confused. He wasn't going to spoil my impression of him by professing to be a photographer and asking me to get into a paneled van and go into the deep woods to model for him, was he?

369

'You want to shoot, you call me.' He slid me a card. 'I run a company that photographs special events. It's not for the starry-eyed. It's hard work and seriously-less-than-famous.' He smiled. 'I'd love to have you on board, purely because I like the way you think and I'm partial to long braids.' He tugged one, but again, it didn't feel predatory. This was the first person in LA other than Marion who seemed to be himself. 'Organize a serious portfolio. I'll pitch you to my partners and we'll see what we can do.'

I looked at his card. It was professional, Woot Prints Photography.

'Wow, Judd. Thanks!' was all I could mange. Was it possible that for once, timing had worked in my favor, planting me next to this guy at this bar?

Judd stood, slinging a camera bag from the floor over his shoulder. 'I've got to go. I've got to cover a fashion event party at Lisa Kline tonight.' He winked as my mouth dropped open. 'I'll try to get some good ones of the seduction for you.'

With those words he walked out the door, leaving me sucking air as some yahoo in a base-ball cap asked me if the seat next to me was free.

I was still there an hour later when TJ cleared away my empty plate and glass. The crowd had thinned and I felt panic balloon at the recollection that I had nowhere to go.

'Anything else?' TJ gleamed, putting a check in front of me.

I shook my head as I paid, wondering what I was going to do next. I checked my watch: 8.30 p.m. Crap. I smiled when I overheard a couple down the bar discussing a studio's intent to make another *Mummy* film. It was the franchise, not the mummy, that would never die. Then I had a brainstorm. I'd see a movie. Genius. Maybe I'd see two, even a midnight show if they had one. That'd eat up hours. Happy now, I hopped off my stool and headed down Main Street towards the Santa Monica Promenade, where there were at least two theaters, maybe three.

I'd only been walking for a minute when my cell phone rang. I answered without looking at the screen. It had to be Vi. Who else would be calling me? My only friend in LA was camping.

It was a shock to hear Noah's voice on the line. 'Maeve?'

I sucked in my breath, frozen. After phantom sightings of Noah all day, the real one was saying my name. Repeatedly.

'Maeve? Are you there? Hello? Maeve, can you hear mc?'

I smiled at his impatience. 'What's up, duck?'

'Oh, there you are.' His voice was relieved.

'I'm here, Big Ears. How the hell are you?' I forced casual cheer.

'At the moment, hungry and in need of a drink.'

Huh. Well. OK. 'Too far away to help, I'm afraid.' Standing alone on Main Street with nowhere to go, pressing the phone hard against my ear as if

I could actually bring him closer. Why was he calling? 'There's this invention called a sandwich, though. First you take—'

'Actually, I'm here.' He cut me off.

Adrenaline shot through my body. 'What?' As ridiculous as it was, I looked around so furiously my braids flew like helicopter rotors.

'I'm in Santa Monica. At the Loews Hotel.'

My heart stopped. Then started like a bird trying to fly out of my chest. He'd come for me! Noah was here to take me home!

'I'm in town for an independent booksellers' conference.'

His words shot the bird like an arrow. But my happiness was only slightly diminished. He was *here*. Near me.

'So I was hoping you'd meet me?'

'You betcha.' I tried not to sound overly enthusiastic. 'There's this great little dive right there called Chez Jay – it's sort of legend for Warren Beatty and Madonna getting it on in the back room once. Or if you want swish, we can go to the poolside bar at the Viceroy. A bit farther out is Wilshire or The Other Room. For Irish pubs we have Finn's and O'Brien's. Or there's—' Excitement had me babbling.

Noah's voice had an unseen smile when he interrupted my verbal flow. 'Why don't you come to the hotel? If it's not too far for you.' Always courteous.

'Sure, sure.' I nodded to no one on the empty street. Anywhere. 'I'm close. Ten minutes?'

'I'll be at the bar.'

I hung up and took a few deep breaths. I had to calm down or he was going to think LA had turned me psychotic. Inhale. Exhale. I surveyed my outfit. My favorite 7 For All Mankind jeans and a black halter top, with jade-green satin ballet slippers. I wouldn't win any fashion icon awards, but it flattered me. My chunky white bangle with a peacock feather painted on it matched the shoes. That showed maturity and good sense. He'd see I'd grown in LA.

I was a little hurt that he'd apparently been in town for a few days at the conference and hadn't called me, but I pushed it away. He'd been busy, and he'd called me now. Feet light, it was less than ten minutes before I was smiling at the doorman as I stepped into the Loews lobby. Loews is one of those lovely hotels where they shoot those scenes on *Entourage* or *The Hills*, with beautiful people sipping drinks by the pool and accepting complimentary frozen grapes and real juice popsicles from jacketed waiters. At night, the lobby exudes understated luxury and the scent of expensive floral arrangements. I located the bar and headed towards it, trying to maintain a measured speed. People didn't run in the Loews lobby. Or at least I assumed. I'd never been.

I spotted his back instantly, and felt the same jolt as earlier. Only this time it *was* his back. Inhale. Exhale. As if feeling my presence, he turned. His face split into a wide smile, and something warm

373

flooded my body. I crossed the distance as he slid off his stool and stepped to me, meeting in a hug that increased from tight to bone-crushing. Finally he released me, and smiled down from six foot four.

'You look great.' He didn't say much, but his green eyes were warm. I grinned back.

'You should've warned me to wear sunglasses, pasty,' I joked. 'Cancer doesn't fall out of the sun on you like rain, you know. You can walk around outdoors, stay a while even.'

'I've been trapped inside a store.' He shook his head, face rueful. 'I just can't keep good staff.' Now my smile spread, and we beamed goofily at each other like awkward teenagers. Noah recovered first.

'My lady.' Ever the gentleman, he assisted me on to a bar stool, hand at my back heating my flesh more than it should. 'I was about to order something to eat. Will you join me?'

I made sure my face didn't change. I'd had the chicken quesadilla appetizer (sour cream on the side) at the Alehouse because it was all I could afford. And that was only because Judd had bought my drinks. My movie excursion would have depended on me talking my way into a student discount.

'I'm not hungry,' I breezed. 'Just ate. Stuffed, in fact.' I patted my non-existent, almost concave, belly. I'd lost weight in LA. A tiny frown suggested Noah had noticed, but he didn't say anything.

'OK. Do you mind if I—' My stomach's loud

rumble would have overpowered a sonic boom, much less Noah's words. He started, then laughed. Without a word, he gave my braid a tug, and turned to the bartender. 'We'll have one filet, medium, please, and one of the halibut, miso broth on the side, peas steamed with no butter. And a bottle of your Cambria Pinot Noir.'

'But . . .'

'And we'll start with the crab cake appetizer.' He looked at me. 'You like crab cakes, right?' He didn't wait for an answer. He knew I did. 'We'll have the crab cakes, lobster reduction on the side.' He shut the menu with a satisfied snap.

I felt a little panicky at the thought of how much it would all cost. 'Noah . . .'

'Maeve, allow your old boss to buy you dinner. You brought me sandwiches often enough when I was on a deadline and forgot to eat.' My nervousness must have been evident, because he laughed. 'Don't look so distraught. This is on the corporate tab.'

That didn't really comfort me, considering I'd seen the corporation. I gestured to the lavish sur-roundings and raised an eyebrow. 'This is pretty swish for an independent bookshop. Dipping a hand into the till, are we? Wait until the boss finds out. You're canned.'

He laughed, but his right eyebrow did the thing where it creased down on one side. It was his tell. There was something he wasn't saying. He noticed me noticing, and looked a little shifty.

'So, tell me about—' he began

'You first.' I wasn't having it. 'Tell me about this independent booksellers' conference.'

His gaze flicked away. 'Nothing very exciting. Just a bunch of dusty bibliophiles trying to figure out how to throw the rock at the Goliath booksellers and stay afloat. Room full of people looking worried.' Definitely. There was definitely something he was withholding. I pondered it. Then horror flooded my body.

'You got married,' I accused, feeling sick. I have no idea what my face was doing since I wasn't stopping it, but it couldn't have been good. I felt miserable. And stupid. Of course that explained the nice digs. 'You and Beth are on your honeymoon.'

His eyes flew back to mine, astounded. 'What? Maeve, no . . . Why would you think that? That's, well, that's just ridiculous. Preposterous, even. Beth and I—'

'There's something you're not telling me,' I interrupted. I didn't want to hear about Noah and Beth. Though I could have swooned from relief at his denial. I still wasn't satisfied. 'You have the worst poker face, Noah. And this hotel . . .'

He was smiling again. He tapped my hand on the bar and absently played with my fingers. 'I never could keep anything from you.' I waited. 'It's not that big a deal.' He gave a laugh and looked away, embarrassed. 'I mean, it's silly really, not worth mentioning.' His eyes returned to my expectant face. 'I've been flown out by a studio. They're interested in *The Boy Who Could Fly*. They've optioned the rights to make a film. They're trying to impress me Hollywood style, hence the highbrow food and hotel.'

'Noah, that's incredible!' I was so relieved my initial supposition was wrong, I was giddy at his good news. I launched across the space between our bar stools, throwing my arms around him. He reflexively wrapped his around me and returned the hug. Or caught me, as I sort of toppled in my enthusiasm. It felt so good to be captured against his chest that I turned to liquid and couldn't move. I blinked back tears at my reprieve. Someday I'd have to face the reality that he belonged to another. But not tonight. We held each other until it wasn't about congratulations anymore, and I realized I'd turned my face into his warm, masculine neck. I didn't pull away until the sound of his cell phone jarred the mood.

'Hello?' He answered, eyes on me. Then his expression became strange. 'Beth.' My stomach plummeted. He mouthed 'excuse me' in my direction and hurried away from the bar, phone close to his mouth. I could see him behind a large plant across the lobby, pacing as he spoke.

After five minutes, he returned, seeming agitated.

'How's Beth?' I faked interest.

'Demanding,' he frowned, distracted. Then he focused on me. 'Maeve . . .'

'OK then, crab cakes for you?' The model-actress-bartender interrupted him, placing a dish in front of us. My stomach indicated its willingness to defect from my body in the manner of Alien to reach the crab cakes if I didn't attend to the matter. I was happy to comply. Beth might be dominant in Noah's life, but I didn't want to hear about it. I wanted to enjoy my borrowed time.

'Wow. These look great.' I seized my fork and took a bite. Noah opened his mouth, then closed it. After a pause, he picked up his fork as well. Diversion successful. 'So tell me more about it. Do they scout booksellers' meetings for frustrated novelists like Catholic girls trolling JDate for doctors?' JDate was the Jewish version of Match.com.

He looked confused. I doubted Noah was hip to the world of online dating.

'My agent called a few weeks ago with an offer. It happened that the conference was coming up, so I suggested this week. They're footing the bill for my trip to meet them and I get a free ride to the conference.' He looked smug.

'It's fantabulous news about the option, Noah. Do you know how many writers would kill for that chance?'

'It doesn't mean they'll actually make the movie,' he warned. 'It just means they've bought the right to be the only ones who can decide to make the movie for the next two years.'

I swatted him. 'I *have* learned a thing or two

378

about Hollywood since I got here,' I teased. 'Like everything is something-meets-something. Hmmmm . . . what would *The Boy Who Could Fly* be? *Harry Potter* meets *The Amazing Adventures of Kavalier and Clay*?'

He looked impressed. 'They said *Calvin and Hobbes* meets *Kavalier and Clay*, with elements of *Harry Potter*.'

'I can't take too much credit,' I confessed. 'No male-coming-of-age-themed meeting would be complete without a reference to *Harry Potter*. For girls it's *Hannah Montana*. Everyone pitches themselves as "the new Harry Potter", or "the next Hannah Montana".' I said this as if I, beleaguered studio head, had to endure endless pitches.

'You've really taken to LA. I was impressed with your social savvy, suggesting all the places we could go.' For once, I couldn't read his expression.

'Oh well, you know.' I gave a dismissive half-wave, as if my velvet-rope lifestyle was an incandescent blur of hot venues. I left out the part that I'd never been inside any of the places I'd walkcd past, but heard about them from Laura-Lola when she came home at night or read out loud to me from *Us Magazine*.

'You definitely don't miss Unknown then, with nothing but Netflix for entertainment.' Noah's voice was funny.

Oh but I do, I wanted to say. Instead I said, 'How's that Ronnie Two Shoes been behaving?'

After a while our main courses arrived. We salted and peppered and somewhere in there a second bottle of wine appeared. Noah asked me about life in LA. I couldn't tell him the truth – that I had no job, no friends, and lived on a futon in a dumpy squat off an alley . . . when I *had* a place to sleep, that is. That would feel like failure. I told him about Marion and the characters on the boardwalk, and my observations about LA.

'The deference cars show pedestrians is amazing. I've nearly plowed down numerous Californians when I'm not expecting them to step trustingly in front of my car. I've stopped traffic dead by merely lifting a foot off the pavement as if I *might* cross the street. It's surreal.'

'Coming from a town with no stoplights and only a few more intersections, I'd be fine with that. I'm the guy that has commuters muttering, "Damn tourist."'

'And everyone's so happy. Like when it rains, they love it because it's a novelty. And I think secretly because it gives them an excuse to lay slothfully on the couch with a remote like the rest of the country as opposed to being healthy happy running outdoors Californians taking advantage of the perfect weather.'

'And you? Are you happy?'

'Yeah, sure.' I didn't meet his eyes. 'Tell me more about Monkey Flower Festival plans.' I felt a pang at the thought of missing the festival.

Noah shook his head and grinned. 'Tuesday's

trying to choreograph the kids into a representational dance about the first time Natives used a monkey flower as a salt substitute, with a modern health message about blood pressure and heart care. And April is composing a ballad that includes the scientific and common names of *all* the monkey flower species in the region.'

'Aren't there hundreds?'

Noah wiggled his eyebrows at me. '*Yes*. And they all begin with *mimulus*.' He began to chant. '*Mimulus debilis, mimulus glutinosus, mimulus luteus, mimulus nudatus, mimulus stellatus* . . .'

'Those can't be real!'

'You doubt me?' He pretended offense.

'You make up stories for a living,' I pointed out.

'Fair point. Speaking of which . . .' He looked at his watch. It was midnight. He looked at me regretfully. 'I should probably get to bed. I have an early flight tomorrow.'

'Wait,' I said, desperate. 'I haven't told you about Laura-Lola and Perez Hilton.' I launched into an expanded version of my story, anxious not to lose my lifeline. After that, I babbled about anything I could think of – dubious star sightings, local haunts, California politics, traffic patterns. Noah listened, eyes drooping more the longer I rambled. I was recapping the weather for each of the forty-eight days I'd been in town when Noah's face split into a wide yawn.

'Maeve, I'm sorry. I love your company, but I've got to go to bed.' His look was kind, but tired.

'But you haven't been to the beach yet! You can't leave without putting your feet in the sand,' I insisted. 'Let's go.'

'Now?' he asked in disbelief.

'Yes. It'll be perfect. Santa Monica by moonlight.' I was already rising from my stool when he stopped me with a hand on my arm.

'Maeve, what's going on?' His face was concerned.

'What do you mean? Nothing's going on. You need to see the beach is all.'

'I don't think so.' He studied me.

'It just seems like we should hang out. Who knows when we'll see each other again.' I had a brainstorm. 'Hey, I know! Let's stay up all night and watch the sunrise!'

'Watch the sunrise?'

'Yes!'

'Unfortunately, I'll practically see the sunrise if I want to make my flight. So I'm going to have to put you in a taxi, I'm afraid.'

'Taxi? Oh, no. I'm not taking a taxi.' I accepted defeat, but refused to have him know the mess I was in. I didn't want Noah to see flighty, silly Maeve in a jam.

'Don't be ridiculous. I'll pay for it. I'm not letting you wander into the night after two bottles of wine.'

'It's not that. It's . . . I mean, I prefer to walk.'

'That's it.' He crossed his arms. 'What's going on?' He gave me his stern look.

I opened my mouth. Then I closed it. Exhaustion washed over me. I was tired of taking care of myself. I wanted someone else to share the load.

'I have nowhere to go,' I confessed.

'What do you mean?' He looked confused. I explained, bracing myself for his upbraid at getting myself into this predicament. Instead, he broke into a laugh. 'God, you had me worried. I thought there were shady characters after you or an arrest warrant. You silly goose, you can stay with me. Why didn't you say something hours ago?'

I shook my head, bemused.

'C'mon.' He stood, and I followed him, like a puppy.

The room he let us into was spacious and attractive, and dominated by a king bed. I felt awkward. Noah caught my hesitation, and tugged my hand.

'C'mon, settle in. We'll watch TV until you're sleepy.'

We flopped on to the bed, burrowing in against the pillows.

'Where's the remote?' I feigned casual, trying not to be aware of his body stretched out next to mine. We both looked around.

'Uh-oh.' Noah pointed. The remote was across the room, on top of the TV.

'Well, go get it,' I said.

'You go get it,' he said.

'I'm the guest,' I argued.

'I rescued you,' he disputed. 'You should show me gratitude.'

I turned on my side, propped up on my elbow. 'Oh yeah? Well I rescued you from being that lonely guy at the bar drinking and eating alone. You should show *me* gratitude.'

'I paid for that dinner.'

'No you didn't. The studio did,' I countered.

'Well I gave you a job when you were broke and desperate.' He gave me a superior look.

'Oh please. You were a mess. I saved that place for you.'

His look was incredulous. 'Cheeky monkey. I graciously hired your unemployable self, *and* I chauffeured you around Arizona, *and* I gave you a modicum of literary education.'

'I made you sandwiches when you would have starved to death, *and* organized your life, *and* made sure you paid your taxes and stayed out of IRS jail.'

He shook his head, smiling. 'It figures that I finally get you into my bed, and we're arguing.'

I frowned at him. Clearly the wine had made my brain a little fuzzy. Surely he didn't mean . . . I dismissed the thought as fantasy.

Noah laughed and pressed his index finger on the crease between my eyebrows. 'Watch out,' he teased. 'Your divot is showing.'

'I see London, I see Kent, I see someone's forehead dent.' I paraphrased childhood lyrics. I thrilled at his touch.

'You seem unperturbed.' He was surprised.

I blew out my bangs and flopped on my back.

'It's funny,' I said. Noah slid down until he was lying on his side, chin on his elbow, listening. Either the wine or his presence was making me brave. Or stupid.

'I worried so much about that divot.' I let the truth come out. 'Lotions, creams, massages, never frowning. If I'd known about Botox, I'd have bought it by the gallon.' I turned my head to look at him. 'Did you know, "Botox" isn't in spell-check for Microsoft Word? That's a fact. It's that new.'

Noah tugged my nose. 'Stay on target, Red 5.'

I resumed my examination of the ceiling. 'Some days they were pumping chemicals in my body designed to kill half my cells and I directed all my energy to maintaining a placid facial expression. I'm not sure why I thought I could control that one wrinkle when I couldn't control my cells, my hair, my dry skin, my chapped lips. Hell, I couldn't keep down crackers. But I was going to block that furrow, no matter what. And you know why?' I looked up at him again, but he waited, listening. 'Because I knew I was going to die,' I said out loud. And paused to catch my breath. The statement reverberated through my system like a bouncing gong. Right to home plate. Noah's gaze stayed steady, and the clanging slowly quieted. I spoke again.

'I knew I was going to die and I didn't want to be lying in my coffin with all my relatives looking at me for the last time with a divot on my forehead. I don't know if I didn't want my parents to think I was worried about going to . . . well, wherever you go. Or if I resented the irony that I'd wear into death the mark of having lived a life, when I hadn't done anything for most of it but be sick. Maybe it was pure vanity. I wanted to be a good-looking corpse.' My laugh was a bark

'And now?' Were Noah's eyes shimmering? I'd definitely had a lot of wine.

'And now I'm going to live a long fucking time,' I gloated. '*I* won. I'm going to do so many things in my life and have so many wrinkles that by the time I'm done I'll be a wizened old crab apple, just like Great-Aunt Ida.'

'You don't have a Great-Aunt Ida,' Noah whispered.

'No,' I confessed. 'But I have a life. And this,' I pointed at my forehead, 'this is the first stamp on my passport.'

I smiled up at him. He leaned down and kissed me. It was so sudden I didn't realize it was happening until it was. The moment his lips touched mine, we locked in an embrace, pent-up longing coursing between us as we kissed intensely. My arms wrapped around his neck as he slid one hand under my head and the other along my back to pull me close, the length of our bodies touching. Time suspended as the kiss went on and on. It was beyond anything I had dreamed of in all my imagined Noah fantasies. His warm skin, solid body, searching lips were real. He made me feel simultaneously like heated carnal flesh and

386

delicate as an eggshell, the way he caressed me and moved his mouth over mine. He kissed my eyelids, my cheeks, before capturing my mouth again. I couldn't believe it was happening, and I didn't want to be *thinking* at the moment. I gave myself completely to the kiss, our tongues tangling.

He pulled back at last, and gently brushed my bangs off my forehead. 'Thank God for you,' he murmured, tracing my cheekbone with his thumb. 'I can't imagine a world without Maeve.' He kissed me again and smiled, bumping his nose against mine.

Emotions were raging through me. They must have reflected on my face, because Noah frowned and stopped stroking my back. His expression became frozen. 'I'm sorry. I overstepped.' He jerked back. 'You weren't expecting to get jumped. I promised you a safe place to stay – I had no intention . . . I was going to control myself . . . Here you were opening up to me and I leapt on you. God, what's wrong with me? I'm so sorry, Maeve.' He released mc and rolled on his back, looking wretched.

I stared at the man I loved. I could hear my heart thrumming in my chest like I'd been running. When we were kissing I hadn't heard, felt or noticed anything but his touch. I wanted him so badly. I don't know if it was a decision or a compulsion, but I grabbed a fistful of his shirt and pulled him back against me.

'Stop talking,' I commanded against his mouth, unbuttoning his shirt. He looked in my eyes for a beat, then our lips locked hungrily and he too reached to slide me out of my top.

I stared at him in the semi-dark of pre-dawn, the low glow of the desk lamp casting shadows on the planes of his sleeping face. I traced the outline of his cheek and ear so lightly there was barely contact. He breathed deeply, evenly. His face was beautiful, with its sharp cheekbones and precise mouth. His whole body was beautiful, naked next to me beneath the sheet. I knew it now. I was intimate with that shapely mouth, the curve of his hip. The finally discovered tattoo was an old friend, a sun symbol spreading between his shoulder blades. But I wanted to know more. How was it he never had bad breath? Even after two bottles of wine and sleep, his breath smelled like pears. And the scar on his jaw, below his left ear. How did he get that? Part of me wanted to wake him, to gobble every second before he left tomorrow. I glanced at the clock and winced. Today.

It had been the most amazing night of my life. We'd alternated between lovemaking and intimate conversation, pillowed heads facing. I'd told him what it'd been like to be sick, and to feel life return in Unknown, like the needles you feel after your foot's fallen asleep. He'd told me about trying to hold his family together as a boy, and the invented characters he escaped into. After a while he said it was my turn to stop talking, that he was going to worship every inch of my skin. And he did, starting with my toes, and slowly, achingly slowly, moving up. That time had been slow and tender, full of whispered endearments. And when he'd joined our bodies, something clicked in me, and my body and soul became one unit again, reunited at last after breaking so many years ago. Afterwards, dozing, I'd clawed my way out of sleep to kiss him again and again. I loved kissing him. I was starved for it. Time suspended like that, our mouths seeking, tasting, exploring, devouring, until we were both aroused again and made love a third time, passionate. Climaxed and satisfied, Noah had gathered me close and fallen asleep holding me to him. It was a perfect fit.

Drowsy now, I consumed him with my eyes, blinking heavily, hating the relentless clock that was going to take him away. Wondering what he was dreaming. I should remember to tell him . . . tell him . . . tell him what? It had seemed so important. I fought to remember, sleep tugging me away . . . Oh yes . . .

'I love you,' I sighed, and closed my eyes.

The whisper was so low it could have been part of a dream, a warm breath fluttering my cheek, a butterfly kiss.

'I'll never regret this night. It will be the treasure I keep in a safe place to take out on dark days and bask in the glow of how beautiful you are and that I was with you. It's beyond belief. You're a miracle.'

Write it down, my sluggish mind urged, *write it down so I don't forget come daylight*. But nothing came out of my sleep-weighted mouth.

'Sleep, perchance to dream. The room is yours until two.' Gentle pressure. Kiss on my temple. Absence. The click of a door.

And with that he was gone, and the savory dream turned to grey mist and the confusion of feeling lost.

CHAPTER 31

BEING WRONG

Vertigo. A specific type of dizziness, the sensation of spinning or swaying while the body is actually stationary with respect to the surroundings. It can cause nausea and vomiting, and in severe cases, it may give rise to difficulties with standing and walking.

I awoke to a boxing match between disorientation and cotton-mouth. Disorientation had an early advantage as I blinked at generic beige walls and absorbed a bed too comfortable to be Laura-Lola's futon. I simultaneously registered a mass-produced print of Native American bowls so banal it screamed hotel 'art', and the fact that I was naked. Shock flooded my system, along with the memory that last night I'd slept with another woman's boyfriend. The nausea of horrifying recollection trounced both cottonmouth and disorientation.

I leapt for the bathroom, and reached the toilet just in time to heave into the bowl. After expelling the colorful contents of my stomach, I rested my splitting head against the cool porcelain. The wine from last night was exacting its penance. As were my sins.

I'd slept with Noah. He was Beth's boyfriend and I'd practically torn his clothes off. We'd made love not once but three times through the night. I'd been ravenous, fighting sleep and reaching for him again and again, storing his touch, feel and taste as if facing a long drought. Fleetingly I rose on a magic-carpet memory of our tangled limbs and whispered words, but quickly fell back to the cold tiles with a bump. It hadn't been love. It'd been sex, and I'd acted like a cheap whore.

I began to cry, a naked hungover tramp sitting alone on some hotel bathroom floor. The nausea of my own bad character was worse than chemo. Noah hadn't behaved above reproof, but I was worse, keeping him at the bar and feeding him drinks long after he intended to go to bed, attacking him when he'd only given me a kiss. He was the wrong 'wrong person' for me. I couldn't fix the ways I wasn't perfect, but I could avoid what made me imperfect in ways I couldn't live with.

I pulled myself up by the bowl and wiped my cheeks. Enough was enough. I'd been waiting for Los Angeles to fix itself for me, and that hadn't happened. It was time to get off my ass. Things were going to be different, starting today.

Right after my walk of shame through the Loews

hotel lobby, that was. I dragged on last night's clothes, and was heading for the door, when I saw the $20 bill on the dresser with a note that said *'for a cab. – N.'* I froze in shock. I'd never felt like more of a whore. Tears started again and I was pulling out my phone to call my sister, when another wave of nausea hit. I raced to the bathroom, stumbling as I reached to brace myself on the toilet. The porcelain knocked my phone into the toilet, and I only had a moment to watch it sink to the bottom before I threw up on top of it.

I didn't spend a lot of time contemplating the contents of my stomach floating over my cell phone once I was upright again. It'd been a cheap phone to start with, and would never survive this. For once I didn't curse my bad luck. This punishment was deserved. I lowered the lid, and turned to go, pausing only to take the $20, and crumple the note. I was going to need a new cell phone after all. So Noah could call and explain why he left me money after cheating on his girlfriend.

When I got back to Venice, Laura was sitting on the sofa, listlessly flipping channels. I tried to gauge her mood. I'd bet my whole twenty dollars on Not Good.

'Hey,' I said.

'Hey.' She didn't look up, but she pulled herself off half the couch.

'Aspirin first.'

'It's here.' She waved at a handy bottle on the coffee table. I sat. I took the aspirin dry.

'Don't you want water?'

'I've got mad skills swallowing pills.'

'Oh, right.'

'So how was last night?'

She looked about to break into tears. 'I'm a complete idiot.'

'Oh, hey! Lau— *Lola*, no.'

She gave a snotty burble of a laugh. 'You can call me Laura.' The laugh caught and her lip started to tremble. 'But really, I think I'm not very smart.'

'Hey.' I scooted over and put my arm around her. 'You are plenty smart.' Technically, 'plenty smart' merely required your brain to remember to tell your lungs to breathe, so it wasn't a whopping lie. 'Besides, smart, schmart. You want to be a wiseass like that Clark guy? You have a heart of gold, sister, and don't you forget it.'

She leaned her head on my shoulder. 'You think so?'

'I know so, bozo. Look at how you've taken care of me.'

'Taken care of you?' she scoffed. 'You're the last person in the world that needs taking care of. You're not afraid of anything. You came all the way out here by yourself. In about a minute you'll have it all figured out and be way more successful than I'll ever be.' From where her head rested on my shoulder, she couldn't see my fly-catching mouth. 'Besides,' she was sniffling again, 'I was awful to you last night.'

'No . . .'

'Yes, I was. Can you believe I thought I was going to hook up with Perez Hilton?' Her tone rose to a wail. I was about to say that I would never have guessed Marion was gay, when she cried, 'He had a *million* girls with him. He didn't even *look* at me. How could I think I'd be able to compete with Nicole and Paris? I'm so stupid.' I shut my mouth. I patted her while she sniffled. 'The worst was this crazy photographer following me around and recording everything! It was so humiliating!' I had to fight my smile, but not that hard. As silly as I might think Laura was, who was I to judge? We all made bad choices when it came to confused hearts. I owned the crown today.

'Where's that badge attitude?' I coaxed. 'We're not supposed to be perfect. We're just supposed to figure out what we can't fix and learn to live with those flaws the best way we can.'

'OK,' Laura said, like an obedient student. Maybe I'd get Marion to explain it better. 'So where'd you stay last night? I'm really sorry I kicked you out.'

I opened my mouth to make a dismissive joke and turn the conversation back to her. Then I paused. And changed my mind.

'You won't believe it,' I said, and began to tell her the story.

A week later, Judd sifted the photos spread on the desk before him. I'd spent most of the week revising my résumé to reflect event photography, darkroom skills and artistic sales out of the internationally recognized Red Gallery of Arizona. I'd also selected my favorite 8" by 10"s to create a portfolio for Judd.

'I'm impressed.' He looked at me. 'We all were. A little too impressed. I'm not sure you'll find the work we do . . . uh . . . artistically stimulating.'

'There's an art to paying rent,' I said. 'Remember the girl in the Pocahontas fringe halter chasing Perez Hilton at Lisa Kline's party? I'm dependent on her charity, and the water stain on the ceiling above her futon is about to be permanently ingrained on my inner cortex. I believe that constitutes medical brain damage.'

'You're hired.'

I exhaled in relief. This had been my last shot. Even Taco Loco didn't want me.

'Now I can replace the cell phone I dropped in the toilet.'

'I wondered about your, er, complicated messaging system.' Judd raised an eyebrow.

I snorted. It'd been a nightmare since I'd lost my phone. I had no money for a new one, and too much pride to accept familial charity. Until I could afford a replacement, I was dependent on Laura to field messages and let me use her phone to return calls. It was my penance. Not that it mattered. Despite making very sure that Tuesday had Laura's number, and strict instructions to disseminate it 'to *everyone*' so they could reach

396

me, especially Noah '*in case he had questions about the store*,' he hadn't called. It hurt.

'You know,' Judd recalled my attention to my pictures, 'these really are good. You should think about how to market them.'

'You think so?' I joined him behind the desk.

Judd extracted a shot of Barney stretched out asleep on the hood of his rusty antique Ford. 'I wouldn't mind having one of these.'

'There are dirty words in two languages going on in that picture,' I warned. 'You just can't see them.'

'I won't tell my mother.'

'I'll bring a copy tomorrow.' I hesitated. 'Can I ask what makes you like it? You don't even know that guy.'

He considered. 'I like seeing people without artifice. All of these,' he gestured, 'you catch real people with their guard down. This one here,' he pointed to a print, 'she's standing still holding a cup of coffee but it looks like she's dancing, right down to her fingers and toes. It makes me want to know more about her. And you. The artist obviously cares about her.'

'She's the best,' I agreed. I couldn't wait to call Tuesday. 'So, you really like them?'

'I expect many people will. The nature shots are strong too. You should sell your work.'

'Here?' I asked hopefully.

'I'm afraid not.' He grimaced. 'Your missions for Woot Prints, should you choose to accept them,

397

you won't find so engaging. It's mostly charity events where no one remembers the charity and a single swag bag would feed East Timor for a month, exclusive private parties that exist merely to be crashed by those higher in the Hollywood food chain – who never do – and promotional launches that attempt to convince meaningless twits that their indistinguishable product is indispensable.' He ticked them off on his fingers. 'Occasionally there's a seasonal special, and you get every twat in Hollywood at some pumpkin patch with fake oh-you-caught-me-in-my-adorable-private-moment shit-eating grins.'

I bit my lip.

'Sorry,' he said. 'If you do this too long, "twat" becomes a staple of your vocabulary.'

'Don't worry,' I reassured him. 'That word is Oliver's divine truth. So what do I actually do?'

'Every gig is swarming with the B-and-lower list. You're there to catch their good side. I try to catch them with chewed-up food in their mouth. But I'll warn you, twits and twats would wrestle Mother Teresa to the ground to make sure you catch their good side.'

'Mother Teresa would definitely lose. Hard to nail the defensive moves when you're dead.'

'*Corpse of Nobel Saint Sustains Red Carpet Tumble In Religious Habit Accessorized By Rope Belt, Cloth Headscarf and Jewelry by Pontius Pilate.* Death is a potentially smart career move if it snags you the cover of *Us Weekly*.'

'That's macabre.'

'Remember James Dean?'

'Gotcha.'

'You'll learn to understand these strange creatures. They're emotional black holes that can never be filled, ravening beasts soothed only by the whirring of the paparazzi shutter. You don't have to worry about not feeding them, because they never eat.'

'Sounds fun.' I wouldn't let myself get depressed.

'Consider it a challenge especially suited to your talents. If you can catch one of these creatures showing genuine self without artifice, the way your subjects do, that'll be a masterpiece.'

I recalled Laura in wrinkled sweats, ponytail and no makeup, on the couch after my night with Noah, laughing at *American Idol*. It was the prettiest I'd seen her look.

I brightened. This would be fun. 'What's my first assignment?'

We considered Judd's booking schedule to see what made the most sense. As excellent timing would have it, my own schedule was wide open. We decided that I would shadow Judd for a few events, learn the dance steps, then start solo with some small gigs.

'Fantastic. See you Wednesday!'

'Just out of curiosity . . .' Judd stopped me as I gathered my things. He tapped a print. 'Who's this?'

Stab of pain. I glanced away from the picture of

Noah, chin resting on his hands as he stared at his computer. 'No one.' I said.

'Right.' Judd didn't buy it. 'See you Wednesday.'

It was the truth. Noah didn't exist for me anymore. I knew my limits – I'd learned from Rondele brand garlic and herb spread that I lacked them. When that succulent cheese spread was in the house, I'd dive in and get dirty with it, swallowing all it had to offer. What permitted me a modicum of restraint was that Rondele didn't have my phone number. I always initiated our late night booty calls.

Noah *did* have my number, or Laura's, at any rate. And he hadn't used it, making it very clear what he thought of me – or rather, that he didn't. No apology, no begging me not to tell anyone, no explanation of the twenty dollars, or even an invitation to engage in more illicit bad acts. Nothing. So that was it. I had too much pride to call him. I'd understood when people had bailed on me when I got cancer – I didn't agree, but I was smart enough to blame the cancer, not myself. With Noah, it was a case of the simplest explanation being true. He hadn't called because he didn't feel like it. End of story.

When I walked into Do You Tattoo, Marion didn't even look up from the *Semper Fi* he was inking on a Marine.

'Go ahead,' he grunted.

I headed for the phone.

'Aloha,' came the lyrical greeting.

'Tuesday!'

'Ay-yi, Maeve! Oh, I miss you!'

'Me too. I got a job!'

'That's great! Pizza Hut or Jack In A Box?'

'Hardy-har-har. It's a photography job. I'm paparazzi now!' As soon as I said it, I worried that it didn't convey properly. 'I mean, I'm an event photographer. There'll be celebrities, of course, but it will be about the events themselves. The challenge will be catching people unawares, you know, food in their mouths . . .' I trailed off. What Judd had made sound artistic, I made sound like the creepy over-hugging Uncle. The blood of Princess Diana was making the phone slick in my hands. 'It's hard to explain,' I concluded lamely. 'You kind of have to know LA.' Out, out damned spot.

'Well Uncle Frank's disappointed you're not in food services, but I'm happy for you. Well sort of happy. I kind of hoped you'd come back. Noah refuses to hire anyone . . .'

'Tuesday,' I cut her off. She was under strict instructions. If Noah didn't care to talk to me himself, I didn't want to hear about him.

'Sorry. I've been working a lot of hours, and we're also trying to get ready for the Monkey Flower Festival. It doesn't help that Ronnie Two Shoes backed into the bandstand when he was setting up lights for last week's dance and now it's collapsed on one side . . .' I let her chatter, drinking in the daily movements of the sleepy town.

'. . . And Helen and Liz have been at each other's throats over the nursery's pink phlox shortage. They both put in orders for four flats each, but only four total came in. Naturally the nursery offered them each two flats, but they won't have it. Ruby and I have been calling it the War Over Four, and neither will budge. It's a good thing Solomon wasn't adjudicating maternity between those two or the Bible would have seen some David Copperfield meets *Saw* action.'

I laughed. 'Can't the nursery dig up some fragrant anemones, mix them in with the Phlox, and *violà*, they 'discover' the lost four flats? As long as the distribution of both plants is exactly even between Liz and Helen's booty, we may yet achieve world peace.'

'Genius! That's why we need you here. *I* need you here. I made the mistake of meeting Samuel at the clinic the same day April picked up Busy's heart medicine. I flipped through one of his health journals and now I'm convinced I have Moersch-Woltmann Syndrome.'

'Nervous system disorder that causes intermittent muscle stiffness in the trunk and limbs, exaggerated upright posture, stiff-legged walk?'

'Oh my God! Do I need a plasma exchange?'

'Been lifting a lot of book boxes by yourself lately?' It was a job we'd usually shared.

'Yes.'

'Do the pains happen to present the day after that?'

'Yes!'

I chuckled. 'Take a hot bath and call Bruce to move the boxes in the morning. You'll be fine.'

'I'm cured! Thank god. I couldn't handle a plasma exchange *and* work *and* the Festival. Noah was enough of a bear about me taking only *one* day off. Of course, he's a bear all the time these days . . .'

'Tuesday.'

'Ugh, sorry. I swear, the two of you. That must have been one humdinger of a fight that neither of you will talk about.'

'Tuesday.'

'Okay Miss Avoidance, what else is new?'

I told her about connecting with Laura, and spending time with Marion and Jacob. I even told her about what I now dubbed the Costco Moment. Soon I ran dry. It felt like dancing at the edge of a crater because there was this giant thing I couldn't tell her, what had happened with Noah. Now that I was accustomed to airing my 900 pound gorillas, I didn't like the feeling. It was unnatural.

"Things sound good,' she said. 'I'm half-astonished you got my message. It took me forever to convince your friend that I was *named* Tuesday, instead of wanting you to call me *on* Tuesday.'

'I'm glad you did. It's good to talk to you,' I was reluctant to end the call, but without means of extending it.

'Aloha, love,' she said, before cutting my connection to Unknown.

The next call was to my brother. I grabbed some apple slices for snacking, and dialed.

'Yo!' I said.

'Yo!' he said.

'I'm calling you back,' I reminded him.

'Oh right. Man, that secretary of yours is whack. It took me forever to explain that I was "Brick your brother" and not "your black lover."'

I laughed at the thought of Laura as my secretary. 'You should see the uniform. So what's up?'

'Hey yeah, I met that old boss of yours, you know, the writer.'

Shock made my lips numb. I sucked in air. 'What?'

'I went to check out the Atlantic Book Festival, and what do you know, he was giving a talk. So I thought I'd introduce myself.'

'You met him?' It bothered me that Noah should have such intimate access.

'Couldn't get near him. Interesting lecture, but he was mobbed by about a hundred boys afterwards. Though they may have been angling for the girlfriend. She was *hot*.'

My hand clenched the phone. 'If you like that sort of thing,' I kept my tone neutral.

'I've always been partial to redheads,' Brick's tone was approving.

I felt a wave of sick wash over me. 'Redhead?' Beth was no ginger.

'Halfway down to her endless legs. I mean, I know you didn't like her that much, but you might

404

want to think before tangling with an Amazon. I
bet she's taller than Jules.' Beth was definitely not
taller than Jules.

'Did he introduce her, let the fans meet the girlfriend sort of thing?' I probed.

'Naw. They couldn't get out of there fast enough.
She practically dragged him to the hotel elevators.
Saucy minx.'

I barely heard Brick prattle on. I felt seriously
ill. How could I have been completely wrong about
Noah? I knew from personal experience that he
was a cheater, but I'd imagined it was because of
our connection. I'd prayed there was an explanation for his silence. And now I had it – he had a
girl in every port. I was nothing more than his
Los Angeles girl. Sweat broke out as I thought
about how many towns Noah visited in a year,
how many he'd visited while I was in Unknown.
I had to get out of here.

I managed a goodbye to my oblivious brother,
gave a half-hearted wave to Marion, and walked
like a zombie back to Laura's.

When I let myself into the apartment, my heart
jolted at the sight of the envelope Laura had left on
the coffee table for me to find. It was old-fashioned
snail mail, my name and Laura's address written in
Noah's familiar handwriting. I held it for a few beats,
feeling the weight of the letter. Then my hurt
bubbled up and I hurled it in the trash. How dare
he treat me as part of some harem?! I couldn't bear
the thought of the lies – or truths – the letter

would hold. I put on my sweats, and was heading for the door when Laura came in.

'Oh, hey!' she said, then her smile faded as she saw my face. 'Are you okay?'

I could only nod as I passed her and headed out the door.

I don't remember running, or how long I was gone, but I registered a change immediately when I walked back into Laura's place. The living room was spotless. Laura had cleared out her clothes, tidied the magazines, picked up candy wrappers, and wiped down the surfaces. A note said, '*I thought I'd improve on your room!!! Hope you feel better!!!*' I didn't have to look to know the trashcan had been emptied. I had no idea where the rubbish went. I didn't care, though. That was how I wanted it.

CHAPTER 32

WELCOME TO THE Z-LIST

Hyperthymesia Syndrome. A condition where the affected individual has a superior autobiographical memory. The two defining characteristics are 1) the person spends an abnormally large amount of time thinking about her past, and 2) the person has an extraordinary capacity to recall specific events.

I was hot, sweaty and irritated.

'I'm not sure you got my best side on that one.' The collagen-enhanced lips moved, as the fake acrylic nails swept the bleached hair off the Botoxed forehead. I dutifully replaced the viewfinder to my eye and snapped a picture identical to the first, wondering if there was a school that taught the wrist-downward hand on hip they all employed. When the 'reality' star turned away, I paused and waited. Within five seconds I was rewarded, and snapped a picture of her gorgeous manicure grasping the expensive silk fabric she wore and unglamorously digging it out of her butt. Click.

I slipped through the party trying not to absorb the vacuous conversation but unable to avoid it entirely.

'I figure if I walk into a room and a man doesn't look at me, he must be gay.'

'So then he asked me if I'd seen Breughel at the Getty. Like I'm supposed to remember all the clubs I've been to! Is Breughel that hot new DJ from Amsterdam?'

'I swear – this meeting with Scott is going to turn my career around three hundred and sixty degrees.'

'It's a once-in-a-lifetime opportunity, and it only comes along twice a year!'

'He got that part because he's bilateral – he speaks English and Spanish.'

'Like, it's hard to maintain a one-on-one relationship with someone if that person isn't going to let me be with other people.'

'I owe a lot to my parents, especially my mother and father.'

I felt my brain absorbing the inanities, words sinking into a corner of my cerebellum where their vacancy would leach the grey matter paler and paler until it would eventually die, the way the souls of Chihuahuas die on the inside when they're dressed in pink satin jackets.

'Oh there you are!' The hostess pounced. 'Come with me. Arabella doesn't feel you got her best side.' She leaned toward me conspiratorially. 'She's one to watch, you know. About to really break out. You should promote her placement.'

I nodded. I'd long since given up explaining that I only took the pictures. I couldn't complain too much. It was a good job and paid just fine. It didn't give me the artistic satisfaction my work in Unknown had, but satisfaction had never paid the rent. There was nothing stopping me from taking candids around Venice. Certainly it was rife with subjects. But it hadn't engaged me yet; didn't seize me with an immediate pull the way the desert had.

Instead of heading home after the party, I walked down Pacific to a small Venice walk street, paper clutched in hand. I found the sign for Ozone, double-checked the address and hurried to number 21. The draping fuchsia bougainvillea reminded me of home.

Ruby's home, I corrected myself. The buzzer sounded, and I took an old-time elevator with a folding iron cage door up to the fourth floor. A door across from the elevator was ajar. I approached it.

When the woman came to the door, I was startled by how pretty she was. Elegant was the word that came to mind. She was tall, taller than me, and had lustrous chestnut hair that looked like it could pull a locomotive if braided into thick shiny ropes. She wore it loose and free, curling down past her shoulders.

'Maeve?'

'Dimple?'

'Nice to meet you.' We shook hands. 'Please come in.' Her smile was warm, gesture graceful. I noticed she had a crooked tooth. Everyone should have a flaw, I thought.

'Thanks for seeing me,' I said.

'It's no problem. My schedule is flexible. I think this might work out.'

I stepped into the apartment and was instantly in love. This was definitely going to work out. I staged a thoughtful hand to my chin to keep from blurting 'I'll take it!' The rent wasn't decided yet. Plus I hadn't seen the shower. An icky shower is a deal-breaker.

I took in the front room. It would have to be a seriously icky shower. The space was all light and windows, with the occasional stained-glass element creating the impression of living inside the light rather than simply letting it into the room. The woodwork was bare cedar, walls vanilla. Everything was designed to welcome, with surprising accents elevating the experience. The full-length mirror doors had subtle Victorian scrolling at the beveled edges. The kitchen wall had inlaid tiles. The corner bedroom was all windows on two walls.

The bathroom was anything but icky, tiled in white octagonal tiles with a decorative black pattern.

'How's the shower?'

'Great.' She eyed me up and down. 'The best

is the tub. You're tall like me so you can appreciate that it's an old-school clawfoot. Even people our height can stretch out fully.' She laughed.

'There's tons of storage, too.' She started opening cabinets. She didn't have to.

We walked back into the airy bedroom. I absorbed the peace of it.

Dimple gave a nervous laugh. 'Don't think this is weird, but I kind of feel like we already know each other from emailing and talking on the phone, so here goes. If you want to see the room's best feature, lay on the bed.'

I didn't skip a beat. I stretched out on the left side. 'What's the feature?'

'Look toward the ocean.'

Without lifting my head from the pillow, I could see an incredible ocean panorama, sailboats dotting the horizon. I bolted upright. 'Holy guacamole, was that a dolphin?'

'Yeah.' She grinned. 'You can see them most mornings. As soon as you open your eyes.' Smile splitting my face, I lay back down. Dimple dropped into a chair.

'So you want to sublet it furnished?' I started the negotiation.

'Mm-hmm. And you're OK with month to month so long as I give you reasonable notice that I'd like to come back?'

'Yep.'

'What can you afford?'

'What do you need?'

She looked over at me and giggled. 'Men would tear their hair out if they saw how women negotiate.'

'It's like watching them try to convince you they don't need to ask for directions.'

As it turned out, we had exactly the same price in mind.

'A true meeting of minds.' I grinned.

'Thank God. I'm so tired of feeling like everything is a battle.' She fell silent.

I figured that if she wanted to tell me more, she would. I was sorry she was going away. She seemed like someone I'd like to know.

'Hey, Dimple?'

'Yeah?'

'Where are you going?'

'I don't know,' said my kindred spirit.

'Tell me how it is when you get there.'

We watched the waves.

'Hey, Maeve?'

'Yeah?'

'Where'd you come from?'

'Unknown. It's nice, you should try it.'

We watched the boats.

'Hey, Dimple?'

'Yeah?'

'Want to meet my bird before you go?'

'Sure.'

I listened to the trees.

'Hey, Maeve?

'Yeah?'

'Want to see your new patio?'

'In a minute.'

'I found a place to live,' I reported to Tuesday without preamble when she answered her phone later that day. Relying on Laura's phone had made my calls efficient.

'That's great,' she said, but her tone was subdued.

'Is everything OK?'

'No. Yes. I mean . . . I'm just tired.' She sighed.

'What is it?'

'I'm heading home from the hospital.' My heart stopped. Then kicked back on in overdrive. Tuesday. Or Noah. Or Ruby. In a split second I swam through a kaleidoscope of far-away faces.

'It's Child.'

'What?' I croaked. My heart now thundered like an adrenaline needle had been jammed to its center. It physically hurt.

'It's OK. He's OK. God, I'm crap at this.' I could see her biting her lip.

'No one's good at bad news,' I managed. 'Please just tell me.'

'I was about to call you. We were waiting for definite news. He's going to be fine.'

'What . . . ?'

'He was having chest pains.'

I was immobile, hand pressed to my eyes, world pulsating.

'He went to see Samuel. The EKG revealed a

significant blockage, so they hustled him to the hospital. They had him on the table within thirty minutes and put in a stent.' Her voice caught a little. 'It was a ninety-eight percent blockage.'

My breath came easier. This I understood. Medical details. 'OK. That's OK. My dad has a stent. In a way this is better. Now we know. Now we're on alert, and we monitor.'

'I know. The doctors said he's fine. *He* said he's fine. It was a little scary, that's all.'

'God. You're telling *me*.' My relieved laugh was a bark. 'That was almost as bad as when I thought Noah and Beth had gotten married!' It slipped out before I could stop it.

'Ha!' Tuesday's snicker was equally relieved. 'Married? As if. Holy vitriol, those two can barely pass a civil word since they broke up. And it was debatable how much they talked *before* it ended.'

There it was again. That moment when time shimmers a beat, like passing through a membrane to another world.

'What did you say?'

'I said I doubt they talked when they were still together. In the beginning, sure, but—'

'No. About Beth and Noah being broken up.'

'What about it?' She was confused.

'They broke up?'

'Of course! Before you left.' My world spun again. Tuesday sucked in some air. 'Are you telling me you didn't know?' she demanded.

'But . . .'

'He was going to tell you when you went to the store to say goodbye. I thought you might even stay. I don't know what the hell happened, since neither one of you will talk about it, but afterwards he moped around like a kicked dog.'

I swallowed. 'But then he—'

'Noah ran into Primrose Tarquin at the Wagon Wheel. She was waiting for Samuel and he was waiting for Bruce, so they got to talking. He did the math and realized you had to have broken up with Samuel before you left. Quite coincidentally, all of a sudden he's got meetings and a conference in Los Angeles and is off faster than you can say full-priced airfare.'

'But Beth called him. When he was here.'

'Probably to tell him she was keeping his Jeff Buckley records or demand that he return the hair she cleaned out of her brush and left in the trash can in his bathroom or something equally witchy.' Tuesday snorted. I was speechless. 'Are you there?' She demanded.

I made a strangled sound.

'Myfriendsaretwomorons,' she muttered. To me, 'I don't know what happened out there, but after he got back he went from being a kicked dog, to being a neurotic teenager asking if there'd been any calls every two seconds even though he had his phone in his hand constantly, to being an aaaaangry bear.'

'So.' I licked my lips. 'So when he was here, in LA, he wasn't . . . he and Beth weren't . . .'

'Weren't even speaking. Correct. She was so spitting mad that he dumped her just when she'd gotten rid of you and thought she had a clear shot at her meal ticket that she was speaking in tongues. It was scary.'

'And now?'

'The good news is you can always get advice from Liz Goldberg on how to avoid a hatchet in your back or a horse's head in your bed.'

'That's not funny,' I muttered.

'Oh, I think it's funny. I think you're both effing ridiculous,' Tuesday asserted. It must be true, because for Tuesday to use even a sanitized swear word was extreme.

'It's not as if he's a saint,' I defended. 'I know for a fact that he's seeing someone already. Maybe he wasn't cheating but that's pretty fast.' Especially considering.

'If you're so *akamai* and *niele*, you can explain how you, in California, know better than me, in Noah's house *and* store every day. *E kala mai!*' In her agitation, she peppered me with Hawaiian.

'My brother saw him, with a girl, at the Atlantic Book Festival.'

'Ooooh, *that* girl. Was she tall, with auburn hair, really pretty?'

'Yes! You know her?' Being vindicated didn't feel as good as I'd thought.

'That's Jan, his publicist.' Tuesday's voice resumed its disgusted tone.

'Mixing business with pleasure then.' Mine matched hers.

'Next time I see her, I'll be sure to ask Jan if she broke up with her *live-in girlfriend of seven years, Kristin,* so she could swing the other way with her long-time client,' she said, with a snort. 'You and Noah, and your rampant imaginations, are *perfect* for each other.' It didn't sound like a compliment.

'What do you mean?'

'You think he's married to Beth yet screwing his publicist. And every time he calls you, he gets some girl hyperventilating about the fact that you're out at some fabulous party so exclusive she can't get in. He's convinced you're living the glamorous socialite's life and want nothing to do with a small town hick like him – his words, not mine.'

'What? That's ridiculous.' I protested. My brain was not processing all this information. Noah had called?

'You know you're my little hibiscus,' Tuesday assured. 'But, you really blew him off.' She sounded disappointed. 'I know I'm not allowed to discuss anything Noah with you, but I don't get it. You return everyone's calls but Noah's. And he was horribly worried you being too broke for a cab when he saw you. He was ready to wire you every penny he had and move to LA to make sure you had enough to eat. He almost went manic when he heard you'd lost your phone. It really hurt him to find out you were out partying every night.'

'I was working! I was photographing events.'

'Good luck getting that through his thick head. After fifty-seven unreturned calls, I can't blame him. Why didn't you just call back?'

'I never got any messages!' I was going to strangle Laura-Lola. 'I had no idea! I thought he was blowing *me* off.'

'You're the only person on the planet who can't see that Noah only has *maka* for you.'

'I hope "maka" means "eyes,"' I muttered as my brain ricocheted. On the one hand, it felt like a huge boulder had rolled off my heart. Noah was who I thought he was. On the other hand, did I want to run backwards to a relationship based on making sure I ate enough? Or did I want to fully stand on my own two feet? For a flash, I appreciated the beauty of illness – there is usually one clear answer as to what's best for you.

'So now that you know, what are you going to do?' Tuesday demanded. My lack of answer was notable.

'Don't tell him anything about this while I try to figure it out,' I instructed. I had thinking to do.

After we hung up, I crossed to Laura's room in two steps.

'Done with the phone?' She looked up from *In Touch* magazine.

'DidsomeonenamedNoahcallme?' The words tumbled out so fast they made no sense.

'What?' Her brow furrowed.

418

'Did. I. Get. Any. Calls. From. A. Man. Named. Noah.' I forced myself to go slow and enunciate.

Laura's face cleared. 'Oooohhh. You mean No One? There was this guy that called, like, a *million* times, but every time I asked who was calling, he said "no one," or "no-one-thanks," like it was one word.' She giggled. 'He was really polite, but never left his name. I didn't think it was worth mentioning.' She shrugged, smile bright. 'Mr No One!'

I sagged against the doorframe. 'Oh. Thanks.'

I rolled back into the living room and collapsed on the couch, staring at what I now thought of as 'my' water stain. So Noah had called. Noah wasn't a cheater. My relief was intense. But, I frowned. Was it about Noah? I was over being 'taken care of.' I was finally doing a pretty good job on my own. Tuesday's question echoed in my mind.

'What are you going to do?'

'I don't know,' I murmured my answer to the water stain. 'I really don't know.'

Two weeks later, I was again surrounded by light and detail.

'Enjoy,' Dimple said, as she handed me the key.

I stared at the alien key in my palm. Was I really about to become an official resident of Venice Beach, California?

'I will.' I closed my fingers around the key. Yes, I was.

CHAPTER 33

VENICE BEACH SEES IT ALL

Aquagenic Urticaria (also known as allergy to water). An extremely rare form of physical urticaria, it is a hypersensitivity to the ions found in non-distilled water. In affected persons, water on the skin causes hives to appear within fifteen minutes and last for up to two hours.

I tripped over a box in the dark living room, and cursed as my shin collided with the coffee table. I'd been living out of suitcases for a month, and I seriously needed to unpack. It wasn't as if I had all that much stuff, but September was the busy season at work, and I'd had no time. All the television premieres held launch parties packed with people craving to be photographed. This was the eighth night in a row I'd gotten home after 2 a.m. Too tired to turn on the light, I only wanted to fall into bed.

On cue, the irritable director who lived downstairs pounded on the ceiling. I'd forgotten to take off my shoes again. It was remarkable how hypersensitive he was to the whisper of rubber soles on hardwood. It's not like I was clomping around in clogs.

'What kind of director never leaves his apartment?' I muttered. 'Is he directing Internet webcam strippers?' No one answered, because Oliver was asleep. Another Hollywood mystery.

Despite the fact that he was an annoying jerk, I was comforted by the director's ceiling-thumping. It was a relationship of sorts. Los Angeles was an isolating place. Where once I'd preferred the anonymity of fading into a crowd, now I missed the community of Unknown. It wasn't so easy to meet people here. I was beginning to appreciate the old joke that the best way to meet someone in Los Angeles was to crash into their car.

I don't have any problems meeting expenses, though. They're *everywhere*, I reminded myself, as I dropped newly arrived bills on the table. I was exhausted from the amount of work I had to take on to make rent. The cost of living in Venice Beach was dramatically different from Unknown. After fourteen-hour work-days covering three to four gigs a day, even Laura-Lola's futon seemed like an appealing alternative. I headed for bed. I wouldn't worry about it tonight.

When I awoke, I experienced the daily spurt of pleasure I'd known since getting my own place. Despite the cost, it was worth it. I enjoyed Dimple's view – it *was* one of the best features of the apartment – but my real joy came from my independence. Every morning I remembered I was living in my own apartment, with my own job, in California, completely self-sufficient. I'd done what I set out to do. My life wasn't exactly as I wanted it, but I was proud of what I'd accomplished.

'Howdy, pardner,' Oliver greeted me when I entered the living room.

'Howdy yourself,' I said. It felt good to speak aloud. Last week, four days had gone by where I hadn't spoken a word beyond 'hi' and 'thank you' to clerks providing me with goods in exchange for money. I'd taken to talking to myself a lot. I resolved to drop by Marion's tattoo parlor for an overdue visit. Being so busy, I barely saw the few friends I had.

I didn't have a job until evening, so I spent the morning sorting out the apartment. The bruise on my shin demanded it. I hung clothes, and put books on the shelves. I wasn't ready to put nails in the walls, even though Dimple had assured me it was fine. Though I'd left over two months ago, I was still too homesick for Unknown to put up my pictures. The one thing I displayed in pride of place was the card I'd received from my parents when I'd sent them my new address. It read: *We couldn't be more proud of you.*

I'd sorted all but a few boxes when my growling stomach would no longer be denied. There were no groceries in the house. I had a growing list of things I needed to buy – a shelf for the bathroom, a toaster oven, a fan – but I wasn't motivated, even for Costco. I collected my camera, and went to find lunch.

I grabbed a salad at the Fig Tree Café, then wandered along the boardwalk, admiring the henna tattoos, jewelry, T-shirts, sunglasses, paintings, sculptures, knick-knacks, CDs, psychics, chakra-adjusters and the 'non-touching healer'. You could purchase anything along the boardwalk. I snapped photos of it all. The Jim Morrison mural, the man in the lawn chair selling annoying bird whistles, a couple in matching Universal Studios T-shirts holding hands, a drum circle on the beach, leather-skinned men drinking beer at the Waterfront, the skate-dancers. I captured scenes of Venice, but it didn't sink into my soul the way that Unknown did. I kept walking, though, taking picture after picture, as if I could force it.

At five I had to return home to get ready for that night's job. The event wasn't until eight, but it was in Studio City, so I had to allow two hours to get there in traffic. Sometimes my round-trip commute was longer than the gig itself. That was LA for you.

'Where are they having the Cannes Film Festival this year?'

'I think he's really deep, you know, 'cause he's all about light, and lightness has to come from a really deep place. Especially if it's true deepness and true lightness.'

'I get to go to lots of overseas places, like Canada.'

'I'm not on a diet. I just don't eat as much as I'd like to.'

'Excuse me, honey.' Fake nails were snapped in front of my face. 'You need to step up the shutter action. You've barely taken any pictures. We didn't have you come to sample the hors d'oeuvres.'

'Of course.' I lifted the camera to my eye.

'Hold on.' She repositioned herself. 'That's better.'

When I got home that night, I'd barely opened my door when the banging came from below.

'The view's nice, but give me a room on the ground floor anytime,' I grumbled to Oliver. He was asleep. I suffered working mom's guilt. Poor Oliver was alone all the time, and it was affecting him. Cockatiels were social animals.

A wave of tiredness washed over me. I was a social animal too. I was proud of getting established in LA, but worn out from everything taking so much effort. I was also tired of being alone so much. It was too late to call Vi or Tuesday, and I was too restless for sleep. Even though it was two in the morning, I decided to finish unpacking. The director could kiss my ass.

By three, I was down to the last box. I sat on the floor and pulled it towards me. It was labeled 'Miscellaneous' and held all the random bits left at the end that I'd thrown together. I pulled out a bath towel, a baseball hat, a pocket calendar, a coffee mug and some unwritten postcards. Then came my framed scan from Samuel. I looked at it for a long time, tracing the pattern with my finger, before setting it aside. Next came a triangular paper football. And at the very bottom, under a jumble of pens and pencils, was *The Girl Who Could*. I carefully extracted the beautiful book. I opened it to the dedication, and slowly turned the pages. By the time I came to the end, I'd made a decision.

'Oliver,' I told the sleeping bird. 'We're going home.'

'I'm glad,' Vi said.

'I had to come here, though, to be able to make the choice.'

'I get you. When are you going to leave?'

'As soon as I can. I want to find someone trustworthy to take over the apartment sublet. I don't want to screw Dimple. I think Clark might take it. I also want to do all the jobs Judd assigned to me. I won't leave him in the lurch. He took a chance on me, so I owe it to him, especially during the busy season. And I want to build a comfortable financial cushion, so I don't get myself stranded like I did on the way out. That part might take me a little longer. LA is expensive.'

'Let me send you some money,' Vi offered. 'You're still calling me from Marion's phone.'

'No.' I shook my head. 'I can do this on my own.'

'Do you have a plan?'

'I do indeed.'

'Well all right then,' she said. 'I won't worry. Maybe I should come visit for this Monkey Flower Festival.'

'Definitely you should.'

A week and a few (borrowed) phone calls later, I put my plan into action. First was a trip to Michael's craft supply store to buy photo paper and inexpensive mattes and frames. Next, an all-night after-hours printing binge at the Woot Prints darkroom, permission of Judd. Finally, setting up my booth on the board-walk one busy Saturday.

I displayed for sale both framed and unframed photos of Venice and Unknown. I initially reserved more space for Venice images, figuring tourists would prefer a local souvenir, but eventually my table displayed prints from both places equally, as avid buyers snapped up pictures of Unknown with enthusiasm. By sunset, I'd sold all my stock.

Three weeks later, Clark and Dimple had agreed on the sublet, I'd had several successful weekends on the boardwalk and amassed a substantial nest egg, and I'd finished my last job for Judd. Elsie had recently had a bath, and my things were in boxes. I had a hotel reservation in Phoenix. I was ready to go, almost.

I smiled as I sold my last photo of palm trees to a tourist in a Hard Rock Los Angeles T-shirt. LA had helped get me where I belonged in more ways than one.

CHAPTER 34

LIFE

Restless Legs Syndrome. A neurological movement disorder characterized by unusual, uncomfortable sensations deep within the calves and/or thighs, resulting in an irresistible urge to move.

Marion looked up when I walked into the tattoo parlor. I'd said goodbye to Judd, Clark and Laura. My last stop was Marion and Jacob.

'How'd it go?' he asked.

'I sold 'em all again.' I was flush with profit. 'Check it out.' I waved my shiny new iPhone at him.

'Nice. But I hate to lose you,' he said.

'You're not losing me,' I said. 'You just have to drive farther. Got any parting advice?'

'Don't spend too much time folding the fitted sheet,' he said. 'It'll never come out perfect.' He handed me a bag. 'I got you these.' Inside were several pairs of touristy Los Angeles knee socks. 'So you remember us.'

'I love you too,' I said. 'I got you this.' I handed him a miniature Oscar statue that said *Best Friend Award*. I was out of kachinas.

Jacob wandered out. 'Hey'ya, chicken.'

My smile broadened. 'Not this time.' I slapped $60 on the counter and tapped the page I'd found in the book. 'This one.'

They both started. I nodded.

'Right here.' I tapped my neck behind my ear.

'Rock on!' Jacob exclaimed. We high-fived.

Marion pulled the book to him and looked at the design. Then he looked at me. 'That's a good one,' was all he said, but his voice was gruff.

I knotted my hair and tilted my head so he could ink me with the Chinese symbol for Life. My decision was permanent.

Afterwards, Oliver and I walked over the soft white sand down to the water. It would be our last time at the beach for a while. I sat cross-legged and watched the mesmerizing roll of the waves. I felt the sun on my face, smelled the salt. I sifted sand with my fingers. I felt the stinging in my neck from the tattoo. Oliver tugged strands from my braids, and a gentle wind blew them across my face. I breathed. Absorbing. I didn't take a picture. I didn't frame the scene. I *was* the scene. Breath, light, warm sand. The graceful cresting of a porpoise shot me with delight. I don't know how long I sat there. I wasn't calculating. I wasn't on the outside. I was the center of everything. Breathing. Feeling.

When it was time, I reached into my pack. There was one last thing I needed to do. I couldn't go back in time and give Cameron this last kachina, but I could say goodbye.

I was perched on the side of Cameron's bed. For a change, it was just the two of us.

'No more,' she begged. We'd been playing 'Would You Rather . . . ?' for almost an hour.

'You just don't want to choose between a hairy mole and a third nipple,' I chided.

'Hairy mole! It'd be the only hair I've got.' Her laugh turned to a cough that turned to gasping for air. She was pallid as onion-skin, except for purple shadows bruising beneath her eyes and freckles standing out like blood spatter on a white wall.

She leaned her head back as she regained control of her breathing. She looked like what I used to imagine I did as a kid, flattening myself in bed so any roaming thief wouldn't see that I was there. A third sheet.

'I think I'm ready for this to be over,' she croaked, without opening her eyes.

A flash of agreement, then revolt. Cameron had been the gift God handed me when I needed it the most. I wasn't ready to give her back.

'Does it hurt?' I asked.

'Don't ask me that.' She silenced me, eyes open now.

'Are you afraid?' I asked.

'No.' Her head was comically large for her twig neck, and her shake was more wobble. 'You know how it is.'

I nodded, but I didn't. I'd never gotten to that place where fear let go. When death had danced close, I'd been afraid. But even when they'd asked if we wanted a priest, they hadn't stopped the fight; chemicals continued to flow. And worked a miracle. Cameron was off the tubes. No more battling. This was a different kind of waiting. I chose to believe that when you were one hair closer, when you could almost smell the lemons, fear died first.

'Tell them,' she made me pledge. 'Tell them I wasn't afraid. Coming from you, they might believe it.'

Again I nodded, wondering what I could possibly say to her family, a twenty-two-year-old girl trying to solace broken sixty-year-olds who wanted to know why God hated them.

A nurse with a fierce unibrow interrupted us. She had a tall glass of Carnation Instant Breakfast drink.

'I'm not drinking that shit,' Cameron said.

'Now, Cameron,' Unibrow cajoled.

'I'm. Not. Drinking. That. Shit.' Cameron closed her eyes and pretended Unibrow wasn't there. Soon enough, she wasn't. She left the drink.

'Flush it,' Cameron instructed. 'I detest that shit.' I did.

'Bargaining time's over,' she said. 'At first I tried to make deals – I would swear less, I'd be nicer

430

to that annoying social worker that wears all the happy-face flair buttons, I'd be a better person in general. I lasted three days before I realized it was stupid and gave up. You can make all the promises in the world and you'll still have cancer.'

I didn't tell her all the bargains I'd been making if God would let me keep her. There were ways you could acknowledge certain death, and ways you couldn't.

Cameron went on. 'For years I was the manic, melodramatic cancer-won't-get-the-best-of-me person. But you know what? It's horseshit. Cancer sometimes will get the best of you, and that's why it sucks.' She grabbed my hand. 'I'm not saying permanently, just sometimes. Remember that.'

'Are you giving me a parting lecture?' I wasn't sure what she wanted from me.

She managed a laugh. 'I want to be as famous as that *Last Lecture* professor at Carnegie Mellon.'

'And as rich,' I agreed.

She rolled her head to look at me. 'I don't know what I would say for my last lecture.' We held eyes, wondering what wisdom we could give one another in our diverging journeys. When she spoke at last, she simply said, '*Live.*'

'As long as I can.' I made the only promise I could keep.

She made a feeble gesture to her long-abandoned desk. 'Get that envelope. It's for you.'

'What is it?' Eagerly I drew out a thick sheet of watercolor paper. Cameron was incredibly talented.

She had been an art student at the Rhode Island School of Design.

It was a watercolor comic map of the United States, scattered with caricature icons – a cowboy galloping across Texas, an Amish buggy cantering through Pennsylvania, Mount Rushmore dominating South Dakota, surfers cresting California's coast. In the middle, hanging out of a bright red convertible, waved a blonde girl with a wide smile, driving, with Cameron's grinning freckled face on the passenger's side.

'It's all the places we said we'd go when we got better.'

I swallowed hard. 'I might not get better,' I said.

'You might,' she said.

'I can't do it alone.' I wasn't talking about the road trip.

'Not to sound like Dr Phil,' we both hated Dr Phil with a passion that burned white hot, 'but you're only as alone as you want to be.'

'I think I might want to be.' My throat was tight. 'For a while.'

'That's a choice.' Her voice was fading as she tired, but she managed a smile. 'But when you're ready,' she indicated the colorful map, 'take me with you.'

I'd cried a normal amount once – skinned knee, dead dog, broken heart. But when I got sick and had a well of legitimate causes, the tears had dried up. I hadn't wanted to wash away in them. In that moment, the valve burst, and every single tear I'd ever held back erupted. I put my head on her knees and sobbed. The watercolor still bears the blotch that stained the corn palace in Iowa before Cameron extracted the map to safety. She made shushing noises, hand on my head.

'I'm going to miss you,' I burbled through the snot.

She feebly tapped the map. 'I'm right here.'

I pulled myself together, and mopped my face.

'If you live, I'll get you a corndog and funnel cake at the Minnesota State Fair,' I begged.

She laughed. 'How did you know what I wanted for my last meal?'

'Crazy in the brains!' I scolded. 'You need to shop on the right-hand side of the menu. Get the lobster Thermidor and baked Alaska.'

'How about snow crab legs and artichokes . . .'

We bantered until her parents arrived, then switched to the safer topic of how unseasonably hot it was and what a relief to be in the air-conditioning. I would not be alone with Cameron again before her death three days later. It was years before I was able to say 'I love you' to anyone, because I hadn't said it to her.

I extracted the jar from my bag. I'd been carrying it with me a long time.

'I hope you enjoyed the trip,' I said to Cameron. 'I'm sorry it took so long.'

I unsealed my portion of Cameron's ashes and gently shook her into the breeze. Soon, I would write her parents and tell them what I had done. I could stop avoiding them.

When the jar was empty, I filled it with Venice Beach sand. In the resulting hollow, I nestled a kachina for Cameron. While her ashes continued her exploration of the world, the seventh kachina would stay on the California beach she'd dreamed of seeing. The statue intertwined a bird, nest, fish and wave. I wondered if my mom had been thinking of my friend when she created it. It reminded me of Cameron's own drawings. To me, the seamless joining of elements and animals meant belonging. I didn't belong to Los Angeles, but I belonged to myself at last, body and spirit. I was grateful to this place for giving that to me. I didn't need to stay until October. This particular marathon was over, though surely there would be others. I was ready for my new home.

The eighth kachina, the mother-figure with the owl, would return with me. It was mine to keep, to remind me of where I began, and of the seven others that marked my journey to where I was now. With a last gaze at the ocean, I walked to where Elsie was waiting to take me to the desert.

'Where're you headed?' The parking attendant looked at my packed car. 'You're loaded.'

What he didn't know was how free I finally was. 'Destination Unknown.' I smiled.

He didn't bat an eye. Venice Beach saw it all. 'Good luck.'

'You know it,' I agreed, and drove east.

★ ★ ★

When I pulled into Unknown it was a far different scene from my shadowy arrival many months ago. Though it was after dark, the town square was vibrant, bustling with preparations for the Monkey Flower Festival. I could see Bruce and Ronnie bickering over how to erect the marquis tent. Liz Goldberg and Jenny Up were hanging paper lanterns on the bandstand, while Helen Rausch skulked nearby ready to pounce on flaws in their work. Fairy lights were strung from every possible branch and structure. I could see Tuesday's work in clusters of misshapen paper flowers. There was no mistaking the existence of a town this time. I was looking at its beating heart. I knew I'd come home as my own heart beat in harmony. I didn't see Noah's tall frame among the crowd, but that didn't worry me. I put the car into drive and headed home to Ruby's. I had all the time in the world.

EPILOGUE

Elevated Mood. An exaggerated feeling of well-being, or euphoria or elation. A person with elevated mood may describe feeling 'high', 'ecstatic', 'on top of the world' or 'up in the clouds'.

'Red wine?'
'Yes, thanks. Did you get the popcorn?'
Pause.
'You remembered to get the popcorn, right?'
Cough.
'Are you kidding me? You forgot the popcorn! What's movie night without popcorn?'
'I had a deadline! I was focused on getting chapters out.'
'Spare me. You spent the entire day distracting me while I was trying to research the impact of Indonesia imports on domestic cement production for *Cement Times: Solid Facts*.'
'I didn't notice you complaining.' Haughty.
'*Whatever*, clever. Let's watch the movie.'
'Where's the remote?'

437

Silence.

'It's on the TV.'

'Well, go get it.'

'You go get it.'

'I cooked the spaghetti.'

'You forgot the popcorn.'

'You picked the movie.'

'I'm the guest.'

'Right. You have more stuff here than I do. There's no room for *my* socks any more!'

'If you can call those socks.'

'There is nothing wrong with black socks.'

Snort. 'Fine. If you won't get the remote, we'll just sit here.'

'Fine.' Quiet. 'I can think of something to do . . .'

'You getting the remote?'

'I was thinking more along these lines . . .'

Giggle. 'That tickles.'

'I can do this instead.'

'Hey! That's shocking, sir!'

Pause. 'Want me to stop?'

'Not on your life. C'mere . . .'

Long silence.

'Maeve?'

'Yes, Noah?'

'What's this I hear about you opening a tattoo parlor in the corner of the bookstore?'

ACKNOWLEDGMENTS

As always, I owe my family a debt of thanks for their incredible support, especially my parents, Paul and Kathy Reichs, and my sister and brother, Courtney and Brendan. I want to welcome and thank Emily Reichs and Brooks Mixon for being brave enough to join our family. I am so glad to have you. A special shout-out goes to Marta Reichs, my ninety-year-old grandmother, who always has been my rock and inspiration. Welcome goes to Jason Tedesco, the newest member of our gang.

I cannot express enough gratitude to my remarkable literary agents Dorian Karchmar, Rowan Lawton and Lisa Grubka. Thanks also to Jennifer Rudolph Walsh, Anna DeRoy, Raffaella De Angelis and Adam Schear. The entire team at William Morris Agency spoils me rotten.

Unlimited thanks go to my incredible editor at Orion, Sara O'Keefe, who turns everything I spin to gold. The entire Orion team gets a resounding cheer for their efforts and dedication, and for always having cookies when I come to the offices.

I am so grateful to the Hedgebrook Foundation

for awarding me a writing residency. Hedgebrook is truly a gift for women writers, and I was blessed to share my time there with other extraordinary women who inspired and improved me.

I could not have invented Unknown on my own. For helping me find a location and hosting me during my research trips to Arizona, I thank Carla Kountoupes, Will Wilson, Zoë Wilson and Cristina Beloud. I do my best writing in London and Los Angeles. I'm incredibly grateful to Matthew Griffin, Peter Dean and Kimberly Cayce for generously providing my homes away from home. And for maintaining my own home when I'm not there, and being a surrogate parent to my cats, I thank Anil Zenginoglu.

I had many technical experts. For assistance with the Portuguese language, I thank Claudio Felix. For his auto mechanical expertise, I thank Paul Tedesco. For helping me write some terrible cop drama dialogue, I thank Ralph Soll. For information to write accurately about shooting a television show, I thank Nina Jack, and everyone at *Bones*. And for the most beautiful drawings in the world, I thank Alastair Sadler.

I had many non-technical experts too, whether it was reading early versions, or just listening. Special thanks always to my reader Ted Robertson. Also to Lisa Ruggiero Hopson, for taking this ride with me from the beginning, literally, one mile at a time. To Hiwa Bourne, for teaching me Hawaiian phrases and demonstrating what it means to look like you're dancing when you're standing still. To Tricia Hale, for demonstrating the power of online reconnectivity. To Julie Lentz and the Gin Mill, for letting me steal you for this book. To Stacey Bowlin, Tasha McGinn, Leslie Norwalk and Sabrina Shea for bedside picnics and helping me with the tricky bits. To Sean Nolan for some inspired gift ideas. To Tom Roberts and Nils Olsen for educating me on deliberate practice and decision making. To my LA 'family', for making it feel like coming home every time I step off the plane. And to my DC 'family', for being so thrilled when I get back. I am blessed in my friends.

Most of all, I thank all those who shared their stories with me. You have my respect, my gratitude and my pledge to continue the fight.

For Dana Ruggiero (1995-2005)
and
For all the survivors.
You represent the fighters out there and you inspire me.

And to the remarkable people who participate in the
Leukemia and Lymphoma Society Team in Training
Programme.
You make a difference.

National Capital Chapter El Tour de Tucson Century
2001
National Capital Chapter Palm Beach Sun Century
2002
National Capital Chapter America's Most Beautiful
Bike Ride (Tahoe) 2004
Greater Los Angeles Chapter Cool Breeze Century
2006
Greater Los Angeles Chapter Honolulu Century 2006
National Capital Chapter El Tour de Tucson Century
2008

Thank you.